BURNING PROSPECTS

To Nancy Gottschang,
I hope you enjoy the story of Prospect Hill Plantation!
Love & Best Wishes,
Melisa Miles

BURNING PROSPECTS

A NOVEL BASED ON A TRUE STORY

MELISSA MILES

Hillcrest Press

Copyright © 2014 by Melissa Miles

All rights reserved.

Cover photo by Julie Brown Cude
Cover Design by Tatiana Jorge
Book design by Lewis C. Miles, Jr.
Edited by Taylor Roosevelt
Clip art swirl used under licensing agreement by Microsoft Word™
Biblical excerpts taken from the public domain King James Version. All other excerpts used in this novel are from nineteenth century publications and were utilized according to public domain copyright laws.

No part of this book may be reproduced in any form or by any electronic or mechanical means including information storage and retrieval systems, without permission in writing from the author.

This book is a work of fiction. Although based on historical fact, creative license has been taken to produce a fictionalized account of actual historical events.

Printed in the United States of America

First Printing: February 2014
Hillcrest Press

ISBN-13: 978-0-9912117-1-5

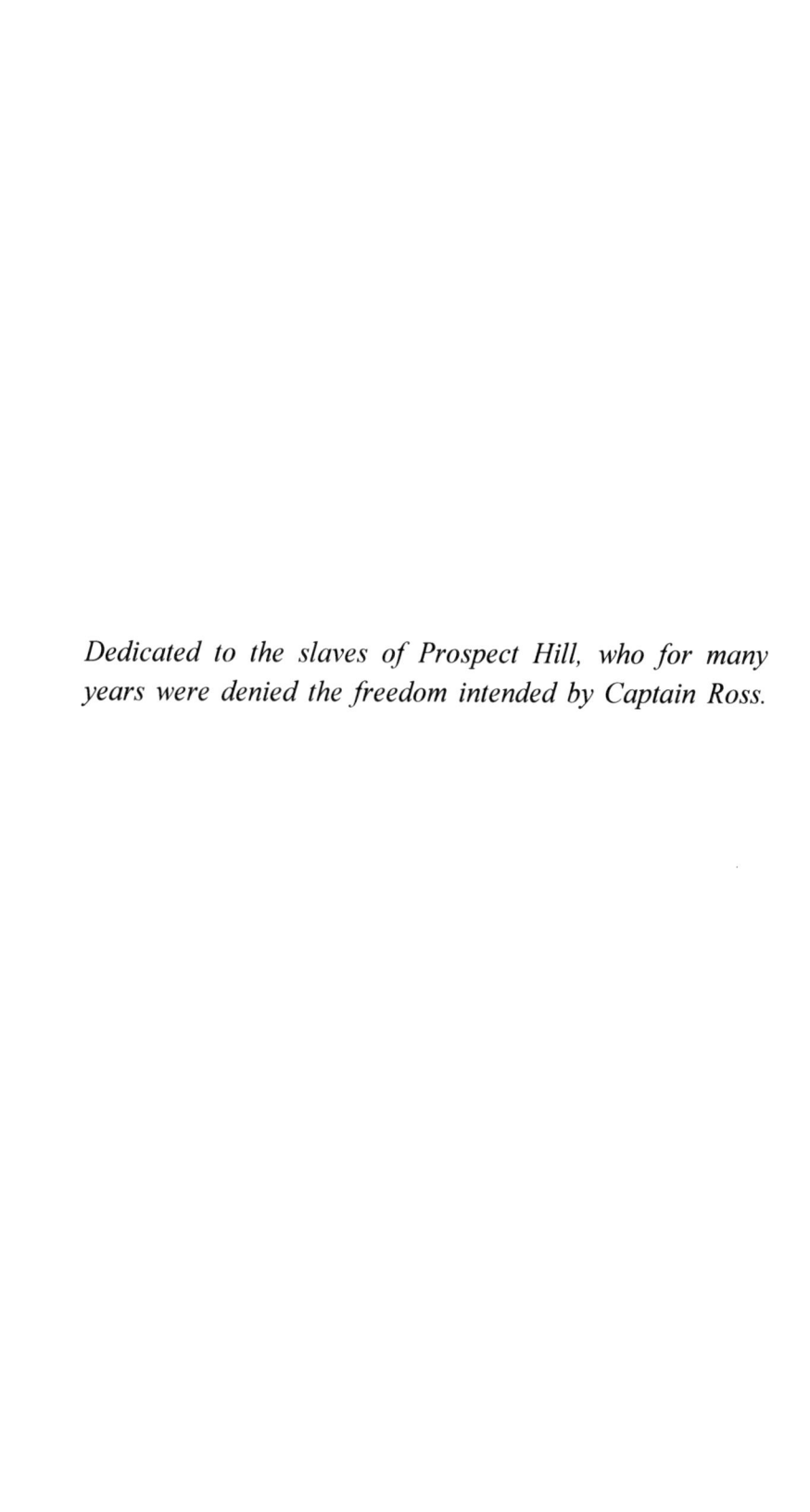

Dedicated to the slaves of Prospect Hill, who for many years were denied the freedom intended by Captain Ross.

CONTENTS

April 15, 1845	1
January 15, 1836	14
January 18, 1836	30
January 21, 1836	39
September 1838	49
April 15, 1840	61
September 1840	82
April 1841	92
July 1843	103
September 1843	111
December 1843	122
March 1844	143
July 4, 1844	165
September 1844	182
October 1844	196
February 1845	207
March 1845	223
April 10, 1845	235
April 14, 1845	248
April 15, 1845 Prospect Hill	263
April 15, 1845 Port Gibson	274
April 16, 1845	288
April 18, 1845	297
April 19, 1845	309
April 22, 1845	317
Afterword	334
Author's Note	338
Acknowledgments	340
Questions for Consideration and Discussion	342
Appendix	345

A slave is one who is in the power of a master to whom he belongs. The master may sell him, dispose of his person, his industry and his labor. He can do nothing, possess nothing, nor acquire anything, but what must belong to his master.

Louisiana Civil Code, Article 35
June 20, 1825

April 15, 1845   Prospect Hill Plantation

Fire! Smoke! I can't breathe!! The words seemed to be screaming inside of Adelaide's mind as she struggled to make her way down the hallway behind Mary. But as loud as the internal dialogue sounded to her, she wasn't making any audible sounds save the occasional cough. The heat from the flames was unbearable as Adelaide began staggering down the regal staircase.

The wood on the stairs under her feet felt so hot. *What's happening? Are we going to die!?* In her confusion, she saw the familiar furnishings becoming distorted by the fire already raging around her.

Am I dreaming? A loud popping sound caused her to momentarily freeze. *No, I have to keep moving.*

But even as her groggy brain was telling her to move, her body was struggling to do so.

Mary, just a few steps ahead of her, kept urging her to continue moving towards the doors on the main floor. It was only these instructions that kept her moving at all. Nothing seemed real; her mind was fuzzy, creating a terrible sense of disorientation.

A deep despair was rising in Adelaide's chest as she moved down the stairs towards the big front doors of Prospect Hill. *Why? Why is this happening? I can't breathe!* As she set her feet gingerly upon the landing, she could see the doors before her. She saw Mary hurriedly glance back towards her once more.

"Adelaide, we must continue on. Really, we must." It struck her that Mary seemed so calm and knew exactly what to do. In contrast, her own brain felt entirely muddled and confused.

Through the thick smoke, Adelaide caught sight of her brother Isaac moving towards her. Surely he could explain to her what was happening. Her spirits lifted momentarily at the sight of him.

"What…what is this, Isaac? I don't understand."

Maybe I am dreaming! She was suddenly aware that Isaac wasn't running or acting frantic. In fact, he seemed to be moving in a slow and clumsy fashion that didn't fit in her mind with the behavior expected in an emergency situation.

However, her brother gave her neither assurances nor answers to her questions. Isaac grabbed the handles of the front doors. He struggled for a few moments, which seemed odd even in the midst of such chaos. She had never known these door to be difficult to open.

At last Isaac was able to throw the doors open. He held his arm out and nodded at his sister and Mary, the young niece of his wife, indicating that he wished for the ladies to exit ahead of him.

Mary was clearly starting to struggle now. It slowly registered in Adelaide's mind that the young woman was holding both Addie and Cabell; the small sleeping children were proving to be difficult for her to bear alone. Somewhere in Adelaide's sluggish mind she realized that Mary must have carried her two youngest children down the stairs and out of harm's way. She felt a sudden rush of gratitude to her.

"Go Adelaide…go!" Mary urged, looking as if she might collapse at any moment.

But Adelaide continued standing completely still. Her brother had already turned and staggered back into the flames. She felt the cool night air pouring into the foyer of the grand plantation and her senses urged her to move out into the fresh air; the life-giving air that her brain was desperately telling her she needed. *Go! Need fresh air! Can't breathe!*

Something wasn't right. She was so groggy, so confused. *Is this really happening? Why am I rooted to this spot? Should I wait for Isaac to return?* The blaze was growing more intense each moment that she hesitated.

"Please! Go!"

The harshness of Mary's last command snapped Adelaide momentarily out of her stupor. She staggered through the double doors and onto the wide, gracious porch directly behind Mary and her two youngest children.

Adelaide stopped abruptly once she reached the safety of the porch to glance back into the burning house. *Something isn't right…I feel so…so strange.*

Turning her face back towards the porch she saw Uncle Esau, one of the largest of the Prospect Hill slaves, standing stock-still in shadow just outside of the door. That alone would be enough to startle her. But Uncle Esau had an axe raised high over his shoulder, and a steely look on his face that Adelaide had never before seen. He was one of her grandfather's longtime slaves, and she had known him since her early childhood.

For a few—but seemingly endless—seconds no one spoke or moved a muscle.

It was Mary, again so cool and calm, who exclaimed, "Uncle Esau, thank goodness! You've surely come to chop down the door to help us escape!"

For a moment, time seemed frozen. The night, already so surreal to Adelaide, just seemed to blur around the edges now. Nothing about the familiar home seemed remotely comforting or familiar to her tonight.

She watched as Uncle Esau slowly lowered the axe. Adelaide felt as if she were watching from some remote vantage point, somehow disconnected from the moment. *This can't be real.* Esau looked over his shoulder quickly and then back at the two breathless ladies and the two small children.

"Yes'm," he muttered before he staggered off down the porch steps and out of sight into the darkness.

Adelaide heard the voice of her nephew coming out of the doorway behind her. "Aunt Adelaide, the house is on fire!" said young Isaac. Adelaide instinctively held her hand out to the young boy who grabbed it, and clung to her tightly. His little face was completely white.

"We need to get further from the house, Adelaide," exclaimed Mary, shifting the load of the young toddlers, who were now beginning to stir. "I can't hold them much longer and we need to be clear if the house collapses."

Mary began moving down the steps, but looked back

when she realized that Adelaide was still rooted to the spot. Mary was truly getting frustrated with her now. *Surely I don't have to do everything myself.*

Still standing partway down the porch steps wanting nothing more than to collapse against one of the tall oaks that surrounded the grand home, Mary was downright cross with Adelaide now. She had always been tremendously fond of her, but tonight Mary felt that Adelaide had behaved like a small child, unable to act on her own accord. In fact, tonight all she had asked Adelaide to do was to wake Martha and bring her downstairs. She had managed everything else herself.

At the thought of Martha, Mary's heart once again began to pound furiously. She only at this moment realized that she didn't see Martha walking behind her mother as she should have been. *Where is she?!*

"Adelaide!" she almost shouted, trying to keep the panic from her voice. "Where is Martha?"

Adelaide slowly made eye contact with Mary. Mary noticed more markedly now that they were free from the danger of the burning house, that the woman was in a stupor—her eyes vague and glazed.

"Martha?" Adelaide replied in a quiet, somewhat slurred voice. "I don't know where Martha is. Don't you know?"

"Adelaide, don't you remember?" implored Mary, now feeling true panic. "I told you that I was getting Cabell and Addie. You nodded at me and watched me gather them into my arms. I told you to wake Martha and bring her down. You repeated my words back to me. Didn't you wake her?"

Before Adelaide could comprehend and respond, several others scrambled out of the house. Isaac Wade and his wife

Catherine appeared followed by Dr. Wade and his business associate, Mr. Bailey. Catherine was carrying her infant daughter and holding the hand of her young son Dunbar.

"We need to move from the house immediately," said Dr. Wade in a commanding voice. Of the group that had recently appeared on the porch, he was the only one who appeared fully awake and was clearly taking charge of the situation.

"Martha?" Adelaide once again said, but louder and more urgently this time with comprehension beginning to dawn on her that her oldest child remained in the upstairs of the house.

"Yes, Adelaide. The children need to move a safe distance away." Apparently taking note of the muddled appearance of his sister Adelaide, Dr. Wade turned his attention to Mary. Her face had drained of all color now and she felt as if her surroundings were beginning to spin all around her.

"Take the children over by the far gate please, Mary," said Dr. Wade. "We all need to get away from the house. It will collapse in minutes."

"I was headed there," Mary replied feeling panic rising in her. "But Miss Adelaide doesn't have Martha."

In desperation, she added, "I told her to get Martha. I told her to bring Martha and that I would get these two." She shrugged her shoulders to indicate the young children now sliding down her front despite her efforts to utilize what little strength she still possessed to hold onto them. *Oh God, why didn't I make sure she had Martha?*

Horror-stricken, but realizing there was little time to act, Dr. Wade shouted, "Everybody off the porch right now!"

Major, Isaac Wade's manservant, appeared in the doorway and addressed his master. "The downstairs is clear, Master Wade. But the stairs is fixin' to collapse."

Some of the Prospect Hill slaves were starting to stagger into the yard now, eyes round as saucers at the sight of the smoke and flames. Mary was sure that she heard some of the slave women praying frantically in hushed tones. She found the sounds profoundly comforting even in the midst of the sheer panic and despair she was struggling to control.

"Martha!" Adelaide repeated her daughter's name for the third time now, only this time it was a guttural scream that seemed to emit from the very depths of her being. "Martha is still in her bed!"

As a physician, Walter Wade prided himself on his ability to stay calm in times of crisis. But this calamity going on around him was testing every bit of his fortitude. *Should I run back into the fire and attempt to rescue Martha? Major just reported that the stairs were beginning to collapse. Perhaps I could climb through an upstairs window.*

He realized instantly that there wasn't a tree located close enough to her window to climb. *If there is any way to save her, it has to be done now!* The internal struggle of making such a decision was weighing on him like nothing he had experienced before.

Mary, remembering Dr. Wade's instructions, led the Wade family to safety and began to take charge of their children. Her Aunt Catherine and Uncle Isaac were acting strangely subdued. Within moments the familiar dark faces that she had known for years began gathering around to assist her.

As Mary took charge of the others, Dr. Wade turned his attention back to his sister, Adelaide. She still had not moved from the exact spot where she had originally stepped onto the porch. But just as he reached out to take her arm and direct her to safety, she took off running back into the house. She was screaming her daughter's name over and over again.

"Adelaide, get back here now!" he shouted as she disappeared from his view. "It is too late to help her. Don't you understand? It is too late!" Terror seized him just as surely as a physical hand had grabbed his throat. He was having difficulty breathing.

Adelaide ignored his voice completely. She ignored her own fear as well. Her only thought as she felt the searing heat of the flames envelop her was to find her daughter. *Martha! I have to save my baby! Martha! Oh God! Help me please! This is all my fault!*

A young house slave named Thomas appeared from the darkness of the yard. He abruptly bounded up the stairs and through the front doors. Dr. Wade yelled for him to stop, but Thomas quickly caught up to Adelaide on the staircase as he was literally running through smoke and flames. He seemed oblivious to the danger around him, focused solely on saving the young girl's life.

Dr. Wade, always one to conceive a logical plan before rushing into action, hadn't yet worked out the best way to save Martha. Now he feared his sister and Thomas would surely perish in a foolhardy effort to run up a collapsing staircase. He knew that his hesitation had wasted precious time. Guilt and shame began to wash over him, and he immediately began rationalizing his actions. *But there never was a chance to save her. Surely even if I had run back in the instant I was told, it was already too late.*

The noise around him was now a deafening roar, with the wooden planks of pitch pine of which the house was constructed cracking and popping all around him.

Crash!

Walter Wade watched in horror as the staircase collapsed with the two figures still making their way frantically up to the second story to save young Martha. This time, he didn't hesitate or even attempt to formulate a strategy of action.

He took a gulp of fresh air and bolted into the foyer, determined not to let a moment's hesitation cost another life tonight. He heard movement behind him and noticed two young field hands nearby, looking determined but clearly terrified of the tumult around them.

"Help me grab them. We have to drag them out as soon as we can. The whole roof is about to come down on us."

Even as he said this, debris was beginning to rain down on the foyer. All three men instinctively covered their heads with their arms and made their way to Adelaide and Thomas, who were both now screaming frantically as their clothing began to catch fire.

"Don't take time to put out the flames! Just drag them out. Hurry!"

Dr. Wade grabbed hold of Adelaide's hands which were not yet burned. He moved as fast as he could towards the doors. As soon as they were clear of the foyer, he rolled her over several times, making sure no flames were still burning on her nightgown. He leaned down and scooped her into his arms. To his astonishment, his younger sister was struggling against him, pushing his chest. Her words were not coherent anymore, but her meaning was clear. She wanted to go back into that house for Martha even if it meant she would die in the flames with her.

The burns on her face and neck raised an alarm which instantly caused his neck hairs to bristle. The location of her burns meant that her airway would be at serious risk of swelling closed due to her injuries. If the swelling became too severe, she would be unable to breathe and eventually die. *Oh God, Adelaide, I'm so sorry. Please don't die.*

The two courageous young slaves, Jack and Moses, were right behind him dragging Thomas out into the night air. Dr. Wade instructed them to pat down any flames burning on his clothing and get him away from the house. He noticed that Thomas wasn't struggling, and appeared to be unconscious.

He felt a stab of dread and prayed silently that the heroic young man had not died in his attempt to rescue his niece. *Dear Lord, this slave did more to try to save little Martha than I did. Her own uncle. Don't let him die. Please don't let him die.*

When Walter Wade joined his brother's family on the lawn, he gently laid Adelaide down in the grass. He was grateful to see that some of the slave women had already fetched cool water and rags. They immediately began tending to the burns of the victims, speaking in calm, comforting tones as they worked. He gave Grace, one of his grandfather's most valued slaves, specific instructions on caring for Adelaide—insisting that he be alerted immediately to any change in her condition.

Dr. Wade took a moment to survey the scene surrounding him. The slaves gathered around now far outnumbered the family members and guests of Prospect Hill. Most of them were busy providing assistance or comfort to his family. *Thank God they are here; we need the help.*

After some time in the cool night air Isaac and Catherine appeared at last to be alert and able to fully comprehend their surroundings, yet no one spoke. The sheer magnitude of the great burning home seemed to compel them all to watch with wide eyes. It would have been impossible to look away.

More than an hour passed and the flames had begun to die down; the last of the roof had collapsed causing sparks to fly into the dark night sky. But still, no one spoke. The children, now under the care of Mariah, a devoted female house worker, were asleep in a huddle against a grand old live oak. The Spanish moss hung so low, it looked like the curtains from a four poster bed draped against the darkness. The sleeping children resembled a litter of newborn puppies, huddled together for warmth and security.

Dr. Wade surveyed the wreckage of what he had once considered a permanent fixture in his life. The grand house, now consumed by smoke and flames, had always been almost a sanctuary for himself and his siblings—a place they felt comfortable and safe. It had belonged to their grandparents, and many of their most precious childhood memories had taken place here: at Prospect Hill.

He wasn't accustomed to feeling helpless. As the oldest of his siblings, he was expected to succeed in his endeavors and engender a certain level of respect. He couldn't have put into words his feelings that night. Random themes burst into his mind at arbitrary times. *Failure? Inadequacy? Loss? Death?*

He glanced back at where the slaves were tending to his sister and Thomas, both badly burned. He had already assessed their injuries and knew that the next few days would be critical. But at least they were still alive. *Thank God they are both alive.* And yet the relief he felt was mixed with grief. *I couldn't save Martha.*

Mary Girault closed her eyes, exhausted and drained from watching the devastating effects of the fire on the once beautiful home. She had always loved to visit her Aunt Catherine at this palatial plantation home with its amazing views and extensive library of leather bound books. This had been a truly wonderful week until this moment. Earlier that night there had been an anniversary party for her Aunt Catherine and Uncle Isaac. Mary had helped to plan it, and it had been such a beautiful affair.

She pushed all of those images aside and forced herself back into the moment. She needed to understand what was happening. *But it hurts to be here now. Oh, how I loved Martha! How will I ever forgive myself for not making sure she was safe?*

With her eyes still closed, Mary's other senses seemed to spring to life. She could hear the soft singing and praying of the slaves, still tending to the family, their voices punctuated with periodic crackles and pops still emitting from the burning house. She could smell the woodsy burning odor of the smoke rising up from the fire. For the first time, she became aware of the dew on the grass underneath her bare feet. A gentle breeze blew across her face and lifted the edge of her nightgown.

Later in her life she would recall all of these sensations experienced on the night Prospect Hill burned to the ground, becoming young Martha's funeral pyre. But by far the most vivid memory she would carry with her from that ill-fated night was the sound of Adelaide's agony and despair. It reminded Mary of a grievously wounded animal, and she couldn't recall ever hearing such anguish from another human being.

Sometimes Adelaide's sobbing was interspersed with words that Mary could comprehend. "Martha. My baby….oh God, I'm so sorry. Martha….my sweet precious girl. My baby…my baby…" But mostly it was just gulping sobs that knew no words. Grace remained by her side for hours attempting to comfort her, and tending to her burns. But no comfort was possible for Adelaide Wade Richardson on that night—or for the many nights that followed.

Though no one had spoken it aloud, they all knew that young Martha Richardson had perished, and that Prospect Hill, the once splendid home of Captain Isaac Ross, was gone forever. His beloved granddaughter Adelaide lay burned and broken on the lawn. Yet two important questions remained unanswered: How did this happen? And why?

January 15, 1836   Prospect Hill Plantation

Captain Isaac Ross knew that his time on this earth was drawing to a close. The doctors had been maddeningly vague and uncertain with him, never providing him with real answers. Neither could they ever provide much relief from his constant discomfort. Eventually he had just told them all to leave him the hell alone. By this seventy-seventh year of his life, he had experienced more than his share of loss: his two sons, a beloved daughter, and his devoted wife. To be honest, he was feeling ready to go on to whatever great adventure was waiting for him next.

There was still one last responsibility he needed to finalize before he drew his last breath. He had come, in his later years, to feel a tremendous sense of obligation to his large holding of slaves. Before he departed this world, he needed to be certain that his wishes were going to be carried out when he was no longer around to make that happen. In particular, he wanted to be sure that his slaves were provided for after his death. Many of them had traveled with him from South Carolina almost 30 years prior, and they had labored for him and alongside him with devotion. It wasn't something that he planned to forget.

But Captain Ross was also pragmatic. He was well aware of the sentiment of his fellow landowners in Jefferson County, Mississippi. He had come to Jefferson County in 1808, following the lead of his older brother Arthur Ross. There was a fortune to be made here, and Isaac Ross had not squandered his opportunity to do just that.

With the invention of the cotton gin, a man could make a fortune on that single crop alone. And owning slaves was the vehicle which had allowed him to earn his prosperity. The closer he came to the end of his life, the more acutely aware he became of the debt he owed his slaves. It was on their backs that he had prospered, and by God, he was going to see that they were rewarded for their years of service.

By the time of his approaching death, he owned around 5,000 acres of fertile Mississippi cotton-growing land with a labor force of just under 200 slaves. Under his direction, his faithful slaves had built Prospect Hill high on a hilltop, surrounded by sloping fields and grassy knolls. As a young man he had never questioned slavery or his inherent right to own another human being. That questioning had only come with age and a great deal of soul searching.

Even now, as he looked around his parlor, his heart burst with pride in his home. Captain Ross had spared no expense in the fine furnishings and artwork adorning Prospect Hill. Glancing around the room, he couldn't help but smile at the floor-to-ceiling bookshelves filled with books from the world's finest authors. It was doubtful one could find a better library in the area. The large windows overlooked the expansive gardens, and he felt a momentary pang of regret that he would likely die before having another chance to once again smell the fragrant camellias and gardenias which filled the yard.

He had designed the main house and other buildings on the property himself, and had worked closely with his slaves to construct them to his specifications. His slaves had been carefully trained to perform an array of expert plantation work. Prospect Hill possessed exceptionally well-built barns, slave dwellings, and all of the other various types of out buildings required on a prosperous working plantation.

His slaves not only planted and harvested the crops, but operated the most sophisticated farm machinery available. His life was intrinsically linked to his large holding of slaves—essentially a symbiotic relationship with both organisms needing the other to survive in its current state. But he had come to realize that it didn't have to be this way. The slaves could be, and more importantly *should* be, independent of him.

The idea to sever those bonds had been on his mind for over ten years now. Surely each could exist without the other under different circumstances. But slavery in its current form required a dependence of the slave on the master—for food, clothing, shelter and medical care. But as much as his white counterparts would despise having to admit it, the master was tremendously dependent on his slaves as well.

The invention of the cotton gin had cinched that dependency in one fell swoop. The dependency, though never freely admitted in the white aristocracy, was the fundamental reason that wealthy planters so fervently opposed any attempts to end the practice.

Hundreds of acres of valuable cotton were not worth a dime without a labor force trained to plant, cultivate, and harvest it. Each party needed the other. But Ross felt strongly that it couldn't go on this way indefinitely.

The abolitionist movement was growing stronger in the north and it was beginning to trickle down to them. It was against the law to import new slaves, and had been for close to 30 years. He felt it was only a matter of time before laws were passed prohibiting the practice of slavery entirely.

Isaac Ross sighed at the thoughts that charged through his weary mind. He was almost glad he wouldn't be around to see the day when it all came to a head. *I'll leave that battle for the next generation. I've already fought my fair share of battles.*

Ross had always had more confidence in his slaves' abilities than did his fellow planters. Perhaps this was because he had fought alongside black soldiers in the Revolutionary War and found them to be fine fighting men. Drew Harris, one such former comrade in arms, had made the journey with him from South Carolina and worked his own property nearby as a free negro.

His beliefs were certainly not widely shared in Jefferson County. A frequent argument heard at homes all across the county was that slaves were incapable of self-sufficiency by nature and design. It was often said that slavery was a blessing in disguise for the colored folks because they were in dire need of people to take care of them. In recent years, he had come to see this argument for what it was: a rationalization for the institution of slavery. And how easy it had been to rationalize! From pulpits across the South, Scripture was used to support slavery on a regular basis. It was therefore quite easy to walk out of church clutching the Bible, feeling completely justified in the continuation of the practice.

But Ross had encouraged his own slaves to be self-reliant in many ways. Each family was provided with pigs to manage throughout the year as a supply of pork. The slave families had smokehouses for curing their own meat. His large cattle herd was primarily used to provide his slaves with fresh beef. In fact, Captain Ross himself had issued orders that no less than two cattle be slaughtered each week for this use.

Anticipating the day when emancipation would come, for he had no doubt that it would, he wanted his slaves to be ready for freedom. Even though it was against the law in Mississippi to teach slaves to read and write, many of his slaves were taught to do so.

It troubled Captain Ross that many of the slaves in his adopted state would be hopelessly inept when eventually freed—not because of an inherent inferiority, but because they had never been taught the skills needed to manage a home and to do business. They had simply been taught to follow orders. He believed that he had an obligation to his own slaves to prepare them for a life of freedom.

Still, even though his relationship with his slaves was different than that of most other plantation owners, he had come to see slavery as a curse. A blight on this nation that he had fought to bring about in the war. It was true that the labor was necessary to run a plantation as large as his own, but it surely couldn't be a just cause in the eyes of God to own your colored brethren and deny them their freedom. He had made it a point to talk to his slaves about their views on freedom. What would they do with it if they had it? What did freedom mean to them?

He was fully committed to the plan that he had laid out in his will in August of 1834. As Mississippi law made it illegal to free slaves within the state, he looked to colonization as an option. He had decided to free his slaves and set aside the bulk of his estate to send them to back to Africa. The responsibility of carrying out his orders would fall to the American Colonization Society. Prospect Hill was to be sold and the proceeds used to pay for their passage to Liberia, the necessary provisions to get started there, and a school built specifically for their use.

A husky voice caused him to withdraw from his contemplations and look up.

"A carriage is a pullin' up, Cap'n Isaac," reported Enoch from the doorway to the grand parlor. "Looks like Missus Margaret's."

He turned his head slowly to face his manservant.

"Thank you Enoch. Show her in as soon as she arrives. We are expecting Mr. Wade as well."

Enoch nodded in acknowledgment and turned to stand vigil at the massive front doors. He, too, knew that his master was not going to live much longer, and the uncertainty of what was to come sent a shiver through his body. To a slave, the death of a master was a terrifying prospect—fraught with uncertainty.

Isaac Ross allowed a long slow sigh to escape him as he recalled the many meetings and discussions that he had conducted before nailing down a concrete way to proceed with his plans. Several very real and pressing issues had thwarted his desires to free his slaves. It would be easier certainly to just go ahead and free the slaves now while he was still alive to see it through, but the passage of an 1822 law gave the state legislature direct involvement in the manumission of one's slaves.

The law gave the legislature the absolute authority to approve—or more likely, deny—all slave emancipations attempted in the state. The purpose of the law had clearly been to limit the number of free blacks living in Mississippi; the possibility of which had created near hysteria among many of the local planters.

Once it was clear to him that the legislature would not approve an application to free such a large number of slaves, he had begun to consider the concept of colonization. Captain Ross had met people who were a part of the American Colonization Society and he had come to believe that his slaves should be given the choice to become free and emigrate to Africa.

The American Colonization Society had been instrumental in founding a colony on the West Coast of Africa known as Liberia. The name of the colony itself was inspiring—Liberia, coming from the Latin word "liber" or free.

Ross realized that none of his slaves had actually been born in Africa, so they would be embarking on a completely new life rather than "returning" to a place of familiarity. Still, surely freedom there would be preferable to enslavement here. At least, that was the consensus of opinion among the slaves with whom he had discussed colonization.

He heaved another heavy sigh as he repositioned himself on his couch. He hated being old. Everything seemed to ache and creak these days. *What happened to the spry young man who fought in the war? He's become an old man, that's what has happened.* He pulled at the collar of his smoking jacket, warding off the chill. *I'll have to ask Enoch to put a few more logs on the fire.*

Ross felt anxious about the arrival of his daughter and grandson, who were due to arrive at any moment. He had asked them to stop by and discuss his last will and testament for what he assumed would be the last time. Without the loyalty and support of his heirs, his desire to free his slaves and provide them with a means to leave for Africa would undoubtedly be impossible.

He smiled broadly when he heard the voice of his daughter Margaret just moments before she swept into the parlor. He had spent many hours of his later years worrying about Margaret, who had twice been made a widow and had remained childless. But of his two living children, she was the joy of his latter days. On every occasion with which he had spoken with her about his intentions, she had readily supported him.

Captain Ross felt confident that he could count on Margaret. In fact, he had recently added a codicil to his will stating that she would have full control over Prospect Hill and the slaves until either her death, or whatever time she deemed appropriate to sell off the estate in order to carry out his provisions made for his slaves. *Yes, I can count on you, Margaret.*

Margaret Reed swooped down to kiss her father.

"Gracious! You are freezing cold."

Before Captain Ross could utter a reply, Margaret had called for Enoch.

"Yes, Missus?" Enoch appeared once again in the doorway to the parlor. Enoch had been the personal manservant of Captain Ross for years, since he had been a young teenager.

"Enoch, my father is cold. Could you please stoke the fire and bring him a blanket? Mr. Wade will be arriving soon and a chill enters the house each time the door opens, I'm afraid."

Margaret sat in a wingback chair closest to the couch which held her dying father. Her prematurely lined face showed the concern and devotion that she felt for him. She wasn't even fifty years old, but much of her life had been filled with loss and grief.

"Margaret, I don't have much time left. I called you here so that we can finalize plans for my estate." He shifted his position again, finding it impossible to be comfortable in one position for more than a few minutes. "And don't argue," he added, seeing that she had opened her mouth to protest his assertion that he was close to death.

She closed her mouth and managed a weak smile at her father. Margaret didn't want to face such things. She had already lost her dear mother, a sister, two brothers, and two husbands. *How much loss am I meant to bear?*

Sensing the words her father needed to hear, she spoke them. "You know that you have my full support."

Margaret and her father had discussed the issue at length on numerous occasions. She cleared her throat and continued, "We both agree that slavery cannot be allowed to continue. And colonization is the only decent option. Our slaves cannot be freed in Mississippi, thanks to the legislature. And even if we could manage their transport to a free state I fear that the opportunities available to them would be extremely limited."

Her father nodded gravely, but managed a smile when his eyes met hers. "If only you had been born a male."

He shook his head slowly from side to side. "I could have easily left my estate in your capable hands. You have a better mind and tougher constitution than most of the men I've known in my life."

A tight laugh escaped Margaret's throat. "Father, what a futile wish."

Margaret tried not to be a sentimental woman. Life was too painful for those who allowed themselves to speculate about what might have been. "I suppose that the fate of your estate is now destined to fall into the hands of my nephew."

As if on cue, Isaac Ross Wade arrived at the front door of the home. Wade was the son of Jane Ross, Margaret's sister. The young man was one of the executors of her father's estate.

The sounds of Enoch's voice drifted into the parlor, followed by the harsher tones of Isaac Ross Wade. Margaret stiffened slightly in her seat as her nephew entered the room in a sweeping manner. Just as she had predicted, a cold chill seemed to follow him into the room.

Margaret had always felt that January was the most dreadful month. The view from the windows seemed barren and frigid—so different from the views during the other seasons. *Prospect Hill is so beautiful in the spring. I hope*

Father can hold out to see the beauty of this place one last time.

"Margaret," Wade nodded in the direction of his aunt. "A pleasure as always."

He took a seat without making any direct physical contact with either his grandfather or his aunt. "Mother sends her best wishes, of course."

He turned his attention to his grandfather, who was grimacing slightly as he once again attempted to find a position of comfort on his couch. His apparent misery was not lost on his grandson.

"No improvement then?" Isaac Ross Wade asked. "I was hopeful that I might find you in better health than on the occasion of our last visit."

"Grace made a poultice for my aches and pains that has helped more than anything the doctors have given me," grumbled Captain Ross. "At least I can get *some* relief from the pain with her remedies."

Wade raised his eyebrows. "I'm not so sure you should be trusting that African tribal voodoo. It might not be safe."

Ross waved his hand in dismissal. "Nonsense. None of it has ever hurt me in all these years. I don't imagine I'll start worrying about it now."

The younger man looked like he had much more to say on the subject, but after a moment simply replied, "The choice is yours, Grandfather."

There was a palpable tension in the room that wouldn't have been there if Captain Ross' will had been a more traditional one. All three of them were aware of it. Matters of death and wills were never a pleasant topic of discussion, particularly when the heirs to a fortune would not receive any significant portion of the wealth for their own use.

In the current will, Wade was designated to receive only his grandfather's fine writing desk and the contents of his library. His grandson would be paid a commission for managing the estate, but not a cash gift—Captain Ross assumed that his namesake had probably been hurt by the decision.

But Ross was resolute in his beliefs that what he was doing was the right thing, and nothing was going to change his mind. Furthermore, when he had tried to explain his stance to his grandson, he had been dismissed from doing so, with assurances that he was free to do as he pleased with his own possessions.

After a few moments of uncomfortable silence, Captain Ross spoke. "You both have reviewed my will and the subsequent codicils that have been added. But now that I'm close to death, I need your assurances. Assurances that the provisions I've laid out—particularly the ones pertaining to the colonization of my slaves—will be carried out according to my wishes."

He addressed them both, but was looking directly at his grandson.

"You've seen the latest codicil, I believe." Wade nodded, and Ross continued, "Nothing goes into effect until Margaret decides that it is the right time."

"Or I die," she added grimly.

Ross cast a loving glance at Margaret. "I want to be sure that you can live at Prospect Hill and make use of the property as long as you choose to."

He turned his gaze back to his grandson. "Are you clear

on the details? You are an executor of the will and now is the time to ask questions if you have them. I'm afraid that you are running out of time to ask anything of me."

Wade shifted uncomfortably in his seat, acutely aware of the two other people in the room intently watching him.

"I'm clear on everything," he rather brusquely replied as he looked from his grandfather to his aunt. "With all due respect, we have been over this before. On several different occasions."

If his grandfather was put off by his abruptness, he didn't show it. "What about the provisions for the cotton crop harvested following my death? The proceeds are to be used to finance the transport of my slaves to Liberia."

"I understand all of the provisions, including the ones in the codicils." Wade's expression was impassive.

Another frosty silence fell over the room. Margaret had said barely a word since her nephew had entered the room. Rumors, however vague, had reached her ears that her nephew had been talking to others about his disdain over his grandfather's will. She had the distinct impression that the words he was now speaking lacked veracity.

"There is something else that I need to discuss with both of you. It involves Enoch." Captain Ross glanced over his shoulder to make sure Enoch wasn't in view, but lowered his voice as he spoke to his heirs. "I'm rather ashamed to say that the codicil I added to my will depriving Enoch of his freedom was petty. It was based on information that I've now concluded wasn't accurate."

Margaret and her nephew did not comment or interrupt, so Ross continued on.

"He has devoted too many years of selfless service to

me not to be rewarded for it upon my death. I fear that I won't have time to get another legal codicil written. So I would like for you both to assure me that you will attest to my intent regarding Enoch. He is to be regarded in my final will as if that earlier codicil pertaining to him—the one I freely admit to writing in unjustified anger—had never been written."

Neither of them questioned what information he was referring to, or any reasons that he might have for this sudden change of heart.

"Just tell me what exactly it is that I need to do, and I will gladly honor your wishes," Margaret replied to her father, leaning more closely to him. "I'm sure that Isaac will also."

Isaac Wade's face conveyed no emotion. There was no way to have discerned what feelings, if any, had been stirred by this latest request from his grandfather. It certainly was of no importance to him what fate befell Enoch after his grandfather's death.

"Certainly I will. I would imagine it would involve the two of us," he nodded in the direction of Margaret, "appearing in the offices of Grandfather's lawyers to document his verbal declaration of intent with regards to Enoch's status under the will. We will affirm his wishes on his behalf and sign the document in the presence of witnesses."

Captain Ross smiled weakly. "That is essentially what I was told by counsel as well. Legal talk that makes little sense to most people."

"I will depend on your guidance, then," said Margaret softly to Wade. "I wish to do everything in my power to honor my father's wishes. In entirety."

"Of course," affirmed her nephew with a terse nod.

For a moment, no one spoke. The crackle of the fire seemed to fill the room with a satisfying sound that captivated the three family members, all momentarily lost in their own thoughts.

"Let's have tea," Captain Ross abruptly announced in as cheerful a tone as he could muster at the moment. He was feeling every single one of his seventy-seven years.

Captain Ross seemed to have concluded that there was nothing more that needed to be said about his will. He was so tired of lawyers and legal discussions. It was not something he enjoyed at all. "I'm afraid we'll have to have tea served in here. I don't feel well enough to relocate myself to a more proper setting for hosting my guests today." He gave them a wan smile.

Margaret rose. "I'll summon Enoch, father."

She walked gracefully out of the parlor but returned almost instantly with Enoch a few paces behind her, carrying a serving tray. As was common with house servants of the period, he moved with the grace of an English Butler and wore a fine livery.

"Enoch must have expected you'd want tea. He's already prepared a tray." She smiled at the servant fondly. "And the cakes look wonderful. Please pass along my appreciation to Grace."

As Margaret returned to her perch on the wingback chair, Isaac Ross Wade looked smugly at the man serving his master. *Margaret actually believes he was busy in the kitchen this whole time. I saw the tray already prepared when I walked in. He has undoubtedly been listening outside of the door to every word we have said.*

As Enoch bent over to pour the tea, Wade was already formulating a strategy for what his first plan of attack would be on his grandfather's will. *There is no way that I am going to watch this fortune pass through my hands without getting what is rightfully mine.*

January 18, 1836   Prospect Hill Slave Quarters

*F*reedom. *They keep sayin' that word. Freedom. But what will it mean for us?* Levi was a slave of only 15 years of age, so he felt proud to have been asked to the meeting. He hadn't said anything, as he felt it wasn't his place to do so. But his mind was so full of questions that he was having a hard time taking in all of the information being discussed. Especially when several of the men started talking at once, which had occurred several times already. It didn't help that Rachael was sitting against the wall looking so pretty. It was hard to concentrate on anything when she was nearby.

Each of the men asked to attend the meeting had been chosen for their perceived usefulness and discretion. Esau was a skilled craftsman with access to the main house. Old Yeary was older, and considered to be wise. Gilbert was the foreman of the field slaves which made him invaluable in disseminating information. Andrew and Levi were younger, but were seen as smart and resourceful. The majority of the slaves at Prospect Hill were not aware of the meeting.

The conversation around the crude wooden table

was being conducted in attempted hushed tones. However, the roaring fire in the stone fireplace that took up a large portion of the wall closest to the table was obligating the slaves to use loud whispers. The energy in the room was palpable, crackling from person to person almost in unison with the crackling of the fire. They all knew their master was nearing death. And as slaves, this represented a frightening uncertainty that would affect every aspect of their very existence.

It was a cold night outside, but the bodies packed into the small cabin in combination with the fire created so much warmth that some of the more ardent speakers were glistening with sweat in the firelight. Tensions were running high, and the occupants of the cabin felt as though they were sitting upon a tinderbox, ready to ignite any second if the wrong words were spoken.

There had been much hearsay, and much whispering around Prospect Hill for months now. Even Captain Ross himself had made rounds about the place in recent times asking certain slaves what they felt of freedom. What they would do with it if they had it? Anything seemed possible now.

They all felt an urgent need to find some answers, but who could they trust to give them the honest ones? Enoch was a trusted source and he had heard most of what had been spoken between Ross and his heirs just days ago. But his information still left many questions unanswered.

The slave women were sitting on the floor, on the pallets that were generally pulled out at night and used for the children to sleep on. However, tonight the children had been relegated to a corner of the room and were already asleep on a pile of blankets. The women leaned back against the rough wooden planks of the wall and felt the chill on their backs seeping through the planks from the outside air, even though the room was stifling. The normal chatter among them was notably absent as they listened intently while tending to their mending.

Edmond Belton slammed his hand down on the table and the room fell silent. A couple of the sleeping children startled enough at the banging noise to raise their heads, but almost instantly returned to sleep. Ed was well respected among the slave population at Prospect Hill, and was looked upon as a leader.

His mother, Mariah Belton, had been one of the original Ross slaves who had come from South Carolina when Isaac Ross had migrated to Mississippi. She held a position of social prominence among the slaves, working in the main house.

All eyes were on Ed as he began once again to speak in an urgent undertone, "I tell you again, I heard it from Enoch myself. Cap'n Ross is dyin'. Ain't no disputin' that. Missus Reed and Mister Wade come by to visit. Enoch heard most of what they was sayin'. Cap'n goin' to free us and give us a choice to go to Africa. Both of the white folk say they is goin' to let it happen but ole Enoch ain't so sure. He says he don't trust Mister Wade no further than he can throw him."

Some murmuring started up around the table and among the second row of men behind the ones seated. "What we got to do," began Ed above the murmuring, which instantly quieted back down, "Is agree on a plan. We can't be lettin' it just be told to us how it's gonna be. We got to know our rights."

The deep baritone voice of Esau rang out clearly and more loudly than intended, "We ain't got no rights! That the point I been makin' all evenin'!"

Several voices shushed Esau at once. He lowered his voice and continued, "We got whatever rights the white men say we got. And that ain't nothin'!"

There was a general assent of agreement to Esau's words running through the room. When Ed's younger brother Wade Belton spoke, his voice was just barely audible above the whispered tones around the table. "You both is right, but we don't need to be arguin' with ourselves. We need to work out for sure what we know is true. Our Master wants to free us. But not to stay round these parts. We'd have to travel a mighty long way to Africa. We don't know what we'd find waitin' for us there neither."

"We'd have our freedom, brother," replied Edmond Belton firmly. The brothers regarded each other for a moment before Ed concluded, "That all I need to know."

After a moment, Ed turned his attention back to the room at large and continued. "Freedom what Americans died for in the war. We fought along side 'em too, but that don't seem to count for nothin' round here. But now we gettin' a chance for freedom that we ain't never gonna have here. They ain't gonna let us. The white men scared of us. Got Nat Turner on they minds every night when they lie down to sleep. They don't want us free and wanderin' round. That why Cap'n Ross has to send us off to free us. But I'm willin' to take freedom however I can."

The slave rebellion of 1831 led by Virginia slave Nat

Turner sent shockwaves through the minds of slave owners across the South. Each wealthy planter was aware that something of that nature could happen in their county, perhaps on their own plantations. The white death toll, at least 50 people, had been high enough to make a lasting impression on them.

"Think on it," said Andrew, a young field worker around 18 years old. "They won't be no white people in Africa to be lookin' down at us. We'd be the ones in charge of everythin' we got."

"But what that gonna be? We got nothin' to take with us!" The conversation was once again growing heated and the attempt at hushing their voices was failing. Esau was a large man, and his very physical presence garnered him a level of respect from the others.

Ed spoke once again, attempting to lower his volume. "Enoch overheard Mister Wade talkin' with Dr. Wade about some place called Haiti a few months back. They said the papers were markin' some anniversary of the black slaves killin' off every single white person on that island. Man, woman, and child…killed them all. Now the black folks make the rules in that place. Mister Wade say it could happen here if they not careful."

More murmuring began around the cabin. Some of the women shuddered at the mention of so many murders, and mutters of "Sweet Jesus" were heard along the wall.

The raspy voice of Old Yeary was barely heard over the murmuring. "All I want is what is supposed to come to me from Cap'n Ross. Nothin' more. I want my sons to get a chance to own somethin' and to make choices. We should go to Africa if we get the chance. I trust Cap'n Ross to know what's best."

The men around the room didn't respond to his comments right away. Old Yeary was getting older and more feeble, but he was a highly respected individual on Prospect Hill.

Esau responded again, but with a slightly deferential tone. "I respect what you sayin'. But we might well die waitin' on these white folks in the family to give us what we been promised. I agree if we given the chance we should go to Africa. There ain't no freedom for us here."

The night was getting late and the discussion was starting to return to points already made. Ed felt the need to take control back and wind it down for the night.

"So, how 'bout you raise your hand if you plannin' to go with your family to Africa if we given the chance?"

He looked around as one hand after another went up into the air, illuminated by the firelight. The raised hands cast eerie shadows around the walls of the slave quarters making it appear as though a hundred hands were raised in favor of freedom.

Ed swallowed hard, filled with emotion at the promise of realizing his dream. He addressed the group again.

"So, we knows that we want our chance at Africa. I suppose we just got to wait and see what happens when Cap'n Ross die. I don't trust that Mister Wade, but there not much we can do 'til we see what he gonna do."

Ed saw determination in the faces of the men surrounding him, and went on. "Keep listenin' for information you can pick up and report it back to me. We'll meet here again when we know somethin' more."

It took some time for the good-byes to be spoken and

the slaves to begin ambling back to their respective quarters. Some walked in slow groups, quietly talking as they moved into the darkness. Levi was talking with some of the other young slaves, his heart full of anxious wonder about what his future might hold. Edmond Belton closed the wooden door, shutting off his view of the other slaves milling along, and turned his attention back to his own small plank home.

Ed moved his sleeping children to their pallets and watched his wife, Sadie, straighten up the room in the firelight. Neither of them spoke for a time. Finally he approached her and put his hands on her shoulders, turning her to face him. She kept her head down, and he took his right hand and gently lifted her chin so that she was forced to look into his face. Her eyes were glistening with tears.

"What'd you have me do, Sadie? Somebody got to take charge."

"I scared. I scared 'bout meetin's and discussions. Master Ross dyin'. That talk about Nat Turner. I don't like all this talk I hearin'."

As terrifying as the Nat Turner revolt had been for whites in the South, literally scores of slaves were rounded up and lynched following the uprising. Many of those killed had not participated in the revolt. There was plenty of fear to go around in the years following the rebellion.

She looked at her husband and felt herself trembling. "You gonna be seen as a leader if somethin' happen."

Then she spoke the words that she hated herself for thinking. "Is things so bad here? We got each other and our young'ns." She knew what freedom meant to Ed, but she was scared. And at this moment, fear trumped her desire to be free.

"Things a changin'. Once Cap'n Ross gone, it won't be like this no more."

Seeing the alarm still blazing in her beautiful face, he added, "But, I be careful. I promise." Then, planting a kiss on her forehead, he said, "We best get on to bed."

He took her hand and led her to the tiny room containing their rope bed and a couple of wooden crates that held their few possessions. The bed was still low to the ground, but preferable to the straw-stuffed pallets the children used for beds. As slaves of Captain Ross, they fared better than most slaves in the state of Mississippi at the time. But a longing for freedom still burned inside of Ed.

His mother, Mariah, didn't share his passions for freedom and had already told him that she and her youngest son, William, would not go to Africa if given the choice. She was mulatto and enjoyed a relative position of status in the Ross household. She hoped to stay on and receive wages for her service. He knew that he would not ever convince her to leave what she knew for a completely unfamiliar existence in a strange land.

He hated the thought of leaving behind people he loved, but he had to think about his own offspring. Although he resented the system that allowed him to be another man's property, he couldn't fault Captain Ross' treatment of his slaves. He had encouraged the slaves to find spouses and had kept family units together—never allowing them to be sold. *But we still is slaves. White men have the control. When the old master dies, someone else will decide which of us can be sold.*

Ed shuddered at the thought of having Sadie or one of

his children taken from him. Perhaps to keep him in line, scare him, or punish him. He held his wife in his arms and eventually drifted into a fitful sleep; his last conscious thoughts were of freedom. Freedom at any cost.

January 21, 1836 Prospect Hill Plantation

The formal living room still bore the traces of the funeral service that had been held just hours earlier. Margaret wandered mindlessly down the stairs and entered the now deserted room after a failed attempt to get some rest in her upstairs bedroom. It had been impossible to rest, as her mind was still racing with images of the day. The clock in the foyer was still frozen in time. The pendulum was stopped by Enoch when Captain Ross took his last breath. The hands on the face of the beautiful clock were stopped at 8:26. *I can't believe he is gone.* She had the familiar heaviness in her chest that she had felt so many times before—each time she had lost a person dear to her heart. There had been too many.

    She comforted herself by thinking of what a proper and respectful service it had been. Everyone who'd received a funeral card had attended the service to honor Captain Ross. Reverend Zebulon Butler of the Presbyterian Church in Port Gibson had given a eulogy. He told of her father's promotion to the rank of Captain in the war. He gave a history of the battles he had fought in, the loyalty he had inspired in the men he commanded, the injuries sustained in battle. He reminded the people in attendance of the fact that her father still wore a glass eye to replace the one he lost in service to the nation. Margaret had beamed with pride remembering her father's life. She felt a smile come to her face. *You would have been proud, Papa.*

She looked around, briefly taking note that the house servants had already removed the black crepe that had been draping the rooms and covering the mirrors in the house earlier that morning. Margaret slowly approached the place where her father's body had been laid earlier to allow mourners a chance to pay their last respects to him. She ran her hand over the polished wooden surface of the bier that had not only held her father's coffin, but her mother's and siblings as well. She allowed her hand to linger on the cool structure and closed her eyes, letting her memories flood over her. Tears slowly began to build in spite of her efforts not to cry. *This is no time for weakness. There is a fight ahead and tears will not serve any purpose in your cause.*

Although her brain told her that she was strong and determined enough to ensure her father's wishes were carried out, her inner self spoke a different message. She was tired, and she had been aware of strength leaving her for some time now. Margaret sighed. She wondered if there was anyone else who would understand how she felt at this moment.

To anyone looking at her, she had a life of privilege and luxury. She possessed fine homes with the best furnishings available. But she had a secret that she had never disclosed to anyone. In truth, in some ways Margaret Reed felt as enslaved as the unfortunate souls that she was dedicating herself to freeing. Enslaved by her role as a woman in a world where only men wielded any power.

She thought back to the conversations that she had had with her father about the injustices of slavery. The lack of liberty, the lack of autonomy, the lack of a vote or voice in their circumstances. It had taken all of her strength not to ask, "But father, where is my autonomy without a husband, father, or brother to speak for me? You admitted it yourself that you wish I'd been born a male."

Her role as a woman in Antebellum Mississippi offered Margaret little more freedom than the slaves she herself owned. And now she had no man tied to her to give her voice in her own circumstances. They had all been taken from her.

Bitterness was often lingering in the shadows in Margaret's lowest moments, and she often found herself turning to Scripture and focusing on feeling grateful for what she did have. *Of course I am better off. Which of them would not trade their own circumstances for mine? Father, forgive my ungrateful heart.* She had known bitter, widowed ladies and had vowed to never become one.

There had even been flashes of momentary envy when she had observed slaves in their quarters so demonstrative and loving with their spouses and children. The stiff inhibitions of societal expectations did not apply to the slaves. *But how can I feel jealous of people in these circumstances? It isn't rational when I have my freedom, and they don't.* But then moments later, the doubt would creep back. *Freedom? What does it even mean?* Then once again, Margaret would chastise herself for making such comparisons.

Of course she was better off than her slaves. It was foolish to suggest otherwise. Furthermore, it was certainly her duty to see to their transport to Liberia. These were the thoughts that churned in her mind and made it difficult to rest. She often wished for a switch to turn off her mind, craving inner peace that she had not felt in a very long time.

Margaret was still lost in thought with her hand resting gently on her father's funeral bier when Enoch walked into the room. He stopped cold when he saw her standing in his path. "Missus Margaret, I thought you was upstairs restin'. I'll go on now and let you be."

"There is no need, Enoch. I was just too restless to nap although I need one desperately." She smiled weakly at the familiar face, actually grateful for the company. "Please don't go. Carry on with what needs doing."

"I was just going to finish clearing up and put these chairs back." Enoch gestured around the room, still partially set up from the funeral service.

She heard the cast iron bells ringing, signaling the end of the work day for the field slaves. The sound was moot today however, as Margaret had insisted they be given the day off for mourning. *Could Gilbert be ringing them today as a tribute to Father?* The thought brought a flicker of a smile across her face. The bells were somehow soothing to her, and she had always liked them even as a child. She and Enoch both stood in the room, listening to the bells until they stopped.

"Missus Margaret," said Enoch breaking the silence. "I is truly sorry for your loss. Captain Ross was a fine man. I hope you don't mind me sayin' so."

Margaret felt a rush of tenderness for this man who had served her father so well. "He felt the same way about you, Enoch. He told me so more than once."

Enoch straightened up and seemed to add an inch to his height. Margaret noticed a tear in the corner of his eye and politely turned away. "Thank you, missus." Enoch walked so quietly out of the room that Margaret, still gazing out onto the fields only briefly caught the back of him as he exited.

Margaret truly did dislike winter months. She would have loved a nice walk to clear her mind, but now that the sun was setting the air would be cold and damp. *The last thing I need is to catch a cold.* She wandered out of the room, not really sure what she was going to do. She just needed to do something.

Maybe I'll pick up my sewing. At least it will keep my hands occupied, if not my mind. Recalling that she had last been working on it in the parlor, she headed that direction. Before she reached the doors, however, she heard urgent whispers that she recognized as coming from her sister Jane and Jane's son Isaac Ross Wade.

"Mother, we have nothing to worry about. I told you that I have consulted Henry Ellett, a fine attorney. He has reviewed the will and told me that there are loopholes in it big enough to drive a carriage through. The 1822 law gave the Mississippi legislature the authority to approve or reject all slave emancipations in the state. Since Grandfather did not obtain the necessary approval, his actions are not legally sanctioned here."

"But what about my sister?" asked Jane with a trace of bitterness in her voice. "She will stop you from whatever you are planning with Mr. Ellet."

"Your sister will know nothing of my plans. She is the one who has control of Prospect Hill for right now, that is true. But upon her death, or earlier if she decides to give it up, the control passes to me. Mr. Ellett and his associates are confident that any will she draws up can be voided upon her death. They've assured me of that."

Margaret reached out her hand to steady herself. She knew that Jane and Isaac were not in agreement with her father's decision regarding his estate. She had prepared herself to defend his wishes knowing they would want her to change the stipulations of the will. But this was such a shock to her, that she felt for a moment as if the room was spinning under her. *He has already consulted attorneys? There is no will I can create that cannot be undone?*

Realizing that the fight she faced was greater than she had even imagined was exactly what Margaret needed to strengthen her resolve. Moments ago, she been mired in pity, feeling powerless. But her father had given her, a woman, the control over Prospect Hill. *And I'm not dead yet, dear sister and nephew. How advantageous that I overheard your mutinous conversation. It gives me time to fortify the strength of my own will so that when the time comes, you will lose your fight.*

"So we wait?" asked Jane of her son.

"For now," replied Wade. "Although things are happening already behind the scenes. The majority of powerful men in Jackson want to make sure that this will does not hold up in court. And we have the law on our side. The legislature only approves the emancipation of slaves following an act of valor. I seriously doubt the slaves in question have performed such acts."

Jane made a scoffing sound. "I don't recall any of those."

"Even if one of the Ross slaves had performed such a deed, the release of the slave would have to be approved by the state legislature. So it brings us back to the point on which we base our legal argument: Grandfather was not within his legal rights to free his slaves. By the time the control of Prospect Hill is in my grasp, I will have the legal argument in place to prove it."

"I should think so. But what about the legal fees?" Jane was still speaking in a hushed whisper, but her voice carried clearly to Margaret's astonished ears.

"Mr. Ellett and his associates are more than willing to wait until I receive my salary as executor. This case will set legal precedents, and be reported in every major newspaper in the state. They are chomping at the bit to be involved in it."

There was silence for a moment. Margaret bristled imagining the smug look that must be gracing her nephew's face. *He thinks he can beat me because he is a man, and I am just a woman. We'll see about that.*

She heard Jane's voice again. "Margaret will be up soon. We will have many written notes to address to those who brought food by today. How I dread the formalities of such occasions."

"I am sure you will manage, Mother. You always pull these things off beautifully." His voice was dripping with indifference, clearly communicating that he had much more important matters on his mind than the trivial social obligations dreaded by his mother.

Margaret heard the stirring from the room alerting her to retreat as quickly and quietly as she could. She managed to get to the bottom of the staircase where she was able to feign a recent descent into the foyer.

Margaret acted surprised to see Jane emerging from the parlor. "Why, Jane, could you not sleep?"

The startled look on her sister's face almost caused Margaret to laugh. But she maintained a completely blank countenance.

"Oh, I only just rose and came down myself," replied Jane with a half-hearted smile.

"The servants should be laying the table for supper. I certainly hope that you will both be joining me," Margaret said nodding in acknowledgment of Isaac Wade's appearance behind his mother.

Margaret took pleasure in seeing them squirm. They were both wondering how long she had been downstairs, and if she had noticed them emerging from the parlor together. She could almost literally see the wheels in their heads turning as she observed their attempts at silent communication.

"Well, I suppose it would be prudent for me to stay the night. It is January and darkness will be falling rapidly." Jane looked coolly at her sister. "May I assist you with any hostess duties, Margaret?"

"Most of the guests have departed. There isn't much left to do, except for correspondence. And I welcome the chance to keep busy."

Margaret held out her arm graciously to her sister. "Come, let's sit and watch the sunset from the sitting room. It is quite a lovely view." After leading Jane a few steps,

Margaret spoke over her shoulder to her nephew, "Of course you will be joining us, won't you?"

Wade followed without comment, confident in his ability to outsmart his misguided aunt. He smiled as he looked around the foyer of the house that he was already counting as his. *I just need to bide my time. And then when that time comes, all of this will be mine.*

***

"So all we do now is wait. That's what I sayin'." Enoch was just outside of the kitchen door speaking with Ed Belton, who had been hanging around the main house as much as he could all day without arousing suspicion. He was hoping to hear good news to take back to the slave quarters. News of freedom.

"But the old Master died. Why don't that make us free like you say before?"

Ed was reeling from the news. Just a few days ago he felt so close to freedom he could almost reach out and touch it. It seemed tangible for the first time in his life. But now, Enoch was telling him that nothing was going to change. He had heard folks in the house saying that Captain Ross had stipulated in his will that his daughter, Margaret would have control over the property, which included all of the slaves, until her death.

"Ain't meanin' no disrespect. I never had no bad feelin's towards missus Margaret. But she could live on another ten, twenty years. And what 'bout us. We just gotta wait?"

"Fraid so," replied Enoch. "Ain't nothin' else to do but wait."

Ed wanted to rage. To scream a primal scream of outrage and betrayal into the darkening skies. He despised himself for getting his hopes up. And even more for allowing the others to feel hope as well. *Hope? Why did I think freedom could ever come to us?*

"You better be gettin' back to the quarters," said Enoch. "Don't want no questions."

Ed turned and headed back to his cabin. He knew others were waiting on him and dread filled his insides as he made his way down the sloping hillside. *What will I tell Sadie?*

He saw Andrew, one of the younger slaves he had asked to attend their meetings, waiting on his return. Andrew's face was full of eagerness to hear what the Fates held in store. Ed felt ten years older than when he had started up the hill, so full of expectation earlier in the day. Now, he wearily headed off Andrew's questions. "Tell everyone there be a meetin' in my cabin tonight. Same time as last."

Andrew opened his mouth to question Ed, but decided better of it. He muttered, "I'll go spread the word," and headed off into the twilight.

Ed didn't rush to get back. What was the point? All he had was time. Time to wait for another white person to die so that he could have a chance to be a free man. *Wait. What a cruel word. Almost as cruel as hope.*

The irony was that this would be one of the few times in life that Ed Belton and Isaac Ross Wade would have the same nemesis—time.

September 1838   Ridges Plantation

Margaret Reed had become mistrustful of almost everyone these days. She positively detested feeling that way, but it had become extremely difficult to know who to believe in. Her own family had become completely polarized over the issue of her father's will. Even trusted friends and neighbors had been whispering behind her back, some even bold enough to accuse her of trying to spread a dangerous influence over the slaves of the entire county.

Her social life, already somewhat limited as a widow, had been negatively affected by her refusal to back down in the years since her father's death. Still, she had made it known what her intentions were regarding the emancipation of both her slaves and her father's, now left in her care. Only days before, she had been caught off guard by her feelings of isolation while walking through her foyer. She had happened a glance at the small round table near the front door which would have normally been scattered with the calling cards of her visitors, but now lay empty.

Tears had began rolling down her now sallow cheeks before she could stop them. Forgoing her constant struggle to resist such impulses, she allowed herself a good cry that afternoon—a release of the pain and torment of going against the status quo in a society full of rules. And in that society, if one broke those rules, the consequences were meted out swiftly and without compassion.

Immediately after her father's death, Margaret had planned for her nephew Isaac Allison Ross, the only son of her dearly departed brother Isaac Ross, Jr., to be her executor. Since her brother's own will from 8 years earlier had provided for the freedom of his slaves, Margaret felt safe in assuming that his son would share the same sentiments. But as time went on, she became unsure if there were any family members other than herself who truly wanted to see the slaves freed.

Ultimately she had summoned her lawyer, Mr. Chaplain, to her property, Ridges Plantation. It was the home where she had moved after the death of her second husband Thomas Buck Reed, a United States Senator. She felt she could be sure of a more private meeting here than she could hope for at Prospect Hill. And privacy was something she fiercely guarded now.

After her husband Thomas' sudden and unexpected death, she could not bear to remain at the home that they had lovingly renovated as newlyweds. Neither could she imagine moving back into to her parents' home again. So, she had sold her marital home to Dr. John Ker and purchased Ridges Plantation. For some time, she had been reasonably happy at Ridges. But since her father's death, the familiar feelings of despair and isolation had washed over her again.

The past two years had been a nightmare of tirelessly crusading for something that at times seemed to be a lost cause. *If only dear Thomas were still here to help me through all of these details.* She missed her husband daily. She was weary and drained from the effort it took to maintain her fight.

Margaret was grateful that Mr. Chaplain would be arriving any minute to obtain her signature on a codicil she was adding to her will. She had had to make more than one revision or addition to the document in her attempt to make it legally binding. This moment was one of many in the past two years that she had wished her father had not left this burden for her to bear.

Margaret had recently decided that she needed to include a back-up plan in her will after hearing further stories of boasting from Isaac Ross Wade's lawyers through the wealthy white planters in the area. The dispute of the will had been rich gossip fodder at every social gathering for the past several years and snippets of the gossip always managed to find their way back to Margaret. She was sure that efforts were already being planned to invalidate her own will.

If that did come to fruition, she and Mr. Chaplain had decided that a codicil stating that if her initial intent was thwarted, her property would instead be given to Reverend Zebulon Butler and Stephen Duncan. Of course, this meant that she was, in essence, making these two men of no blood relation her heirs. But both of these men were members of the Colonization Society who were dedicated to seeing slaves returned to Africa. In her state of desperation,

Margaret felt like this was her best option.

Mr. Chaplain's arrival was announced by Hattie, one of Margaret's oldest servants. Hattie had the distinct shuffle of advancing age to her walk now. As she watched her retreat from the room, Margaret hoped that Hattie would choose to live with Adelaide after her own passing. The thought of her niece, Adelaide, always her greatest source of joy, now pained her. *Oh, dear Adelaide, how I've loved you. Even Father loved you so much that he left a bequest of ten thousand dollars for your care. Do you support his dying wish? If only you understood how much this means to both of us.*

Adelaide's brother Isaac Ross Wade was Margaret's fiercest enemy at the moment and her most recent encounters with her niece had seemed rather strained. *Is it paranoia on my part, or are you siding with your brother? If only I could know for sure.* The Wade children had lost their father at a young age, and both Margaret and her father had taken on a great role in their upbringing and education. The pain of her nephew's betrayal had been extremely difficult, but the thought that Adelaide could have joined forces with him was almost too much for her to bear. A small cry of despair escaped her throat in spite of her best efforts.

Mr. Chaplain's entrance into the room broke her reverie. "Mrs. Reed, you are looking well."

The outright lie by her attorney almost caused Margaret to audibly snicker, but she managed to restrain herself. Despite her fragile emotional state, the decorum of her upbringing was firmly ingrained in her. Besides, she certainly didn't need to provide any more fuel for the talk running rampant through Jefferson County speculating that she had completely lost her mind.

However, the cold hard fact of the matter was that she looked anything but well, and she was fully aware of it. Dark circles had formed under her eyes, and she had lost a good bit of weight despite all of the delicious food at her disposal. She just didn't have an appetite anymore. The loss of weight had only exaggerated the lines on her face. The strain of the legal wrangling and family disputes had taken a tremendous toll on her health—and it showed.

She managed a gracious smile and replied, "You are far too kind, Mr. Chaplain." Then gesturing with her right hand in a sweeping motion towards an armchair, she added, "Please have a seat."

Mr. Chaplain sat on the designated chair, and opened his briefcase on his lap. He pulled out some papers and handed them to Margaret. "Please feel free to take your time reviewing them before signing."

She began reading the legal jargon, which was becoming more familiar to her than it would have ever been to a genteel southern lady under different circumstances. *Under normal circumstances.*

Hattie entered the room carrying a tray. *Shuffle, shuffle, shuffle.* "I remember Mr. Chaplain like coffee. So I bring some for him."

Margaret momentarily looked up from the technical details dividing up her life, and thanked Hattie.

Mr. Chaplain, obviously pleased that the old woman had remembered his preferences, also smiled and began placing his case on the floor to better manage his cup and saucer.

Hattie fussed over the coffee, adding the cream and

sugar to his liking as Margaret continued to read through the papers.

When she was satisfied with the content of the document, she looked up at her lawyer. Hattie quietly took her leave. *Shuffle, shuffle, shuffle.*

Margaret cleared her throat softly before speaking, "Mr. Chaplain, I know what people are saying about me. My very neighbors and friends that I have known most of my life have told me that I'm acting recklessly and foolish. I've been told I'm not a lady because I am going through with this 'misguided farce of fanaticism,' I think it was recently called."

The gentleman leaned forward to set his cup and saucer down on the table. His expression registered concern. "You have indeed borne a great deal of scorn and ridicule. Are you having reservations about your decisions?"

"Certainly not. I'm simply clarifying my position for you before placing my signature on these papers. You may well be asked about my state of mind on this day. I want to make it clear to you, that if anything, these attempts to shame me into backing away from my father's desire to liberate his slaves have done nothing but make my determination stronger."

"I will testify to such if need be," replied Mr. Chaplain. "You are clearly sound. And plainly determined. There is no doubt about that."

"I bear the burden of knowing that the fates of more than three hundred souls rest in my care. When I add my own 120 slaves to the numbers waiting at Prospect Hill, I often can't sleep at night thinking of what will come of them if these testaments do not hold up to the rigor of the courts."

The gentleman regarded his client for a moment. "I believe that we've written a document that will hold up to the most stringent legal challenges, Mrs. Reed."

"With all due respect sir, my nephew feels differently, and has not hesitated to crow it from the rooftops. His counsel is undoubtedly giving him similar assurances to the contrary."

She didn't intend to be rude, and felt chastened by the stung expression that appeared on Mr. Chaplain's face. But Margaret was feeling tired. She was ready to bring this to a close. Ready to close her eyes for a few hours. *Ready to stop fighting.*

"Have you a pen, Mr. Chaplain?"

The lawyer, a bit flustered by the suddenness of her request stammered a bit before handing over his steel nib pen to Margaret. She picked up the papers that made up her last will and testament and carried them over to her writing desk. She wanted to be sure that her signature was neat and legible. She wanted nothing left to chance that could possibly be contested at a later date. After carefully signing her name, she returned the stack of papers and the pen back into the hands of her legal counsel.

"Is there any way that I can assist you further, Mrs. Reed?"

Mr. Chaplain surveyed his battle-weary client. He wished that he genuinely had as much confidence as he had recently expressed in the ability of the will to hold up to the inevitable scrutiny it would face. *But then if I could predict the outcomes of legal proceedings with any certainty, I would be the richest man on the earth.*

"Thank you, but no, Mr. Chaplain. I think that will be all

I need for today." She smiled graciously at him, grateful for his assistance but anxious to be alone with her thoughts again.

She called softly for Hattie, who appeared with Mr. Chaplain's overcoat and hat.

He looked as if he wanted to say something more. Perhaps to reassure her further. She did not look well, despite his false flattery at their greeting. After a brief moment in which no words naturally came to him, he simply said, "Have a nice day, Mrs. Reed," and walked through the front door, which Hattie held open for him.

"Can I get you somethin', missus?" asked Hattie, a look of concern coming over the deep creases in her mahogany face.

"Hattie, I would surely appreciate a hot cup of tea. But I think I'd like to take it upstairs in my room. I'm feeling a bit tired."

"Yes'm. I bring it right up to you."

"Thank you, Hattie." She felt a deep affection for Hattie and so many of the other slaves that she had come to know over the years. It was probably the only thing that had given her the strength to keep fighting, to keep resisting her family. *They are counting on me. I have to stay strong for them.*

Margaret held onto the railing as she made her way up the staircase. She thought again of Adelaide as she approached the landing of the second floor of her home. Adelaide had married the April after Captain Ross died. She had seemed very happy then, and Margaret had acted as Adelaide's second mother during the planning stages of the ceremony and wedding trip. Jane wasn't the most nurturing type of mother, and Margaret had always been more than happy to provide that support. *Lord knows I love her as if she is my own daughter. The daughter I will never have.*

Margaret reached her bedroom and eased onto the chaise lounge by the fireplace. *Maybe I am just imagining a tension that isn't even there. Perhaps she hasn't been keeping up on all of the details of the proceedings at all.* She began replaying conversations recently held with her dear niece. It wasn't unusual that she would see less of her now that she had become a married woman. She had obligations to her husband and to her household after all.

When Hattie shuffled into the room, Margaret suddenly felt a stab of remorse at the realization that Hattie seemed a bit out of breath. *Why did I have her come all the way up these stairs carrying a tray? I should have realized that it would have been much easier for her to serve the tea in the parlor downstairs.*

But if Hattie resented the climb upstairs, she didn't show any sign of it to her mistress. She poured the tea and prepared it in the way that she knew Margaret enjoyed it. Reaching out with an ever so slightly trembling hand, Hattie handed her the cup and saucer.

"Now, you let this here tea warm you up and help you rest." Hattie pulled the throw from the end of Margaret's bed and laid it gently in her lap.

"Thank you again Hattie. You take such good care of me." Margaret couldn't help but notice that Hattie's face beamed with pride at the recognition. She watched as Hattie disappeared into the hallway and started back down the stairs.

Margaret recalled her meeting with Mr. Chaplain. She had spent the past two years devising the best plans to keep both her estate and her father's from being squandered, rather than going towards the slaves' liberty and new life in Africa. She was well aware that the slaves had no legal rights whatsoever in the hierarchal structure of Mississippi in 1838. They would be totally dependent on the two men she left in charge: Zebulon Butler and Stephen Duncan.

If I'm wrong about trusting them, then our cause is lost. These two men are truly my last hope. Our last hope. In an irony not lost on her, she had cast her lot—that of a wealthy white woman—in with that of the slaves. If she were to fail in her efforts, then it was a failure for all of them. Only, as she well knew, her failure would have much more drastic implications on their lives than it would on her own.

She made up her mind that she needed to reach out to Adelaide. Perhaps she was just being foolish in allowing her bitterness towards her sister and nephew to affect her always warm relationship with Adelaide. After all, she was a grown woman now and didn't need to seek approval from her family—she could make her own decisions about what is right and what is wrong. *I'll send her a note tomorrow asking her to come round to Prospect Hill for a visit.* She felt a small surge of energy pass through her at the opportunity to see Adelaide again and having the chance to catch up with her latest news.

Sadly, the long two years of fighting had worn Margaret down. She never had another visit with Adelaide. By the end of the week, Margaret Reed had taken her final breath; forever ending any hopes she may have held for reconciliation.

***

October 1838   Prospect Hill Plantation

Isaac Ross Wade stood on the wide front porch of his grandfather's home and surveyed his domain. At twenty four years of age, he felt as if his life was entering a new phase that would bring with it the wealth and privilege that he believed to be his birthright. Everything he could see stretching out before him was now his to manage as he saw fit. *Who is going to stop me now that Aunt Margaret is gone?*

His mother, Jane Brown Ross, walked out of the front doors and stood beside her son, feeling secure in their right to be there. This had been her parents' home after all. She had advised her son to wait several weeks after Margaret's funeral to formally move into the house. Many of Margaret's personal belongings had to be dealt with. Jane and Adelaide had taken care of distributing her clothing, shoes, china and other trivial items that were of no consequence to Wade whatsoever. He was concerned with much bigger sources of wealth than his aunt's baubles.

To Jane Brown Ross, appearances meant everything. She viewed it as crucial that her son's outward appearances were beyond reproach. She had big plans for the fortune that they were going to share and she knew that their hands must be artfully played. The tide of public opinion in Jefferson County needed to be on the side of the legitimate heirs of the Ross estate. *Surely they will agree that we would be more desirable beneficiaries of Prospect Hill than a group of slaves who wouldn't know what to do with freedom if they had it.*

The signs of the changing seasons were evident around them as they stood on the porch. The leaves were changing colors, and the air was becoming crisp. It seemed to them as if nature itself was joining them in heralding the great changes that lay ahead at Prospect Hill. Isaac Ross Wade cast one last glance in the direction of the slave quarters before escorting his mother back into the house. *There are going to be plenty of changes around here.*

April 15, 1840   Prospect Hill Plantation

Mary Girault was feeling extremely grateful to be at Prospect Hill on this beautiful April day. Her Aunt Catherine would marry Isaac Ross Wade later today and she was to be one of her attendants for the ceremony. She gave a twirl in her dress, admiring herself in the long oval mirror standing in the corner of the room.

At thirteen, she felt so grown up having been asked to be a proper maid of the bride and not a mere flower girl like her younger sister. The dress, covered in sheer white organza with a pale blue sash, made a full circle when she spun.

There had not been much happiness for Mary in recent months. She had been born in Natchez, and remembered the beautiful homes lining the bustling streets. It had been a vibrant and exciting place to live; especially when compared to where she currently resided with her parents. Her earliest memories had been happy ones.

Now they lived in Tuscahoma, a little-known town which had been founded by her father Major James Augustus Girault in 1834. His appointment by President

Van Buren through a special commission had been a great source of pride for the family. The appointment made him the receiver of public money for land sold in the area. At the time, her father saw opportunity in relocating his family from Natchez and seized it eagerly.

At first, it seemed rather exciting to young Mary to move to former Choctaw Indian territory and live in the wilderness. By 1836, their home, Bellevue, was built and it was a large and comfortable home in the stately Colonial style. But Mary had grown weary of being schooled at home. Her teacher was from New England and barely managed to keep her contempt for Southerners a secret. She missed the company of other people her age and opportunities for precious time away from her siblings.

Mary had been strictly forbidden to speak of her family's troubles before leaving home for the wedding. But holding onto the secret of their recent misfortunes had been weighing on her. She longed for someone with whom she could talk to about it, but she didn't dare break her word to her mother. She stopped spinning and primping in the mirror for a moment and contemplated the seriousness of her situation at home.

Her father had invested most of their money in the Mississippi Union Bank, which he had been certain was a sound investment at the time. However, the bank was unable to pay their European creditors and went under. Her father had secured his investment with their plantation Bellevue, most of their slaves, and other properties which now might have to be sold to pay off his personal debts. Mary knew only what she had overheard plus the little she had actually been told by her mother. But it was enough to give her a terrible sense of unease.

But what was giving her the biggest knot in her stomach was what she had overheard her parent's whispering about the morning her family had left to come to Prospect Hill. She had been so excited about her trip—her trunk sat by the front door of Bellevue waiting to be loaded into the carriage. Her brothers and sisters were playing with a ball in the courtyard but she had grown bored of the game, feeling anxious to depart.

She had started to run up the staircase in search of her mother, but quickly remembered that she was thirteen now and was never supposed to run. She slowed herself down, making as elegant an ascent up the stairs as she could manage with her ungainly build. When she reached the upstairs landing, she approached the door of her mother's dressing room which stood partially open. She had wanted to ask her mother yet again when they would be departing for Prospect Hill, but had begun to think it wouldn't be wise. After all, her mother had admonished her only an hour earlier for asking that very question.

Just as Mary decided to return back down the stairs, she heard her mother's voice. She felt sure it was her voice, but it sounded strange—higher pitched and almost frantic. Mary froze and listened, knowing that she shouldn't be eavesdropping, but unable to pull herself away.

"What do you mean a lawsuit? The federal government itself is naming you as a defendant?"

"It is a possibility, yes." It was definitely her father speaking.

"How can you be so calm? Isn't it bad enough we may have to sell everything? What will this mean to our family?" Her mother actually sounded scared. Her fear was immediately transferred onto Mary, still standing outside the door, transfixed by what she was hearing.

"Susan, you worry too much. I don't need you becoming frantic. I am only telling you this because I don't want you to hear of it from some old pea hen."

Her mother was crying now. Neither of her parents spoke for several moments. She could hear muffled sounds she knew to be her mother, and a shushing sound coming from her father.

"There are lawyers available to take on cases such as this. I've been informed that there is a gentleman by the name of Cocke who has a great deal of expertise in handling these matters."

Still more silence.

"Susan, I have not done anything wrong and I won't have you doubting my integrity. I issue receipts for monies received for the purchase of land as you know. I'll be turning over further monies with matching receipts in June. The records will bear up to scrutiny. I feel certain this will not go to the courts."

Mary heard sniffing and more shushing. She didn't want to hear any more, already feeling like she had violated her parent's trust in her by listening to this much. *I really must go back downstairs now.*

She had done so, and neither of her parents knew that she had overheard them talking. By the time her parents had walked into the courtyard giving instructions to the slaves for the carriage to be loaded, Mary was once again in a circle with her siblings who were still playing with the little brown ball. She had just convinced them to switch to a game of Blind Man's Buff when her parents appeared.

She had been relieved to finally take her seat in the interior of the carriage, but had been unusually quiet on the journey, something her mother apparently noticed. Mary replied to her mother's inquiry, "I was excited last night and did not sleep very well." The explanation had seemed to placate her mother for the time being.

As Mary had looked out the window at the scenery changing, she was aware of the soft chatter of voices of their house servants accompanying them on their trip. Nellie and Minny were sitting on the back board of the carriage facing rear with their feet swinging to and fro over the edge. She had occasionally hear muted laughter coming from behind her and would wonder what they were laughing about. Sam and Joe were sitting on the driver's seat.

Sam had been driving the family's carriage for as long as Mary could remember, and she always enjoyed hearing the conversations he would have with the horses. She believed that Sam could get those horses to do just about anything if he asked them nicely enough. The roads in this part of the state were very rough and difficult to travel.

Luckily, they only had to travel by land as far as the Mississippi River. From there, they would travel by steamboat downstream to Rodney. From there it was a fairly easy journey to Prospect Hill.

She remembered the words of reassurance that her father spoke earlier and felt momentarily more at ease. Still the future seemed scary and uncertain to Mary. She was grateful to have the chance to escape all of it for a few glorious days of wedding festivities. Once she had arrived at Prospect Hill, the excitement had pushed the worries out of her thoughts. She was around some of her favorite people, including her mother's parents James and Marbella Dunbar. Grandmother Marbella had made a big fuss about how beautiful she had become, and Mary felt quite pleased at the compliment. It was only in her few quiet moments alone that the fears crept back into her mind.

She again caught a glimpse of herself in the mirror and managed a small smile. *The dress truly is quite lovely, isn't it?*

Her musing was interrupted by the entrance of Adelaide. Adelaide Richardson, the groom's sister, was one of Mary's favorites out of her newly acquired family at Prospect Hill. Adelaide and her husband John had just had their first child, a precious baby girl named Martha. She was only 3 months old, but Adelaide had let Mary hold the little baby without hovering over her as if she feared Mary unable to maintain her grasp of the precious bundle.

Mary became immediately enchanted with little Martha: the way she grasped Mary's finger with her tiny little fist, the shapes she made with her little mouth, and the tiny wisp of fuzz that crowned her head. Even though Mother said it was nonsense, Mary was certain that Martha smiled at her when she was holding the tiny creature.

"Admiring the beautiful dress, I see?" Adelaide wore a gracious smile on her face. "You look absolutely lovely, Mary."

"Thank you very much. I love to watch it move with me when I do." She couldn't help but laugh and twirl around again.

Adelaide laughed. "Catherine's family ordered those

dresses from a fine shop in New Orleans. I hear the fabric is from Paris. But that silk organza was likely spun in China.

"Do you want to hear a secret?" Adelaide came closer to Mary, who nodded vigorously, delighted to be taken into her confidence.

"Catherine told me that she wanted a new wedding dress made for herself like the one Queen Victoria wore when she married Prince Albert this past February. The newspaper out of Port Gibson, *The Correspondent*, contained such a vivid description of the satin and lace gown. The fabric was a creamy white color. Imagine wearing a dress like that and not having to worry if you soil it. Such an impractical color!"

Mary again nodded and for once actually felt grateful for her condescending teacher. She had read the articles describing the lavish wedding to her, but with the purpose of disparaging the ostentatious display of wealth shown by the European royals. But Mary had been fascinated by the whole affair and had questioned her own mother about it later.

She knew that America had fought a war to be free from the tyranny of royalty, but that didn't mean she wasn't interested in such a grand wedding as that one. Her favorite stories had kings and queens, princes and princesses; of course she was fascinated by the real ones living in actual castles. *Maybe one day I will travel to Europe and see a castle for myself.*

Adelaide continued, "Apparently the dressmaker in New Orleans told Catherine that white dresses were now becoming the fashion of choice for brides. She suggested that Catherine save the dress she was planning to be married in for a later occasion and have a new dress made in white silk and lace. Modeled after the royal version, of course."

She lowered her voice to a whisper now. "The dress she suggested would have cost twelve hundred dollars."

Mary could tell that she was supposed to be shocked at this figure, and dutifully gasped. In all honesty she had no concept of what a dress should cost and what was considered excessive.

"Well," continued Adelaide, "Catherine's father, your grandfather, was furious and refused to have a new dress made. I won't even repeat the exact words he said, but needless to say your aunt is going to be wearing the original dress today when she marries my brother."

"I can imagine him being furious. I've seen him mad a few times before." Mary smiled. She felt so grown up being included in family secrets.

"I told Catherine that she looks lovely in her dress and will be a most beautiful bride." Adelaide nodded for emphasis before adding, "And so she will."

Adelaide's own dress for the occasion was hanging up in the room and she would be getting dressed herself as soon as Grace, or Grace's daughter Fannie, came up to assist her.

Earlier that morning Adelaide had shared with Mary that her beloved Grandfather Captain Isaac Ross had left Grace and her children to her in his will. Her Aunt Margaret had made sure that the bequest was honored before her death, and Adelaide had offhandedly commented that she couldn't have lived without them. Mary knew that Adelaide had meant it to be a compliment to the usefulness of the workers' abilities, but found her claim to be a bit dramatic all the same. She also knew from what she had overheard that Grace would be allowed to leave Adelaide's service and emigrate to Liberia if she was given the chance to do so by the courts.

Captain Ross' desire to free his slaves had been quite the talk throughout the state since his will was probated in 1836, including in her own home. He was among a handful of notable wealthy plantation owners who were taking this controversial action. Mary's father was worried about the precedent that it was setting, and she could recall one rather heated discussion arising between her parents after her mother had commented that she found Captain Ross' intentions to be noble.

Her mother had let it go in deference to her husband, but Mary had agreed with her and wished that she had argued her point better to her father. Why did her mother always have to back down? Mary was determined to have her own opinions, even after she married—not simply parrot her husband's beliefs.

Mary had been fascinated to discover upon Catherine's engagement that she had been coming to the very plantation owned by the famous Captain Ross. In fact, she had felt an inexplicable thrill at passing over the threshold of the main entrance for the first time. She had been instructed by her mother not to mention the will or the pending legal action while visiting here, saying that it would be "in poor taste" to do so. Still, Mary had hundreds of questions that she would love to ask Adelaide about the will, but she was too fearful of losing the easy rapport she felt with her new family to risk it.

A flustered Fannie came rushing into the room. "Missus, I sorry to be so late in coming to help you get dressed. You can't imagine the goings on down there 'mongst the colored folk. Momma's been helpin' with the cookin' so much I don't reckon they'd pulled it off without her."

Adelaide rose and walked towards Fannie. "We have plenty of time still. I'm so glad that Grace is helping make Catherine and Isaac's day special."

Fannie was already unbuttoning the long row of tiny buttons running down the back of Adelaide's dress as she stood holding onto the back of the chair at the dressing table. "My corset sure seems tighter these days, Fannie."

"I expect that's due to little Miss Martha. But she sure is worth it," said Fannie smiling at the thought of the precious baby that had so enchanted Mary. Evidently she wasn't the only one who was taken with the new arrival.

Mary watched as Fannie lifted the dress over Adelaide's head and somehow became mesmerized by watching her step into the stiff crinoline skirts that would be worn under her dress. She felt a sudden shock of realization that she was supposed to be attending to Aunt Catherine right now, having been told to return once she had gotten dressed.

She gasped and told Adelaide that she had to go before exiting the room as gracefully as she could manage. *I hope I wasn't missed. I would hate for Aunt Catherine to think she was wrong in trusting me to attend her today.*

Once she walked into the large upstairs bedroom that Catherine was using to get ready, she realized that there is no way anyone would have noticed her absence. There was so much activity going on around the bride that it made Mary's head spin. She had never thought of her aunt as being a particularly pretty woman, but she had to admit that she did look quite lovely in her wedding dress—a long gown of satin in a robin's egg blue color that seemed to bring out the blue tones in her eyes. Catherine's dark hair appeared smooth and shiny in the sunlight.

The collar of the dress was embroidered with cream-colored thread in an intricate pattern that was truly an impressive piece of sewing. The sleeves were full on the upper arm, but tapered at the wrists which had smaller embroidered designs on them to compliment the pattern at the neckline. Mary could see why her grandfather, ever the pragmatist, would have never considered having a different dress made at the last minute to follow a fashion trend. In any case, this dress seemed to Mary to be exquisite enough for Queen Victoria herself.

When Mary approached the circle of ladies attending her aunt, she noticed orange blossoms being woven into her hair. They had a sweet fragrance that perfumed the air in the bedroom and traveled on the breeze coming through the open windows. The blossoms had been shipped up the river from New Orleans especially for the wedding. Mary caught site of Catherine's veil which was hanging near an open window, and became transfixed with the delicate fabric's fluttering.

However, a momentary sadness came over her at the memory of her younger brother James, who had died several years before of yellow fever. With a wistful smile she thought that if he were here with her now, he would have been spooked by the fluttering veil thinking it to be a ghost. *My sweet silly brother. How I miss you.*

When Catherine turned to allow access to the back of

her hair, she caught sight of Mary and smiled broadly. "What do you think, Mary dear?"

"I think you look lovely, Aunt Catherine. That dress is the prettiest thing I have ever seen."

Catherine's smile brightened even further. "I do hope Isaac feels the same way. You look quite pretty yourself. Do you like the dress?"

Mary twirled for what must have been the twentieth time that day and enthusiastically replied, "Yes, I like it very much!"

Catherine laughed. "I am so glad you do. It is almost time now. Your Nellie has been helping to gather flowers for the ceremony. I was hoping for a church wedding, but Isaac wanted to hold the ceremony here. Apparently the minister at the Presbyterian church in Port Gibson is no friend of his, and he didn't want him officiating in any way."

"So who will be performing the service then?" Mary had not heard this bit until now and was intrigued at the thought of her new uncle having an acrimonious relationship with a local preacher. *I wonder why he doesn't like him? I had better not ask about that either.*

"Father asked our minister to travel with us from Pine Ridge to perform the ceremony. He baptized me as an infant, so I am quite pleased to have him officiate today. He was most kind to make the journey."

Catherine turned to gaze out of the window overlooking the sloping hills and perfectly tilled fields. *This will be my home now. The place where I will raise my children.* The wisteria was coming into full bloom now, and the plantation was a beautiful sight to behold. She knew that the cotton crop would be planted the following week and that her wedding had been timed with this in mind; all hands needed to be available to work hosting their guests.

The calendar ruled life in the agricultural plantation world of Catherine's upbringing, which had taught her the highs and lows of farming firsthand. Her family home of Belmont was located in neighboring Adams County. *We'll pray there is no late frost this year.*

Still focused on the view outside, Catherine murmured wistfully, "The only thing that would have made today more perfect is if my own dear mother could have been here with me."

Mary gasped. She had always thought that Grandmother Marbella *was* Catherine's mother. *There are so many secrets in my family. Why has mother never told me?*

Catherine turned back at the sound of her niece's gasp and looked at Mary with kindness. "Mary dear, whatever is the matter?"

Mary felt foolish. "What happened to your mother, then?" She wondered immediately if she would be admonished for asking such a blunt question. But Aunt Catherine smiled kindly at her.

"I thought you knew that my mother died when I was only two years old. Marbella has been as much of a mother to me as she possibly could have been and I am grateful for that. But on my wedding day, my heart yearns for my natural mother who will never meet any of my future children. I suppose weddings make one nostalgic. Please forgive me."

Mary was going to respond to assure her aunt that there was no reason to seek her forgiveness. In fact, she was extremely grateful that Aunt Catherine was always honest with her and did not treat her like a child. Before she could answer however, her older cousin Helen swooped in to focus Catherine's attentions back to the matter at hand. Mary didn't like the snobbish look that her older cousin had given her, and Mary had made a contentious sound under her breath; immediately grateful that her mother wasn't around to hear it.

Mary wasn't going to let her older cousins ruin this day for her. She was the youngest of the maids asked to attend the bride today, but she was determined to prove herself capable. She stood at once and fussed around, imitating the actions of the older ladies as best she could. Her heart was pounding with anticipation of the wedding. She loved weddings, and this was going to be a grand one.

Mary had been enthralled with the transformation she had witnessed in the house in preparation for the wedding. The staircase had been wrapped in greenery, with flowers woven into the garlands. Flowers had been gathered from the property and purchased especially for the occasion. Mary had overheard that some flowers had been sent all the way from St. Louis.

Her own delicate nosegay held roses, hyacinth, pansies, and tulips. She had been asked to distribute them to each of the bride's attendants before the ceremony began. Uncle Esau, one of the slaves at Prospect Hill, was an excellent craftsman and had constructed two ornate stands to flank the wedding party holding large arrangements of lilies. Each one had been crafted from native tupelo, carved with scroll work and sanded to a smooth finish. The overall effect was spectacular and the house was breathtaking in its beauty.

Guests had started arriving, and the Prospect Hill slaves were busy attending to the carriages and horses of the visitors. The elder members of both families stood at the entrance greeting the guests as they arrived. Mary frequently stole glances out of the upstairs windows catching glimpses of the fashionable people streaming out of carriages. She took in every detail of the gowns the ladies wore, the dapper gentlemen escorting them, and the hustle and bustle of the slaves working in every direction she looked.

When the music began to drift up the stairs, Catherine's father James Dunbar entered the room where the female members of the wedding party stood waiting. He walked over to his daughter and slowly lifted the veil from her face and kissed her cheek before letting the veil drift gently back into place. Mary noted that there didn't seem to be a need for words, because neither the bride nor her father spoke. She watched her grandfather hold his arm out for Aunt Catherine to take and they walked in perfect timing with each other's steps to the top of the stairs.

Adelaide appeared briefly and took Catherine's hand. She gave it a squeeze and whispered, "In a few moments we will be sisters," before making her way down the stairs. Once Adelaide had cleared the bottom stair, the wedding party began slowly descending the adorned staircase.

When Mary reached the landing, she could see the musicians responsible for creating the beautiful sounds she had been hearing. Her teacher had instructed her on classical musical instruments and she recognized the piano, harp, and the violins. One by one, the attendants walked slowly into the room full of guests. When it was Mary's turn to enter, her stomach felt as if it were full of butterflies. She was acutely aware of all of the people watching her and suddenly felt self-conscious. Before long, however, the eyes of the crowd were on the next attendant, and she could relax and enjoy the wedding ceremony.

After the service concluded, there was a formal dinner larger than any meal Mary had ever seen. Besides the large hams and turkeys brought out from the kitchen on platters, there were potatoes prepared in a variety of ways, vegetables, fruits and cobblers.

Mary began wishing at once that she could loosen her undergarments to allow her to sample a bit of every single item on the tables, but she just couldn't manage it. While she looked around the room at the many faces, some familiar and some completely new to her, she thought about her own wedding one day and wondered if it could possibly be this beautiful.

***

The guests had been seen to, the tables cleared, and the food stored away. The white folks spending the night in the big house had been served their coffee and the beds had been turned down. The fireplaces were lit, and the windows closed in preparation for the crisp night air which was already beginning to settle on them. Grace had received assurances from her mistress Adelaide that leftover food could be carried down to slaves' quarters after dinner. There was going to be another wedding at Prospect Hill before the day was through.

As Grace took charge of loading food into crates to be carried down the hill, she thought back to the days when Captain Ross owned everything. Slave weddings had been held in the house more than once. Captain Ross provided the bride and groom with several useful gifts and had attended the weddings himself. He had encouraged weddings between his slaves even though the law of Mississippi did not recognize the unions as legal. *Things sure is different around here nowadays. This new master sure ain't nothin' like Captain Ross.* Grace was grateful that she and her children were no longer living here, but with Adelaide's family.

Permission for the wedding tonight between Levi and Rachael had been granted by Mr. Wade, but nothing had been offered in the way of gifts. He had merely commented, "Make sure it doesn't interfere with the duties you have on the plantation, understand?"

Levi had eagerly agreed that it would not, and got busy planning. He secretly thought himself quite clever to have chosen this night as there would be plenty of leftover food and decorations from the large formal wedding held earlier. *This here is goin' to be the fanciest wedding round the quarters in a long time. Maybe just the finest one ever.*

Sure enough, the meeting room built in the first years of the plantation's existence had never looked more festive. As many flowers as could be inconspicuously moved down the hill had been placed around the room. Everyone seemed to be in the mood to celebrate an occasion for one of their own—especially after having worked seemingly endless hours for the past weeks to prepare for the wedding and feast of the master they felt no loyalty to.

Rachael looked truly beautiful in the dress that Grace had given her for the occasion. It had been one of Adelaide's that had been passed down. Rachael didn't care how it came to be hers. She had never seen anything so pretty—it was a more beautiful dress than she had ever imagined.

The dress was a peach-colored frock of muslin with a fitted bodice. There was a cream-colored silk lace overlay on the bodice of the gown and satin edging around the bottom of the skirt. Rachael had no proper undergarments, but the snug fit of the bodice and the crinolines sewed to the inside of the skirt gave her the distinct hour glass shape that she had never imagined herself possessing. Her heart burst with pride and happiness. *I can't wait to see the look on Levi's face when he see me. I hope he like what he see.*

Levi had borrowed a jacket from Enoch, Captain Ross' manservant, and had put a white rose in his lapel for the occasion. Enoch had chuckled and told him he looked "quite the gentleman" when he had pulled the jacket together in the front and stood up straight. Indeed he felt like one, and it felt good to look good. As a field slave, this type of garment had never been provided to him, even when Captain Ross was living. He could tell from the way Enoch was looking him over that he would impress Rachael when she saw him. *Right now I don't feel like a slave to no one. I just feel like a man—a husband to my Rachael.*

Sure enough, Rachael and Levi each got emotional at the sight of each other standing up in front of the little wooden building reflected in the flickering firelight. Since no preacher had been called upon, old Aunt Dinah had agreed to officiate. A woman who garnered much respect from the slaves on Prospect Hill, Dinah was seen as a spiritual leader to the younger members of the community. They sought out her advice and knew they would be admonished if they acted in a way unfitting the dignity she thought they should possess.

Dinah gathered the group in a circle around the couple for prayers of blessings on the union. She prayed that the couple would continue their strong loving feelings for each other, and she prayed for them to have lots of children. Then she placed a broom in the doorway right over the threshold to the outside. She instructed Levi and Rachael to grasp hands and said in a loud, though slightly trembling voice, "In the eyes of God, step into the holy lands of marriage."

The couple jumped over the broom in unison onto the hard earth outside the door. Cheers and shouts erupted from the group that had gathered to witness their union. The men clapped Levi on the back as the women grabbed hold of Rachael to hug and kiss her.

Sadie Belton had joined the throng of people around the newest couple among them, but Ed held purposefully back. He had caught the eyes of Esau and Wade who discreetly made their way over to where he stood. In the chaos of the evening, especially once the fiddler started playing, not a soul noticed the hushed whispering going on among them.

"I saw Mister and Missus Parker up at the big house. They say they want to help us. Mister Parker respect Captain Ross and want to make sure he honored by doin' what he wanted doin'. He said he goin' to arrange for Reverend Zebulon Butler to come an meet us here."

The Parkers lived near Prospect Hill. Although wealthy slave owners themselves, they were sympathetic to the plight of the slaves and felt that the intentions of Captain Ross should be carried out.

"Ain't no white man goin' to come an meet us with Mr. Wade up there in that big house," said Esau with a look of contempt.

Ed shook his head. "Reverend Butler a preacher. He ain't favorin' slavery at all Mr. Parker say. And Missus Reed left him in charge of everythin' when she die."

"What he want to meet about?" asked Wade. His brother seemed to light up at his question.

"Answers, my brother. We goin' finally get us some answers 'bout whats goin' on." Ed was actually smiling at the thought of hearing what he hoped would be good news.

Esau had noticed the large crates of food being laid out. "Better get goin' afore the ladies come a lookin'."A broad smile covered much of his face.

The other two laughed knowing Esau had lost all interest in the conversation at the sight of the large ham being set down. And who could blame him? This was a feast, the likes of which they hadn't seen in some time. So they followed him back into the crowd and joined in on the festivities. After all, there was nothing more to do for now but wait for the preacher to come and share what he knew.

It was the early morning hours before the festivities drew to a close and the slaves started making their way back to their cabins. Most of the food had been eaten and the fiddler had finally put down his instrument in exhaustion.

Levi took his bride by the hand and led her to the door

of their home. "You happy?" he asked her. She put her arms around his neck and looked up into his earnest face.

She nodded. "You happy?" she repeated back to him.

He laughed heartily as he picked her up and swung her in a circle. As he lowered her gently back to the ground he couldn't recall a time he had ever been more happy. *Our freedom is a comin' Rachael. One day I will love you as a free man.*

September 1840   Prospect Hill Slaves' Quarters

Reverend Zebulon Butler had to be careful not to be seen coming onto the grounds of the large estate. He had waited until night had fallen and he had left his carriage out of sight as a precaution. Ed Belton had met him at a designated location in the woods just off the main road. It would have been foolhardy to pull his carriage onto the drive leading up to the main house. He was not entirely comfortable with the secrecy, but didn't intend on giving Isaac Wade any more ammunition to use against him in the courts. This meeting tonight would certainly be viewed as conspiring with the slaves in the eyes of many people in the area. *The other white people.*

Ed knew the grounds of Prospect Hill Plantation like the back of his hand; the woods, the fields, the outbuildings, and certainly the slaves' quarters. He skillfully navigated the fallen logs, briars, and tree limbs that might have induced injury to Reverend Butler without his guidance—which is exactly why he had insisted on meeting him near the road. After a 15-minute walk through what Reverend Butler had now deemed as rather treacherous terrain, the pair of men arrived in a clearing that marked the area of the plantation that housed a large number of slaves who lived at Prospect Hill. The cabins were small, but sturdy, and were kept meticulously clean.

Before the two men had fully entered the clearing, the sounds of a song drifted through the crisp night air. The voices were deep and rich, full of intonation that made the words seem to dance right up to their ears.

Come down, angels, trouble the waters
Come down, angels, trouble the waters
Come down, angels, trouble the waters
Let God's saints come in

Zebulon Butler had always enjoyed hearing the spirituals, and secretly preferred them to the more staid hymns often sung in his own congregation. Something about the soulfulness appealed to him at a visceral level—there was a genuine nature to their singing that just came through in a way that he didn't experience in most white churches. He had told another member of the Colonization Society recently that he imagined the Good Lord smiling up in Heaven when He heard the slaves singing to Him despite their circumstances.

Not all of the slaves were aware of the meeting, and Ed Belton wanted to keep it that way. Too many tongues wagging just spelled trouble. He had become the unofficial, but generally agreed upon, leader of the slaves who wanted to get answers about their status. And Ed took the responsibility of this position seriously.

Many of the Prospect Hill slaves did not seem to share his impatience to get answers. Much to his vexation, a number of them seemed satisfied with the status quo and didn't push for answers. "There no point in it," several other field workers had told him while walking back at the sound of the bells that evening. "When there somethin' to know, some white man come an tell us I reckon."

Ed couldn't for the life of him understand this way of thinking. This was their very freedom at stake. It meant the difference between being a free man and an enslaved one. To Ed, this issue ranked just under life and death as a matter of urgency and importance. Sadie had run into the same mindset in her conversations with the other women. Some were scared of the unknown, and figured that at least they knew what to expect here. "No tellin' what we find in Africa."

When they reached his cabin, Ed held the door open and said, "After you, Mister Butler."

The minister stepped over the threshold and into the cabin, quickly surveying the bare furnishings; his expression unreadable. Ed was pretty sure that this was his first time being a guest in a slave home and even though it was a humble dwelling, he felt pride in the tidiness of the place and the little decorative touches that Sadie had given it. There was a small fire burning but it wasn't yet cold enough for much more than embers. *Just somethin' to keep the chill off us.*

Only six other slaves were present in the cabin when the two men returned. Sadie had taken leave to another cabin with the children to provide the privacy required for such a discussion. Ed pulled a chair out for Reverend Butler and once again thanked him for coming. He could feel his heart pounding in his chest. He wanted more than anything to hear some good news. Something that would give him hope—hope that he could pass along to Sadie and his children.

"We'd appreciate anythin' you can tell us sir," began Ed feeling the need to start the talking.

Butler scanned the faces of the men around the table. He cleared his throat and asked them to introduce themselves. The men appeared a bit alarmed to have been asked to give their names. In unison, they looked to Ed who nodded almost imperceptibly in reassurance.

"Well, sir, you know me already. Name's Ed Belton," he said, taking the initiative and hoping to relieve the anxiousness evident in the others.

"I's Wade Belton," his brother added. The remainder of the men followed suit.

"Andrew, sir."

"My name Old Yeary."

"Levi."

"Esau, sir."

"Name's Gilbert."

As each man gave his name, Reverend Butler gave him a nod and a smile to offer encouragement. "I think you've all been told who I am," he said, and each man around the table nodded in affirmation. "And why Mr. Belton has arranged for me to be here this evening." Once again, they nodded.

Butler cleared his throat. "I, along with Mr. Stephen Duncan, have been left in charge of Mrs. Margaret Reed's estate. That estate includes her home Ridges, as well as her…" he hesitated, not wanting to use the word 'slaves' and instead he finished with, "servants."

The firelight illuminated the faces around the table and

he saw them waiting patiently for him to continue. "Unfortunately the estate of Captain Ross has fallen under the control of his grandson, Mr. Isaac Ross Wade, and several other executors now that Mrs. Reed has departed us."

He shifted in his chair slightly and addressed his next comments primarily to Ed, as he sensed that he would be doing the majority of the talking tonight. "Mr. Wade has made it clear in the past that he would fight his grandfather's will in court, and we have received official news that a lawsuit has indeed been filed in the probate court to appeal the wills of both Captain Ross and Mrs. Reed."

"Could you tell us 'xactly what the wills say?" asked Ed, his heart sinking when he heard the definitive news that the courts were now involved in deciding his future. *Bunch of white men. They not goin' to want to see us freed.*

"Certainly," replied Reverend Butler. "But I will have to just relate it to you in my best recollections without having the document here to read the exact words."

Ed and the other slaves nodded. They preferred having him shorten it for them. They were not the least bit interested in hearing legal terminology and jargon. They merely wanted to know what all of this meant for them.

"When Captain Ross died, he left provisions to free all of you. His home and lands were to be sold to pay for your passage to Liberia, a colony in Africa. Monies left over were to help get you started there, and to build a school. However, nothing was to be sold until after Mrs. Reed's death unless she decided on her own to take action sooner. Before she went on to her eternal reward, she left myself and Mr. Duncan from the Colonization Society in charge of seeing out the terms of her own will. But fearing that Captain Ross' will would be struck down by the courts, she stated that if that happens Prospect Hill and Ridges would both be left to Mr. Duncan and myself. She did this knowing that we would honor her wishes and sell both properties, providing for your freedom."

He paused to let this all sink in. The men around the table had barely moved while he was talking. They were listening intently. Ed's brain was latching on to every word Reverend Butler spoke, knowing that he would be questioned by the others about it later.

"As you know, Mr. Wade has moved into Prospect Hill and assumed control. Legally, he is within his rights to do so. I can tell you that the other executors are not happy with the way he's been handling things around here. He has some legal troubles of his own with regards to those gentlemen."

He tried not to sound too smug as he reported this last bit of news. He had taken some personal pleasure upon hearing the news that Mr. Wade wasn't going to be granted free license by the other executors to squander the fortune that his grandfather intended for much nobler purposes.

"Mr. Duncan and I are well on our way to getting Mrs. Reed's will upheld. We are hoping that within a year, we can have those of her servants who wish to emigrate to Liberia leave for the colony. But her will is much more straightforward than that of Captain Ross, you see. Because Mr. Wade had control of that estate, not us."

Ed looked directly at Reverend Butler. It was something that could bring trouble down on the head of a slave—to look a white man directly in the eyes. But Reverend Butler didn't appear at all disconcerted by his boldness. "Reverend, what this all mean for us?"

He regarded the men seated around him. None of the other slaves had spoken a word, and it confirmed his initial assumptions that Ed was speaking for them tonight. Undoubtedly a lively discussion would be held after he had been returned to his carriage. The pastor chose his words carefully. As an executor of Margaret's estate, he needed to be sure that he followed her will to the letter of the law. Not being an attorney, he wasn't entirely sure what could be used later against him to undermine his friend's intentions for her slaves. One of these men might inadvertently slip and a piece of information could get back to Wade's ears.

"Well, gentlemen," he said looking from Ed and then to his companions. "I know these are not the words that you want to hear. And you may grow even more tired still of hearing them before it is over with. But for now, we have to wait. Wait for the probate court to rule on the legal action brought by Mr. Wade and his mother, Jane Ross."

"So, if the judges in them courts say that Master Wade has to follow what that will say to do, he has to set us free?" Ed felt an infinitesimal flicker of hope cross through his chest.

Now Zebulon Butler felt truly uneasy for the first time tonight. He had been advised by his lawyers that it was almost a certainty that Isaac Ross Wade would take this fight through every court at his disposal until he ran out of legal options. It could drag out for years—and almost certainly would.

"Well," he said shifting in his seat again. "Not right

away. He could appeal the ruling. That is to say, he could disagree with it and ask a higher court to hear the case and make their own ruling."

Ed felt deflated. *How long is all of this goin' to take? We could grow old and die waitin' on these courts to decide what to do with us.* He sat up as straight as he could. He didn't want anyone or anything to allow the pride he still felt to drain out of him. If these men were looking to him as their leader, he was sure going to act like one.

"We sure hope you will keep us up on what's happenin' with things in the courts," Ed replied once he was able to regain his composure. He hoped that no one had noticed the struggle going on inside of him as he wrangled over what to do next. Ed felt like there was no physical way that he could just sit and wait, doing nothing while strangers decided on his fate. Not only his fate, but that of Sadie, the children, and everyone else filling these small cabins that made up his community. He would certainly be working on a plan in his mind. *Every day while I is out in that field workin', I be plannin' on how to beat you Master Wade. You can count on that.*

Reverend Butler spoke about the plans of the Colonization Society and about his feeling towards slavery. Ed had stopped listening. His mind was racing with uncertainty. When Butler had finished speaking, a few moments of silence went unfilled by anyone.

Finally, sensing there was no more to say, Butler spoke again. "Mr. Belton, could I trouble you to escort me back to my carriage? Unless you have more questions that I can answer for you first."

Reverend Butler was already standing up. "And I'm

sorry to have not brought better news."

Ed sensed that he was growing uneasy and was anxious to leave. But the fact that Butler had addressed him as 'Mr. Belton' had not been lost on him. He had never had a white man bestow a respectful title on him like that. Ed nodded in response to the man's request, having to remind himself that Butler was just the messenger. *He on our side. No need in forgettin' that.*

Ed retrieved the pastor's coat and hat off of the chair by the door and handed them back to their owner. After allowing the man to put on his coat, Ed opened the door. He gave a meaningful glance back at the men still seated at his table before pulling the door shut behind them. There would be a great deal of talking before this night was over. *But talkin' ain't goin' to get us nowhere.* However, before he was more than a few steps from his doorway, he could hear the voices from inside his cabin in feverish whispers.

The two men didn't talk as they made their way back towards the main road. Both of them had the same goal, but the stakes were much higher for one than the other. The journey was even more difficult now than it had been earlier as the night had gotten darker. A thick layer of cloud cover blocked out the moonlight that could have illuminated their path through the dense undergrowth. Ed was holding a crude lantern, but it wasn't giving off much light for both of them to see where to put their feet.

When they finally reached the carriage, Ed untied the horses and held them steady until Zebulon was seated before handing him the reigns.

"I will arrange a time to come back when I have something new to tell you. Mr. Parker has agreed to be a go-between for us and I will be staying in his home on the nights I come to met with you," said Reverend Butler. He sat momentarily holding the reins in his hands before adding, "I sincerely do regret not having better news to bring you."

"It ain't your fault. I thank you for comin' out here."

Ed nodded as he watched the carriage pull away and disappear down the main road. He stood there for a while; he couldn't have said for how long. His head was reeling with all of the information that it held regarding his future prospects. As a slave, he had grown accustomed to being powerless and having little control over his fate. But there was something about knowing that he was *supposed* to be free by now that made his insides churn with resentment and anger. *Supposed to be free, and yet still a slave.* And there was no way to know how much longer they would be waiting for answers.

Tonight was the first time he truly realized how much of Captain Ross' money was getting spent. Mr. Wade was spending up the money that was meant to send them to Africa and start a school. Somehow the thought of that had never occurred to him until now. *What goin' to happen if the money all get spent before we get out of here?* There were so many questions and so few answers.

As he made his way back to his cabin to face the others, he practiced what he was going to say out loud to himself. He knew he needed to be strong and keep his head down. Sadie would need to hear reassurances from him that things were going to work out in the end. But he was finding it hard to think of all the right things to say to everyone else when he had a hard time believing them himself.

April 1841   Oak Hill Plantation Parlor

Isaac Ross Wade had made the two mile trip to his mother's home alone this Sunday afternoon. Catherine was expecting their first child in a few months and was staying close to home these days. It was just as well that he was unaccompanied, as his main motivation for the visit was to discuss a recent turn of events in the state legislature in Jackson.

He had fumed over his perceived betrayal by people who had been close to his grandfather the whole trip over. Even now, as he waited for his mother to join him in her well-appointed parlor, his mind kept replaying his disappointments. *John Ker keeps meddling in our affairs. What self respecting white man would take the side of negroes over a gentleman such as myself?*

Wade knew that he had many powerful allies in Jackson who wanted to see the wills of his grandfather and aunt overturned. In fact, in his estimation the majority of property owners in the entire state of Mississippi would side with him on this issue. Since filing the first suit, however, he had also discovered that there were equally powerful people lined up to support the colonization of the Prospect Hill and Ridges slaves. He regarded these people with severe disdain.

Dr. John Ker was Wade's staunchest opponent in the legislature. A prominent area physician, he had been a surgeon in the Seminole War and one of Wade's grandfather's oldest friends. When Wade was a boy, the two men would smoke cigars on the wide front porch at Prospect Hill and tell war stories, each one trying to best the other.

"Hell, I lost an eye, for God's sake!" he had heard his grandfather proclaim more than once.

The men were friends for more than twenty years before his grandfather's death. Remarkably, Wade had always admired and respected Ker but now felt nothing but animosity towards the older man.

After Aunt Margaret's husband had died, Dr. Ker had purchased Linden Plantation. It was a truly remarkable place, and if truth be told Wade had always secretly coveted the sprawling home. It sincerely chafed him that Ker, with all of his wealth and prominence, could be so sanctimonious about this fundamental issue of slavery. *Aren't I entitled to inherit that which is due me? And even if I can manage to buy back Prospect Hill when it is sold, land in this part of the state is worthless to me without slaves. Ker knows that all too well.*

Now Ker was using his position in the state Senate to undermine Wade's attempts to circumvent the wills. Wade had come so close, he could almost taste the victory. The House had already passed the bill that would invalidate the wills. But the Senate, under the strong admonitions of Ker, had defeated the bill. If the law had successfully been enacted, his grandfather's will would have been rendered illegal. The best part was that it would have been retroactive in nature, so even though the will was probated before the law would have gone into effect, it would have nullified the wills of his grandfather and aunt.

Ker and his allies would not be able to stop the passage of a law making it illegal to free one's slaves by testament—Wade had been assured by many lawmakers that the law stating such would be in place by early the next year. But Ker had effectively won his battle by keeping the retroactive effect out of the law. Meaning, since Isaac Ross and Margaret Wade's wills were probated before the passage of new legislation, it would not apply in their case.

Wade could still hear the strong and sure voice of Ker in his mind, and it caused him to ball his hands into fists out of sheer frustration. Ker had argued that it was a gross violation of a man's human rights to limit his ability to do whatsoever he deemed right with his property. Tensions were running high in the Jackson halls of power as well as in the courts. Wade's frustrations with the courts of law were causing him to panic for the first time. *I am going to run out of options before long. The legislature was my last best hope.*

Jane Brown Ross swept into the room with all the grace that she had been raised to possess. Wade stood as his mother approached him, reaching out to grasp her shoulders. He pulled her close enough to plant a quick kiss on each cheek before releasing her. She motioned for him to sit and then did so herself in the chair opposite him.

"You look weary," she said after scanning him intently

for a moment. "How are things at Prospect Hill?"

"Fine, just fine," he replied with a wave of the hand. "Catherine is well."

"Good, good. I'm most happy to hear it. Any problems with the slaves?"

"Nothing I can't handle. Peter Stampley is one of the best overseers in the county." He wasn't interested in small talk. *Hopefully Mother will allow me to just get to the point.*

He continued, getting to the heart of what had been troubling him on an almost constant basis. "These legal battles are taking a toll. I'm growing increasingly frustrated with the judgments of the courts. Our state legislature requires approval to free slaves, and has done so since the 1822 manumission law went into effect. Something grandfather failed to recognize and respect. Mr. Ellet had been so sure that we had a strong case to overturn the wills. And yet, here we sit, still waiting for the outcome we so desire."

He leaned forward and lowered his voice. "I am truly beginning to fear that the courts will continue to rule against us from here on out. We have little recourse beyond the judicial system. And Ker has derailed our best chance in the legislature."

"The American Colonization Society is a strong opponent, I agree. They've retained counsel that makes a strong case for preserving the provisions of my father's will. They are mostly using scare tactics rather than valid legal arguments. We must be patient, son. This will be a long, slow process, and we both know that."

Wade fidgeted in his seat. He hated feeling patronized.

But his mother continued, "The High Court of Errors and Appeals made their ruling based on bad information. Once they are apprised of the true nature of the Colonization Society's intentions they will have little choice but to ultimately rule in our favor."

"How can you be so sure?" He wondered, as he had on occasion before, if she was keeping something from him. Almost instantly he was chastising himself for having the thought. *I should be ashamed of myself not trusting my own mother. This entire debacle is making me paranoid.*

"I am sure because we have the law on our side. And, even more importantly, we have Scripture." She reached for the Bible laying on the table beside her. "Never underestimate the power of Scripture. The judges know that one day they will meet their maker like the rest of us."

"Yes," Isaac replied, "But perhaps they are not as certain as you regarding the interpretation of the Scriptures." He had heard the arguments from abolitionist materials renouncing biblical references to slavery as being misinterpreted. They made him sick.

"I marked a couple of references for you earlier this week. I thought they might bolster your resistance to the despair you are feeling." Her gaze left him, and she focused her attentions on her Bible. She pulled a ribbon from the pages of the large black leather Bible, allowing it to fall open in her lap. She ran her finger across the page until she found the verse she was looking for.

"I'm reading from the book of Ephesians, Chapter 6, verses 5 through 8. 'Servants, be obedient to them that are your masters according to the flesh, with fear and trembling, in singleness of your heart, as unto Christ; Not with eyeservice, as menpleasers; but as the servants of Christ, doing the will of God from the heart; With good will doing service, as to the Lord, and not to men: Knowing that whatsoever good thing any man doeth, the same shall he receive of the Lord, whether he be bond or free'."

She looked up from the book in her lap into the face of her son. "I've heard it directly from the pulpit many times that *servant* in this text refers to slaves. And Saint Paul himself directed them to obey their masters at all costs. It is really quite clear, darling."

Wade nodded grimly. He had heard all of this before. It was just words to him now, and words were not going to change anything. *It isn't dear old Saint Paul I need to convince, Mother, it is the judges of the great state of Mississippi.*

Apparently taking his silence as a sign to continue, Jane went on. "Here is another one from the book of Titus, Chapter 2, verse 9. 'Exhort servants to be obedient unto their own masters, and to please them well in all things; not answering again'."

He was not impressed. "Mother, I know that there are numerous passages of Scripture that uphold the divine right we possess to own slaves. What I need to know is that the courts are going to uphold our rights as well. Those lawyers from Montgomery and Boyd did a brilliant job of arguing the case against having free blacks in the state. The dramatic scenarios about the free slaves inciting rebellion and creating discontent among the enslaved were highly effective. By the time they were done every judge on the bench wanted to see each one of the Ross negroes on the first boat back to Africa."

Jane's face remained neutral. If she was concerned, it certainly didn't show. "We are staying one step ahead of them always. We certainly are doing everything in our power to retain what is ours."

"What really infuriates me is the way the American Colonization Society tries to come off as noble in their intentions. When their true motives are completely nefarious." He felt the color rising in his cheeks.

"You worry too much. We are in a position of good standing."

Jane stood and walked over to her son, holding out a hand to him. "Join me for a walk around the gardens. I need some air."

He understood that she was done discussing the matter, and was tactfully changing the subject. Wade obediently stood and escorted his mother onto the grounds. *I certainly hope you are right, Mother.*

***

That evening many of the slaves on Prospect Hill gathered in the meeting house to sing and hear the stories of the gospel. Captain Ross had made sure that many of his slaves were instructed to read and write, which some had taken to well. Others had Bible verses memorized that they liked to share and pray over. Like many enslaved Africans, the Ross slaves had adopted Christianity while still incorporating elements of ancestral worship passed along from their elders. Dinah was often the one to preside over the religious services held in the quarters, as was the case on this particular evening.

"Holy God tells us in his word this very truth. 'There neither Jew nor Greek, there neither slave nor free, there neither male nor female: for ye all one in Christ Jesus'."

Her words were punctuated with "Amens" and "Yes Lords" from all around the fire-lit cabin.

Dinah's hands were high in the air now. "So I tell you Jesus don't care nothin' bout whether we slave or free, black or white. We all goin' to the same place in the end."

More "Amens" came from all around her.

"Saint Paul hisself told old Philemon to take back Onesimus like he were his own brother an treat him right." Dinah repeated for emphasis, "A brother, he told him!"

There was a general murmur of consent around the room and still more "Yes Lords" and "Amens."

The Benton brothers stood in the back of the room, certainly not engaging in the worship. They were only in attendance because their wives had asked them to come. Ed especially felt it hard to hear this talk of a better life waiting. *Waiting for freedom after I'm dead? I want freedom now while I can live a free man on this here earth.*

Even the story old Dinah was talking about had gnawed at him. Why did Paul send the slave back to his master at all? If Onesimus was free in Jesus, why couldn't he live as a free man? Slavery was an institution designed to break a man's spirit. The Bible talks about a man having authority in his home, but it sure didn't seem to apply to a black man enslaved in Mississippi. So many of the others in the room seemed to draw great comfort from the words of that great big book, but he had a hard time finding the comfort.

When the singing started back up, he motioned to his brother to step outside. The volume inside the cabin had reached great heights. Both Belton wives were engrossed in the service and their absence would likely go unnoticed for quite a while.

When they were far enough from the meeting room to be heard, Ed spoke to his brother.

"I seen Mister Parker today. He told me Reverend Butler been told in a letter about Master Wade spendin' money for his own uses. He breakin' the law, but he don't think no one can stop him. Cap'n Ross' will say that the crops supposed to be sold to put towards sending us to Africa. Not to make Master Wade richer than he is already."

Wade Benton shook his head. "I don't know how much more of this we's supposed to take. Ain't there nothin' we can do?" He felt an anger burning inside of him that made him want to lash out at something. *We just supposed to wait. Waitin' and more waitin'.*

Ed replied, "You know we waitin' on the final say from the high courts. Reverend Butler say things goin' our way."

He knew these very words would frustrate his brother. He could hear his unspoken words as if his brother had said them out loud. It frustrated Ed himself to have to say them. But the hopeful part of him felt they were getting close. If they could only be patient a while longer, they could be farming land of their own within the year. Free men on a free continent. He didn't expect there would even be white folks anywhere nearby once they got there. Certainly not ones that held the kind of power over them that white men had here.

The sounds of the voices were faint behind them now. But if Ed concentrated he could pick out Sadie's voice, and the sound of it made him smile. He wanted a better life for them. More than anything he wanted his children to have a chance to dream. Dreaming was a dangerous thing for a slave, leading only to heartbreak and disappointment.

But there were free black men in the world earning a living and supporting their families, and in his heart he knew that he should be out there right now doing just that. The bitter sting of Isaac Wade's betrayal, spending their hard earned money right out from under them, was like rubbing salt in a festering wound.

Ed and Wade were quiet for a few moments, each deep in thought. The brothers were different in temperament, with Ed being the natural leader of the two. But Wade was equally as determined to become a free man. The impotence of their situation weighed heavily on them both. They listened to the lyrics of the spiritual drift across the yard.

> *The talles' tree in Paradise*
> *The Christian call the tree of life*
> *And I hope that trump might blow me home*
> *To the new Jerusalem*
> *Blow your trumpet, Gabriel*
> *Blow louder, louder*
> *And I hope that trump might blow me home*
> *To the new Jerusalem*
> *Paul and Silas, bound in jail,*
> *Sing God's praise both night and day*
> *And I hope that trump might blow me home*
> *To the new Jerusalem*

"A new Jerusalem. You think that could be what we find over in Africa?" asked Wade hopefully.

"I thought about it so many times. It got to be better than living under Master Wade. At least with Cap'n Ross we knew our family goin' to stay together. Ain't none of us know what this master goin' do."

Wade nodded vigorously in agreement. It was something they hadn't spoken of before, but for the first time on Prospect Hill there lurked a real possibility that slaves might start getting sold to pay off legal fees. This was but one more reason the Belton brothers so desperately wanted an end to the waiting. If they waited too long, someone they love might get left behind. The thought caused an involuntary shudder to pass through Ed.

Something in him shifted ever so slightly. Maybe it wasn't so bad after all to seek solace from the worship going on just through the doors. Wade seemed to have had the same feelings, and after a moment he spoke again.

"You know, I feel like singin' all of a sudden. You want to go back and join 'em?" Wade shrugged with a grin on his face that Ed hadn't seen in a long time. Hope could do that to people, and Ed understood his brother's need for it. They were down to nothing but hope at this point.

"It would make Sadie happy, anyway," Ed replied with a shrug. "For some reason, she alway say she like my singin'."

He followed his brother back inside the cabin where all the cares of this life seemed to have been momentarily forgotten by the worshipping crowd. Ed Belton willed himself with all his might to believe the gospel story of hope and freedom and allow himself to escape his worries for one night. *Just one night.*

July 1843   Port Gibson

Zebulon Butler leaned his head back against his chair. A long, slow sigh escaped as he reflected back on the whirlwind of the past few months. Many times he had wondered why Margaret Reed had left this burden upon his shoulders. The legal wrangling and opposition from the community, many of them his own parishioners, had taken a toll on him. *And it is not over yet. Not nearly over.*

For a moment, he forced himself to focus on the positive aspects of recent events. A large number of Mrs. Reed's slaves had sailed the month before to Liberia. It was clearly a success for his cause and he felt tremendous satisfaction that this feat was accomplished without any violence or last minute legal complications. The courts had ruled in favor of the Colonization Society time and again. There was no doubt to Reverend Butler that God's very hand was instrumental in releasing these souls from bondage.

But even as he reveled in the victory, he had a bitter taste in his mouth. The very lawyers that he and Stephen Duncan had retained to plea the case to the courts had not argued against the practice of slavery itself. Neither had they argued that the negro population languishing on the plantation had a legal and moral right to freedom. To Butler, those arguments would have been noble ones that supported his own ideology of abolitionism. Had the lawyers secured a victory on these arguments, he would have felt total jubilation and vindication, rather than the conflicting emotions that he was currently feeling.

Even though the eventual outcome of the case was exactly what he had been hoping and praying for, did the ends justify the means? The persuasive argument made by the lawyers advocating for the manumission and colonization of the Reed slaves was, in essence, that it benefited Mississippi to rid herself of these problematic individuals before they had a chance to create discord. He pulled his reading glasses into place and reached for a stack of paperwork he and Dr. Duncan had received from their attorneys.

The lawyers had made an argument explaining the rationale for the restrictive 1822 law limiting the rights of owners to manumit slaves. With another sigh he began reading parts of the argument for what must have been the thirtieth time:

> *The practice of manumission was productive of great evil, by the rapid increase which it caused in the free negro populations. This kind of population was found by experience to be both oppressive and dangerous, constituting a heavy charge upon the public and a great nuisance to the community. It became, therefore, the necessary policy of*

these states to rid themselves of this evil, and as far as practicable to prevent its further extension... it may be safely asserted that every such limitation or restriction of the right of manumission, was intended by the legislature only to relieve the state from the accumulations within its borders of an obnoxious free black population.

He lowered the papers back into his lap. The unfairness of this argument caused him to swell with righteous indignation. He had attempted to express his concerns to Dr. Duncan, but found to his surprise and disdain that Duncan had found nothing remotely concerning in this line of argument. He had agreed fully with the reasoning employed by their counsel and praised their accomplishments.

Of course, Butler had to remind himself on numerous occasions that Stephen Duncan reportedly owned at least one thousand slaves spread across numerous properties. The two men were made allies in this matter by the decree of Mrs. Reed, but Zebulon Butler did not align himself with the tactics employed to accomplish it.

When he had met with the Belton brothers shortly after they had won the final decision allowing them to begin arranging transport for Mrs. Reed's slaves to Liberia, he had been careful not to disclose any of the language used to win the decision. It would have been so terribly insulting to insinuate the truth to them. He chose not to inform them that judges were more concerned with the trouble they would stir up here in Mississippi than in their inherent right to freedom. As the matter had been settled, it was too late to go back and second-guess the tactics used. He instead attempted to focus on the fact that a large number of slaves were going to be free men and women on their native shores.

Ed and Wade Belton had demonstrated tremendous joy in the good fortune of Mrs. Reed's slaves. It was obvious to Butler that they were sincerely happy for the ruling and the opportunities that were being provided to them. However, it brought up further questions regarding their own situation. Once again Butler had no good news for them, and it pained him to have to relay that fact.

The truth was that Mrs. Reed's will had the fortune of having executors who wanted to see it carried out according to her wishes. Captain Ross' will, on the other hand, possessed an executor who wanted to undermine the very core virtues of the document and render it null and void. This created a terribly difficult and frustrating situation for the Prospect Hill slaves and it pained Butler on a daily basis.

He had reiterated some points that had been previously related to them, hoping to at least remind the Belton brothers that people were working on their behalf, even if the results were proving to be painstakingly slow. He reminded them that the High Court of Errors and Appeals had ruled in their favor, which was to be taken as an encouraging sign even though Isaac Wade was contesting the ruling. He reiterated to them that even though the state legislature passed a new law the previous year making it illegal to free slaves by will, it would not apply to them since the will was written before the law went into effect.

He once again conveyed the pending suit filed against Wade by the Colonization Society attempting to force him to abide by the decree of the High Court. Finally, he relayed to them his beliefs that it was a sign of the court's frustration with the obvious delay tactics being utilized by the heirs of the estate that the Chancery court had forbidden Jane Ross in March from filing any further claims until the current matters were settled.

Each time he met with the slaves of Prospect Hill, he found them to be in full understanding of the matters at hand. Certainly their manner of speaking indicated their lack of formal education, but nothing was lacking in terms of intelligence. In fact, to his surprise many of the Ross slaves could read and write. It explained the stipulation in Captain Ross' will that part of the proceeds from the sale of his estate were to go towards establishing an institution of higher learning in Liberia for his slaves. The thought of Isaac Wade squandering this money month after month as the slaves toiled in the fields galled him to no end. He left after each meeting with the slaves full of fresh contempt for Isaac Ross Wade.

The offensive arguments used to win the legal battle, and the loathsome character of his nemesis were not the only things putting a damper on his celebratory feelings of seeing the Reed slaves on their way to Africa. A few hours earlier, a copy of the *New Orleans Commercial Bulletin* had been delivered to his home. He didn't subscribe to this paper, but an acquaintance who knew of his interest in the case thought he might want a copy. He noted the date on the paper of May 11, 1843 and began flipping through the pages. It only took him moments to see what indeed piqued his interest.

An article appeared reporting the imminent departure of the Reed slaves for Africa, and briefly recounting the nature of the will and the resulting litigation. As he read further into the article, he felt the surge of indignation once again mounting in him.

> *We are sure that none of our readers will fail to share with us the pleasure with which we feel in noting today the departure of a vessel freighted with human souls of the African race, destined for their fatherland and prepared by a long and faithful pupilage for freedom. It is by these periodic departures from our port of industrious, honest and intelligent manumitted negroes, that we see practical exemplifications of the beneficent uses to result to Africa herself from the transfer of her children to this continent, and their subjection to the whites. The emigrants are carrying out to the rest of their race, laborious and thrifty habits, civilization and the Christian religion, and dotting the African coast with prosperous and intelligent communities.*

He restrained himself from crumpling the paper into a ball in his fist. He hurriedly went back and reread a few of the sentences that he had found the most offensive before slinging the paper to the side. He leaned his head back on his chair once more. *So the rich planters of New Orleans would like for us to believe that these slaves benefited greatly from being held here in bondage. Not only did they benefit, but the entire continent of Africa owes us a tremendous debt of gratitude.* He could already hear the sermons ringing down from the pulpits across the state of Mississippi proclaiming this to be true. That missionaries of our Christian faith have departed to convert the heathens of Africa. This would be touted as following the directive of Christ himself in The Great Commission.

There were days he longed to return home to Pennsylvania. He felt as if he were a voice of reason crying out in the wilderness. But he reminded himself that he was led by the Spirit to come to this place. And he would do everything in his power to serve his God to the best of his ability. He picked up his Bible and began reading scriptures that bolstered his resolve and renewed his strength.

He was determined not to stop fighting on behalf of the Ross slaves. The battle was only half won, and he knew that a long road lay ahead. He bolstered his inner strength by reminding himself that he had been named after a great military leader. Colonel Zebulon Butler had been a hero in the wars that dotted our nation's history and he had always been proud to bear his name.

He wouldn't allow himself to become mired in the dirty politics of slavery. He knew that many of his allies in the colonization movement must have the sentiments that he had heard expressed in court. Sure, they put forth a much more honorable face to the matter, but he suspected the secret that lay buried beneath the façade. He couldn't let it stop the progress that was being made.

Feeling a surge of optimism and vigor, he walked to his

desk and began writing. One of his most useful and powerful allies had been Dr. John Ker. He set forth immediately writing a letter to Ker recounting his meeting with the Belton brothers. He was unwavering in his resolve to utilize the influence of these wealthy slave owners even if they shared completely different views on the morality of slave ownership. *Maybe the ends do justify the means after all. The most important issue facing humankind today must be resolved regardless of the methods utilized in doing so.*

September 1843   Prospect Hill

Isaac Ross Wade had grown weary of the meddlesome do-gooders who'd become so fond of interfering in his private affairs lately. Earlier in the afternoon, he had received a letter from Person and Company, his cotton factors in New Orleans. This was not unusual in itself. Wade was accustomed to correspondence with Person and Company and received frequent letters advising him on everything from cotton prices to the availability of pork shipments from the west.

What was upsetting him today were the contents of the letter. His respected business partner was informing him of a merchant in Rodney who had been advised to watch out for Prospect Hill cotton being sold under the brand of another plantation. Legal papers had apparently been brandished along with the suggestion of complicity to fraudulent activity if a sale was made under these terms. Apparently the merchant was spooked and had contacted the cotton factor with his concerns.

Wade had never expected to receive this type of news. His reputation was being besmirched by these allegations.

In his mind he was only protecting his own interests by setting aside cotton whose sale wouldn't be included in the proceeds of the estate. Who could have tipped off the agents in Rodney? Even without proof, he knew that his enemies in the Colonization Society were behind it, and anger boiled inside of him.

He had always enjoyed cordial relations with the merchants in Rodney, where his cotton was shipped via steamer to New Orleans. He wouldn't tolerate Peter Stampley or any other agent representing Prospect Hill being subjected to unpleasant questions regarding his personal business. He would have to make sure this season's crop of cotton was sold by the books. Furthermore, he would go to Rodney himself, since all transactions regarding Prospect Hill were obviously going to be done under the watchful eye of troublemakers.

He certainly didn't mind making the trip to Rodney. It was a booming port city on the Mississippi just a few miles away. It offered opera and theater which kept Catherine happy, as well as plenty of whiskey and card games for himself. *We will just make the best of it. We could both enjoy a trip to Rodney after all.* The hotel in town was extremely comfortable and rivaled those he had stayed in while in New Orleans and St. Louis.

He stood and walked to the windows overlooking the sloping meadows in front of his home. *All of this should have been left to me in the first place. Then none of this would be happening.* He had grown up with so much admiration of his grandfather. When his own father had died, his grandfather became a father figure to him. He was a larger-than-life hero in young Isaacs' eyes and he took tremendous pride in being his grandson—especially as he bore his name.

He had listened avidly to his war stories as well as the fanciful tall tales that his grandfather made up for him. There had been one about a small mouse who wore boots and went into a saloon to avenge the loss of his tail. Even years later, Isaac chuckled at the thought of some of these imaginative stories. His memories of his grandfather had been such good ones.

But something changed in the old man over time. He lost his zest for living and, in young Isaac's view, he just gave up on life. In fact, after the death of his daughter Martha, he literally disappeared for about a year. He was even feared to be dead, and Isaac thought back to how profoundly sad he felt at that time imagining that he would never see his beloved grandfather again. It was also during that time that Isaac's mother Jane became bitter. *Something changed within her as well.*

And then one day he had turned back up at Prospect Hill with even more stories to tell of his travels. There were more adventures about falling ill in Indian territory and visits to the north. But his views on some very fundamental issues had changed. He began talking about his slaves much more than ever before. Eventually he came up with his harebrained scheme to sell everything that he had spent his life building and just give it all away. Not to Isaac Ross Wade, or other legitimate heirs. But to his slaves in order to send them to some God forsaken continent full of famine and pestilence. As long as he lived, Isaac Ross Wade would never understand this decision. And he would never support it.

At first people tried to talk Captain Ross out of his decision. They called colonization a scheme devised by abolitionists with their own liberal agendas or by religious fanatics. Ross was a firm believer in a higher power, but was certainly no fan of any religious denomination. Finally, Isaac Wade's mother Jane had decided that the best course of action was to just play along with him while he was still living, but fight the will in courts when the time came. And that is what ultimately happened.

Except for Margaret. She genuinely seemed to understand her father's plan and support it. This had come as another bitter shock to Wade. Margaret was a very intelligent woman and managed her own home better than most men he knew. He had always admired her for the way that she had stepped in to help him and Adelaide during the difficult period following their father's death. But she had ultimately betrayed him too. And bitterness swelled within him at the thought. If only Margaret had seen her father's plan for its foolishness this could have all gone so differently.

But it didn't help to recount past losses, and Wade was a pragmatic man. He needed a plan to limit the ability of others to meddle in his affairs. He suspected that James Parker and his wife Mary had been sending letters to John Ker and Stephen Duncan with their suspicions. They didn't openly oppose him, but he was aware of their sentiments all the same. But where were they getting their information? And then it came to him. *Those damned slaves are running to them like crybabies.*

He resolved at once to have his overseer Stampley keep his ear to the ground for any information he might overhear in his role as overseer. He had much more contact with the slaves than Wade himself. In fact, he made a point of limiting his contact with the Prospect Hill slaves as much as possible. If he had a message for them, he would send his own manservant Major to relay it. *I need a firm hand here. If I make an example out of a few of them, it might stop them from running to the Parkers.*

Wade took a moment and did a mental inventory of the other planters in the area. He had confidence that the majority of them support the stand he had taken to fight for his rights to inherit his grandfather's property. They had expressed that opinion to him on numerous occasions: he was the legitimate heir. Who else should inherit? His cousin Isaac Allison Ross, his sister Adelaide, and a few others. He would be glad to make sure they received a portion. Of course his mother was the last living child of Isaac and Jane Ross, and as such was entitled to legacies even though her father left her none. *But Prospect Hill is rightfully mine. The house, the land, and the slaves.*

He had received offers from many of the other planters in the area when Margaret's slaves were freed a few months earlier. Fearing the time was nearing that he would be ordered to release the slaves from Prospect Hill over to the custody of the Colonization Society, neighboring planters offered to help him resist these attempts. Wade made sure that the word trickled out among the county families that there would be several hundred armed men on hand to defend his home against outside influences. His lawyer, Henry Ellett had assured him that they would be able to obtain an injunction to keep the Jefferson County sheriff at bay at least temporarily if he tried to remove the slaves by force.

Catherine entered the room, and walked to where her husband still stood; looking thoughtfully out of the windows. She slipped her arm around his waist. "It is beautiful isn't it?"

"I love this place, Catherine. I don't know what I would do if we lost it." He didn't face her. He couldn't bear to see his perceived failures reflected in his wife's eyes.

Catherine seemed to sense his doubts. She gently placed her hand under his chin and turned his face to hers. "Look at me, Isaac. We will pray that we can remain here. It is what we both want and I support you completely. But I want you to understand something with no doubts in your mind."

She met his gaze fully and smiled tenderly at him. "You are my husband and I have a great deal of love and respect for you. Our home is ultimately where we live together with our children. And if by chance it cannot be here…" he opened his mouth, but she continued before he could speak.

"If it cannot be here," she repeated, "We will make the best life for our family somewhere else. We will certainly not be destitute by any means."

He was grateful to his wife for telling him the exact words he needed to hear. And she was right, of course. But this fight had become personal, and he just couldn't foresee anything that could cause him to back down from it.

Wade smiled at his wife. "Thank you, Catherine." They embraced for a moment, before he remembered his thoughts regarding the trip into town.

"What would you think of getting all dressed up and spending a few days in Rodney soon? I've got some business to take care of, but we could take in a show or two. We could book a room at the finest hotel."

"I think it would be the perfect tonic to relieve the toll this business has taken on you. We'd take Major and Mariah of course, but leave the children here. It would be nice to be alone, like our honeymoon in New Orleans. When you gave me this." She lifted an ornate locket that she still cherished. It had been a wedding gift from Isaac.

"Certainly. We will begin making plans then. I need to lay the groundwork for the sale of the cotton crop next month. That shouldn't take long. After that I am all yours, my dear." He smiled and opened his arms wide. She nestled back into them.

"I came down here to tell you that your presence has been requested. Young Isaac has something he wants to show you. I told him that I would see if you were free to come upstairs." She whispered conspiratorially, "He is very proud of himself, so please be sure to make a big production of your pleasure."

He laughed. His son was his pride and joy. It warmed his heart that he enjoyed showing off his little tricks for him. "Tell him that I will be right up."

Catherine smiled and left the room. He surveyed the room around him and ran his hand over the simple, but elegant secretary desk. The one thing besides some books that his grandfather had actually bequeathed to him in the will.

He was looking forward to a time in the near future when he would own Prospect Hill outright, with all of the slaves as part and parcel of the property. The courts had been a disappointment, but he blamed the inflammatory statements made by the American Colonization Society lawyers for his losses. He just needed to regroup and come up with a different tactic. It was beyond his comprehension that he could lose this place that meant so much to him to a bunch of enslaved Africans. *They wouldn't know what to do with freedom if they had it. Why couldn't Grandfather realize that?*

Wade was going to raise his children here and teach his sons to run the place. He would watch his daughters marry here. And he and Catherine would grow old here together. Catherine had been tremendous support through the trials and ordeals of this unpleasant conflict. He was eternally grateful to her, and wanted her to experience the joys of this grand old home just as he had. *In time, Catherine. In time.*

***

Levi had just finished reporting to the group of men gathered around the table in Ed Belton's cabin. He had been the one to volunteer to make the trip to Mr. and Mrs. Parker's home to relay the concerns of the slaves regarding the cotton. They were all aware of the stakes involved here. If the money earned from the cotton crop was diverted away from the estate, it would not be there for their transport to Liberia. Already the growing frustration regarding the delays and the high costs of the court fees had caused tempers to flare. Some of the slaves were tired of waiting and wanted to take action now. Ed Belton was urging them to continue being patient. For now.

But it was about time to harvest the cotton crop again.

They needed to know that this crop was theirs. That this crop was going to be for their benefit as their true master had intended. None of them felt any sense of loyalty to Mr. Wade. He had power over them, but he had not earned their respect. That was one issue that they were unanimous on.

James and Mary Parker were sympathetic to the plight of the slaves, but were cautious to keep their role in assisting them quiet. They had seen the way that Margaret Reed had become an outcast and had no plans of following in her path. Mrs. Parker had assured Levi that she would write a letter to Mr. Ker immediately alerting him to the possibility that Prospect Hill cotton would come to market under the brand of a different plantation.

She had also given him a nice meal and said a prayer for his safe return. Upon his return to Prospect Hill, he had told both Ed and Wade Belton that he believed her to be an honest woman who would do her best to help them. Even though he had been back for a while, this was the first chance to meet together for Levi to inform the group at large what had transpired during his absence. Most of them agreed that the Parkers could be trusted, but not all of them were sure. It was hard to know who to trust, and fear was difficult to keep in check.

As a servant in the main house, Mariah Belton was always a good source of information for her sons. She overheard many conversations that went on in that big house and knew how to be discreet and fade into the background. Ed felt that he could stay a step ahead of his master by having this inside information. It wasn't much, but to a man who had no legal position in society, he had to take whatever luck he could get.

Their hopelessness and despair regarding the situation were always hard to keep at bay. It was already autumn and soon the cotton crop would be harvested and sold. It was backbreaking work that would be for naught if Isaac Wade squirreled it away for his own use. The only thing that could keep Ed's spirits up through the grueling weeks ahead would be to think of the profits putting him one step closer to freedom.

At night, before he fell asleep, Ed thought about what life would be like in Africa. He imagined building a grand home of his own with tall white columns and a big front porch. He could envision a house full of sons and daughters, attending school and not having to work all day for another man's profit. He could picture Sadie, looking beautiful in a big full skirt and tiny waist drinking lemonade on the front porch. *We might even have us some servants.*

It was becoming more and more difficult for Ed to control some of the more hot tempered among them. His brother Wade was a big help, and he had been very impressed with Levi. For such a young man he had shown exceptionally good judgment and never seemed to get caught up in emotions that clouded his thinking. Ed was glad to have Levi in his confidence, helping him protect the rights of the group still living here in the quarters.

For Levi, as it was with Edmond Belton, nothing was more important than working to ensure his freedom. He wanted a fresh start with Rachael, who was expecting a child now. In his mind, he pictured raising his family as a free man. Free to own a business. Free to buy property.

Free to vote and have a say in his future. He knew that he was treading on dangerous ground running messages to Mr. and Mrs. Parker. There was no doubt in his mind that he would be punished if Master Wade discovered what he had been doing.

He refused to let fear keep him from fighting for the chance to go to Africa with his family. It was what Captain Ross had wanted for him, and he would die trying to achieve it if that is what it came to.

The word *free* became his mantra, and Levi said it over and over as he worked in the fields. *Free, free, free.*

December 1843   Natchez, Mississippi

Mary Girault was trembling with a combination of excitement and anxiety. Natchez was the most exhilarating place she had ever been, and the Christmas season had the city decked out in holiday charm, adding to its appeal. There was little to bring her cheer at home these days. It seemed at times that life held little else than watching her mother give birth to siblings, only to watch her parents bury their tiny lifeless bodies, felled by illnesses not responsive to any known treatments. Her father's legal and financial troubles did nothing to ease the sense of gloom that fell over the home. The isolation she felt in Tuscahoma compounded all other problems.

Mary had helped her mother care for her younger siblings and tried very hard to be a dutiful and loving daughter. As the eldest, she felt the greatness of this responsibility on an almost daily basis. She worked hard at her studies and she learned the ways of a genteel Southern lady, even though she had always preferred running free outdoors or simply being left alone to read great novels.

But recently her mother had given her the most

wonderful surprise. She had made arrangements for Mary to attend a holiday ball being given in the home of Stephen Duncan himself! His gracious mansion, Auburn, was the envy of Natchez society and an invitation to the ball of the season was highly coveted. She could hardly believe her good fortune. She had written to both Aunt Catherine and Adelaide right away, and they had each sent eager responses expressing their own excitement and pledges to assist in any way.

However, in one letter, Aunt Catherine had made a request that Mary found odd. *"Please don't specify the exact location of the ball to your Uncle Isaac. He and Dr. Duncan are adversaries on legal matters and it would be quite awkward to explain that I'm assisting you in your efforts to attend. I am sure that you understand, Mary dear. Love and devotion, Aunt Catherine."* Mary honestly had not understood, but as long as Aunt Catherine was helping her attend this wonderful event, Mary would gladly do as she asked.

Despite Mary's compliance with her mother's admonitions regarding mentioning her family's misfortunes, she knew that Aunt Catherine was aware of their dire situation. She was at least aware that times were difficult financially, because she sent lovely gifts to the children on occasion and had invited Mary to spend time at Prospect Hill after young Isaac had been born. Mary loved those occasions when she could visit the sprawling plantation and experience new things. The best times were when Adelaide also came with her children. Martha was growing into the most precious child and Mary was still besotted by her.

Mary's mother had made arrangements with a spinster woman whom Mary recalled meeting on several occasions, to serve as chaperone while she was in Natchez. She was known to the Girault children as Aunt Cecelia, although it was unclear how they were related, if at all. Mary really didn't care, as long as she could stay with Aunt Cecelia and attend the ball at Auburn. Both Nellie and Minny had accompanied her on her long journey to the vibrant city on the high bluff overlooking the Mississippi River.

Aunt Cecelia's home was just lovely. Located just off of Canal Street in the heart of Natchez, it was built in the Greek Revival style and was graced with majestic white columns. It seemed so regal to Mary, who literally had to tell Minny to close her mouth, which she had left gaping open too long for Mary's taste, after pulling up in front of the structure. Upon their arrival, she learned that the house was shared equally between her hostess and her brother Samuel and his family. However, according to Cecelia, Samuel's family spent very little time in the house. Mary got the distinct feeling that Cecelia did not care for her sister-in-law. When she spoke her name, she did it with a nasally tone that caused her nose to wrinkle.

Mary's bedroom during her stay was at the top of the stairs, overlooking the street. The bed was an enormous poster bed with lovely hangings adorning it. The mattress was the most comfortable thing Mary had ever laid upon and she made a note to ask what it was filled with. A fire was lit and crackling in the fireplace when Mary entered the room. Her heart had positively leapt in her chest from sheer delight when she saw the floor-to-ceiling bookcase on the far wall of the bedroom. The secretary in the corner held a pen and ink well which she was pleased to see. She was keeping a journal of her trip and had promised correspondence with Aunt Catherine, Adelaide, and her own mother of course.

There were three oil lamps burning in the room in addition to the light of the fire. *My own room at home is as dimly lit as a cavern compared to this room. Such opulence!* In the glowing light of the room she was enthralled with the garlands of pine draped over the mantel. It gave the room a delightful smell in addition to its obvious beauty. *I could move into this place and never leave.* Nellie appeared a few minutes later. "Will you be needin' anythin' for I go on down?"

"Oh, nothing at all Nellie. I will see you in the morning." Mary was glad to see her leave, eager to continue her explorations of the massive room. She was drawn to the window and spent an unknown amount of time just watching the comings and goings on the street below. She could hear music coming in and out as doors to the streets opened and closed. She heard the gaiety of laughter from ladies in fashionable frocks escorted by gentleman in equally impressive attire. For sixteen years of age she was hopelessly naïve regarding the proper way to conduct herself in the company of a gentleman. *That is exactly why mother has sent me here—undoubtedly Aunt Cecilia has been enlisted to help me find a suitor.*

Mary paused for a moment to study her reflection in the mirror hanging over the vanity. Her cheeks were flushed from the cold wind of the December day and her hair had been mussed by her bonnet. *If I were a stranger looking upon this image, what would I make of her?* Mary pondered this for a moment. She had the strong Huguenot features of her grandfather Colonel John Girault. Her cheekbones were high and aristocratic in appearance producing striking features. Her hair was rich and dark in color and fell into thick waves past her shoulders.

Colonel Girault had died before she was born, but her father had remarked on her resemblance to him on numerous occasions. Her grandfather had been born in England but left for America as a young man with his brother. Unfortunately his brother hadn't survived the journey. Mary loved hearing stories of her grandfather's early years, including his service to George Rogers Clark during the Illinois expedition. His life seemed so exciting and adventurous to Mary. She was glad to resemble him. Last year she had entered the parlor at her own home to hear her father's voice. He was hunched over something and Mary overheard the words, "…disappointed in me, father."

When he had noticed her presence in the room, he had immediately straightened his countenance and called her to join him on the sofa. When she did so, she saw that her father was holding a clipping from a newspaper. It was yellowed and delicate and she noted the care with which he handled it. She leaned closer to read the words printed on the friable paper. She saw that it was from the Washington Republican dated 16 June 1813. It read:

> *Died at Bayou St. John in the 58th year of his age, Col. John Girault, for many years a resident of Natchez. He has left a widow and a large family to deplore his loss, a calamity*

over which every heart must bleed. By his death a numerous circle of friends has lost the society of one whose memory among them will be forever cherished and whose name they will ever embalm; calumny never sullied his name; nor perhaps ever lived a man more universally esteemed and loved.

On Friday morning last after a tedious illness, which he bore with fortitude, he resigned his life into the hands of the Almighty, fully persuaded that in leaving this troubled world, he would join the great assembly of the just—and dwell in the midst of everlasting joys.

He was an honest man and a sincere Christian, "Mark the perfect man and behold the upright, for the end of that man is peace."

"This is one of the obituaries printed when my father died." She watched in silence as he gently laid the clipping back into the center of the large family Bible where it had been previously. "I'd like to think if he could see me now, that he would be proud of the man that I've become." Mary was stunned. Her father had never taken her into his confidence in this way. She didn't want to let him down. She placed her hand lightly on his and smiled at him. "I am certain that Grandfather would be very proud of you."

James Girault turned to face his daughter. "You remind me so much of him. He had the same slender nose with the slightest bump to give it character. You will be a fine and beautiful woman, Mary. And with your intelligence and fortitude, you will make an excellent wife to whomever is lucky enough to earn your hand."

Mary smiled now recalling that tender moment shared with her father. He had been so preoccupied and tense lately, that she had come to cherish moments such as those. She walked away from the mirror and stood in front of the bookshelves. She ran her hands fondly over the volumes lining the shelves. It was an impressive collection of titles including works by James Fenimore Cooper, Ralph Waldo Emerson, and Nathaniel Hawthorne. There were leather bound collections of poetry, volumes in foreign languages, and so much more. *It would take a lifetime to open each book and examine the contents!*

She reached up and carefully removed a particularly grand volume having decorative embellishments on the spine. Gingerly, she held the leather book in her hands, enjoying the feel of it. The book bore the name of Sir John Hawkins and was titled *A General History of the Science and Practice of Music.* A thrill rushed through her when she realized the book was published in London in 1776. *Grandfather came from London!* She had become so entranced with the book, that she hadn't noticed Aunt Cecilia standing in the doorway until she cleared her throat pointedly. Mary jumped, startled and turned to face her hostess.

"I am quite sorry, Aunt Cecelia," Mary blurted. "I should have sought permission to remove any of your books from the shelves. Please forgive me."

"Nonsense Mary." Aunt Cecelia smiled. "You have no

idea how delighted I am to have your company. It will be the excitement of my entire holiday season, I am sure. Please act as if this is your own home. It will be as such while you are staying here."

Motioning to the bookshelves behind Mary she added, "My brother has added to the extensive collection of books begun by my father, the bulk of which is housed downstairs. What you see here is simply the overflow. So please explore the remainder of the library at your leisure. When you've rested from your journey of course."

"Thank you, Aunt Cecelia!" Mary gushed. She couldn't remember when she had been this happy.

That night before climbing into the huge bed, she had come across a magazine in the top drawer of the bureau. Intrigued, she pulled it out and examined it further. The title on the top read Graham's Magazine and was dated 1841. She took it to bed with her and began reading a story called *The Murders in the Rue Morgue* by Edgar Allan Poe. She knew after the first few paragraphs that her mother would not have approved of her reading the story, but, feeling a bit defiant, she continued reading.

The short story was set in Paris, which immediately titillated Mary who had fully committed to finishing the story by this point. Even when it became quite graphic and terrifying, she kept reading. When the bodies of Madame L'Espanaye and her daughter Camille were found badly damaged, she gasped but kept reading. When the crime is solved and the brutal killer turned out to be an escaped "Ourang-Outang," Mary gave a sudden yelp of horror.

It didn't take long for her to regret finishing the story. She wanted to return the magazine to the bureau drawer at once, but was terrified to get out of bed. *What if something is lurking under this great bed that I'm in?* The grand bedroom, such a source of wonder and joy only hours before, was now sinister and the shadows cast by the fire made every unfamiliar object suspect.

It was only the strong desire to be a thoughtful guest that forced her to extinguish the flame in the lamp nearest her bed. She had thought of leaving it lit during the night lest she wake up frightened in the strange room. Ultimately, she thought better of it, realizing that she didn't want it noted that she had used too much oil during her first night in the home.

As it turned out, Mary was so exhausted from her journey that she didn't wake until the morning light began flooding into the bedroom. That day and the several following were a whirlwind of excitement and activity unknown to Mary prior to this trip. They visited the finest homes in Natchez including Green Leaves, The Elms, and Gloucester. At each home Mary mirrored the gracious movements and mannerisms of Aunt Cecelia, taking in every bit of each day as if she were a sponge absorbing sea water. Mary's mother had taught her the social graces, but there was little opportunity for her to practice them with people outside of her family in Tuscahoma.

The day of the ball finally arrived, and Mary had a knot in her stomach from the moment she woke. She had seen Auburn, the home of Dr. Duncan and his wife Catherine, on their travels about Natchez and could scarcely believe that she would be attending a ball in that grand place that night. Even from the street, it was clearly a remarkable home and her anxiety was becoming palpable.

Her Aunt Catherine and Adelaide had conspired to give Mary a suitable wardrobe for her trip and especially a gown for the ball. She was overwhelmed by their generosity and thrilled beyond imagination when the packages had begun arriving at her home weeks earlier. Her mother had needed to make some adjustments, but for the most part everything was just perfect. She had felt fashionable during her visit to this point and hoped that she would look to everyone in attendance at Auburn like she belonged perfectly.

Nellie and Minny helped her dress beginning in the early afternoon as it was quite an undertaking. She had been told by Aunt Cecelia earlier in the day that there was no need to rush as it was expected that guests be fashionably late for occasions such as these. But Mary was so eager to see herself in the dress again that she had badgered poor Nellie to the point that she agreed just to get peace and quiet.

Once she was in her dress, she perched at the vanity and allowed Minny to style her hair. She had been advised by Aunt Cecelia as to how to wear her hair for the evening and was fortunate that her hair was full of natural waves and volume. Minny lightly applied some scented oil to her hair and brushed it through carefully. Then for what seemed to the restless Mary to be hours, she painstakingly applied pins in her hair to hold the hair in place. The pins on top were adorned with little jewels.

Mary walked as gracefully as she could muster over to the mirror when Minny had pronounced that she was finally finished. She froze for a moment, hardly believing that the creature gazing back from the mirror could possibly be her own reflection. Both of her servants let out a low gasp of approval at the sight of Mary's image in the mirror. The stunning creature reflected back at her was wearing an emerald green gown of satin crepe adorned with lace trim on the sleeves. The neckline came together modestly in a slight 'v' shape in folds of delicate fabric. Nellie had pinned a diamond broach with a large emerald in the center just where the neckline reached its lowest point.

The effect was stunning, just as Aunt Cecilia had predicted it would be when she insisted on loaning her the broach for the evening. The fitted bodice also formed a 'v' surrounded by a full skirted effect on the lower half of the gown. Mary marveled at how tiny her waist looked, but then realized that she could scarcely breathe in her tight corset.

Before exiting the foyer of her hostess's home that evening, Mary pulled on her gloves and allowed Minny to drape her shawl about her shoulders. It would be a cold evening, and the carriage ride to Auburn would expose her to the night air. Mary was impervious to the temperature due to her nerves, which steadily worsened as they came nearer to their destination. Aunt Cecilia attempted to make small talk, but her chatter was unintelligible to Mary at the moment. Not wanting to appear rude, however, she did manage the occasional one word reply when she felt it was expected.

"You are going to be fine tonight," Aunt Cecilia said. Mary did not reply and sensing that she was being waited on to answer she murmured, "Oh yes, I think so."

Cecelia laughed. Mary turned to face her perplexed. "What was that, Aunt Cecelia?"

"I don't think you have heard a word I've said tonight," she said with a smile. "I know that this is new to you. But trust me, you are going to be one of the prettiest girls at the ball tonight. And you will have more dance partners than you can manage."

The intended effect of easing Mary's nerves was unfortunately ineffective. At the mention of dance partners, Mary's stomach gave an uncomfortable lurch. She knew that there would be many attractive gentleman at the ball and their attentions would throw her into a realm she knew nothing about. She had spent the past few evenings watching ladies in Natchez effortlessly chattering away at their suitors. *How easy they make it appear.*

The carriage rolled to a stop in front of Auburn. Mary began to rise, but Cecelia gently placed her arm across Mary's lap. "Not yet. We are still a few places back. When we are directly in front of the entrance steps, we will be escorted from the carriage. Just follow my lead." She smiled genuinely at her.

Mary nodded. *There is so much I don't know.* They sat in silence a few moments waiting for the carriage to reach the appropriate location to disembark. Mary fought to keep her stomach contents down. She swallowed hard several times and took deep, even breaths.

Music from inside the house had begun wafting towards them through the open entry doors. The red brick mansion with four imposing white columns had a large portico in front where people were milling about greeting each other as the crowd made its way slowly through the doors. As Mary and Cecelia were assisted out of the carriage, Mary attempted to discreetly take in the Christmas decorations already impressive in their lavishness. The iron railings flanking the brick steps leading up to the portico were entwined with pine boughs laden with pine cones, holly berries, and to Mary's surprise whole red apples. She wondered how they were securely affixed, being so heavy, and she had to resist the temptation not to pull on one as she passed by.

The Duncans stood near the entrance personally greeting the arriving guests. Mary had practiced these polite introductions many times and felt quite confident that she had been perfectly charming. Relieved that one hurdle was successfully behind her, she walked with Cecelia into the foyer and froze instantly. The staircase was magnificent. It was an absolute marvel in that it stood in a perfect spiral completely unsupported.

"Aunt Cecelia, what is holding up the staircase?"

Cecelia looked a bit perplexed, and simply answered, "Why, I have no idea. Smarter minds than mine have worked that out." It was obvious to Mary that she hadn't given it a moment's thought.

Soon Cecelia was talking to acquaintances and laughing animatedly. Mary looked around the magnificent home. It was the finest house she had ever seen. She walked closer to the staircase and stood almost underneath it gazing upright hoping to see some form of attachment to the upper floor of the house. She glanced quickly to make sure Cecelia was still in sight, and then back up at the top of the spiral staircase searching in vain for a means of support.

"It's an amazing bit of architecture and engineering, isn't it?"

She jumped a bit, as she had been intently studying the staircase. Her eyes immediately fell upon a tall, broad shouldered young man who looked to be about eighteen.

She had certainly never seen him before and thought it a bit improper that he hadn't made the suitable introductions generally required before initiating a conversation with a young lady. Furthermore, his voice sounded strange. *What was that accent?*

Her stomach gave another lurch as she became aware of his gaze falling on her. His eyes met hers fully and yet he still had not made proper introductions. She cleared her throat and shifted restlessly unsure as to what her next move should be. Aunt Cecelia was no help. She wasn't even looking in Mary's direction. The young man had a thick mop of blonde hair that was a trifle untidy in contrast to his neatly tailored suit and tails. His smile was completely unnerving her and she had the feeling that he knew this. She was beginning to wonder if he was a true gentleman at all when he finally spoke again.

"I apologize for startling you. I saw you admiring the staircase and my words tumbled thoughtlessly out before I could stop them. I'd been doing the same thing, you see." And then seeing her puzzled expression hastily added, "Admiring the staircase that is."

She smiled at him in spite of herself. *He is so familiar. It is discomforting, and yet I feel drawn to him somehow.*

"You must think me dreadfully rude." He extended his hand out to her, still smiling with twinkling eyes. "My name is Henry Willcox. And it is my distinct pleasure to make your acquaintance."

She held her hand out for him to take and he leaned forward, brushing it with his lips. The butterflies in her stomach had now turned into hummingbirds and she felt a bit lightheaded. It did nothing to calm her nerves that his eyes remained locked on hers as he straightened back up.

"Mary Girault." The words spilled out too fast.

She suddenly couldn't remember her well-rehearsed speech. She felt completely tongue-tied in the presence of this stranger. Luckily, he spoke again without seeming to notice her distress.

"So did you work out the question of what holds the staircase in mid-air?"

Mary gave a laugh. "Certainly not. I remain quite perplexed by it. It seems to just be floating in the air as if by magic."

"And yet," Henry replied with a broad smile, "I am quite certain that there is a completely logical explanation. Dr. Duncan told me earlier that the house was designed by an architect by the name of Weeks from New York."

Henry leaned closer to Mary and lowered his voice to a conspiratorial whisper. "Apparently this Mr. Weeks was the center of quite a torrid scandal involving a mistress found dumped in a well. I know nothing further however, for when I was being told this remarkable story, Mrs. Duncan hushed him before he revealed any more details. But Mr. Weeks made a new start down here, and quite a start it was. The house is a masterpiece."

Mary had gasped audibly at the casual mention of a young woman being left in a well, but Henry hadn't seemed to notice. *He is certainly not from Mississippi. Such improper talk for having just made my acquaintance. I feel sure mother wouldn't approve.*

Finally, Cecelia made her way over to the young couple at the foot of the staircase. While she and Henry were making their own introductions, Mary found herself studying his features. There was the slightest crinkle around his eyes when he smiled. His face was extremely handsome and she realized at once that she found him very attractive. It was still proving impossible to form an intelligent sentence in his presence. After a moment, Cecelia suggested that they make their way into the other rooms of the house that were open to receive guests.

Everywhere Mary looked revealed extravagance and elegance. Flowers and greenery were on every available surface of the house. The musicians were so numerous, Mary thought it must be a full orchestra hired to play tonight. There was a room filled with food and beverages, even though Cecelia had told Mary that there would be a formal dinner served later. There must have been hundreds of people in the home, but it didn't seem as crowded as Mary would have thought. It was a testament to the sheer size of the mansion.

Cecelia's predictions had been correct. Mary was a highly sought after dance partner during the course of the evening. But none of the other young gentleman had unnerved her in the same way that Henry Willcox had. She had some well-practiced small talk ready for them, and she danced beautifully having practiced at home with siblings and her own father. She had chanced a few glances around the great room for Henry but hadn't spotted him again. She felt a bit disappointed that he hadn't asked her to dance and wondered if she would put him off with her awkwardness.

When it was time for the guests to make their way to dinner, she quickly spotted name cards on the tables. They were hand printed with a beautiful ruby-colored ink, with swirls and flourishes that Cecelia later told her were called calligraphy. Each card was seated in a small arrangement of greenery and red berries that seemed almost a perfect match for the ink. When she and Cecelia found their seats, she was a bit disconcerted to realize that Mr. Willcox was seated right beside her. When he saw her approaching, he stood and pulled out her chair. She thanked him as graciously as she could and took her seat beside him.

The food was unbelievably lavish. There were mince pies, and meats of all sorts. Each dish was garnished with intricately placed herbs and fruits. Rich desserts appeared in all varieties. She tried to remember her mother's admonishments about eating too much in public, but it was so tempting. *Why does being a lady have to come with so many restrictions?* She became aware of Henry's gaze falling upon her and turned her head to face him. She immediately began to wonder if she needed to wipe her mouth. *Why is he watching me?*

"Mr. Willcox?"

"Isn't the food delicious?" He looked directly into her eyes again. It was as if he could see right past the pretenses of social etiquette. He just went straight to the heart of whatever topic was on his mind. "I couldn't help but notice that you haven't eaten much at all."

She didn't know how to respond. This was a very direct thing to say, and not something she would expect a southern gentleman to blurt out. Then she thought about the accent, and was overcome with curiosity.

"You are not from Mississippi, I presume."

He laughed at once. "No, I am afraid you have me on that one. I hail from Pennsylvania. Dr. Duncan and I have mutual friends who arranged my visit here. He and his wife were kind enough to extend an invitation to the ball tonight. I'm here on business, really."

Now she was truly baffled. He certainly looked too young to have business dealings with someone of Stephen Duncan's stature. *Perhaps he only looks younger than he really is.*

Seeing her confusion, he added. "I am beginning my studies at the University of Pennsylvania. I've been studying the Colonization movement and one of my professors told me that Dr. Duncan in Natchez was pivotal in the success of the movement in this state. I must admit I was surprised to realize he owns so many slaves himself." He said this last part in a low voice, aware of the many guests seated near by.

"Well certainly he has slaves. He is probably the wealthiest cotton planter in the state. Would you expect that he would plant and harvest it all on his own?"

He smiled his large uninhibited smile again. "No, of course not. However, since he is so involved in supporting the colonization effort, I suppose that I expected him to have more abolitionist tendencies, you could say."

"Are you an abolitionist?" Mary said this as if it were a dreaded disease. Mainly because that is the way her father always spoke the word. She knew that her father had the utmost contempt for these sorts of people. Especially when they hailed from Northern states.

"Would you have a problem with it if I were?" He looked at her directly. Not smiling now, but with no offense in his expression.

Mary was taken aback. This type of conversation was far too familiar and direct. She should be talking about the weather. She had made a point of learning about the great tornado that hit Natchez several years earlier. Anything but slavery and abolition. That was almost as bad as religion or politics. However, at this moment she felt that the latter would actually have been an easier subject to navigate with the handsome stranger unnerving her so.

He waited for her answer without comment. She thought about changing the subject, but couldn't think of a good way to do it. Finally she blurted out, "My father says that I should stay away from people with revolutionary ideas." She regretted it the moment it was spoken. How stupid and childish she must look to him.

"He does, does he?" Now Henry's grin was beginning to grate on Mary's nerves. "I suppose it is a good thing you weren't around in 1776 then. There were a good number of revolutionary thinkers who signed a certain document declaring us free from tyranny. I do suppose that you are familiar with it."

"Of course I am familiar with it!"

Mary realized too late that she had raised her voice above a polite tone for dinner conversation. Her Aunt Cecelia abruptly looked her way, and Mary felt the color rise in her cheeks. She was beginning to regret the seating arrangement immensely.

"I apologize if I offended your sensibilities, Miss Girault. Please forgive me."

She chanced a glance at him, still flushed and aware of her heart pounding in her chest. He was still wearing that maddening smile.

"No need to apologize," she said stiffly. "You are entitled to your opinion, just as I am to my own."

Finally the smile faltered a bit and he looked at her rather imploringly. "I shouldn't have sounded so flippant about the Declaration of Independence. It was rude of me. Of course you have learned about it in your own schooling."

Just when she was beginning to regain a sense of ease in the conversation, his grin flickered again and he added, "It is always difficult when someone with such revolutionary ideas makes you question your own way of thinking, I imagine."

Heat rose to her cheeks again. *How arrogant he is!*

"First of all," Mary replied as courteously as she could manage, "You have not caused me to question anything. And second, I would appreciate it if you would stop mocking me."

At this Henry looked genuinely stunned. "It is not my intention to mock you, Miss Girault. I apologize again for anything offensive that I have said tonight. I must admit that I detected some hostility in your tone when you inquired if I were an abolitionist. Perhaps I am too defensive."

Her mind was reeling. "So you do believe that slavery is wrong?"

"Yes, I do," he replied simply. "I believe that it is the paramount evil that exists in our great nation."

Mary didn't know what to say. Never in her life had she heard such things. She knew that her teacher had similar beliefs but also knew that her father would not tolerate her voicing them to his children. She wanted to ask him more, but she felt as though she were betraying her father for speaking to this young man at all. He was the archetype of her father's perceived nemesis: a northerner with radical ideas who comes down to stir up trouble. *Is that what he is here to do?* She thought about her Aunt Catherine and Uncle Isaac as well. They had financially supported her visit to Natchez and she was having somewhat polite conversation with a self-declared abolitionist.

They were quiet for the rest of dinner. She was aware of every movement he made, and felt quite uneasy. She noticed with slight indignation that he had begun making small talk with the gentleman on his right. When guests were summoned back for more dancing, Henry stood solemnly and pulled her chair slowly back as she stood. They stood facing each other for a brief moment, before Henry bowed slightly and said, "It was a pleasure to meet you, Miss Girault. I hope that you enjoy the rest of your evening."

He turned and walked away leaving Mary's mind swirling with questions and emotions that she had never experienced. And though she had vehemently denied it, he was right. He had challenged her lifelong beliefs, creating just a flicker of a question in her subconscious. She danced late into the night until her feet ached terribly, but she didn't see Henry again that night. She wasn't sure if she would ever see him again. And the thought made her feel somehow empty and alone although she was in a house full of people.

March 1844   Prospect Hill Plantation

Adelaide Richardson sat on the front porch watching Cabell toddling around attempting to keep up with his older sister. She so enjoyed being here, surrounded by family in a place that had always been so special to her. Her husband John was a good man, but he was quite ambitious and spent much time away from home. At Prospect Hill her children were with their cousin, which held a great appeal to her. Soon there would be more cousins to grow up playing together here, and the thought of it made her smile.

Her grandfather, Captain Ross, had instilled in her a great devotion to family as had her dear Aunt Margaret. There wasn't a day that passed that her heart didn't long for them both. She despised the fact that the legal battles surrounding their wills would forever tarnish her memories of them. It was unavoidable, but caused her to grieve for the way things had been before.

She recalled many a conversation on this very porch with her grandfather in which he talked of his slaves as if they were his extended family. She knew of his intentions regarding his slaves, and it pained her that her brother Isaac was not honoring these wishes. But Isaac had been a loyal and loving brother to her, and had directed that Adelaide's legacy left for her in the will be carried out to the letter. It was about the only directive in the will he had not defied. She had promptly received the $10,000 Grandfather had bequeathed to her.

Her grandfather's will had also stipulated that Grace and her children were to be given over to Adelaide for her own uses. Having Grace around to cook for her was a wonderful thing, but Adelaide understood also that the provisions of the will allowed for Grace to choose to leave for Liberia with the others if she so desired. She was resolved to accept that decision when the time came as graciously as she could. *I at least owe that much to you, Grandfather.*

Her feelings about the controversy surrounding the wills was so difficult to work out. Her husband and brother staunchly believed it was the right of the heirs to oppose the will and claim what was rightfully theirs. The land, she knew, was of little worth without the slaves. Still, it seemed that wages could be offered to them if they would agree to stay. But when she brought this up early on, Isaac had scoffed. "That isn't how our dear Grandfather left things, Adelaide. If they don't go to Liberia they are to be sold in family units. Either way, without a legal battle, we lose Prospect Hill. Don't you understand that?"

She had never outwardly questioned anything since. She truly did understand that her brother found it unfair not to inherit the estate, but didn't their grandfather have the right to decide what becomes of it? When the conversation turned to the case as they so often did, Adelaide allowed her mind to wander elsewhere or excused herself from the conversation all together—leaving that talk for the men and her mother. She had grown tired of her mother's unpleasantness, and her resentment of Aunt Margaret. Couldn't she allow the poor woman to rest in peace?

The sentiment in the county was clearly aligned with her brother's views. The notable exception was the Parkers, who seemed quite sympathetic to the plight of the slaves. They were not entirely open regarding their position, as they too felt the tremendous pressure to conform to popular opinion. But Adelaide knew of their sympathies and had heard murmurings of the Parkers writing letters to Dr. Ker and the Colonization Society on their behalf. Part of her respected them a great deal for doing so. Another part saw it as a betrayal of Isaac. Thus, the feelings of confusion seemed to constantly battle between themselves in Adelaide's psyche.

Adelaide knew that she didn't have the strength of character to withstand the ostracism that her Aunt Margaret had endured in her last years of life. She knew that about herself, and it pained her to no end that she hadn't spent more time with her in those last few months. *Why didn't I let you know how much I loved you and appreciated all you have done for me?*

Martha and Cabell's laughter punctuated her thoughts as she relished the warmer air signaling the end of winter. It was the first warm day of the year and she and the children were enjoying every moment. Grace appeared with a pitcher of fresh lemonade and some glasses. "I thought you might like somethin' to drink Missus Adelaide. I made it fresh."

Martha ran to her mother's side instantly. "I want some. I want some!"

"Of course darling. Let me help you." Adelaide intercepted Martha's quick hands which were already attempting to grab a glass off of the tray which Grace had set down on a side table. "But first, how do you ask?"

"May I please have a drink?" said Martha in her most polite tone of voice.

"Take a seat, Miss Martha, and I get it for you." Grace was, as always, concerned with making sure that Martha was developing proper manners for a young lady. She took on the responsibility with great importance. She felt pride when the children that she helped to raise behaved in a way that represented the family well.

"Yes Grace," the little girl replied in the sweet soft voice that warmed Adelaide's heart. There were little beads of sweat forming on the child's forehead to confirm the warmth of the day.

Adelaide leaned over and lifted Cabell off the ground, and placed him in her lap. She kissed the top of his little head and smiled at him. He returned the smile and said, "Drink."

"'I would like a drink please,' Cabell," Adelaide responded to him, knowing full well that he couldn't repeat the phrase exactly, but still encouraging him to learn the proper responses that would be expected of him in society.

"Like drink please," said Cabell with a fierce look of determination on his small face. Adelaide laughed as she put her glass to his lips and allowed him to sip the refreshing beverage. She noticed Grace reaching for a napkin as Cabell sloshed the drink down his chin. *Yes, I will miss you if you decide to leave us, Grace. Especially with the new little one arriving this year.* Adelaide allowed her free hand to rest on her already protruding midsection, revealing the impending arrival of the newest Richardson baby.

Catherine came through the doorway and took a deep breath of the spring air. "Here you are. What a beautiful day to be outside. I think I'll join you."

"Certainly. I'd love that."

Grace poured a glass of lemonade for Mrs. Wade before quietly taking her leave and returning inside the house.

Adelaide smiled as her sister-in-law took the seat on the other side of Martha. She enjoyed Catherine's company very much. "Did you rest well?"

Catherine had been upstairs lying down, and Adelaide assumed that her young son Isaac was still in the nursery upstairs.

Catherine nodded, stifling a yawn.

"No sign of Mary yet, then? I am so looking forward to her arrival."

Adelaide had to admit that she was as well. She had become quite fond of Catherine's vivacious young niece and enjoyed the times they spent together. And Martha positively adored her. She had been asking all morning about Mary and when she would be arriving.

Adelaide hoped that she would make it today. But there were no rail lines connecting that part of the state and determining the exact time of an arrival was impossible. Furthermore, it was a long and arduous journey from Tuscahoma to Prospect Hill, involving rugged, often washed-out roads to the Mississippi River port of

Greenville. Once in Greenville, which was an eighty mile trip from her home, Mary would book passage on a steamboat going downstream to Rodney. William Belton, Prospect Hill's carriage driver, had been lodging at the Hunt Plantation near Rodney since the previous day to bring Mary the rest of the way. According to her letter, she would be traveling with Nellie to attend to her needs and with Joe for protection.

"Her letters are so descriptive and entertaining. I simply love to read them," said Catherine.

"Yes they certainly are," agreed Adelaide eagerly. "I loved the descriptions of the ball and of Cecelia's home. I wouldn't mind having a few days to peruse the library there myself. I'd grown up thinking that Grandfather had the most magnificent library in the state. Little did I know that my view of the world was so narrow."

Catherine laughed. "I'd like to get more information about her suitors. She gave woefully little details about that particular aspect of her visit. Did you notice?"

"Yes, and even when I gently pressed for information, her response back to me contained very little on the subject." Adelaide gave a small "humph" of mock indignation.

"Well, we can question her in person when she gets here. She'll have little choice but to answer then!" Catherine laughed again as she spoke.

Adelaide joined in on the laughter. "Oh, the poor girl. I'm beginning to feel a bit sorry for her now with both of us ganging up on her."

They spent the next hour chatting amiably about the weather, their husbands, the servants and the latest fashions. Both of them had spent the last few years of their lives either expecting a child or just having given birth to one, so they almost felt as if they were living vicariously through young Mary Girault and the topic of conversation came back to her before long.

At the sound of Mary's name, Martha who had been busily working alongside Cabell constructing an unknown structure from their wooden blocks skipped over to the ladies.

"I want Mary to get here!" It was a proclamation rather than a question. But her mother responded kindly, "She is on her way as we speak, Martha. You must be patient."

"I don't like being patient." Martha stuck her bottom lip out and crossed her arms across her chest.

"None of us do darling, but we have to learn it." Sensing the need for a change in subject, she added, "What is that magnificent arrangement of blocks going to be when you finish?"

Martha looked back at the pile of blocks that Cabell was now smashing. "It was Prospect Hill, but now it isn't anything."

"Prospect Hill?" Adelaide inquired. She never would have dreamed that was what the young children were building.

"Yes. We love it here," replied Martha simply. She looked back over her shoulder rather contemptuously at her younger brother who had now reduced her masterpiece to shambles.

"Would you like to go up to the nursery and see if Isaac is awake?" Catherine asked the children. "I can summon someone to take you up."

Catherine was expecting her second child any day now. She was quite large and found it difficult to move with much ease. Adelaide had become momentarily caught up watching Catherine adjusting her position in the chair when she became vaguely aware of Martha jumping up and down.

"Martha, please stop jumping." Adelaide could feel the porch shaking beside her and it was grating on her nerves.

"But I see a carriage!"

Sure enough, a cloud of dust in the distance directed her eye to a small black speck in the distance that she recognized to be an arriving carriage.

Soon there was a palpable excitement among the group on the front porch, and moments later Mary arrived to quite a welcoming committee.

She was genuinely happy to see the Martha and Cabell again and lavished them with loving hugs and kisses, much to their delight. After several minutes however, Catherine stepped in and told the children that Mary needed to freshen up from her long journey. Mary smiled at her and turned to greet her aunt.

"Thank you so much for inviting me here again, Aunt Catherine."

Her aunt clasped her hands around those of her young niece. "It is my pleasure. We so enjoy having you here with us. How was your journey?"

"Well," Mary replied, "The river was quite exciting on this journey! We reached Paw Paw island at nightfall, and a gentleman on board began telling a quite inventive tale regarding ghosts who inhabit the island. Many people aboard the steamboat were actually frightened by his story!

Some of the ladies even believed that they should duck if the ghosts threw fruit at them while on deck! Nellie was positively hysterical with fright when I recounted the tale to her, which I came to regret immediately. But we made excellent time. I heard the captain boasting that we were averaging at least twelve miles per hour."

Catherine and Adelaide both laughed. "Ghosts on Paw Paw island? I've never heard such a thing!" exclaimed Catherine.

"Because it is utter nonsense, but the gentleman got some passengers mighty worked up." Mary went on, "But Vicksburg was delightful. I picked up something for you Aunt Catherine. To thank you for your hospitality. I will present you with it after dinner."

"There was no need, I assure you," replied Catherine with a smile. "But I do thank you, Mary dear."

Adelaide's eyebrows drew closer as she registered her concern for Mary's report. "Twelve miles per hour? Is that safe? John tells me that the lower Mississippi is quite treacherous and these steamboat captains are known for being reckless. Apparently there are snags everywhere."

"Gracious, I hope so," Catherine agreed, now also looking mildly concerned.

Mary felt eager to change the subject, not wanting anything to come between herself and future visits to Prospect Hill. She exclaimed suddenly, "Mother sends her love, of course. I must tell you at once before I forget!"

Her tactic seemed to work, as Catherine laughed. "I will be sure to let her know that you did so the moment you arrived. Please, come inside and refresh yourself. You and Adelaide will be sharing a room upstairs. There should be fresh water in the basin and a clean towel waiting for you."

Over the next several days, Mary fielded numerous questions regarding her trip to Natchez and the grand ball at the Duncan home. She offered extravagant details regarding the ball itself; the gowns ladies were wearing, the prominent guests in attendance, the full orchestra, the lavishness of the home and the decorations. She had described the dinner so thoroughly that Catherine insisted it had made her hungry just hearing about it. She demonstrated the face that Cecelia made when she mentioned her sister-in-law which made both Catherine and Adelaide giggle.

"Did you receive any calls from the young men with whom you danced at the ball?" Catherine knew only what Mary had offered up in her letters, but felt it was lacking in specifics.

"Aunt Catherine, I wrote to you about it remember?"

"Please refresh my memory then Mary. Which gentlemen would you like to see again?"

"I am not sure that I will see any of them again. It isn't as if I am frequently in Natchez. I sincerely doubt they will trouble themselves to call on me in Tuscahoma."

"Hmmm," replied Catherine thoughtfully. "That is probably true. Are you corresponding with anyone at least?"

"Yes, Aunt Catherine. There is a young man named Robert with whom I have been exchanging correspondence. He writes very well, but he is busy learning the business of the family cotton planation from his father."

"Robert? What is his surname?" asked Adelaide. She and Catherine were determined to get answers out of Mary no matter how much questioning it required.

"His family name is Newell," Mary replied rather wearily.

Noticing the glance that was exchanged between the two women, she hastened to add, "They are not one of the better known families in Natchez. But he has been taken under the wing of Dr. Duncan, who spotted promise in him apparently. He just goes on and on about how brilliant Dr. Duncan is and marvels at his wealth and prominence. I find it a bit pretentious to be honest."

Mary didn't have the slightest bit of interest in Robert Newell. She found him to be a bore at the ball and subsequently when he visited her at Aunt Cecelia's. However, she was polite and entertained his letters partly to put off the questioning she would have received from her mother if she were not maintaining any contact with a suitor from her trip.

Catherine and Adelaide didn't admonish her for her feelings, for which she was grateful. She had told no one of Henry Willcox. He had infuriated her with his arrogance to be sure, but he had also ignited a spark inside of her that she had never felt before. She was intrigued by this handsome stranger from an entirely different background than hers. She wished now that she hadn't become so cross. Perhaps if she had responded differently, he would have asked her to dance. Maybe even visited her at Cecelia's home.

She had hoped in vain that he would call on her in Natchez. She had remained there a week past the ball in order for her to fulfill the social obligations that were part of the expectations of a well-bred young lady in

Mississippi. She had been a gracious hostess when receiving callers at Cecelia's home and she had also left her own engraved calling card at the home of the Duncan's in acknowledgment of the invitation. She was quite fond of the new cards that she had received in preparation for her trip. Aunt Catherine had ordered them for her and the script was lovely. *Mary Elizabeth Girault*

However, Henry Willcox did not materialize again while she was in Natchez. Aunt Cecelia had practically dismissed him when recounting the evening as he was a visitor from the north. Her only mention of him was of his dashing good looks. Mary had been amused that the spinster woman had quite a twinkle in her eye as she spoke of the much younger man. But she could certainly understand his effect on her.

Mary had departed to spend Christmas with her family in Tuscahoma and most of the journey home kept her mind occupied with thoughts of Henry. She tuned out most of the chatter between Nellie and Minny as she recounted each word of their conversation at dinner. *What would father say if I told him that I fancy a northern abolitionist?* She gave a small shudder at the thought. He was clearly not an appropriate beau for her, and in any case he would be returning to his studies in Pennsylvania at the end of his Christmas holidays. In spite of her hopes to the contrary, she knew that she would likely never see him again.

Before Mary left Prospect Hill, her Aunt Catherine had given birth to a son they had christened Dunbar Bisland Wade. He had been born with a strong, healthy cry and Mary was pleased to see both baby and mother looking so well. She enjoyed every aspect of life at her Aunt's home. Uncle Esau had built a wooden rocking horse for the children complete with a leather bridle and saddle. The slaves of Prospect Hill seemed to excel as craftsmen and when she had asked her Uncle Isaac how they had learned to make such beautiful things he had replied, "My grandfather indulged them. A bit too much if you ask me."

Still Mary had thought that it was a good thing to have taught them so many useful skills. Everything here was so well built and well maintained. Sometimes she wandered through the house running her hands lightly over the polished wooden railings and wainscoting. She had gazed at the portraits of Isaac Ross and his wife Jane Allison Ross wishing that she had gotten the chance to know the man responsible for bringing this magnificent place into being. She had even played the massive piano and marveled at how beautifully the room accommodated the large instrument. She ran her fingers across the keys creating a playful glissando before walking to gaze out of the window. *I feel so happy here. I honestly think that this is the one place where I feel completely at peace. I wish I didn't have to return home so soon.*

***

Henry Willcox had found his calling. His trip to Natchez in December had completely changed his way of viewing the world. He had expected to visit with Dr. Duncan and learn a great deal under his tutelage, then to leave feeling honored to have been welcomed by a man he greatly admired. But what he had learned had transformed him from a carefree young man into an idealistic crusader.

Stephen Duncan was a brilliant businessman, a prominent member of society and a member of the American Colonization Society—as Henry had known before arriving in Natchez. But Duncan also was a man who prospered greatly on the backs of enslaved men and women for whom he held little regard. He owned a thousand slaves, and the sheer number was staggering to Henry. He had trouble comprehending how that was even possible. It had been difficult for Henry to reconcile these differing aspects of his mentor's character. And even though he had come to learn more about Duncan's role in the colonization movement, the businessman had little interest in discussing it; much preferring to tutor Henry on investing and earning profits.

His trip south had stirred something inside of the young student who'd became acutely aware of how sheltered his life had been to this point. He realized that he could not just return to his university career immediately, as he had fully intended to do. His father had been furious when he had received the news and Henry knew that there would be hell to pay when he finally made his way home. He had explained in his first letter to his parents his reasoning and his intentions in staying in Mississippi longer than originally planned. There was nothing more that he could do to appease them at this point, so he pushed the thoughts of his parents from his mind and focused on his higher calling.

Providence had intervened in keeping him in Mississippi longer than planned. Henry was sure of it. Days before his scheduled departure from Natchez, a letter had been delivered to Dr. Duncan's home bearing the return address of Zebulon Butler. Henry found the name to be strange when he noticed the letter sitting on the edge of the desk in the grand office Duncan kept for himself at Auburn. Henry had commented on the odd name to Dr. Duncan, as their conversation had reached a momentary lull.

"Ah, Butler," Duncan had replied. "A co-executor of mine involving the estate of a wealthy woman wishing to free her slaves and colonize them to Africa. I'm sure that I've mentioned it to you already."

Henry answered in the affirmative, now anxious to hear more.

"We had to fight the heirs tooth and nail to see it done, but eventually we proved our case. Butler is a Presbyterian minister in Port Gibson and a bit sanctimonious for my taste."

Duncan pushed away his ledgers, removed his glasses and rubbed his forehead. "I imagine the letter is entreating me to assist with the Prospect Hill slaves again."

"Prospect Hill?" inquired Henry with only mild curiosity.

"The name of the plantation owned by the father of the woman whose estate I helped to settle. He died more than two years before she, and yet those souls are still laboring at the plantation of their former owner. Only now under their new master, his grandson Isaac Ross Wade. From what I hear he will deplete every cent from the estate to keep the provisions outlined in the will from being carried out."

This piqued Henry's interest. "I remember hearing mention of that case at the university. Those slaves were also to be freed. They have been waiting all of this time for freedom? How many years has it been exactly?"

"He died in 1836 if I remember correctly. Captain Ross directed for all of his slaves to be given the option of emigrating to Liberia. He even wanted a school built over there for them and funds to get them started. I doubt any of his slaves will ever see the coast of Africa. There won't be money left to make it happen."

"And the courts have allowed this to happen?" Henry was surprised that the legal directives of a prominent citizen could be so easily disregarded simply because they went against the wishes of his family.

"Mr. Wade has lost every single legal case that he has filed," replied Duncan. "But he just files new appeals to stall for time, I suspect."

Henry reeled at the injustice being perpetrated upon these unknown slaves. He knew that none of this was his concern, but felt a strange compulsion to offer his assistance.

He cleared his throat and spoke, a bit unsure of how he would be perceived by his host. "Dr. Duncan, could I be of assistance in this matter while I am here? It does sound like an interesting case."

Duncan appraised his young guest's earnest expression. "I suppose it couldn't hurt to see what he wants. But I am a busy man as you well know, and I have fulfilled my obligations. I don't know how much more involved I wish to become in this ugly business."

He picked up the letter from his desk and carefully opened it with his ornate polished silver letter opener. Henry watched intently as Duncan scanned the letter, his face impassive.

After a few moments, Duncan let out a long slow sigh and placed the letter on the desk in front of him.

"It is just as I thought. Reverend Butler is becoming increasingly frustrated by Mr. Wade's refusal to comply with the directives of the estate of Captain Ross. He has been in contact with the Prospect Hill slaves who report that the cotton crops are being sold under an assumed name in order to avoid being credited to the estate. Some of the slaves are being sent away to the homes of family members to work there. Captain Ross did not believe in separating slave families, and so this has apparently caused them considerable upset."

Duncan's voice did not convey any emotion, and certainly not any indignation at this blatant disregard for the welfare of the unfortunate Prospect Hill slaves. Henry found this disconcerting as he himself was feeling almost outraged at the thought of this unknown stranger getting away with such things. He did not want to betray his feelings and made a great attempt at keeping his tone neutral. "And Reverend Butler requests your assistance in rectifying this situation sir?"

"Yes, he feels that I have more influence in these matters than I actually do. This disagreeable business over in Jefferson County has stirred up quite a bit of controversy around the region. The papers in New Orleans are even covering the legal wrangling that has been going on. I do have an interest of sorts as I am a member of the Colonization Society who was directed in his daughter's will to oversee the settlement of those slaves. But I do not see the point in getting personally involved with particulars here. This is something for the lawyers to hash out in the courts."

For once, Henry did not stop to think through his actions. All of his life, he had been careful to conform to the expectations of society; of his parents, his teachers, his friends. But in this one moment, he was thinking entirely of something else; of righting a wrong that he could not sit by and watch happen. Yes, it would be easy to travel back to his comfortable life and resume his studies. Within a matter of weeks he would likely forget about this business going on in Mississippi. But what of those suffering on Prospect Hill? *I am going to stay and help this Butler person fight for them.*

"Will you send a letter to Mr. Butler inquiring if I may be of assistance? I may need to lodge with him briefly until I determine the availability of hotels in the area."

Dr. Duncan did not immediately respond. He studied the sincere young face of Henry Willcox for a moment.

"And what of your father? This venture to Port Gibson is sure to interfere with your education."

"My father will understand."

Henry knew this was a lie the very moment that he spoke the words, but Dr. Duncan thankfully didn't challenge him on it.

Duncan regarded him for several seconds before replying. "All right then, if that is what you wish, I will write the necessary letters."

Henry excused himself from the room, his mind swimming with uncertainties and yet filled with a strange exhilaration that he had never before experienced. He had been helping Dr. Duncan with some accounts most of the morning and wanted to splash some cool water on his face and maybe take a brisk walk around the grounds.

As he reached the door, Duncan said, "And I will be sending a bank draft over to Port Gibson in your name. You have been of great assistance to me these past weeks and have earned a just compensation for your efforts."

When Henry turned back to thank him, he noted a small wry smile on Duncan's face. "In case your father doesn't understand as well as you are imagining he will."

Henry suddenly realized that Duncan was likely right. It was improbable that his father would continue to send him the financial means with which to stay in this part of the country.

Recognizing the charitable nature of his act, Henry responded, "Thank you sir."

"It is my pleasure, Henry. I admire your spirit. I caution you, however, not to become emotionally involved in the matter."

Reflecting back now on that day in December made Henry feel a bit foolish. He had learned so much since then that recalling that memory felt as if he were evoking the musings of a naïve child. *Perhaps I had been but a child then. But I see the world much more clearly now.*

The night before, he and Butler had been in the slave's quarters at Prospect Hill meeting with a group of men. It wasn't the first time that Henry had made their acquaintance. The night of the first meeting, he had been amazed at the knowledge the slaves held regarding the legal case. Mr. Butler had done a good job of keeping them apprised and Edmond Belton had a book containing notes on the case. He had been surprised to learn that the slaves could write, but felt immediately ashamed of his assumption. Reverend Butler had assured him later, however, that he had been right to assume it as the vast majority of southern slaves were not taught to read and write.

What made the meeting unusual was the mention of a familiar name in such a strange new place. One of the slaves, Esau, had joined them late. He didn't appear to be vexed, but rather amused when recounting the cause of his lateness. With a chuckle he said, "Miss Mary kept on askin' me questions bout how I made the rockin' horse. How you cut the wood to curve like that Uncle Esau and how does it keep from rockin' too far and tippin' over?" He shook his head from side to side. "That missus asks more questions than I ever heard of!" There was a general congenial murmur of agreement from around the cabin as Esau took his place. *Mary?*

Henry recalled the beautiful young lady at the ball in Natchez a few months earlier. Her name had also been Mary, and the first words that he had heard her speak were, "Aunt Cecelia, what is holding up the staircase?" Henry attempted to put the notion out of his mind. *Mary is one of the most common names in America. Surely it could not be the same young lady.* But the seed had been planted and during the rest of the conversation that evening, Henry found it very hard to concentrate.

The young Mary from the ball had cast quite a spell on him. He had run through their dinner conversation countless times in his mind and could not believe he had been such an idiot. He wanted to pay her a visit in the days following the ball, but could never get up the nerve to bear the almost certain rejection he would face. So he did the only thing he knew to do; chalk it up to a learning experience and move on. But now, on this warm spring night in Jefferson County Mississippi he was reminded of the longing he felt for Mary Girault, whose beautiful visage now seemed to float in front of his eyes.

When the meeting was coming to an end and Reverend Butler was saying his goodbyes, Henry took the opportunity to speak to Levi. He was the closest in age to Henry of the slaves they had been meeting with, and Henry had taken quite a liking to the young man. "Does a young lady by the name of Mary Girault live on this plantation, Levi?"

He almost held his breath waiting for a reply. Levi looked puzzled. "You know Miss Mary?"

Henry's heart started pounding as he replied, "I met a young lady by that name last December in Natchez. When Esau mentioned the way this young lady was asking questions, it brought her to mind for some reason."

"Miss Mary's the niece of Missus Catherine," Levi replied. "She don't live here, but she visits here quite a bit."

Henry's heart leapt, but then almost as suddenly crashed again. *What would she say if she knew I was here helping to defeat her Uncle's efforts? Or if she understood the level of contempt I have for him? If I'd ever had a chance of winning her forgiveness, that is gone forever now.*

Still he felt as if he had just consumed a hot beverage, as the thought of Mary being on this exact same place warmed his insides. Even the slightest possibility of a chance meeting with her excited him more than he had imagined possible.

"Levi, I almost forgot." Henry pulled a small book out of his pocket. It was his favorite book of poetry, *Ballads and Other Poems,* by Henry Wadsworth Longfellow. "This is the book that I promised I would bring on my next visit. I hope your wife enjoys it."

Levi smiled and gingerly took the small leather volume from Henry's hand. "My Rachael goin' love hearing these poems. And I need more practice with my readin'. Thank you kindly Mr. Willcox."

"Will you please call me Henry?" he asked for at least the third time even though he knew it to be a fruitless exercise.

Henry felt great affection for Levi. Levi's life was so different than his own, and yet he had such a spirit of optimism in his view of the world. It was humbling to be around him. Especially when Henry recalled the long evenings of his university days, spending hours in discourse with other elite young men of privilege complaining about the politics of the day.

It shamed him now, in retrospect, to think of his pompous notions about liberty and democracy. He realized that he had known nothing of what life was like for people like Levi who literally had never been given any of the rights that he and his classmates took for granted. *What did we ever have to complain about?*

July 4, 1844   Port Gibson

Henry Willcox was feeling as weary as a man three times his age. He prayed for the optimism and ability to see the good in his fellow man that he so admired in Levi. Earlier in the week, he had received a package from his father. When he opened it, he found a pamphlet titled *Thoughts on African Colonization* by William Lloyd Garrison. A small note penned by his father fluttered out of the large envelope when he pulled the pamphlet from it. It said, "Please read carefully. Is this what you want to postpone your education to support?"

He had read through the pamphlet twice immediately. Then he had gone back and read certain portions of it again. One portion particularly troubled him.

> *Of this I am sure: no man, who is truly willing to admit the people of color to an equality with himself, can see any insuperable difficulty in effecting their elevation. When, therefore, I hear an individual—especially a professor of*

religion—contending that they can never enjoy equal rights in this country, I cannot help suspecting the genuineness of his own republicanism or piety, or thinking that the beam is in his own eye. My Bible assures me that the day is coming when even the 'wolf shall dwell with the lamb, and the leopard shall lie down with the kid, and the wolf and the young lion and the fatling together;' and if this be possible, I see no cause why those of the same species—God's rational creatures—fellow-countrymen, in truth, cannot dwell in harmony together.

He needed to believe that colonization was a noble endeavor worth fighting for. Garrison's words held a certain truth that troubled him. The argument that black men and white men cannot live together in harmony once slavery is abolished was bandied about quite often in his social circles. It had become an accepted notion among many. But why did this need to be so? Wouldn't it be a much more noble cause to fight for the abolition of slavery without any conditions? Colonization was beginning to seem such a conditional solution, and one that offered the black man little choice in his own future. So many questions churned through Henry's mind.

There was progress being made towards allowing the Prospect Hill slaves to leave for Africa. At first that seemed cause for great celebration, but it wasn't long before he felt compelled to bring his newfound concerns regarding colonization to Reverend Butler's attention. He also presented him with a copy of Garrison's writing. Henry was surprised to find that Butler had the identical concerns and had already read the same pamphlet.

"This issue has troubled me for some time. When Mrs. Reed's slaves were finally released and sent to Africa, I tried assuring myself that they were better off. Surely, freedom was always better than bondage." Butler gave a rather bitter laugh, "Oh, I told myself they were given the choice. But really, the choice was to go to Africa or remain here as a slave. What kind of a choice is that?"

Henry didn't know what to say. He had never known that Zebulon Butler had even the slightest doubt in the cause of colonization. He so fervently supported it.

Butler went on. "What I've come to conclude is that colonization is the lesser of two evils—slavery being the greatest evil. I still pray for the day that we can live peacefully with our black brothers and sisters in this country. But I fear that that day is still beyond my own lifetime."

"Have you asked the slaves at Prospect Hill what they want?"

"I actually have had discussions with several of the slaves on more than one occasion. Did you know that Ed and Wade Belton's mother will not consider leaving? Their younger brother refuses to leave his mother behind, so he will also stay."

"I did not know that. It must be hard for their mother to see them leave."

"Captain Ross was very specific in his final will that the slaves be given the choice to emigrate. But the only option for the majority of them was to either go to Liberia or remain here and be sold as family units. Of course once they have a new master, they can be sold at his whim in whatever manner he chooses. And they are quite aware of this fact. So most of the slaves have chosen to go. They are just waiting for the chance."

"But why support 'the lesser of two evils' as you call it? Why not support the more noble cause of the outright abolition of slavery?" Henry was feeling a disillusionment that was nagging at him terribly.

"I do support that cause. However, my idealism has been replaced by pragmatism. We are in the largest cotton growing region in the world. Slavery is viewed as the only viable means of sustaining the lives of landowners here. I've found that there are people here who will listen and support the colonization movement. You will find no one in these parts who will support abolition."

Henry opened his mouth to protest further but Butler cut him off. "Henry, I see much of myself in you. I understand your indignation and I share it. Please understand that you will only undermine your own efforts if you go too far in fanning the flames that are already burning just under the surface."

"I just cannot stand seeing Isaac Wade cheating them out of what they were left by Captain Ross. He wanted them to have a chance at a new life. It can't happen now, can it?"

"I'm going to focus on the positive. Mr. Chambliss has accepted the legal appointment to be the receiver of the Ross slaves. Even though it is likely that Mr. Wade will object and attempt to block his efforts to take possession of the slaves for the Colonization Society, I have to believe that the sheriff will offer Chambliss the necessary protection to do so."

"When we were last at Prospect Hill, Esau told us that Mr. Wade was going to have numerous fellow citizens there on the property with loaded guns when they attempted to come for them."

"Surely he is just posturing. Even Mr. Wade has to know at some point when he has lost the battle."

Henry shook his head. He had learned nothing of this man to indicate that he had any intentions of backing down. *Ever.* But he was glad to have a powerful ally such as Stephen Duncan supporting him. He suddenly realized that he had forgotten to tell Butler of his latest correspondence.

"I've received word back from Dr. Duncan. He assured me that if the court-appointed receiver is turned away, he will assist in hiding a group of Ross slaves until they can catch a steamboat to New Orleans. He is willing to arrange their passage to Africa."

"If we can succeed in getting small groups to freedom it is a good thing. But eventually I would like to see the directives of the will carried out as they were intended. Otherwise, Wade wins in the end. And more importantly, the provisions Captain Ross intended to be in place to establish them in Africa need to be fulfilled."

Reverend Butler exhaled and clapped Henry on the back. "We've been working hard, son. Let's allow ourselves a celebration. Today is a holiday, let's not forget. And a holiday of ironic significance to us at the moment."

Henry smiled at his newfound friend. "Independence Day."

"And that means good food and good music around

here. It is still morning. If we eat quickly, we will have time to ride out to the slaves' quarters at Prospect Hill. We need to give them the news about Mr. Chambliss. Progress is progress, even when it comes slowly."

"Agreed," answered Henry with a smile.

God it feels good to smile. They deserve some good news for once.

By the time the two set out for Prospect Hill, Henry was so full of good food that he actually had a bit of difficulty climbing up into the wagon. "I never should have eaten so much today!"

He could tell that Reverend Butler shared his sentiments, even though his only response was to rub his own slightly protruding belly.

By now, Zebulon Butler had become familiar enough with the trail from his parking place on the edge of the woods to the slaves' quarters to make the trek alone. The path, now better worn, was not nearly as treacherous as it had been the first night he had visited here. It seemed like a lifetime ago.

When they arrived in the clearing in which the first of the cabins appeared, it was obvious that a great celebration had been going on here as well. There was still music ringing in the air. The remains of food were on a great makeshift table set up outside of the gathering house. It appeared that the slaves were given the day off, and there was a general mood of gaiety in the air. The hot sun of late afternoon was greatly diminished by the large number of trees blocking its rays.

The two men were greeted with enthusiasm and smiles.

Even though the majority were not present during meetings, it was commonly known that these men were helping them win their freedom. Both men initially tried in vain to politely refuse offers of food, asserting how much they had already eaten. Now after just a few bites more, Henry was feeling the need to walk a bit.

Prospect Hill was made up of thousands of acres of land. Most of it was forested, but the fields were extensive and the lands in the vicinity of the large main house were cleared of many of their trees. Henry had never before seen any of the place besides the path from the road to the slaves' quarters. He mouthed to Butler that he needed to walk off some of the food, and Butler nodded his understanding while still immersed in deep conversation with a small group of men.

As he walked to the edge of the quarters, Henry glimpsed Levi and his wife Rachael sitting close together. He noticed that Levi was reading to her from the Longfellow book of poetry. Rachael was holding their son, who was sound asleep across her shoulder. She was leaning in close to Levi and the obvious bond they shared warmed Henry. He decided that it would definitely be rude to interrupt this tender moment and crept by them unseen.

He continued walking just inside of the tree line. To the left of him were cleared grounds containing outbuildings and sheds. He could see tools in one, larger farm equipment in another. It was almost evening, but being summer, the day was still fairly lit.

He wondered as he walked around this place what it would have been like when Captain Ross was alive. If only he could have devised a plan to free his slaves while still alive, all of this could have been avoided. He found that his feelings towards this man whom he would never meet were strangely conflicted.

He was cresting a big hill when he heard laughter in the distance. There were voices as well, but the exact words could not be made out. He walked cautiously closer to the sound of the voices. He knew that he was not an invited guest here and wasn't at all convinced he would receive a friendly welcome if spotted.

When he discovered the source of the laughter he froze. *Could this be?*

Mary Girault was holding a bright red rubber ball as she briskly walked across the grass. The large stately mansion was visible in the distance behind her. *Who else is with her?*

A young girl of about four came into view running towards Mary and laughing. "Throw the ball, Mary. Please!"

"Try to catch it this time, Martha. Here you go!" Mary was smiling at the young girl as she tossed the ball lightly towards her.

Martha squealed and threw her arms up too early to make the catch. The ball landed near her feet but began rolling down the hill past the girl.

"You get it this time Martha!" called Mary with a laugh. The little girl nodded and took off down the hill.

Henry watched Mary intently. Her face was flushed and her dark wavy hair was flying loose from its pins. She was laughing and cheering on her young charge as she chased after the ball. *She is even more beautiful than I remembered.*

When Martha returned with the ball, she stood with her little feet wide apart and planted firmly on the grass.

"I'm going to throw this ball really far, Mary. Watch me!" Martha threw it so fast that Mary barely had time to react. It whizzed past her head just as she ducked quickly out of the way. The ball sailed past her and into the woods.

"You are certainly getting strong. I am very glad that I got out of the way in time."

Martha laughed, delighted to have thrown the ball so hard. After a moment, however the laugh turned to a small pout. "Do you think we can find it?"

"Don't worry Martha, I will get it."

Mary saw that Aunt Catherine was walking down the front steps of the house towards them. She ruffled the top of Martha's sweaty little head. "It looks like it is time for you to go inside. You run along to Aunt Catherine, and I will go look for the ball. Will you please tell her where I am going?"

Adelaide was still recovering from the birth of her little girl Addie, and it had been a rather difficult one. Martha and Cabell were spending the holiday here, and Mary had been enthralled with the precious girl as always. Her own mother and siblings had accompanied her on this visit, and although the house was quite crowded, it had been a wonderful holiday.

"All right, Mary. Will you promise to come and see me before I go to bed?"

"Of course I will. I will tell you a story, I promise."

The little girl smiled and turned to skip towards the house. Mary watched her for a moment and heard the sing song voice of the little girl announcing her intentions to get the ball before coming inside. She saw Catherine wave to her in acknowledgment. Mary returned the wave and turned towards the trees that held the missing toy. *How far could it have gone with all of those trees to block its progress?*

Henry watched her moving closer towards him. He knew that he should retreat quietly and return to the quarters. Everything that made sense in the world told him to just go. *Take no chances, you idiot! Just make your exit now.*

But he was transfixed by her—the way she tilted her head when she was thinking, and the soft fullness of her lips. Some force seemed to be keeping him rooted to the spot, unable to move. After a few moments it was too late for any course of action other than to try to stay out of sight.

Mary was intently focused on finding the ball. She was scanning the ground in the vicinity of where she had seen it enter the wooded area. She was so close to him now that Henry was sure that she could hear him breathing.

A snapping sound behind him caused both Mary and Henry to turn, startled, in the direction of the noise.

Levi and Rachael were walking along slowly, holding hands. The baby must have been entrusted to someone back in the quarters as they were now alone. The couple stopped when they spotted Mary.

"Evenin' Miss Mary," said Levi with a smile. "You walkin' by youself?"

Mary laughed. "No Levi, not walking really. Little Martha lost her little red ball in the woods here. I promised her that I would retrieve it and bring it inside."

"I see it over there," said Rachael pointing at a spot a

few feet behind where Henry was frozen against a tree.

"I get it for you Miss Mary," Levi called out, already moving in the direction of the now stationary ball.

Henry watched him trot over to the ball, stoop down to pick it up and then freeze as he was half way back up. He had spotted him. Henry frantically motioned to Levi not to reveal his presence. Levi looked puzzled, but straightened back up slowly and looked away.

"What wrong?" Rachael inquired. She had noticed his hesitation.

"Just makin' sure it ain't a snake over here. But it just a stick."

At the word snake, both Mary and Rachael made an immediate investigation of the ground around their feet.

"I'm very glad to hear it," exclaimed Mary. "I guess I should get on back in the house anyway. They will be wondering where I am."

Levi handed the ball to Mary and she thanked him for recovering it. She watched as he and Rachael began walking back towards the group of cabins through the trees. When she listened intently, she could hear the laughter and music coming from that direction.

Henry felt dishonorable watching her like this without her knowledge. The shame of Levi seeing him standing there in the shadows flooded over him. Without stopping to think, he took a step away from the tree.

The crunching of the pine straw and twigs under his feet caused Mary to turn and gasp. She didn't say anything to him right away, but he saw her eyes narrow somewhat when she recognized his face.

After a moment Mary said, "What on earth are you

doing here?"

His head was reeling in an attempt to come up with the right words, but instead he stammered, "I'm not sure if you'd believe me if I told you. I didn't know that you would be here. Then I saw you playing in the grass with the little girl. And of course I recognized you."

"And you have been watching me all this time? Why didn't you make your presence known to me sooner?" Mary's eyes flashed with anger.

"I should have." His head dropped ever so slightly. "I truly do apologize."

Mary regarded him for a moment. Her anger had faded, but she was utterly confused in finding him here. This is certainly not how she would have imagined meeting him again when that thought had crossed her mind. And the thought of meeting him again *had* crossed her mind. More than once.

"You still haven't told me what you are doing here," she finally said.

Henry was unsure of what to say. Reverend Butler had told him when he had first arrived that these meetings needed to be handled discreetly as the legal case was complicated and full of animosity. Yet Mary had asked him a direct question and he didn't want to give her further cause to distrust him. *What reasonable explanation can I possibly have for lurking in the trees spying on her?*

He decided that his only good option was to be honest with her. Henry took a deep breath and replied, "I am on this property today with an associate, Reverend Butler. After eating far too much food, I felt the need to take a walk and I ended up here. I happened upon you here and I recognized you from the ball in Natchez."

He watched her expression carefully as he spoke, but it was inscrutable. He went on, "Dr. Duncan who hosted that gala event is the one who arranged for me to visit Reverend Butler. I am currently on leave from my studies in Pennsylvania and have extended my visit in Mississippi." He hoped that bringing the Duncan name into the conversation would add to his credibility.

"I'm still not sure that I understand why you are here at Prospect Hill. What interest could you have in this place?" Her expression had softened somewhat but he still felt a bit of suspicion emanating from her.

Henry chose his words carefully. "The man who originally owned this plantation directed the American Colonization Society to manage the relocation of his slaves to Africa after his death. Reverend Butler is trying to honor those wishes and is here to further those efforts. He believes that the slaves who were given their freedom by law deserve representation and assistance in this matter." Henry tried desperately to read her expression, but found it impossible. He rather lamely added, "And I do too."

"So the two of you snuck onto the plantation to meet with the slaves in secret? You do realize that Mr. Wade is my uncle. Why shouldn't I go back to the house and alert him to your presence here?"

This was all going terribly wrong. Henry felt a stab of desperation. *I've been such a fool! I could undo all of the work that Butler has put into assisting these people.*

But Mary made no show of moving towards the house. She continued studying Henry's face.

"What interest do you have in helping the slaves?" she

finally asked.

"I just feel like it is the right thing to do. All of my life I have had things handed to me, never having to work for anything. I thought I understood the ways of the world and I was going to be some important part of it. A few months ago, all I wanted was a chance to come down here and work with Stephen Duncan so that I could advance my place in the world. I told myself it was to learn more about his involvement in colonization. But when I did some soul-searching, I knew that what I really wanted was to learn how to become rich and successful."

Mary waited for him to continue. When he didn't, she prompted, "And now?"

He had a pained expression on his face that Mary had not seen even once on the night of the ball. That evening he had been so cocky and sure of himself. There was no resemblance of that young man here in the woods tonight.

"Now?" Henry chuckled, but the pained expression remained. "My father is livid. I've disappointed him terribly. I've discovered that there are many people in this country who were not born into the same life of privilege that I've enjoyed. Some that were born into bondage and have no rights at all. I think now I need to at least try to make some sort of difference for some of them."

"But what do you intend to do?" Mary inquired. "How can you help them?" Mary, who'd always secretly admired Captain Ross' decision, was intrigued by Henry's involvement.

"We are not doing anything that is against the law, I can assure you of that. The courts have already ruled in favor of the slaves. Your uncle is refusing to comply with the court's order."

Mary wasn't sure whether to believe this or not. She was certainly aware that a long and protracted legal battle had been going on. *But surely if ordered by law to honor the provisions of the will, Uncle Isaac would have done so.*

Henry saw the doubt in her eyes. "I'm sorry to be the one to tell you. I certainly have made a mess of things and I really am sorry."

He had concerns that she would discuss this matter with Mr. Wade, which would create problems for the ultimate goal of liberating the slaves. But he felt that asking her to keep his secret would only further alienate her.

"I only ask that you allow me to return to the slaves' quarters undetected. Mr. Butler and I came here to deliver news to them about a man named Mr. Chambliss who has been appointed to retrieve them from this place and assist them in their departure. I'm sure that Reverend Butler has already done so in my absence and is concerned regarding my whereabouts as we speak. We will be gone within the half hour, I assure you."

Mary contemplated his words, taking in his sincere expression. There was no compelling reason she could think of for her to assist him. *I barely know him. And yet...look at the ways his eyes are imploring me.*

"Just go," she finally replied in a low voice. "I will do nothing to hinder you."

"Thank you, Miss Girault." He had taken the slightest turn in the direction of the quarters before he turned back to fully face her. "I would have liked for our second meeting to have been under very different circumstances. If only I had been able to muster the courage to visit you in Natchez.

I would like to think it would have gone quite differently."

He turned and began walking away from her.

Mary's heart seemed to swell at his words. *I can't let him leave this way. He clearly thinks that I despise him.*

"Wait!" she called out to him. "I *wanted* you to call on me in Natchez. I waited a week hoping you would come by, but you never did."

Somehow the knowledge that he had thought of her and wanted to see her again had moved her. She felt a tenderness for him and the anger from moments before had completely disappeared.

He stopped and turned back at her words. He smiled weakly, "I was afraid that you would not receive me if I called on you. I was smitten from the moment I heard you question how the staircase was built."

Mary could not believe her ears, but she returned his smile. *He was smitten with me? I thought he found me foolish.*

He went on, encouraged by the change in her demeanor. "You see, I'd been in the foyer of Dr. Duncan's home for nearly an hour and absolutely no one had marveled at the staircase until you came in. That is when I knew that you were different."

"Different in a good way, I hope."

"Definitely a good way."

They regarded each other in silence for a moment before Mary broke the silence. "If only you'd come," she said feeling the regret in her chest. "I would have received you."

He hung his head slightly and replied, "Then I was a complete and utter fool."

With that he disappeared into the falling darkness

leaving Mary bewildered but more exhilarated than at any other time in her life. Somehow this display of self-effacement made her all the more fond of him. Gone was the swaggering boy of the ball. In his place she found a sincere and humble man, yearning to make a difference in the world.

The rest of the night she went through the motions of reading to Martha and talking with her mother and aunt. But her mind kept returning to her conversation with Henry Willcox. She was filled with confusion and questions that she had no hope of getting answered. However, the sentiment that overshadowed every other thought in Mary's head was relief. She had seen him again after all—just as she had hoped she would.

September 1844   Rodney Mississippi

Rodney was bustling as always. Catherine usually enjoyed her visits here tremendously. The city had an air of ungainliness about it indicating that it had sprung up suddenly out of nowhere. There was an interesting mixture of the rough and rowdy in town combined with the more refined set. The Presbyterian church had been the first real attempt to bring a sense of culture and sophistication to town, and other establishments soon followed suit.

It was true that the saloons and businesses of ill repute did a thriving trade in this town, but Catherine found it easy to overlook the more unsavory elements of the city. Its advantageous location along the Mississippi River between St. Louis and New Orleans made it full of possibilities for growth. There was an exhilarating thrill one experienced just being amidst the hustle and bustle of the town.

Today however, she felt hot and uncomfortable as it was unseasonably warm. More importantly, she was worried about Isaac. He brushed off her worries any time she had expressed her concerns to him so she had stopped doing so. But she remained apprehensive about their future, and his state of mind. The legal battles and disputes with members of the Colonization Society had worn him down. He was edgier than normal, and seemed preoccupied much of the time.

He had left earlier to "attend to business" and she had been waiting for him at the hotel for a while. He would likely be gone for hours dealing with the cotton merchants in town. The room was growing stifling and she was becoming restless. They were planning to attend the opera that evening, but she knew that Isaac would not really "be there" with her at the theater. He would sit beside her with his mind on other matters. *Thank goodness Mary is here with us. She is such a breath of fresh air.*

Their fifth wedding anniversary was coming up in the spring, and Catherine had recently asked him if he would like for her to plan a party to celebrate. She had been so hopeful, latching on to an opportunity to take his mind off of this awful business. But, his complete lack of enthusiasm had caused her to cry; her hopes dashed. Of course Isaac had apologized profusely, assuring her that he would love for her to plan a party. Although she knew that he had no interest in one, she had begun planning all the same. It gave her something to look forward to. She despised feeling helpless, and yet that was becoming the norm for her. *Oh Isaac, I love you so. Please don't shut me out of your problems. I want to help you.*

She sat near the window, hoping to take advantage of the slight breeze that was coming in through the opening. She watched the comings and goings of hundreds of people below her, allowing her mind to drift back over the years that she had been Mrs. Isaac Ross Wade. She had been happy at Prospect Hill with her husband. She knew that if they had to move elsewhere, she could be happy there as well. *But could Isaac?*

A soft knock on the door snapped her back to her senses. She walked gracefully across the richly carpeted room and opened the door. Mary stood in the hallway with a hopeful smile on her face.

"Aunt Catherine, can we please go for a walk? There is so much to see and do here. It is so difficult to stay indoors on such a lovely day."

Catherine smiled at her niece. *Some fresh air would probably do me a world of good.*

Mary leaned closer conspiratorially, "Nellie is being frightfully annoying! She keeps looking out of the window making disparaging remarks about the way that the ladies…um, some of the women, are dressed in public. I'm terribly fond of her, of course, but I think it would do me good to get away for a while."

Catherine laughed, imagining Nellie's shocked response to the saloon girls walking about. "I absolutely must be back to the room before Isaac returns from his business. But I think we could walk about if we stay near the hotel."

"Thank you!" gushed Mary as she took her aunt's hand and pulled her towards the staircase.

When they were out on the street, Catherine did feel her worries begin to melt away. The warm sun actually felt good when combined with the breeze. As they walked by the Presbyterian church, she told Mary about the bell in the tower which tolled periodically.

"Apparently it was made from melted silver dollars

donated by the parishioners. Imagine so much money going into a bell! Needless to say, it isn't your average church bell."

"No wonder it sounds so lovely!" offered Mary enthusiastically. The two-story brick church built in the Federal style had always appealed to Mary and she found its history to be fascinating.

As Catherine looked out over the Mississippi River, she was reminded of a story that Isaac had told her. She recounted it for Mary as they strolled along the streets of town.

"Years ago Isaac's grandfather, Captain Ross, had a beautiful daughter named Martha who was engaged to a lawyer. His name was Mr. Samuel Frye."

"Martha? Is that who Adelaide's Martha was named for?" interrupted Mary, unable to stop the thought from blurting out.

"I imagine so," answered Catherine patiently. She knew that she was supposed to be cultivating Mary's manners, but she covertly took some pleasure in her exuberance and impulsiveness.

Suddenly Mary realized on her own that she had interrupted the story. "I'm sorry, Aunt Catherine; please finish." She appreciated the fact that her aunt was never as quick to chastise her as her own mother would have been. She could relax more when she was with Catherine.

"Well, the evening before Martha's wedding, she received news that her dear Samuel had been inflamed to enter into a duel with another local lawyer named Daniel Beasley. Frantically she and her father raced here, but did not make it in time. Samuel was killed in the duel and

Martha's heart was broken. She was your age I believe. Seventeen."

Mary gasped and put her hand up to her mouth. "That is terrible!"

Catherine nodded her assent. She pointed out a spot on the opposite side of the river. "There is a sandbar over there where it happened. Evidently it is located in Louisiana technically, and therefore outside the reach of the law here in Mississippi. Otherwise, Beasley could have been charged with murder."

"He should have been! The poor gentleman was killed just as he was going to marry Martha."

"Sadly Martha's heart was later broken again with the death of another fiancé. She herself died at only twenty-five years of age, never experiencing the joy of matrimony. According to Isaac, Captain Ross was devastated by the loss of Martha. He had a special fondness for her." Catherine's expression was wistful as she gazed across the river at the scene of the duel.

"It isn't fair that Mr. Beasley got away with murder!" declared Mary with rising indignation that someone who had caused Martha such grief would get off scot-free.

Catherine gave a small shudder. "Well, he honestly ended up faring worse than if he had gone to trial I believe."

"What happened?" Mary was completely enraptured with the tale now. "What is worse than being charged with murder?"

"Don't tell your mother that I told you this," began Catherine, but Mary was already shaking her head vigorously assuring her aunt that she was more than old enough to keep her confidence.

"He went to Indian territory. A place called Fort Mims. He had requested an Army commission after his shameful actions regarding the duel. He was made a Major and sent to the frontier. Major Beasley was in command of the fort when it was attacked by Creek Indians."

Again Mary gasped. "What happened to him?"

"Apparently," replied Catherine, "Beasley was warned more than once that the Indians were coming, but ignored the warnings and didn't even properly close the front gate. Some even say he was drunk in the middle of the day."

"Surely not!" replied Mary. "But what happened to him, Aunt Catherine?"

"He was killed. Most agree he was even scalped."

"How awful!" Mary now felt sorry for the man even though he had killed Martha's fiancé. She wouldn't wish that awful fate on anyone, no matter how terrible he might have been.

They were still strolling the streets when Mary spotted a figure high on the bluff near town. It was too far away to be sure, but there was something very familiar about him. She knew that Catherine was heading back to the hotel, but she wanted a better look at the man who was now descending the bluff. She had a much better chance of it if she stayed out near the street than if she went back inside the hotel. *But how can I convince her to allow me to stay out here alone?*

"Aunt Catherine," Mary said, attempting to sound casual. "Could I stay on the porch outside of the hotel for a bit? My room is quite hot, but should cool down soon. I won't stay out long as Nellie will be getting anxious soon about dressing me for the opera tonight anyway."

"I told your mother that I would keep watch over you." Mary could tell that Catherine wasn't sure about it, but felt her heart leap when Catherine said, "Do you promise that you will stay right here outside of the front doors?"

Mary could hardly believe her luck. *Aunt Catherine must be very anxious to get upstairs and beat Uncle Isaac back to the room.* "I promise Aunt Catherine."

True to her word, Mary stayed near the hotel entrance. She watched people scurry past coming in and out of the businesses on the main street of Rodney. Before long she saw the figure in question just coming into view. Just as she had suspected, it was Henry Willcox, and he was walking in the direction of the hotel. She wasn't completely sure what she wanted to happen, but she certainly didn't make any move to go inside of the hotel and out of sight. She felt the familiar flutter in her stomach, the one she had experienced at both of their previous meetings.

Just when she thought he was going to walk right past without taking any notice of her, he looked up. The flicker of recognition was immediately evident and he came to an abrupt stop, causing much indignation to the woman behind him who crashed into his back and dropped her packages.

Mary watched with a laugh as Henry attempted to assist the woman in picking them up, in spite of her attempts to swat at him. *Perhaps she thinks he is trying to steal them?* Mary couldn't make out the words that the woman was shouting, but they were clearly not very nice. After several moments of dodging her swinging hands and stammering his apologies, Henry held out several of the dropped items as a peace offering. As the woman took her items with a "humph" Henry looked back at Mary. She smiled at him, and he felt his heart leap in his chest. Looking both ways, he began carefully crossing the busy street feeling encouraged by her smile.

When he finally reached the spot where Mary stood waiting for him, he greeted her warmly. "Mary Girault, it is so wonderful to see you again." He attempted the utmost formality as he sensed that is what she had expected and wanted from him at their first meeting in Natchez.

"Hello Mr. Willcox." She offered her hand to him once again, which he took in his own. He bent to kiss her hand softly and they both felt a surge of exhilaration pass through them.

"Are you here with your family?" Henry asked. He was making every effort to keep their conversation clear of anything unpleasant that might lead to any sort of disagreement.

"With my Aunt Catherine and Uncle Isaac," replied Mary.

She wanted to tell him that she had kept his secret. She had in fact not said a word to anyone about finding Henry at Prospect Hill, or that Reverend Butler had also been there. But somehow confiding this in him felt like even more of a betrayal to her family. Ultimately, she decided not to offer the information. And Henry didn't ask her.

"There is a great deal to see and do here. I was surprised when I first arrived in Rodney. He pointed in the direction of the place where Mary had spotted him. "I was just up on the bluff. The view is amazing from up there. Have you seen the steamboats? Some of them are quite luxurious."

"A bit different than what you see in Pennsylvania?"

Mary had never been that far north and really couldn't imagine what it must be like there.

"It is very different," he replied. "But this place has a unique beauty unlike anything I've seen before."

Something about the tone of his voice, combined with his intense gaze caused Mary to flush. She couldn't understand it herself much less explain to anyone else why she felt this way around him. No one else on earth had ever had this effect on her.

Henry seemed to just notice where they were standing. "Are you staying here?"

The hotel was well-appointed with a grand ballroom and plush rugs from the orient. It was the finest establishment in Rodney, and Uncle Isaac had insisted they stay here.

"Yes we are. Where are you staying while in Rodney?"

"We are staying at one of Mr. David Hunt's homes right over there," he answered pointing once more. "His holdings are so numerous, it is staggering."

"We?" asked Mary. She raised her eyebrows as she posed the question to him.

"Reverend Butler and myself," he replied simply. "Mr. Hunt is a generous benefactor of the Presbyterian church here as well as many other charitable organizations."

"Like the American Colonization Society?" Mary asked him directly.

Henry contemplated her question for a moment. *How quickly we arrived here. Why can't I keep the conversation on a lighter note for once?*

"Yes, that is one of them," he agreed. "I see that we've touched upon a topic in which we see things very differently."

"Perhaps I want to learn more about how you see things," Mary said quietly—so much so that he wasn't completely sure that he had heard her correctly. She knew that she was treading on dangerous ground, but something inside of her burned to learn more about the world outside of southwestern Mississippi. She didn't want to become like her mother and simply mimic what her father believed. She wanted to think for herself and form her own opinions after hearing what people had to say. *Why would my parents bother providing me with an education if I'm not meant to question anything?*

"I would like nothing more than to talk to you about what I believe." He looked at her desperately attempting to gauge her sincerity. It only took seconds to read her expression correctly. Mary was open to really listening. He somehow knew without her saying it that she had kept his secret. That alone told him a great deal regarding her intentions.

It was true that Henry would cherish a conversation with her about issues that mattered to him. In fact, he would like to listen to her and to learn more about her family and her home. He wanted to know what books she liked to read and discuss ones they both had read.

But at this moment, beyond anything else he wished to have a few moments of gaiety and laughter, perhaps even dancing. A few blissful moments to forget that they came from completely different backgrounds. An opportunity to court this beautiful and exciting young woman without any of the complications that their situation created.

Gazing into his eyes, she replied, "I would like that too."

She swallowed hard, aware of the pounding of her heart.

He was standing close to her and his penetrating gaze was both disconcerting and thrilling at the same time.

They regarded each other in silence for a moment. Both of them having wished for this meeting often. Now that it was happening, they were neither one sure how to proceed.

"When can I see you again?" Henry finally asked her. "Would your aunt and uncle allow me to call on you?" He felt strongly that he wasn't willing to wait for chance to bring them together again. *If I'm reading her correctly, she wants to see me again as well.*

"I honestly don't know," she answered. *How would I explain my relationship with Henry to them? Aunt Catherine asked me not to mention being at Auburn. And Uncle Isaac has such contempt for Zebulon Butler.* "The situation is complicated. Without them knowing your background I can't imagine they would allow it. And how would I explain your background without discussing the reason you are in Mississippi? I wouldn't feel right lying to them."

"I would never expect you to lie. We will figure this out. I can't imagine not seeing you again, Mary."

The words just tumbled out without thought. But he didn't regret them. He wanted to be honest with her, and it felt refreshing to have his feelings out in the open.

"I feel the same way."

She appreciated his candor. Each time she spoke with him, she felt as if she were seeing more of the true Henry. No blustering or posturing, but just the very heart of him.

A thought suddenly occurred to her. "We have tickets to the opera tonight. At intermission I could make an excuse to walk outside for some fresh air. We could talk then."

Stealing a few moments in secrecy wasn't exactly what Henry had in mind. However, he would take whatever opportunity presented itself to see her again. And to be honest, he had certainly not come up with a better plan yet himself.

"I will be just outside the doors to the opera house at intermission tonight if I have to move heaven and earth to do it." He gave her a gallant smile and bow.

Mary giggled at his exaggerated show of chivalry. Henry was just straightening back up when he realized that a man had stopped right beside them. His smile faltered immediately.

"Mary?" Isaac Wade had appeared without her noticing his approach. Mary felt a bit flustered by his sudden appearance, but covered well.

"Oh, Uncle Isaac. This is Henry Willcox. We met while I was in Natchez attending a holiday ball there. You might remember that I made that journey. What a surprise to see him here." Then looking towards Henry, she said, "Mr. Willcox, this is my uncle, Mr. Isaac Wade."

The men shook hands and exchanged pleasantries while Mary's mind frantically worked to make sure the situation wouldn't implode on her. She couldn't allow the two of them to begin a conversation. Only a couple of questions and answers would be a disaster.

"Uncle Isaac," said Mary desperately, just as he was opening his mouth to ask Henry where he was from. "Aunt Catherine is waiting for you upstairs in the hotel room. She wanted me to tell you as soon as you appeared."

Isaac looked surprised to have been cut off so abruptly, but thankfully he didn't question Mary. Isaac knew that he had been inattentive to his wife's needs lately, and certainly wanted to make it up to her.

"My apologies then," he said to Henry. "I hope we will meet again under different circumstances when we have more time to become acquainted. I should like to learn more about what brings you down here. If I had to make a guess, the accent that I detect would be a Pennsylvania one perhaps?"

"Very good sir," replied Henry. "Next time then?"

Isaac Wade nodded and turned to Mary. "I expect you should be getting ready for the evening?" It was obvious that he didn't like the idea of leaving his young niece outside in the company of a young man without either himself or Catherine present. Mary certainly recognized his intent, and saw no sensible way to question it.

"Yes Uncle Isaac. You are right, of course."

Turning to Henry she hoped to convey in her eyes that she wished she could stay there with him so much longer. *Thank goodness we agreed on our next meeting already. Otherwise we might never have spoken again.*

She said her goodbyes to Henry with her uncle at her side. When Henry turned to leave, Isaac escorted her inside the hotel. The lobby was elegant with fine furnishings and real chandeliers. Rodney was becoming a major stop along the Mississippi River and the buildings reflected its growing importance. Wealthy planters threw around money like water, and local businesses were thriving.

As they walked together towards the staircase, Isaac commented on Henry. "He seems like a respectable young man. What do you know about his family?"

"I only just met him briefly. I believe he mentioned

being a student at the University of Pennsylvania."

In truth she didn't know much about him at all. And it scared her that she had such a strong connection with him in spite of that fact. Of course, for Uncle Isaac, Henry's family would be of paramount importance. That was to be expected and she accepted it without much thought.

"Well, perhaps we will have the opportunity to see him again."

She nodded at him in agreement, holding fast to the secret that she would see him in a few short hours.

When Mary returned to her room she brought the back of her hand to her lips. He had kissed her hand ever so lightly and yet it almost seemed as though she could feel his lips still lingering there.

She told Nellie that she needed a few moments to rest before getting dressed for the theater. But in truth she lay on her bed recounting each conversation that she had ever had with Henry Willcox, and imagining what the next one would be like. With crimson rising in her cheeks she imagined kissing Henry the way she had seen lovers kiss each other. Not a mere brushing of the lips across her hand, but a real kiss on the mouth with his hands wrapped around her tightly.

October 1844   Prospect Hill Plantation

Edmond Belton had convened a meeting with his small group of followers for this evening. After a discussion with his mother, Mariah, had revealed the Wade family's recent trip to Rodney, Ed had become concerned. Through bits and pieces of conversation overheard in the big house, Mariah had determined that the master had been meeting with cotton merchants in Rodney to secure a deal for himself that would shelter some of the proceeds of the cotton crop for his own personal use. The details were not clear, but what little they knew raised anxieties to a higher level.

    He was dreading the meeting tonight. Tempers were rising, and it had become increasingly difficult to justify the position of waiting. The others wanted action. *But what can we do that won't get us all whipped, or worse?* Ed felt angry at himself for believing that Mr. Parker and others had been able to intervene on their behalf and force Isaac Wade to conduct his business dealings relating to the estate legally. He had let his guard down and allowed himself to think the problems had been resolved. Once again, he despised his dependence on white men to settle his disputes. *Once I have my freedom, I won't never be obligated to a white man. I will be my own master.*

The time was nearing for action to be taken. Real action that could bring about real change. Edmond Belton knew this, but he had also promised Sadie that he wouldn't do anything rash or dangerous to bring trouble down upon them. The bleak reality of their situation was that slaves like Levi who had been a mere boy at the time of Captain Ross' death were now grown men with children of their own—and yet still not enjoying the freedom they were promised so many years ago. The injustice of it was becoming more than Ed and the others could bear.

Levi had once again agreed to relay a message to assist them in making a decision. This time he had hitched a ride with a wagon of Parker's going to Port Gibson. He had spoken with Zebulon Butler and asked him to come meet with them. They had set up this meeting for tonight. As much as Ed hated to depend on a white man for assistance, he was willing to swallow his pride and do what needed to be done to ensure their freedom. He had come to realize that the best hope they had of peacefully resolving this issue was going to only come about through the assistance of men who had legal standing in the state of Mississippi.

As usual, Sadie had already cleared out to give them a private place to discuss matters. Ed stood alone in his cabin looking around. He was afraid. Even if they got their freedom and went to Liberia, what would life be like there? He kept trying to convince himself that anything would be better than remaining in bondage.

But it was difficult not to fear the unknown when facing

the possibility of such a drastic change in circumstances. He had some good memories in this cabin, despite their circumstances. He loved his family and felt such pride in them. The images of his children's faces drifted through his mind. Ultimately, it was thinking of his children that gave him the resolve he needed to stay strong through these struggles. *I got to keep hopin' for somethin' better. Better days are comin'.*

Soon the other men began arriving. They didn't have long to wait before Reverend Butler knocked on the door softly. His young companion was with him again. At first Ed and the other slaves had been distrustful of someone new entering the fray. It was certainly understandable given the circumstances. They had grown wary and were careful about whom they trusted. But over the months, Henry had proven to be genuine and they knew him to be an ally.

Reverend Butler listened without interruption as Ed Belton filled him in on all of the snippets of conversation that Mariah had overheard. She was their best source of information now that Enoch, his wife Marbella, and their children had been given their freedom. Isaac Wade had honored that provision of the will for whatever reason. To the slaves, it all just seemed to be based on the whims of Master Wade. Their very fate, in fact, was subject to his impulses.

When Ed had finished his account, Zebulon Butler spoke. "Even though the high courts have affirmed the will, Mr. Wade is attempting new legal maneuvers almost daily. As you've heard there is talk of locals arming themselves and coming here to stop any attempt to remove you from this plantation. Dr. Ker, Dr. Duncan, Mr. Parker, myself and others are working with the Colonization Society to force his hand. The sheriff has been ordered to make this transfer to Mr. Chambliss happen. But I think he is afraid."

Levi asked, "What does the sheriff have to be afraid of?" It wasn't issued as a challenge. It was typical Levi, thinking through things and wanting to see each situation from every angle.

"May I offer up my own opinion?" Henry seldom spoke out at meetings with the slaves. He was an observer more than a participant and had always left the talking to Reverend Butler.

The reverend smiled at him. "Of course. You've been here long enough to have earned the right to an opinion." He had grown very fond of this exuberant young man from his home state.

"I believe that he is scared of incurring the wrath of these rich and powerful planters. When this is over, he fears having to live here among them after having opposed them in this matter. They could run him out of town, I'm sure, and leave him and his family without a home or a job. It will take a great deal of courage to stand up to these men and do the moral thing."

"Well said, Henry," replied Zebulon. "Any of us who oppose the status quo here are seen as trouble makers and we have to tread carefully."

For a moment no one spoke. And then Ed verbalized the thought that was on all of their minds. "Where do this leave us?"

Henry's heart was so burdened by the plight of these men. His many talks with Levi had left him humbled beyond description. He had been writing of their conversations in his diary each night, trying to make sense of why a smart and sensitive man like Levi could be facing such dire circumstances. Where was the justice in any of this? He had been such an idealistic young man just a year ago. Now the world seemed like such an unfair and ugly place to live.

In his last journal entry, he had written of Levi:

> *When I compare the character of this young man against my own, I must admit with great humility that his is the far nobler one. Despite his disadvantages, he views the world with optimism, trying always to see the best in others. I doubt that hate and bitterness would stand a chance of existing within the soul of this man. The brightness of the light within him would force these evil emotions into the deepest shadows within mere seconds.*

Tuning back in to the discussion going on around him, Henry heard Zebulon Butler once again reiterate the work that was being done on the behalf of the slaves. He admitted that ultimately it came down to the same word he used each time he had met with them. *Wait.* The word itself almost caused Butler pain to speak at this point. He knew that it was an empty word to speak to them this many years into their battle for freedom. But it was the only option he could see. Things were moving in their direction, albeit at a snail's pace. If they would give him just a bit longer, he felt sure they would eventually be rewarded for their patience.

Conversations broke out among the group of men.

Tensions were higher than on the occasion Butler had last spoken with them, and tonight it was literally palpable in the air. Henry's opinion suddenly rang out above the murmuring voices.

"It seems to me that Isaac Wade is the one and only problem. Without his interference Mr. Chambliss would be free to carry out the court's instructions. We need to come up with a way to get him out of the way." Henry had just blurted out his sentiments without asking again for permission to speak. He looked to Butler, slightly abashed.

Reverend Butler didn't look angry, but asked, "How would you propose doing this? The lawyers representing the society have explored every possible avenue to remove him from his position as executor. I can't foresee him voluntarily stepping aside from managing Prospect Hill when he has come this far and fought this hard thus far."

"I don't have the answers to that sir. I apologize for blurting out nonsense."

"No need, Henry. We all share your frustration, you can be sure."

There wasn't much more that could be discussed or decided further, so Ed dismissed the group and small discussions began to break out around the cabin.

Henry approached Levi. "Have you begun reading *Nicholas Nickleby* yet?"

"I been readin' it to Rachael." Levi's smile spread across his face. His reading had been steadily improving since he had been borrowing books from Henry. The pride he felt was so obvious, that Henry couldn't help but smile too. Levi's enthusiasm was contagious.

"So what do you think of the story so far?"

Levi thought a moment before commenting, "That uncle of his, Ralph. He a hard man. I feel sorry for him."

The answer wasn't what he had been expecting to hear.

"Why do you feel sorry for him?" Henry had not felt the slightest trace of that particular emotion when he had devoured the serial published by Charles Dickens several years ago. He had waited eagerly for each new installment when they first became available.

"'Cause he could have been loved. Those poor people came to him in a time of need and would have been a lovin' family for him if he weren't so hard. He goin' miss out on a chance at love."

Henry had never thought if it that way. But Levi had a good point. Instead of viewing the mean and indeed hardened man with loathing, he began to see him with pity instead.

"I got somethin' else to tell ya'," said Levi with another huge grin on his face. "Miss Mary comin' to visit next month. I thought you might want to know."

Henry was taken aback. He thought about protesting or pretending not to care whether Mary Girault was here or 100 miles away, but the playful grin on Levi's face told him that it was no use.

"Well, thank you for the information," Henry replied casually. "I will put it to good use."

Levi pulled two small objects out of his pocket and offered them to Henry. "I made these for you."

Henry reached out and took the objects from him. He looked down and inspected the small wooden figures carefully. They were meticulously carved and had the smooth edges to indicate that Levi had worked hard to sand them down. One of them was clearly a dog. And one was a man. Henry had told Levi recently that he had grown up with a big lovable dog named Jake. He missed him during his more lonely moments down here in Mississippi. Levi must have felt these wooden carvings would be a pleasant reminder of his much missed canine friend.

But he also understood the truest meaning of the offerings. Levi did not want to accept gifts from Henry without having something to offer in return. Henry felt touched beyond words. All that came to him was a simple, "Thank you, Levi. I shall cherish them always."

He felt a sudden rush of determination to help these men, women, and children be free of this place. *No matter what it takes.*

***

Isaac Wade stood in front of one of his grandfather's treasured paintings of the *Bonhomme Richard,* a warship of the Continental Navy.

He recalled a conversation with his grandfather in his much younger years about the ship. He could still remember his grandfathers words. "She eventually sunk, but what a fight she fought for our navy! Even though she was shot full of holes, burning and taking on water, the old girl stayed afloat for almost two days. I have a great deal of respect for her."

"You speak of the ship as if it were a real person," he had replied to his grandfather's description of the sunken ship.

"I suppose I do. It was much more than just wood and

other materials. It was a home to her crew, and she provided a great service to our nation."

Captain Ross had made a sweeping gesture with his hand around the room and continued, "I feel the same way about this place, son. I created it out of nothing, and now she represents so much more than just shelter. My blood, sweat, and tears went into building Prospect Hill, so she is now a part of me."

"You built this house yourself?" Young Wade was in awe for a moment.

But Captain Ross shook his head firmly. "Not by myself, no. My slaves worked as hard as I could have ever expected them to work. They put their own blood, sweat, and tears into Prospect Hill right alongside my own. A home is much more than four walls and a roof. It is the place where your treasured memories are stored up and you will always feel like you belong."

Wade sighed now, recalling those happier days with his grandfather. *Oh how I looked up to you, and wanted to be like you. Why did you choose not to leave Prospect Hill for me to cherish just as you did?*

When Wade's own father died of yellow fever, his grandfather became his legal guardian. He had always expected the house to be his, especially since his two uncles had died so young.

As a young boy he had loved hearing his grandfather tell stories from the war. He had fought under Colonel Charles S. Myddleton as a part of the South Carolina 2nd Regiment of State Dragoons. He had fought in many battles, sustained many injuries, but felt great pride in his part in helping defeat the British.

Isaac Wade remembered each story in great detail, even so many years later. It just served as a reminder of how much the stories had mattered to him. As a young boy he had tagged along in his grandfather's shadow wanting to learn how to do what he did. To learn how to run Prospect Hill himself one day.

Another favorite topic of Captain Ross was his migration to the Mississippi territory, almost 10 years before it became a state. The trip from South Carolina had been challenging, but the hope of adventure and opportunity waiting for him in the west drove him forward. He recalled his grandfather saying, "Good or bad, whatever I found here, I was staying. I vowed to never make that trek again. I'll be buried right here in Mississippi come hell or high water."

And so he was. Buried under a colossal monument erected by the Colonization Society. Wade still bristled at the thought of the $25,000 that was taken from the estate to construct the monument. He felt with the utmost certainty that his grandfather would have wanted a much more modest grave. Even the inscription written on the structure was too pretentious in Wade's opinion to have suited his grandfather's nature. Grandfather used to complain about people that he viewed as "putting on airs." But his old friend Dr. Ker wouldn't hear of anything less, selecting the expensive monument personally and asking Mr. Coulter to write the inscription which read:

> *His last will is graced with as magnificent provisions as any over which philanthropy has ever rejoiced and by it will be erected*

on the shores of Africa a monument more glorious than marble and more enduring than time.

Even now when Wade looked out over the family cemetery, with the monument towering over all others buried there, he did so with conflicted emotions: hurt, pride, sadness, regret, resentment. They all swirled together, flooding over him as he reflected on his relationship with his grandfather.

He felt determined now, above all else, to protect his own interests and that of his wife and children. He pushed whatever regrets he felt about the betrayal of his grandfather's wishes aside and resolved to do what needed to be done. He had certainly come too far now to back down and hand this place over to the slaves.

As if to strengthen his stance and remind him of what he was fighting for, his son entered the room with Major.

"We back sir," reported Major with a smile. "Young Master Isaac is mighty smart for his age."

"Daddy, I picked this!" He was holding some perfect looking cotton, pulled free of the boll.

Wade stooped down and picked up his son.

"He was askin' all kinds of questions. We walk down to the ole' cotton gin by the creek. He real interested in what goin' on round here." Major was still smiling at the young boy.

"It's good for him to see the workings of the plantation," agreed Wade. "Thank you, Major."

As Wade listened to young Isaac recount his morning with excitement, he was also actively reviewing his options for preserving his way of life. *Just as Prospect Hill was your home, Grandfather, it is mine as well. And I won't ever regret any actions that I am forced to take to keep it.*

February 1845   Prospect Hill Plantation

Catherine Wade was in her element as she planned for the dinner party to celebrate her and Isaac's fifth wedding anniversary on April 15th. She had been distressed when Isaac originally seemed disinterested and then quite perturbed when he had mentioned off-handedly that he would be leaving on a business trip the afternoon of the 15th. After quite a bit of placating he had been able to convince her that moving the celebration up one day would not be a problem.

Catherine didn't want to admit to Isaac that she was extremely superstitious about such things. She had never celebrated a birthday early, even by one day, fearing it to be bad luck. It didn't seem much different to her with an anniversary. Somehow it just seemed to Catherine to be tempting fate to celebrate an event which took place on a certain date before actually reaching that anniversary date. She knew that Isaac wouldn't be bothered with such nonsense. And waiting until a later date when he would have returned from his business trip would be disappointing. Reluctantly she had agreed to the event being scheduled for the evening of April 14th.

Now, several months later, the ominous feelings she had felt regarding celebrating her anniversary early had faded into the background. They had been replaced by a wonderful sense of optimism and excitement. She had written to her sister Susan requesting that Mary come visit for an extended stay on the pretext of needing her help with the planning. In reality, it had been Mary who had asked her aunt to make such a plea to her mother. Mary had explained to Catherine that she was much happier at Prospect Hill. Catherine had protected Mary's confidences and made the request appear as if it were her own idea.

Catherine could understand Mary's wishes. Bellevue was still in the Girault family's possession, and Catherine was aware that her brother-in-law was working to ensure that the family remained there. In addition to his financial troubles, James had gotten into a legal battle regarding some land transactions and monies received. The Federal Government was claiming that he was indebted to them for $100,000. He was fighting the charges and suits but it was taking its toll on the family.

To be honest, Catherine relished the time that she had Mary here with her. She was delightful company during these months that Isaac had been so preoccupied. Her assistance in making preparations for the party had been invaluable. Mary had been with them when they celebrated her 18th birthday earlier this month. Catherine had commissioned her dressmaker in New Orleans to create a beautiful gown for Mary to wear to the ball held in Rodney in the glittering ballroom of the hotel. Mary had been so excited that she had literally cried tears of happiness and gratitude.

But Catherine Wade didn't know the primary reason for Mary's desire to spend more time with her family. It was true that Mary had always cherished her time at Prospect Hill and looked forward to each visit. But being here full-time allowed her opportunities to covertly see Henry Willcox. At first Mary had been extremely hesitant to sneak around meeting Henry alone without a chaperone. Imagining her mother's horrified expression if she were to be discovered was enough to terrify her. However, her desire to be with him, and the impossibility of doing it through the proper channels had eventually convinced her that this was the only way.

Henry had always been a complete gentlemen when they had met each other, as she had known he would be. Mary had rationalized to herself on more than one occasion that nothing had yet or would ever happen between them that would be considered improper had he been considered a suitable beau for her. A few times, she had attempted to work up the courage to confide in her Aunt Catherine that she was secretly seeing Henry. But then reality would crash down on her and she would realize that no one in her family would ever approve of her being courted by a self-declared abolitionist.

Through their many conversations, Mary had learned to respect and even admire Henry's opinions. However, she refused to completely accept his notions that slavery was immoral. She had grown up hearing slavery justified from the pulpit of church with passages taken directly from the Bible. To completely agree that the institution itself was evil was in essence condemning her father, her uncles, and everyone else in her family's way of life. But her opinions were gradually changing ever so slightly.

For instance, even though she did not wish to judge her family's choices, she could see herself moving to a free state and living happily without slaves. Henry had spent hours relating to her his upbringing in a house full of domestic servants; none of whom were slaves. Mary had agreed that she would prefer that arrangement for herself one day as well.

For his part, Henry was grateful that Mary was asking him questions and really listening to his answers. He understood her reluctance to fully see his point of view, knowing full well that he would feel the same way if he had been raised in the south. He secretly hoped that with enough time and reflection, she would eventually come to see things his way. He admired her refusal to accept the existing state of affairs and her willingness to challenge notions that most of her contemporaries would never dare to.

On their first meeting, in the carriage house, Mary had confided in him, "As much as I dearly love Adelaide, I cannot understand her assertions that she couldn't live without her slaves. Surely she could offer wages to free blacks if slavery were abolished."

"She would become accustomed to it more easily than she fears. What she fears is the unknown." After a moment's contemplation Henry added, "To be honest, I think we all do."

They had climbed into one of Captain Ross' fine handcrafted carriages and were sitting with a respectable space between them. The clandestine nature of their meeting was sending a small electric shock through Mary's body. In spite of the nagging fear of being discovered, she had never felt more alive. She had always been so obedient and dutiful that this act of rebellion against her parents' wishes was rather thrilling.

Henry had taken a room in a boarding house with the money he had received from Stephen Duncan. Reverend Butler had insisted for the longest time that he stay in his spare room, but Henry desired the freedom to come and go without need of explanation. There was a livery in Port Gibson where he could hire a horse and ride to Prospect Hill much faster than he and Butler ever made it in the carriage.

Even though he hadn't openly admitted to visiting Mary, Henry felt strongly that both Butler and Levi knew exactly what he was doing—and each had qualms about his decision to do so. Both men had urged caution in their own very different ways.

Zebulon Butler had told him that as a gentleman he must think of Mary and the consequences that their discovery would hold for her. "You would be free to return to Pennsylvania unscathed and move on with your life. Mary, on the other hand, would find her future prospects extremely limited. People in this area do not recover from scandal easily. Please take heed of my concerns, Henry."

Levi had simply made a vague reference to the goodness of Miss Mary. In case his point had been lost on Henry, he added, "It won't do her no good to be found in the company of someone not approved of by her family."

Levi had looked sheepish for a moment after offering his opinion. But Henry had reassured him that he completely understood his meaning, and appreciated his concern for Miss Girault.

On Mary's birthday, Henry had purchased a copy of the book *Poems on Various Subjects, Religious and Moral* by Phyllis Wheatley. After Mary had unwrapped the present and thanked him, Henry asked her if he could read a few of his favorite poems to her. Mary listened as attentively as she could. However, it was clearly written long ago as the style of writing was very old—requiring her complete concentration. Henry had finished reading a poem titled, *Hymn to the Morning*, that Mary had found quite lovely when she noticed that he was looking at her rather gravely.

"What is it Henry? You look troubled suddenly. I truly do love the poems. Please continue." Mary worried instantly that she had offended him in some way. *Perhaps I looked bored while I was attempting to concentrate on the words of the poem?*

"There is a poem that I wanted to read to you, but now I find myself hesitating." He paused for a moment, flipping through the pages until locating the work in question. "I fear now that it may be too personal. In fact, it may cause you pain."

Mary was alarmed. "Why would you think that?" She was gazing intently at him, and her sincerity encouraged him to continue.

"When I was thinking of a gift to give you, I recalled you telling me of the sadness you felt at losing your younger brother and other siblings. And of how the grief ravaged your mother each time, and the difficulty of witnessing that again and again."

Mary nodded, "I remember. But what does this poem

have to do with any of that?"

"Phyllis Wheatley wrote a poem called, *To a Lady and her Children, on the Death of her Son and their Brother.* She articulates so beautifully the same emotions that you shared with me that evening. I thought you might like to hear it." He paused briefly, choosing his words carefully. "But now it seems as if it could be hurtful to read it to you."

Mary contemplated his words. Henry's expression was so earnest and his intentions so pure. She felt that it would be unfair not to hear the selection of poetry that he had chosen expressly for her.

"Please read it to me. I'd like to hear it."

Henry nodded and looked at the book by the glow of the lamp Mary had carried down from the house and began reading slowly and clearly. It was obvious why Henry had chosen this particular poem to read. It truly did express her emotions at losing her younger siblings in an elegant way. Mary was unable to stop the free flow of tears down her cheeks when Henry read:

> *But see from earth his spirit far remov'd*
> *And know no grief recalls your best-belov'd:*
> *He, upon pinions swifter than the wind,*
> *Has left mortality's sad scenes behind.*
> *For joys to this terrestrial state unknown,*
> *And glories richer than the monarch's crown.*
> *Of virtue's steady course the prize behold!*
> *What blissful wonders to his mind unfold!*

Mary thought of her little brother James, imagining him

running through the streets of Heaven experiencing joys that she couldn't imagine. When Henry had finished reading, she leaned against his shoulder, ignoring the physical boundaries they had both insisted upon initially, and sobbed without care for any proprieties. Henry placed his hand against her hair and shushed her gently over and over as she cried. He made no attempt to rush her grief, but allowed it to flow freely. He could feel her body shuddering against him, racked with sobs.

When all her tears seemed spent, Mary sat upright and wiped her face with her sleeve. She noticed that she had soaked Henry's jacket, but knew he wouldn't mind. In fact, at that moment she felt so perfectly at ease with him that she didn't care how puffy her face must be or how disheveled her hair would surely look. She had never felt comfortable in a man's presence before and she felt immense gratitude to him for providing this sense of security to her.

Henry looked into her face intently. "I am sorry to have caused you to cry, Mary. Please forgive me."

Mary shook her head. "No, I needed to cry. I think I have been holding in my feelings for too long. I loved the poem tremendously. It was so beautifully written."

She reached out and took the book from his hands, turning to the cover page. It was dated 1802, which immediately affirmed Mary's initial feeling that the writings were from an earlier era. After a moment of perusing the cover page, she gasped audibly, and then read aloud, "By Phyllis Wheatley, Negro servant to Mr. John Wheatley, of Boston in New England."

She looked at Henry, who was wearing a bemused

expression.

"These poems were written by a negro woman?" Mary was incredulous. She knew that many of the Prospect Hill slaves could read and write, but she hadn't thought that a negro would have published a book. Especially not a woman.

Henry smiled broadly now.

"Phyllis Wheatley was a slave initially. She was captured as a young girl in her native West Africa and purchased by the Wheatley family. They named her Phyllis and allowed her to learn to read and write. Eventually she was given her freedom. This is actually not even the first edition of this book as her writings are from the previous century."

"I have never heard of her," Mary said softly. "But I will cherish this gift forever, Henry. Thank you."

They spent the remainder of their time together discussing Catherine's big plans for the anniversary party. Mary had been enjoying her role in helping prepare for the event. Henry listened attentively as Mary described the flowers being sent from St. Louis and the negro fiddler coming over from Rodney to provide music. Henry claimed to be famished after listening to the menu Mary recited for the affair. He relished the ease with which he could talk to her. It felt as if they had grown up together.

Henry walked her to the back door of the big house before taking his leave. They arranged the next time they could meet. As Mary started through the door, she turned back for one last glance at Henry. He was still standing, waiting for her to disappear from view. She smiled at him in a way so uninhibited and genuine that his heart literally leapt in his chest. He returned her smile and watched the door close softly behind her. *God help me, I've fallen in love with you, Mary Girault. There is simply no denying it.* In spite of the furtive nature of their relationship and the hopeless reality that it would ever be sanctioned here, he loved her.

As Mary quietly ascended the staircase to her bedroom, she realized that she felt the exact same way about him. In one fell swoop he had caused her to fall head over heels in love with him. The fact that he had found the precise poem that spoke to her grief and despair had erased any doubts she had previously had regarding her feelings for him. She felt tremendous gratitude for the cathartic experience of crying into his shoulder after hearing the poem—in fact she felt ten pounds lighter after her cry. The fact that he was able to select that perfect poem confirmed in Mary what she had felt for quite some time; that when she shared herself with Henry, he really listened to her.

***

The anniversary party was not the only thing being planned on Prospect Hill in the months leading up to the auspicious occasion. Edmond Belton and his group of followers had finally had enough waiting. Ed had seen it coming for some time now, but had tried vainly to head it off. He was torn between his promises to Sadie, his own desire for justice, and his loyalty to the others who'd put their faith in him. The turning point came when he noticed Esau, Old Yeary, Andrew and Levi talking in hushed tones several nights before. As soon as he and Wade approached, the talking had abruptly stopped.

At the time, Ed did not force the issue, but he had gained a pretty clear sense of what was being discussed. The urgent looks on his friend's faces conveyed that this had been much more than social chatter. His suspicions were confirmed by Levi the following day. Levi, always honest to a fault, wanted to reconcile the group. "We can't afford to be fightin' 'mongst ourselves." It wasn't the first time Ed Belton had heard those words from Levi. He knew he was right.

The other men had decided the time for waiting had passed. Ed asked them to talk with him, reiterating Levi's wise advice. "We all dependin' on each other," he had said.

So the night had come to decide what to do. Ed hadn't asked for Reverend Butler to come this time. This was their fight now. They had appreciated his help and were glad for the slaves who'd gone to Africa before them. *But now it is our turn. And we ready to go.*

Once they had gathered in Ed's cabin old Old Yeary was the first to speak. "We gonna have to do somethin' to make Master Wade see things our way."

Esau laughed—not in his rich baritone they had all become accustomed to, but rather a bitter laugh that took the Belton brothers by surprise.

Everyone had looked in his direction, and when the laughter died down Esau said, "See things our way? When he ever seen things our way? That man see things one way and one way only. The way that suit him best. He ain't never gonna see anythin' our way. We fools if we think so."

No one in the fire-lit cabin knew what to say. Old Yeary

had long since been a respected member of their community and Esau had basically just called the old man a fool.

However, Old Yeary did not back down. "Son, you can think I is a fool, and you might be right. But every man has some good inside him. Even Master Wade."

Esau did not laugh again. He looked a bit abashed when he responded. "But how you suppose we gonna get him to see what be right to do?" His voice was still tinged with bitterness but it was clear that he was making an effort to provide his elder with proper respect this time.

Old Yeary hung his head slightly as he replied softly, "I don' rightly know."

Esau looked at Ed Belton with the clear message, "I told you so" left unspoken.

"Remember what Mr. Henry say a while back?" Andrew spoke out this time. The other men looked at him. "He say we got to get rid of Mr. Wade in order to get what we deserve."

Wade Belton shook his head ever so slightly and added, "But Reverend Butler told us the lawyers tried that."

"We ain't talkin' 'bout lawyers." All eyes reverted back to Esau. There was no laughter, no bitterness. But something about his tone sent a shiver through Ed. It was clear to everyone in the room that Esau and Andrew had decided something between themselves.

"What are we talkin' 'bout then Esau?"

Esau looked at Ed directly before he gave him an answer. The answer that Ed knew was coming before the word reached his ears. "We gotta get rid of him for good. So he ain't never gonna get in our way again."

Ed exchanged a quick glance with his brother before he responded to Esau. *I wonder how many times they meet without me? What exactly they plannin' to do? Somethin' that gonna get us all killed most likely.*

"You talkin' 'bout killin' a man so he can't keep us from somethin' we deserve?"

"That's right," said Esau simply.

Wade Belton was looking around at the faces of the men he had known for years. They were set in fierce determination, considering the possibility of what might need to be done. All except for Levi. He looked as though he had just seen an apparition. Terror was inscribed onto his face.

"Levi?"

Levi turned his face to Wade, who had spoken his name in a tone that conveyed no emotion.

"What you think 'bout this?"

Levi swallowed hard and glanced around the room. As the youngest man here, he had always felt as though it were an honor to have been asked to participate in their meetings. He didn't want to do anything to jeopardize his place among them. However, he couldn't believe that they were discussing the murder of another human being. The consequences of such an act could bring down a heap of trouble upon all of them, including their wives and children.

Finally he answered, "I can't say that I know what I thinkin'. I don' like the thought of killin' no one. Let alone a man with children. But I don' have no answers for how to make him change his mind neither."

Levi's heart felt full: full of fear, grief, and longing. He wished for the first time that he wasn't a part of the leadership and was instead with Rachael laughing and free from this worry.

Andrew spoke up again. "Esau think we can cause an accident. Maybe loosen up the boxin' that cover the axel on his carriage wheel."

Old Yeary replied to Andrew's suggestion before Esau, who'd already opened his mouth, could speak. "We got no way to be sure he be the only one hurt. Sides that, ain't gonna hurt him too bad less the carriage be goin' fast 'nough."

Ed felt as though he had totally lost control over the direction of this conversation. He repeated his early question. "So we sure we want to kill Master Wade?" He looked once again at his brother.

Wade Belton knew what was on his brother's mind. They had had many conversations about his concerns for their safety. "I don' like it either brother. But we gotta do somethin'. I can't honestly say it would grieve me much to see him gone. Lord forgive me, but it be the truth."

Ed knew with certainty that it would cause him no grief if Isaac Wade perished, but there was still the risk of their role in any sort of accident being discovered. Even if he could get himself to the point of agreeing to a murder plot, it would have to be one that would almost certainly be attributed to an accident. The thought of what would happen if they were found to have a part in any disaster caused him to shudder.

Levi was shaking his head slowly back and forth. He took advantage of the window of silence and said, "I got no respect for Master Wade. But we no better than he is if we do somethin' like what we talkin' 'bout."

"Sometimes you gotta do what needs to be done when you a man, and 'specially a father. Just cause you don' like it, don' mean it don' need doin'." Esau was calm, but he clearly conveyed that he made no apologies for what he felt needed to be done. And to Esau and Andrew that was killing their master.

"When Mr. Henry say we need to get rid of him, he didn' mean killin' him." Levi was sure of that, and had been thinking it over ever since Andrew first brought it up.

"You think you friends with that white man?" Now Esau was laughing again. "He ain't your friend. How you think you know what he mean?"

Levi replied simply, "'Cause I know him."

"You know what he want you to know. He think he doin' some good deed comin' down south to help us poor folk. But we don' know nothin' 'bout what he think." Andrew looked to Esau for affirmation, and was instantly gratified by the latter's vigorous nodding.

"He think no one notice him sneakin' up to the big house? How we suppose' to know what he talkin' 'bout with Miss Mary? She family of them folks ain't she? She think like they do." Esau sat fully erect in his seat as he spoke in a raised voice.

"He been nothin' but kind to us. Why you gotta make him sound…" but Levi's voice trailed off. He refused to let his emotions reveal the wounds inflicted by the words of the others. He felt in his heart that Henry was his friend, and he wasn't going to let anything get in the way of his belief in his friend's sincerity. Even though Levi didn't approve of Henry meeting with Mary, he resented anyone mocking his friend's actions.

Ed intervened. "I think Henry tryin' to help us best he can. What important now is decidin' what need to be done now. Think about what best to do. Why don' we give it till tomorrow. We meet back here and talk again."

Ed was relieved to get no argument from any of the others. The tension in the room was high and Ed was grateful for the break from it and for the chance to regroup. When they met again, he would be ready with a plan of his own and he would be able to take back control.

Levi's heart had never felt more troubled. *How can I gain my freedom at the cost of another life?* For a few moments he considered running away with Rachael and their son Gabriel. But it wasn't long before he dismissed that possibility. The chances of him making a clean escape were slim to none with a wife and small child in tow.

He couldn't see any good options laying ahead of him. Perhaps it had been naïve of him, but he had really believed that if he were patient enough the legal system would clear the way for them to go. *Our only hope now is that the law gives us justice before we got to do somethin' like murderin'.* Levi sat on the step outside of his door for a long while before going inside. It gave him time enough to fully compose himself—he wasn't going to let Rachael see how scared he was.

March 1845   Prospect Hill Plantation

Levi hadn't been sleeping well for the past couple of weeks. The most recent discussions involving how to best handle the "problem with Master Wade," as it had come to be called, had left him shaken and disheartened. By nature he was a peacemaker and he had tried in vain to come up with a way to solve their problem in which no one was hurt. It was a fruitless effort, he had come to realize, due to the fact that both sides were firmly entrenched in their beliefs. And both sides believed that they were in the right.

At night, while Rachael slept beside him, Levi would ponder their future for hours. Both their future if they left for Africa, and their future if they remained in Mississippi. Each of these potential lives he pictured for his family held a degree of uncertainty and apprehension. Some of the Reed slaves had written letters to people left behind asking for supplies and other assistance. He felt certain that if he and Rachael emigrated to Liberia they would face new diseases, unfamiliar climate and terrain, the indigenous peoples of Africa who may not welcome their arrival, and so much more.

But remaining enslaved here felt too disheartening to even consider it as a viable possibility. It was one thing when Captain Ross was alive. Levi had been quite young, but remembered him fondly. Sometimes the other slaves would reminisce about Captain Ross in the evenings, recalling how much better life had been then. Levi understood their need to do so, but he was uncomfortable with the notion of glamorizing the past and their previous owner. While he listened to the wistful recollections, he forced himself to remember that even while Ross was at Prospect Hill they did not have freedom. *We still was just slaves. We still belonged to him and had no choice to walk off this place. There ain't no gettin' around that.*

During the meetings with the Belton brothers and the others, it had become increasingly clear that killing Wade was the only option now being considered amongst them. Levi didn't feel judgmental towards the others who wanted to get rid of their master in this way. He figured that every man had to do what he thought was right. He could certainly understand their sentiment. But every man also has to make the choice he can live with. *And I just don't think I can live with a plan that involves killin'.*

Levi had essentially withdrawn from the discussions, which hadn't been lost on Ed. He had taken Levi aside and asked him pointedly if he was backing out of their plans. Levi responded truthfully that he didn't know. He tried to explain his objections clearly, without bringing anything biblical into the discussion, remembering Ed's recent comments on how the Bible was 'always bein' used to justify somethin'." But even though Levi didn't bring up the Bible to Ed, it was a factor in his decision. He had been raised to have the fear of God in him and prided himself on living a righteous life.

In truth Ed really just wanted Levi's assurance that if he did back out of the eventual plan, he would do nothing to block it from being carried out. Levi gladly offered those assurances without reservation.

During his long wakeful periods during the night, Levi was left to search his soul for what he felt was the right thing to do. He felt obligations to so many people. Not only for himself, Rachael and their little son Gabriel. He also felt a responsibility for the other slaves at Prospect Hill with whom he felt a strong familial connection. And finally for Zebulon Butler and Henry who'd given hours of their time and efforts to help them.

In his deepest moments of introspection, it had even crossed his mind what Henry's condemnation of him would feel like, should he be discovered being party to killing a white man. Seconds later, the ludicrous nature of the worry had resulted in him laughing out loud, ultimately waking Rachael. *If you get caught in a plot like that, you better worry 'bout your neck in a noose and not Henry's opinion of you.* But he still couldn't shake the feeling of shame he would feel if Henry learned of his role in a murder plot.

Levi still met with Belton's group and felt pride in his leadership role among the community in the quarters. He told Ed, honestly, that he was still giving the matter consideration. And that was a true understatement, as Levi considered this matter above all others. He was still working to come up with a different way to get what they all wanted. *A better way.* Ed seemed to respect Levi's right to do so as he had promised not to interfere with any plan—even one which he felt strongly opposed to.

Some nights, he would slip out of his bed and sit outside with his back against the door. He would look up into the night sky, sometimes even talking to the stars as if they could hear him. He wondered if they would look any different in the African sky. He wondered if he would ever get the chance to find out. *Lord, if you really up there, please help us out down here. Show me the way. Show me the way.*

***

Mary truly was enjoying helping Catherine plan for the anniversary party. But it was becoming increasingly difficult for her to keep her mind off of Henry. They had continued meeting secretly in the carriage under the cover of darkness, but several times she had snuck down during the day to sit on the seat and reminisce over their conversations.

She would run her hands across the spot on the leather seat that Henry had occupied hours earlier; closing her eyes in order to create a mental image of him sitting there beside her. She longed every day to be able to come out into the open with her true feelings for him. She had grown to cherish every moment that they were able to spend together.

Several times over the past weeks, Catherine had been forced to repeat questions to Mary, as she had been too distracted to hear her the first time. Earlier today, Catherine had asked, "Are you sure that you are all right, Mary? You haven't heard a word I've said. Where on earth is your mind this morning?"

Mary suddenly snapped to attention, looking at her aunt's smiling face. "I suppose I have a great deal on my mind thinking of my family back at home Aunt Catherine. I apologize for not being more attentive. It was rude of me."

To Mary's relief Catherine was still smiling. But the relief turned to alarm when Catherine said, "I keep thinking the most logical explanation for a young girl to act this way is a new beau. And yet, I can't imagine who it could possibly be around here." Her expression was hopeful, as if possibly she could be correct in her hunch that there was a dashing young planter's son who'd been covertly sending Mary love letters.

Mary laughed as gaily as she could manage given her fear that her expression would convey the truth. "Aunt Catherine, of course there is no beau. I'm here with you every day, aren't I?"

Oh Aunt Catherine, how I wish I could tell you the truth!

Catherine's smile faltered instantly. "Oh Mary, I am sorry. Of course you are worried about your dear parents, and here I am teasing you about a suitor. Now it is you that must forgive me!"

The two women embraced. "There is nothing to forgive, Aunt Catherine. I love being here at Prospect Hill with you."

"And I love having you here. But I do understand that part of your heart remains back at Bellevue with your family as well."

Catherine suddenly said, "Let's take a break from working." She pushed aside the fabric swatches that she had been asking Mary's opinion on moments earlier. "We can walk a bit outside in the gardens. Would you like that?"

The offer to stop this tedious task and stroll the lovely grounds of the planation was quite welcomed.

"I would love that!" Mary replied enthusiastically. Mary would have been interested in fabric swatches for a new dress or bonnet, but it was hard to muster up much fervor for new chair coverings. Especially when the image of Henry's face kept wafting in front of her, causing a major distraction.

Mary had learned that planning for the party included other seemingly unrelated tasks such as replacing the sun-faded fabric on the chairs in the sitting room. As Catherine had commented several times over the past weeks, "Everything at Prospect Hill must look top notch for the party."

Catherine stood and held out her arm to her young niece. They strolled through the open front doors, down the front steps, and around to the gardens. It was a particularly beautiful spring day, and a nice walk outdoors seemed just the prescription she had needed to clear her head.

As they walked, Catherine said, "I love this place. I hope to grow old and eventually die here. Hopefully, if I get my heart's desire I'll be buried just over there." She gestured to the small family cemetery where the large monument for Captain Ross stood towering in the bright noonday sun.

Mary shuddered. "I don't like thinking about where I'll be buried, Aunt Catherine. It is a bit too morbid."

Catherine smiled at her. "You are young still. Once you bring children into the world, you begin to think of your legacy. What you will leave behind, and how you will be remembered. I think it is only natural."

They walked in silence for a few moments before Catherine went on, "I am beginning to have fears that we will lose this place. It makes me question things that I thought were certainties merely a few years ago."

Mary noticed that her aunt had a pensive expression as she surveyed the rolling hills and forests around her home, her eyes misting with tears. Mary thought of her mother, always admonishing her not to ask questions. But she felt as if Catherine wouldn't mind and plunged forward, pushing her mother's lectures aside.

"Why would you lose Prospect Hill?"

Catherine stopped walking and looked into Mary's earnest eyes. "You've become a grown woman right in front of my eyes. Yes, I suppose you are wondering. We don't discuss it in your presence of course, as it is business. But there are times when business greatly affects our personal lives, doesn't it?"

It seemed to Mary as if Catherine were just musing aloud rather than actually responding to her question. But she had been bold enough to ask her aunt the question and wasn't willing to press her any further.

However, after a few minutes of wistful thinking, Catherine said, "There are some men in the area who are trying to help the slaves get the freedom that Isaac's grandfather granted them in his testament. But you see, Mary, Isaac believes strongly that Captain Ross was not within his legal rights to do so. The lawyers gave him such hope at first. But now it has been years and every court has ruled against him. Against us."

Catherine looked as if she were about to cry in earnest,

so Mary did not press her to go on. They continued strolling the grounds in silence before Catherine spoke again. "If we lose the ultimate legal battle then Prospect Hill will be sold, and the slaves…" her voice caught. She swallowed hard, composing herself. "The slaves will be sent to Africa leaving us with no resources to run this place. Even if Isaac could manage to buy it when it is sold."

Mary felt as if she had been physically stabbed in the heart. It required her greatest efforts to keep her composure while her aunt was saying, "There are some men in the area…"

Mary knew instantly that Henry was one of *those men*. One of the men who could cause Catherine to lose Prospect Hill. The very place she dreamed of raising her children, growing old with her husband and dying.

Suddenly Mary had a fleeting image of herself as some giant rope in a cosmic game of tug-of-war. Henry was pulling one arm and Catherine was pulling the other. She loved them both. *How can I love a man who is causing my aunt so much pain and worry for her future? But how can I just stop loving him when he is everything I've ever dreamed of?*

***

Isaac Wade stood inside of the parlor and looked through the windows. He had seen his wife and niece walking together and noticed that their conversation seemed intense. It always pained him to see Catherine unhappy in any way, and he hoped that there was nothing seriously troubling her. He made a mental note to ask her later what the two had been discussing in the gardens.

He glanced at the discarded fabric samples laying on the table, mentally tabulating how much this party was going to end up costing him before it was over. He didn't begrudge Catherine the joy of planning it, or of her spending money for that matter. Isaac Wade felt that he had a duty as a southern gentlemen to indulge his wife's wishes as much as he possibly could. *She merely wants our home to look beautiful for our friends and neighbors. And why not? I've worked hard and it is satisfying to have something to show for it.*

Today, however, his mood was sullen. Every bit of news he had gotten lately had been bad. Mr. Ellet, his lawyer, was demanding money again. He had received official injunctions forbidding him to remove any of his grandfather's slaves from Prospect Hill to be sent to "other family plantations." How the court found out that he had sent a few slaves to Adelaide's and his mother's homes was more upsetting to him than the order for him to desist. It meant that people were continuing to meddle in his private affairs, and that infuriated him. *The whole lot of them belong to me now, and I will do with them whatever I please.*

However, this wasn't entirely the case, and he knew it. The truth was that Wade had to keep records for the courts as the executor of the Ross estate. Therefore a paper trail was in existence which could be used as evidence in a trial. Some of the words used in court documents he had received such as "fraud" and "illegal activity" would give any law-abiding citizen reason to be concerned. Adding to his frustration was the fact that every time he contacted

Ellet for assistance, he was reminded that he still owed Ellet for services rendered and would "do well to remember that before making additional requests for legal counsel."

Wade slammed his hand against the hard surface of the desk, which he immediately regretted. "Damn!" He began shaking his hand to ward off the stinging sensation when he heard Catherine's voice drawing nearer. *I have to pull myself together and let her believe that everything is going well for us.*

He walked into the foyer to meet his wife and niece as they walked through the large double doors. Forcing what he hoped to be a sincere looking smile on his face he crowed, "Why, if it isn't the two most beautiful ladies in Jefferson County!"

"Isaac darling, how are you?" Catherine left Mary's side and walked to her husband.

"I am just fine, Catherine. My expert sleuthing abilities lead me to believe that you ladies had your fill of cloth swatches and needed a bit of air?"

Catherine smiled and nodded. "It is a truly beautiful day today. Spring has finally arrived. The tiniest little signs of life are popping up in the gardens. By the evening of our anniversary, it will be just as lovely here as it was on our wedding day!"

Mary was pleased that her uncle had distracted Catherine. She felt a strong desire to be alone and sort out her feelings.

"Aunt Catherine, may I please go upstairs and lie down for a bit? I am feeling tired."

"Of course you may," answered Catherine, but not without walking over and placing the back of her hand on

Mary's forehead. "But I was just about to call for some fresh lemonade. Please be sure to have some when you come back down."

Mary nodded and offered up a rather feeble smile to her aunt before beginning up the staircase. She could feel her aunt's eyes on her as she climbed the stairs, but did not look back. As she reached the upstairs landing she heard the conversation resume downstairs, but did not attempt to discern what was being discussed.

Mary's head was spinning from the conversation that she had just had with her aunt. Now that she had heard the argument over the will fervently recounted from the opposing viewpoint, it was causing her mind to swirl with questions. Lately, she had been spending so much time hearing matters from Henry's vantage point that she felt somewhat shamed not to have been more concerned about how the matter was going to affect Catherine.

She removed her shoes and stretched out on the great four-poster bed thinking over her conversation with Catherine, alternating with conversations she had had with Henry on the same topic. *How could two people that I care for so deeply see the same exact situation in such different ways? And both of them feel so justified in their beliefs.*

As fruitless as it seemed, Mary hoped against all hope that when this matter was finally resolved she and Henry could have a future together. Regardless of the outcome, someone that she loved was going to be hurt. She didn't want to take sides. It was true that she had been affected by Henry's passion on the subject of slavery, the readings he had shared with her, and the book of poetry by Phyllis Wheatley which was currently stowed inside of the lining of her trunk.

It seemed to Mary that the stakes were very different for the two people that she loved. On one hand, if Henry's side lost their fight, his pride would be wounded. But if Uncle Isaac lost, the whole way of life for the Wade family would change forever. *But it isn't that simple is it? Henry's side includes the slaves themselves. What about the effect on their lives?*

Mary spoke aloud, as if the answers would come to her more easily if she did so. "Yes, what about the slaves? What about Levi, Rachael, Mariah, Grace, and all of the others? Shouldn't Esau have a chance to sell his beautiful wood work and support his family? Their way of life is also at stake."

But no answers came to her. This was all beyond her ability to influence in any way. *This is a matter for someone with wisdom and insight far greater than my own.*

Mary slowly rose to her feet, knelt by the side of her bed, and prayed.

April 10, 1845   Port Gibson

Zebulon Butler was concerned about the Prospect Hill slaves. Ed Belton had been distant the past month or so, and reluctant to schedule another meeting. He had tried reassuring himself that the group was just tired of hearing the same old "wait and see" message. To be honest there really was no additional news to share with them, and he understood their frustration in being told to wait. But something was nagging at him, and try as he might, he couldn't push the thought from his head.

A few nights earlier Henry had made a comment when they had dined together to discuss strategy. He mentioned that he had seen Levi, the young slave in whom he had taken quite an interest. When Butler had pressed him for the details of this meeting, Henry had been maddeningly vague, offering only, "I ran into him while riding near the area." Butler suspected the true reason Henry had been at Prospect Hill, but it seemed pointless to express his concerns regarding the potential harm to young Mary's reputation yet again.

Henry recounted Levi asking him, "What 'xactly you

mean by getting Master Wade out of the way?"

Henry reported that he had been baffled by the question and not sure how to answer, but ultimately responded, "I just blurted out something without thinking, Levi. I have no idea of how you can get him out of your way. Apparently even experienced lawyers haven't been able to successfully remove him, so I should not have opened my mouth at all."

Henry had reported that Levi seemed rather distraught during the conversation, as if he had been giving his comments quite a bit of thought and consideration. Henry's only reason to bring this to Butler's attention had been to express his regret in causing Levi to fret over a situation that couldn't be resolved in the manner in which he had suggested.

But to Zebulon Butler, the alarm he felt at hearing Levi's comments ran much deeper. *Does the young man think that Henry meant to get rid of Isaac Wade by doing him bodily harm?* The thought had immediately come to him as Henry was recounting his conversation with Levi. Although Butler pushed the thought out of his mind dismissively, it had crept back and nagged at him for days now.

Butler truly cared for Henry and was grateful for the optimism and enthusiasm he brought to the cause at hand. He had been like a breath of fresh air around the town—instantly likeable to the citizens of Port Gibson. Many of the female parishioners in his church had been trying to make a match with their daughters. But Butler had the distinct impression that Henry's heart had been spoken for. However, rather than being a cause for celebration, it filled Butler with concern and apprehension for his young friend.

The young man, he was sure, had been making trips under the cover of darkness to see Wade's beautiful young niece. A very dangerous situation that he had attempted to warn Henry about to no avail. Henry had been polite, heard him out, and expressed appreciation for his concern—and then gone right on with his visits to Mary Girault. The ramifications of him being caught with Mary on the grounds of Wade's home would be grave, and he prayed nightly that Henry was exercising the utmost caution.

Butler understood that Henry was enamored with the young lady. He had fallen under the spell of a few lovely young southern belles himself when he had first arrived in Mississippi. Ultimately he knew that a wife would distract him from the noble work of the church and worked to make himself impervious to their charms.

A recent graduate of Princeton, where he had attended seminary, he had arrived in Mississippi intent on converting as many souls in this wilderness as possible. His father had been overbearing and difficult to please. The disdain for continuing to live in his shadow and his domineering manner was a major factor in his decision to move far from Wilkes-Barre in his native Pennsylvania. At the time it had seemed like a good plan for an idealistic young man in his early twenties desiring both a challenging career in ministry and some distance from home.

Settling originally in Vicksburg, his fiery sermons and stringent doctrine helped him to make a name for himself. But he had a fire in his belly for mission work and the more rural areas of the state beckoned him. Captain Isaac Ross' son Arthur Allison Ross had been a classmate of his at Princeton, and had been the one to ask him to come pastor in Port Gibson in 1827. Unfortunately his friend died a few years later, preceding his own father in death by two years. But Butler continued serving God the best way that he knew how: putting the fear of hell and damnation into the hearts of every man, woman, and child in his congregation. His trademark soon became pointing one finger upwards to the heavens reminding his congregation that God was always watching.

Upon reflection, he had been happy in Port Gibson for the most part. But the issue of slavery drove a wedge between himself and most of his friends, neighbors, and parishioners. Having spent so much time recently with Henry Willcox had been a blessing, serving to recharge him for the ongoing battle of ending slavery he seemed to fight on a daily basis. The two men had spent many hours engaged in philosophical discussions about slavery to be certain. But they also conversed about politics, religion, familial relationships, literature, poetry, and so much more. In fact, it was with more than a twinge of regret that Butler regarded Henry's interest in a young lady, as Butler was now missing his company.

The fact that Henry's relationship with Mary was clandestine in nature and unlikely to ever progress beyond mere infatuation made it even more regretful to Reverend Butler. To a practical man such as himself, it seemed a great risk to undertake for very little potential reward. *Perhaps if Miss Girault was willing to cut ties with her family here and move to Pennsylvania with Henry?* But as soon as the notion came to Butler, he had dismissed it. *What future could they have under those circumstances? And besides, Henry's relationship with his own family is strained at best currently considering his decision to leave the university.* However he mentally played the scenarios regarding a possible future for the young people, it never seemed to add up to a workable situation.

Suddenly that nagging thought emerged once more from the recesses of Butler's mind, momentarily interrupting his internal dialogue about Henry's personal life. *What if the slaves decide that getting rid of Wade is truly the answer to their problems. Could that account for Edmond's reluctance to see me again?* He tried to put himself in their position; waiting for all of these years and still denied of freedom. *Would I be desperate enough to kill a man who was standing in my way?* When he forced himself to be honest, he believed that his answer might well be yes. Desperation plays tricks on the mind, allowing people to justify things that otherwise they would never have considered. He had seen it before.

Then even more disconcerting thoughts came to the forefront. *If the slaves do kill Wade, are Henry and myself culpable? If not legally, then possibly morally?* Butler tried to recall the exact words that Henry spoke that evening in Belton's cabin, and the reaction his words had received. *Surely they understood that Henry was simply referring to a way to remove Mr. Wade from the case?* He tried in vain to remember any looks that might have been exchanged between the slaves or whispered discussions around him.

For his part, Butler had not given up his quest to help the Prospect Hill slaves. He was actively working with the American Colonization Society to carry out the orders of the courts, but was being thwarted at every turn by the influential people Isaac Wade enlisted to help block the rulings.

He wondered what the slaves must be feeling as they were right now busy preparing for the grand and lavish party being planned in the upcoming week to celebrate the Wade's fifth wedding anniversary. He tried to imagine it from their point of view: toiling for a master who is cheating you out of your inheritance while lording his wealth over you. The very wealth intended to send you to a new life of freedom on another continent.

He felt that time was even more of the essence now with his new concerns about a possible plan to be rid of Wade. Butler resolved to devote even more of his time and energies to getting the slaves safely off of Prospect Hill before anything dire could occur. *I won't give up fighting for you. I promise you that. Please don't do anything rash that will jeopardize your chances of realizing your dreams of freedom. Hold on just a bit longer. Please.*

***

Henry was initially worried that Mary seemed distant upon their meeting. She had smiled and greeted him as always, but there was something missing. The warmth that usually shone in her eyes seemed to be subdued and her very smile appeared a bit forced. Even after they had climbed into the carriage that had become so familiar to them, Mary was unusually quiet. After a few moments of gentle coaxing, Mary eventually shared with him the conversation she had had with Catherine and the effect it was having on her.

Henry listened as Mary discussed her father's opinion

on Captain Ross' will. She told him that Catherine had dreams of staying at Prospect Hill for the rest of her life. For the first time Henry came to understand the full extent to which the new ideas he had been introducing her to were in direct conflict with her upbringing. The last thing he wanted was to threaten her sense of connectedness to her own family. *Perhaps I've pushed too hard, trying to share my views with her.*

Henry's heart felt heavy for Mary. *How difficult this must be; wanting to remain loyal to your family and yet true to what you believe to be right.* He pulled her close to him, relieved when she made no attempt to resist the gentle pressure on her upper arm. She rested her head once again upon his shoulder and prayed that a happy outcome was possible for them. Even in moments where neither of them spoke, it seemed as though words were passing between them silently. *I know how hard this must be for you, Mary... Thank you for understanding, Henry. I truly do love you... I love you too.*

They remained in this manner for over an hour, barely speaking, but neither of them concerned with the lack of conversation. Mary's head resting comfortably against Henry's shoulder. It was as if they had progressed to a new level of companionship where words were unnecessary. Both Mary and Henry silently wished that things could just stay like this forever—never having to face the difficult decisions that would surely be in their future. However, they were no longer children and had long since learned that 'happily ever after' only exists in fairy tales.

***

Levi felt the panic rising in his chest. *I can't breathe! Stay calm. You got to stay calm.*

Edmond Belton had gathered the group together with some urgent news. News that changed their entire strategy. Mariah Belton had overheard Master Wade making plans to send some of the slaves to Oak Hill permanently. He had been speaking to his mother Jane who'd visited Prospect Hill earlier in the day.

According to Mariah, Mrs. Ross reportedly said, "I am in need of some strong men for chores and heavy work. Please don't send me any too old to be of real use to me Isaac. I have enough aging slaves as it is; they have slowed down substantially and I don't like the idea of introducing outsider negroes to my brood."

Mariah reported that Mr. Wade then began writing down some names, speaking them aloud as he did so. One of the names had been Levi. The shock of hearing his own name among those being considered to ship off to a neighboring plantation had not yet worn off of Levi. And the thought of leaving Rachael and Gabriel was creating an ache within him that he could barely tolerate. He was forcing himself to be strong, but finding it terribly difficult.

The conversation between Master Wade and his mother had reportedly continued. "I also could use at least two females. I wouldn't ask you to send a trained house servant, of course. Merely ones who show potential for such work. I'm sure old Aunt Sally can train up some new girls, but she's getting on in years and needs help."

Mariah's account is less reliable at this point because she had been forced to move from the spot where she could hear the conversation well, due to the descent of Catherine

Wade down the staircase. However, she felt sure that she had heard the name "Sadie" from Master Wade as he continued making his list, followed by Wade's voice saying, "Of course this transfer will have to wait until after the anniversary party."

Catherine entered the room where her husband and mother-in-law were speaking, allowing Mariah the opportunity to return to her earlier position nearer to the open door.

"What is this about the party, Isaac?" Catherine was heard to inquire.

"I will be sending some slaves to Oak Hill to aid Mother," he had replied coolly. "*After* the grand affair you've been working so hard to plan, of course."

"Thank you," Jane replied to his statement. "I hope this won't make it difficult for you."

"Not at all, Mother. I can list the negroes as chattel on the inventory forms in a way that shows they've remained here at Prospect Hill. I've grown weary of outsiders meddling in my business affairs, and refuse to cow under to bullying. I'll do what I please with my property. And it pleases me to be able to assist my mother."

Mariah had taken leave to report her news to a young housemaid who ran down to the quarters immediately. Ed and Wade Belton had been in the fields, but she had found Esau repairing some tools and he had promised to convey the news to the others.

By the time Esau had located Ed, he was irate and demanding something be done. When Esau spoke his wife's name, Ed's stomach had clenched violently and he had thought for a moment he might be sick on the spot.

Sadie leave here for good?

As Levi sat now and listened to the conversation around the room, his eternal optimism was failing him. He had run through a list of mental options: *I could ask Master Wade to let me stay. I could ask Master Wade to let Rachael and Gabriel come along too. I could run away during all of the commotion from the party and sneak my family out too.* However, each possibility seemed flawed and Levi was rapidly losing hope in any of them.

"I say we burn the house while they all sleeping," Esau said in an undertone. "It was slaves what built that house. I say we set it blazin' and ole' Master Wade won't be botherin' us no more."

"What if they wake up and escape?" Ed was surprised to realize that he felt no qualms regarding burning a family alive. He felt nothing but hatred for Isaac Wade and all his kin. Perhaps hearing that his wife would be sent away had hardened his heart to the point where nothing else mattered. Whatever the reason, he didn't feel any reluctance to torch the house. *Master brought this down on himself!*

"We get Ole' Cook to drug the coffee. Party is goin' to be in the afternoon. Guest'll all be leavin' 'fore dinner. Cook say they always drinkin' coffee after dinner. They sleep through anythin' with the drug in 'em." Andrew spoke as though he had evidently given this a great deal of thought before now.

Ed still wasn't completely convinced. One thing he felt certain of was that their plan had to be successful. Allowing Wade to survive was not an option. The consequences of that were too dire to contemplate. "Just suppose he don't drink the coffee that night?"

Esau spoke now. "I will grab me an axe from the shed and wait by the door. His room right there off the front doors. If he come out, I take care of him."

Levi shuddered. He couldn't believe that it had come to this. "What about the little children? Are we saying they goin' to burn up too?"

No one replied to Levi immediately. It was clear that the others were resolved to what had to be done, but no one in the cabin relished the idea that innocent children would be a casualty of their plan.

Finally Wade Belton responded. "The way I see it, he left us no choice. We tried doin' this the Christian way. We been tryin' for years and years. It ain't done us no good 'cause he got all the power. Only choice we got left is gettin' rid of him. Now we can just get rid of the one man, and that what we wanted to do at first. But now he forcin' us to do somethin' right now to stop him takin' our people from here."

Levi understood what he was saying on an intellectual level. But his heart was pounding in his chest and he felt nauseous. *How can this be the right thing to do? Those little children ain't got no party to this matter.*

Belton went on. "If I come across a rattler nest, do it solve anythin' if I jus' kill the grown-up viper? I goin' to kill all the vipers. Even the youngins'."

"But we ain't talkin' 'bout rattle snakes brother. We talkin' 'bout children." Levi spoke softly, with a catch in his voice, but he made sure that his words were clearly heard. "It just ain't right."

"Children who goin' grow up to be just as dangerous as that man up there. More dangerous than any ole rattler." It was Old Yeary who spoke now. "I don't think I ever woulda seen this comin' a few years back. But now I can't see hows we got a choice. We goin' die here if we just keep waitin'."

The room fell into an uncomfortable silence. Then in voices barely over whispers the plan was created, and responsibilities delegated. Who would get the herb used to drug the coffee? Who would actually put it into the coffee pot? Someone needed to have the torches prepared with oil ready to light. Andrew knew some men who could be trusted. Esau was going to station himself outside of the door. Lookouts were needed at certain intervals. More names were offered up as people that could keep quiet and be trusted. Someone inside the house needed a signal for when everyone was asleep. Ed thought Mariah would be willing to do that. There were so many possibilities for error, and all contingencies needed to be planned for.

Ed realized that Levi had been completely silent during the past hour that the rest of them were planning out the minutia of the plan that would end their captivity once and for all. He looked around to make sure Levi was still there, and found him sitting on one of his children's empty sleeping pallets with his head hanging down between his knees.

"Levi?"

Levi looked up slowly. Ed didn't think he had ever seen him more miserable. Even when Rachael had been laboring to birth his son and he was too worried to eat or drink for hours.

"You told me you goin' to let me know if you goin' to be a part of this."

Levi felt agonized. For most of his life he had had a clear idea of what was right and what was wrong. It came to him without him even having to think about it. But this was different. He felt as if his very soul had been torn into pieces. But he just simply could not be a party to a plan where innocent children would burn to death. He knew that from deep inside himself to be true. *What good is freedom if you can't live with yourself?*

Levi looked directly into Ed's eyes and gave his response. "No. I can't be a party to this." His words were barely audible.

All eyes had now directed their attention to Levi. A couple of expressions did not even attempt to mask the contempt they were feeling at Levi's refusal to go along with their plan. But Ed felt no contempt for Levi. He felt now as he always had—that Levi had earned his respect and deserved to be treated as such.

"We got your promise you won't breathe a word of this to nobody?" asked Ed gravely.

Levi nodded. "You got my word on that."

It pained Ed to lose Levi, and he knew that his brother felt the same. It had been Wade who had originally felt that Levi, though young, would be invaluable. And he had been until now.

"You better go on now, then." Ed spoke the words without malice, but his meaning was clear. *If you are not a part of the plan, you are no longer a part of us.*

Once again, Levi nodded and slowly rose to his feet. He exited the cabin with one swift glance back at Ed, whose face remained impassive.

When Levi was clear of the cabin and completely alone,

he collapsed against the foot of a tree and sobbed like a young child.

April 14, 1845   Prospect Hill Plantation

The day of the big anniversary party finally arrived. Though it had been initially conceived mostly as a vehicle for distracting Catherine from her worries over the legal matters, she was truly excited when the day finally dawned. She and Mary had meticulously planned every detail, preparing for every possible contingency they could imagine. When she woke that morning Catherine felt sure that Prospect Hill had never looked lovelier. *Even on my actual wedding day.*

The slaves had outdone themselves for the event with both the grounds and the interior of the home looking immaculately cared for. A fresh coat of paint had been recently applied to the doors and window sills, the porch railings had been scrubbed, and the garden didn't sport a single rogue weed. The rugs had been beaten, the floors swept, and Catherine would have been shocked if a speck of dust could be located in her home on this fine morning. She gave a sigh of contentment as she surveyed her fine home. *I am blessed in so many ways.*

Adelaide had arrived the day before with Martha,

Cabell, and Addie which had created an added level of gaiety and excitement at Prospect Hill. Adelaide brushed off Catherine's concerns that her husband John was not making the short trip with her, merely replying, "He stays very busy with his career. He sends his regrets."

It filled Catherine with such joy to see her own dear children playing with their cousins. Mary's preoccupied manner of late had lifted instantly the moment young Martha had run into her arms exclaiming, "Mother said you'd be here already, Mary! I couldn't wait to see you!"

As Adelaide was asking Catherine how she could help with the final preparations, Martha was peppering Mary with questions.

"What's a manimersary?" asked Martha. "I heard mother calling the party that."

Mary laughed lightheartedly. "It is called an ann-iv-er-sa-ry, Martha. It is like a birthday in a way. But instead of celebrating the day you were born, it celebrates the day you were married."

"My birthday was in January!" exclaimed Martha. "I turned five!"

Then looking rather serious, she added. "But I'm not married, so I don't get a manimersary."

Mary laughed again, "I don't either, Martha. Maybe one day I will. I remember when Aunt Catherine was married here. I was a bridesmaid."

"A what?" Mary loved the way that Martha's little face scrunched up when she asked questions.

"It is a tradition that a bride chooses people to help her prepare for her wedding. In my case, I was only thirteen, so I wore a pretty dress and carried flowers. That is about all I really did, but it was truly wonderful. I remember how grown up and special I felt that day."

"I want to be one of those when you get married, Mary! Can I please?" She looked excited now at the thought of the dress and flowers.

Mary scooped Martha into her arms and planted a kiss on her cheek. "Of course you can, sweet Martha. But I have to find a husband first." *Martha Ross Richardson, you were just the distraction I needed! I am so glad you are here. I met you for the first time at that wedding, and have loved you ever since.*

There became a great deal of bustling about when the hour for the party drew near; almost a frenetic level of activity seemed to be going on around the plantation.

Mary helped as much as she could, but sometimes she would get distracted watching the various happenings she had come across. She watched a group of slaves, including Jack, Thomas, Moses and Andrew unloading crates of oysters from the back of a wagon. She remembered hearing Uncle Isaac specifically request them, saying, "It will be summer soon and we won't be able to eat them for months." Mary knew that oysters were only consumed in months containing the letter 'R' for safety reasons, making June, July, and August off limits. Catherine had gladly acquiesced to his request and made arrangements for a large shipment from New Orleans to be delivered the morning of the party.

In fact a portion of the side yard had been specifically set aside per Isaac's request to hold an oyster roast for the gentlemen in attendance. Several slaves were shoveling raw oysters onto a metal sheet over a fire built in a large round pit made from stones. Mary watched as they wet large pieces of burlap and covered the oysters to create a way to produce and capture steam. Periodically the burlap would be pulled back to check the oysters. When the oysters opened, they would be transferred to large pails set up on crude wooden tables in the shade of the oaks. This would be the domain of the men during part of the afternoon, Mary realized. No lady would stand at these tables shucking oysters in her finery.

Another part of the yard, a good distance from the oyster roast location was set up for croquet. Martha and her young cousin Isaac had already played several games, however if they were following any rules at all they were certainly ones they had invented themselves. Extra chairs had been brought out onto the porch for the guests who fancied observing the outdoor activities from their shady perch. The comfort and pleasure of each guest had been of the utmost importance to Catherine Wade. To look around Prospect Hill in the hour before the guests were due confirmed that fact.

The music from the hired fiddler began to fill the air in the final half hour before the guests arrived, and Mary was consumed with a sense of excitement for what was to come. She had plans to see Henry after dinner that evening, and she felt the familiar quivering in her stomach that preceded their meetings. She had felt a stab of remorse that she couldn't invite him to the party, but they had discussed the possibility of him attending before ruling it out entirely. Each scenario they imagined would involve small talk which would eventually lead back to his reason for being in

Mississippi: advancing the cause of the colonization movement. In particular, colonizing the slaves from this very plantation. An action that was being fiercely opposed by her family.

Henry had even suggested that he could pretend to be a deaf mute, which would eliminate any chance of his secret being discovered. Mary laughed as she reminded him that Uncle Isaac had already spoken with him once before and wasn't likely to forget that he could hear and speak quite perfectly. Ultimately they decided to just meet when the party was over and Mary could free herself to get away.

Much of the party itself was a blur for Mary. She was helping Catherine with her official hostess duties, trying to make sure that all of the guests were having a good time, making small talk and suggesting activities for anyone who was at risk of lapsing into boredom. Most of the ladies in attendance knew each other, however, and had formed little groups to gossip.

When their bellies were full of oysters, the male guests took their leave to drink brandy, smoke cigars, and talk politics. The recent inauguration of James Polk was heartily celebrated among the men of Jefferson County who were present at Prospect Hill. As both a Southerner and a Democrat, Polk gave the planters hope that he would continue Andrew Jackson's legacy of supporting states' rights and slavery in the western states.

Texas was another hot topic of conversation. Congress had recently passed a joint resolution to annex Texas into the United States. The Texas Constitutional Convention still had to vote to accept the proposal. If they did so, the voters of the state had to approve it as well. Texas would enter the union as a slave state, so the support of annexation around the room was unanimous. Times were prosperous, the outlook seemed favorable and the brandy flowed freely until late in the afternoon.

The wealthy planters of Jefferson County saw themselves as modern day feudal lords; an aristocratic ruling class. Ingrained in them since childhood was the belief that they exclusively possessed the capability to provide a noble way of living for their families. Sheer contempt and disgust was felt towards anyone who sought to interfere with their way of life. Women and children were certainly owed protection and guidance, but were expected to be obedient in return. They were among the elite of society—and they were fully aware of that fact.

The conversation at Prospect Hill that afternoon over liquor and furls of smoke mirrored those views. Several planters complained about the laziness of their darkies and shared remedies for dealing with these "adult children" clearly lacking the intellect and work ethic to be useful without a strong hand overseeing their labors. If any of the planters in attendance differed with these views regarding the intellectual capacity of the black race, those views were suppressed. Certainly Isaac Wade, still feeling the indignity of his grandfather's shift towards overindulgence of the negroes on Prospect Hill, supported any negative portrayals expressed.

The state of Mississippi in every way possible supported these commonly held beliefs when its first constitution was written. Restrictive laws made it nearly impossible for free blacks to earn a living in the state. Only wealthy white landowners could vote. In fact in the original state constitution, unless one owned at least 600 acres of land, he was ineligible to become the Governor of the state. Similar requirements existed to earn a seat in the state legislature. Many of these requirements were removed regarding suffrage and political office in late 1832, but the laws regarding blacks in the state only became more restrictive with the passing of time.

In this way, the laws of the state made justifying the elite's views on the roles of both women and black citizens of Mississippi extremely easy. Since many white preachers of the day quoted scriptures to support these views, including the assumptions that the black race were descendants of the shamed biblical figure Ham, the plantation owners felt completely justified legally and morally in their views. By the time that the conversation began winding down, each man set out for his own domain feeling empowered, his chest puffed out in pride.

The ladies in attendance played their own roles to perfection all afternoon, observing the social graces with elegance and charm and dishing out compliments freely to the other ladies, even if sometimes lacking in sincerity. Dresses were admired and fawned over, and pleasantries exchanged. To the wives of the elite planters of the county, appearances were everything. To this end, Catherine Wade had spared no expense to prepare her home for the critical eyes of her contemporaries. She was the consummate Southern hostess and no one could have found fault with the lavish party she had organized to commemorate her wedding day.

It was with exhaustion and relief that Catherine bid

farewell to the throngs of guests heading to their carriages for the journey home. Both Adelaide and Mary had been invaluable to her, assisting with the guests. Food had been plentiful and beautifully presented. Grace, who'd come with Adelaide to help, and the other kitchen servants had certainly outdone themselves for the occasion. Catherine's heart swelled with pride and gratitude that her reputation as a superb hostess would be affirmed by the success of the afternoon. *People will be talking of this gathering for weeks. It was definitely a success.*

As the last couple departed, Adelaide congratulated her sister-in-law on a beautiful fête. With a laugh, both ladies agreed that it was an exhausting but delightful afternoon. Catherine sent word to the kitchen that dinner would need to be served late, as she was going upstairs to rest. Adelaide was going to stop by the nursery to check on the children before sending for Fannie to help remove her from her fitted dress so she could take a nap.

Mary attempted to blend into the woodwork in order to slip out undetected to meet Henry. She was eighteen now, and would not be required to go upstairs for a nap. If she was questioned, she could simply claim to have been reading a book while the other ladies of the house napped. For good measure, she went into the library and removed one from the shelf at random to carry with her.

She slipped out the back door, near the kitchen. Large trays of leftover food were being removed from the house and returned there to be packaged up and carried down to the slaves' quarters. Mary paused until there was a break in the foot traffic and walked the short distance to the carriage house. The doors were open and Mary could see William

Belton polishing the carriages. It seemed like there were activities going on everywhere she looked.

Mary decided to walk into the gardens and wait for William to finish his responsibilities with the carriages. She couldn't think of a good reason to explain her entrance into the carriage house now. Darkness would be upon them soon, and most of the slaves would be returning to their quarters shortly. *I won't have to wait long.* Mary sat down on a bench at the edge of the garden which offered her a view of the carriage house doors.

For the first time since removing it from the shelf, she looked at the book in her hands. She smiled when she read the cover. It was one of her favorite books, *Pride and Prejudice* by Jane Austen. She opened the book and flipped to one of her favorite scenes in which Mr. Darcy approaches Elizabeth at the piano. Mary admired Elizabeth's spirit and looked at her as a sort of role model. She continued to peruse portions of the book, looking up occasionally to see if the doors of the carriage house remained open.

At last, she noticed William coming out closing the doors behind him. Several small groups of slaves passed by, engaged in conversations. Mary greeted them as they passed, trying to appear casual as she flipped through the pages of her book. When she could see no other group approaching, she stood slowly and walked to the carriage house.

She opened the door slowly and peered inside. Even though the sun had not set outside, it was rather dark in the interior of the structure. *This really isn't proper, is it? What would Mother think of me sneaking into a darkened building to meet a young man?*

This was the internal dialogue that came to Mary in moments of doubt. At her age she should be finding a suitable match. Young Martha's mention of being in her wedding had been running through her mind on and off during the day. *My wedding.* The problem was that Mary couldn't imagine anyone she would rather marry than Henry. *But how can that ever happen?*

One of the large doors creaked softly as it slowly swung outward towards the yard. Almost instantly, Henry's silhouette appeared in the crack of light flooding in from the outside. Mary's heart soared at the sight of him, and the doubts she had been entertaining moments earlier evaporated like mist.

Once he had shut the door behind him, Henry lit his lantern and the carriage house filled with a soft glow.

"I just got here," Mary said breathlessly. "Your timing is just perfect." She felt her face flushing, as it so often did when she came into close proximity to him.

He smiled. "I know. I was watching from the trees. What were you reading?"

"You were watching me?" asked Mary. "That hardly seems fair. What if I had done something unladylike?"

"It would have given me something to tease you about mercilessly!" Henry laughed, but there was no malice in his expression and Mary laughed with him.

"I am beginning to wonder if you are a gentleman at all," retorted Mary playfully. "Honestly! Spying on a lady? It seems that I've caught you doing that very thing before actually. Remember?"

"I remember, but can you blame me?" Henry was still

smiling, but there was a twinge of melancholy in his expression that hadn't been there a moment before.

"Whatever is the matter? Can I blame you for what?" Mary was concerned now. *Have I said something that I shouldn't have?*

"Blame me for seizing any opportunity that I can find to see you. Since I am not able to call on you in your home officially, it leaves me to sneak around. It isn't honorable is it?"

Mary felt flustered now. *Is he having doubts about continuing to meet me?*

"But Henry, I understand why you have to do it this way. It has nothing to do with your honor. Surely you know that I understand that."

He moved even closer to her, both of them still standing just inside of the large double doors. He reached up and hung the lantern on a nail that was protruding from a large wooden beam. Mary stood frozen to her spot, watching him intently; unsure of what he was going to do.

He reached for her hands. She gently dropped her book to the ground and placed her hands into his. Looking deeply into her eyes, Henry said, "I want more for us than this Mary. I want to travel to your home, Bellevue. I would very much like to speak to your father and ask him for his permission to court you. I would explain that we met in Natchez, and attempt to answer his questions as truthfully as possible without inflaming his sensibilities."

Mary's heart began to pound furiously. "But what if Father refuses? It would be almost impossible to arrange meetings with you in that case." Her conscience troubled her as she added, "To continue to see each other after he had forbidden it would be an outright betrayal of his wishes. And of his trust."

Up to this point Mary had been quite successful in rationalizing what she had been doing. After all, she wasn't being expressly disobedient if her parents or aunt had not forbidden these meetings with Henry in the first place.

"Of course I won't speak to him without your blessing. But it is what I wish to do. You deserve better than what I can offer you here." He swept one hand around in a sweeping gesture. "Like this."

Mary didn't know what to say. She didn't doubt the love she felt for Henry. But she was terrified of disappointing her parents and Aunt Catherine. They were her family, after all. *Why does this have to be so complicated?*

Henry went on, "I need to ask you something very important. I don't expect for you to give me an answer right away, but please promise you will think about it."

Mary nodded earnestly.

"Even if your father refuses my request, would you agree to come to Pennsylvania with me? My sister's home has plenty of room. If I wrote her, I am sure that she would eagerly agree to have you stay with her until we could arrange to marry. I have some fences to mend with my own parents first. But they will come around once I am back."

Mary was stunned. She suddenly felt unsteady on her feet, and felt her grip on Henry's hands tightening. She didn't know what to think. *Pennsylvania? I don't know anything about life there. How would I be received by his family? Would they look down on me like my old teacher always did?*

This was not the marriage proposal Mary had pictured as

a young girl, with a handsome suitor bent down on one knee. Even so, the knowledge that Henry wanted to marry her was overwhelming and beautiful. But it was also extremely confusing; she found herself filled with conflicting emotions.

"Once my father gets over his displeasure with me, he will grow to love you dearly. I know that for a fact. What is there not to love about you?" His gaze was so tender and imploring that Mary's uncertainties began melting at once. "We have some time. I've told Reverend Butler that I want to stay as long as he needs me to. But after the slaves from Prospect Hill are gone, I will return home."

"I promise I will think about it, Henry. I do want to marry you. I want that more than anything. But I want to get married here with my family around me. I want them to approve. Otherwise, my joy will be dampened by their absence."

Henry nodded. "I understand. You love your family very much. If they do give their permission, would you come with me to Pennsylvania then?"

Mary thought about it. She knew nothing but Mississippi, and yet something in her yearned for the life that Henry had described to her. The tenets of slavery that she had come to question would not be an issue for them there, as it was a free state. She could always visit her family and they could visit her. As long as her marriage was sanctioned, she would always be welcomed here. After a few moments, she eagerly said, "Yes. If Father gives his permission, I will."

Henry's face lit up, and a broad grin spread across it. "Mary Girault, you have made me the happiest man around for miles."

Bolstered by her acceptance, he mustered up the courage to ask, "May I kiss you? I know it isn't proper and I know I haven't gotten permission from your father, but…"

Mary nodded and leaned towards Henry. Her heart was now pounding so furiously, she wondered if her ribcage could contain it for much longer. She felt Henry leaning closer, his hands releasing hers to reach around her back. He kissed her lightly and tenderly at first. When she didn't pull back from him, he kissed her more eagerly.

It was Henry who withdrew himself from the kiss after a few blissful moments had passed. He wanted to look at her beautiful face again. To reassure himself that he wasn't dreaming. *I've really just been kissing Mary. My beautiful Mary.*

"Do you know how much I love you, Miss Girault?" Henry asked her with a smile.

"If I didn't before, I certainly do now." Mary smiled and blushed, the kiss still fresh on her lips. She had imagined many times what it would be like to kiss Henry, but it had never lived up to the reality she had just experienced. *I could kiss him every minute of the rest of my life.*

Henry laughed. "I am glad. I want you to know that I love you. And I plan to show you every day."

Mary's heart was bursting with happiness. *If Father will see reason and make an effort with Henry, he will see how happy he makes me. Surely he will not object.* But the happiness began to falter as she considered the alternative reaction from her father. *Will I be able to stand up to him if he refuses to accept Henry? Will I be willing to leave everyone else that I love behind for Henry and a new life in*

Pennsylvania?

Henry seemed to sense her doubts as if having just gained private access to her thoughts. "I promise that I will do everything in my power to make this work. I want us to have the benefit of relationships with both of our families. I love you Mary."

"I love you too Henry."

He kissed her again briefly; this time barely brushing his lips against hers.

"I need to get back inside. I will be missed soon." She leaned down to pick up her book and walked to the door, stopping as her hand gripped the lever to look back at him. He was watching her intently.

"You never told me what you were reading." He hated to see their time together end. He would say anything to keep her around for just a few precious moments longer.

"*Pride and Prejudice*," she replied holding up the book for him to see.

"A romance," Henry said with a smile. "How appropriate."

Mary slipped through the doors and made her way carefully to the back porch door. Her heart was so full of happiness and her mind so full of potential scenarios that she barely took notice of Andrew passing down what appeared to be bundles of sticks and rags to another set of hands reaching up through the cellar doors.

April 15, 1845   Prospect Hill Plantation

Mary had been lying awake in bed for over an hour. Her mind was replaying her encounter with Henry from earlier in the evening. She knew it was after midnight now, as she had counted twelve full chimes heralded by the grand clock downstairs. *Mrs. Henry Charles Willcox.* She repeated the name several times, still having a hard time acknowledging that it was real. *He really wants to marry me. To take me back to his home and spend his life with me.* Her insides squirmed each time the image of their kiss floated across her mind.

During dinner that evening, Mary had been so distracted that Aunt Catherine had asked her brother-in-law, Dr. Wade, if Mary looked ill. "I am fine, Aunt Catherine. I should have rested with you and Adelaide earlier rather than reading. The party has left me quite tired."

"You should retire early tonight, then," Aunt Catherine replied. She was quite fond of Mary and felt an obligation to her sister to ensure that Mary remained well during her visit. She wanted to be sure that she returned to Bellevue appearing rested and healthy; not weary and bedraggled.

"I will, Aunt Catherine." Noting the concern in her aunt's expression, she added: "I am fine, really I am. I will be as good as new in the morning."

There were several guests present at dinner, helping to remove the focus from Mary. Adelaide had decided to stay the night, as well as Isaac's brother Dr. Walter Wade and his business partner Mr. Bailey. When the two visiting gentlemen were describing their business ventures to Uncle Isaac over coffee around the table, Mary had grown so bored that she began seeing various amusing shapes in the wallpaper pattern in the dining room. She had concluded that the swirls in the pattern appeared to be small ivory squirrels lined up around the room when she heard Aunt Catherine suggest that the gentlemen take their conversation into the library over some sherry.

Relieved, Mary left her coffee cup untouched and followed Catherine and Adelaide into the parlor where the sisters-in-law chatted amicably about the afternoon's festivities. Mary made her best efforts to smile, laugh, and appear as if she were following every word of the conversation. In reality, she was reliving her first kiss in vivid detail, complete with the sensation of butterflies fluttering inside of her.

The children had long since been fed and put to bed. Mary was glad that she had come back inside from her meeting with Henry in time to say goodnight to Martha and little Isaac. They had begged her to tell them a story, so she had snuggled them around her in the nursery and made up a tale about a pair of grasshoppers that lived in the trees at Prospect Hill. She smiled now as she remembered the tale:

Once upon a time there was a beautiful green grasshopper named Katydid. She lived on a particularly lovely dogwood flower in a tree right here outside the window. She shared her flower with her handsome husband, named Billydid. Katydid and Billydid loved the children that lived at Prospect Hill, and their cousins who visited them. They enjoyed watching Isaac, Dunbar, baby Catherine, Martha, Cabell, and Addie play in the nursery, on the porch, and especially when they played near the tree where they made their home. They kept a special watch over them. At night, they enjoyed singing songs to the children in the house. They always sang the loudest in the warm months when the windows were open at night to provide beautiful music for the children to fall asleep to. Even though they would rather eat leaves, sometimes they would swallow pesky mosquitoes whole if they looked as if they might bite one of the children.

During the daytime Katydid and Billydid had grand adventures. Sometimes they would ride on the back of a blue jay named George as he flew through the air over Prospect Hill. The grasshoppers enjoyed these flights tremendously as they had the best view of the house and the trees when they were soaring above them.

Sometimes William would let them ride on the back of the carriage when he drove into town so that Katydid and Billydid could enjoy all of the excitement going on there.

But one day in town, a bad-mannered little boy grabbed Billydid from his perch on the carriage and held him a little too tightly in his warm grubby hand. "Look what I got, Ma!" he shouted at the top of his lungs as he went running towards his mother.
"Put that disgusting thing down this instant!" she shouted to her son.
"Do I have to?" the boy whined.
"This instant, young man!" his mother insisted.

So the boy slung poor Billydid to the street roughly without a look back at him and followed along behind his mother. Katydid jumped down to help her husband move out of the way of the many pairs of shoes tromping down on either side of him. Quickly, she roused the stunned grasshopper who was still a bit dazed from his hard fall to the ground. They scampered out of the way just in time before they would have been squashed under a large boot.

But when they headed back for the carriage to return to Prospect Hill they saw to their horror that the carriage had pulled away. William had not noticed that his tiny passengers had run into trouble, as he was preoccupied navigating the carriage down the busy streets. So in our next story, we will have to see how the two little abandoned grasshoppers will find their way all the way back to their home at Prospect Hill.

When she stopped talking, the children, who'd been hanging on every word, sat bolt upright. "You can't stop there Mary!" Martha protested. "We need to hear how they get home!"

"I will tell you more of the story tomorrow Martha. It is bed time now." Mary smiled at her eager expression, glad that she had enjoyed the story. In truth Mary had no idea how the pair of adventurous insects were going to get back and needed some time to come up with a continuation.

"I like your story, Mary," Isaac assured her.

"Me too!" Dunbar and Cabell parroted.

Mary turned the children over to Fannie to put to bed after kissing each of their tiny foreheads.

She gave Martha an especially tight hug and whispered in her ear, "See you tomorrow, sweet Martha. I love you."

"I love you too, Mary. This much!" She held out her little arms as wide as she could possibly stretch them.

Now, hours later, Mary was still awake trying unsuccessfully to turn off her brain so that she could get a few hours of rest. The upcoming weeks held so much uncertainty for her. *When Henry speaks with Father, what will he say?*

Unlike Mary who was tossing and turning, Adelaide was sleeping so deeply that she had not even moved once since lying down on the bed several hours earlier. Adelaide's children were soundly sleeping as well: Martha and Cabell on the small bed which had been pulled out from under the large poster bed and Addie in the large wooden cradle brought in especially for her use.

Mary thought about getting up and walking down to the library for a book. But she dreaded the thought of being miserably tired the next day. Especially if it would be her last chance to visit with Martha for a while. And of course, she had to have the rest of the Katydid story worked out for the children. With her mind still churning through her plans for the following day, her hopes for the future she would share with Henry, and her thoughts regarding the children's story, darkness gradually overtook Mary's consciousness.

***

Mary was on a pond covered with lily pads and surrounded by flowering trees. The sky was perfectly beautiful with wisps of white clouds scattered throughout the crisp azure canopy. She was seated on the bench at the bow of a slender mahogany row boat; a parasol held in her left hand to ward off the rays of the sun. Facing the center of the boat, she was trying to make out the face of the man rowing the boat. The scene was idyllic and romantic, so surely the man must be her beau. Yet she couldn't make out the details of his face. *He seems so familiar to me somehow. Who could it be?*

But before it was possible to discern the identity of the rower, Martha appeared in the center of the rowboat; directly between herself and the mystery gentleman. "Mary, I can't swim. What if I fall in?"

"I will save you if you fall in, Martha. But that won't happen. This boat is very sturdy. You are safe here with me. I promise."

Suddenly Martha jumped up to run into Mary's arms. The sudden movement upset the stability of the boat and they began to rock back and forth violently. Martha's little arms flew out to the sides in a desperate attempt to balance herself.

"Mary, I'm falling. Help me!"

Mary's heart pounded as she reached out to grab Martha, but she couldn't reach her. She watched in horror as Martha hit the water flailing about and screaming.

Mary turned to the faceless rower. "Do something!" she screamed. "Help us!" But he did not respond. Mary began to doubt he even existed.

Looking back to Martha, Mary was suddenly gripped with fear as the little girl had begun coughing and sputtering as water entered her mouth. "Help me Mary!"

Mary stood, preparing to jump into the pond to save her precious Martha. But strong hands were gripping her. "Let me go! I have to save her!" She fought off the hands desperately, thrashing back and forth trying to shake them off, but they were too strong.

"Mary! Mary, wake up. The house is on fire."

Mary Girault opened her eyes. Panic filled her immediately. She wasn't on a boat in a pond. She was in the familiar bedroom at Prospect Hill where she had spent many nights before. And Martha was safely asleep in her bed, wasn't she? But then why was Dr. Wade shouting at her?

"Mary, did you understand me? The house is on fire. We

only have minutes to get out. Wake Adelaide. The two of you need to bring down her children. I will make sure everyone else is up. Hurry!"

"I understand." Mary sat bolt upright, as wide awake as if she had slept the full night. She watched the back of Dr. Wade running out of their room and onto the next one, fulfilling his intentions of rousing everyone in the house.

She began shaking Adelaide. Gently at first, but then quite roughly when there was no immediate response. When Adelaide opened her eyes, Mary shouted, "Adelaide. Wake up. We have to get the children downstairs right now. There is a fire!"

Adelaide slowly sat up. "A fire?" Her eyes were somewhat unfocused, yet wide open.

She sounded groggy, which Mary attributed to just having been roused from a deep sleep.

"I can carry Cabell and Addie. Since Martha can walk, you can bring her down. Just tell her to follow close behind you." Mary was already scrambling to gather the younger two children and realized that Adelaide was still sitting on the edge of the bed.

"Adelaide!" Mary shouted even more loudly. "You have to wake up Martha and bring her down. Do you understand? I have Cabell and Addie. You get Martha!"

"Get Martha," replied Adelaide as she stood beside the bed. "Yes, get Martha," she repeated to herself walking slowly towards the child's bed.

Mary, with Cabell over her left shoulder, leaned to scoop Addie from the cradle. She struggled a bit as the boy was beginning to slide from his position on her shoulder. After a moment, she had a decent grip on both children and felt she could at least manage long enough to get down the stairs and through the front doors. Something she planned to do with as much speed as she could manage.

She dashed for the doorway, and the smell of smoke hit her senses with a sudden shock. The air in the hallway was filling with the thick smoke, pungent and blinding. Mary turned back to see that Adelaide was standing over Martha's sleeping figure. "Bring her down, Adelaide. We must go now." When she got no response, she said once again, "Adelaide, do you have Martha?"

Adelaide turned to face Mary and slowly nodded at her, still appearing somewhat stupefied.

From Mary's vantage point in the doorway, Mary could not see past Adelaide's form to notice Martha's body still curled into a fetal position in the center of the bed; her favorite way to sleep since infancy. All Mary could see was what appeared to be an empty bed with its rumpled sheets and quilted coverings.

Mary turned her attention back to the hallway. She could just make out the top of the staircase, and felt she could navigate to it safely. Adelaide had come to stand so closely behind her that Mary could feel warm breath on the back of her neck. Not sparing the second it would take to glance back once more into the room, Mary began walking briskly to the staircase. *We still have time, but we have to keep moving. I need to stay calm.*

Adelaide followed silently behind her. A couple of times during their descent down the stairs and out onto the porch, Mary had been forced to urge Adelaide forward. This perplexed Mary greatly. Why would Adelaide not feel the same innate desperation to get to safety that she was feeling? The two children she was carrying seemed to grow heavier with each passing minute and the smoke was causing Mary to feel as if she were suffocating. The primal urge she felt to escape the burning home was unlike anything she had ever experienced.

Her initial exhilaration at seeing Uncle Isaac at the foot of the stairs didn't last long, as he was clearly not fully coherent either. He did manage to open the front doors for her, necessitated by the heavy burden she was struggling to carry. But even that simple task, normally quite effortless, seemed to be difficult for her uncle to manage. *Maybe the smoke has addled his senses?*

It was with tremendous relief that Mary finally reached the familiar broad covered porch and eagerly gulped the fresh night air. Her relief almost immediately turned to terror and shock however, at the sight of Uncle Esau with his axe drawn ready to swing down on her at any moment. *What on Earth? He looks positively murderous. If I scream, I fear he will swing that axe!*

Thinking as quickly as she could, Mary thanked him for coming to their rescue. *Hopefully if I disarm him with kindness, he will snap out of this state he is in. What is going on here?!* She forced herself to smile at the enormous man and looked him directly in the eyes as she spoke. In reality she had always liked Uncle Esau and greatly admired his craftsmanship. To see him looking at her with venom in his expression sent a cold shiver through her entire body. *Could this still be just a dream?*

Her words seemed to reach Esau somehow, even as lame as they had sounded to Mary as she spoke them. He glanced around nervously; whatever his initial plan had been was obviously disrupted. The uncertainty in his expression during his moments of hesitation had given Mary a small flicker of hope; his steely determination was clearly faltering.

When he lumbered off into the darkness, Mary felt her entire body shaking. But somehow, even now Adelaide did not seem to realize the danger they were in. She was acting as if they had all the time in the world to leisurely stroll out into the grass where they would finally be safe.

And then in one horrifying moment just before the rest of the family came spilling out onto the porch, Mary had realized that Martha was not with her mother. After that instant of realization the rest of the night was experienced by Mary in a fog-like state.

She followed Dr. Wade's instructions and was fully aware of everything happening around her. But nothing seemed real. Nothing seemed possible. The thought of having lost Martha to the flames was too painful to comprehend. Throughout the night, as her senses were bombarded with Adelaide's cries and images of an inferno where a grand home once stood, the same plea kept running through Mary's mind. *Please, God, let me still be dreaming.*

April 15, 1845   Port Gibson

Bam, bam, bam! Zebulon Butler raised his head off his pillow and looked around his bedroom. Pale light was just starting to filter in through the cracks in his curtains. *Bam, bam, bam!* He realized that the pounding noises had not been a part of some dream, and rose to sit on the edge of his bed groggily. *Bam, bam, bam, bam!* The urgency of the pounding caused him to spring out of bed headed in the direction of the sound. As he approached the door of his home, he could hear a man's voice calling his name.

"I'm coming!" he yelled in reply, hoping to silence the unknown caller from any continued yelling and pounding at this early hour. His housekeeper had not yet arrived for her daily duties.

He opened the door moments later to the flushed and anxious face of James Parker. Parker, a neighbor of Isaac Ross Wade at Prospect Hill, had been invaluable in providing him with information regarding the happenings around the plantation. It was immediately clear from Parker's countenance that something was terribly wrong.

Butler took a step back from the doorway. "Come in, come in. Tell me what has you so troubled this morning." He kept his voice calm and reassuring, reminding himself that one could always think better when in control of one's emotions.

Parker shook his head vehemently. His breathing was ragged and heavy. "I can't this morning, minister. I'm needed back as soon as I can get there. So much to be done. But I felt you would want to know right away, so I came at first light."

Parker looked at him expectantly, causing Zebulon Butler to wonder if Mr. Parker realized that he hadn't actually told him the reason he had awoken him yet. After a brief moment, he prompted him, "What exactly has happened?"

"Oh, I'm sorry. This situation has me rattled, I'm afraid." He took a deep breath before continuing, "Prospect Hill's been burned to the ground. The fire started in the cellar under the main staircase."

Parker looked at the Reverend, his face ashen. "There is talk already going around that it was the slaves that burned the house. That they got tired of waiting and took matters into their own hands."

Butler felt as if he were going to be sick. All of the doubts he had been attempting to push from his mind regarding how the slaves might have interpreted Henry's comments came rushing back into the forefront. "They are blaming the slaves?" he asked weakly. Gone was the commanding voice that carried from the pulpit with ease. Gone was the attempt to keep complete control over his emotions.

Parker nodded vigorously. "Blaming the slaves and anyone they think may have helped them."

"Surely no outside forces in this area helped them. If it even *was* them at all." Again Butler's voice was thin; betraying his conscience. Then without warning, absolute fear for the slaves seized him. "What will they do to the slaves if they suspect them guilty of arson?" He began to envision whippings and interrogations that made his stomach clench.

"It's worse than that, I'm afraid," Parker replied. "It isn't just a matter of arson—as if that wasn't bad enough. There was a death. Wade's little niece Martha Richardson."

"Oh dear Lord, that is terrible. Was anyone else hurt?" The fear was quickly becoming panic in spite of his best efforts to control it.

Parker's expression answered before he had even formed his response. "Wade's sister, Mrs. Richardson was badly burned. It isn't known if she will survive. Several slaves ran into the house to try and save the little girl, and were also burned. The scene over there is one of sheer devastation. The house is a complete loss."

Before the preacher could ask anything more, Parker had already taken a step back towards his horse. "I really do have to get straight back. All the planters in the area are meeting to assist in salvaging anything that can be saved. Our wives and servants are boxing up anything from our own houses that can be of use to the Wades. They'll be staying over at Oak Hill with Mr. Wade's mother for now."

"Yes, of course you need to help then," Butler managed.

"It's more than that. When the talk gets back to what should be done with the slaves suspected of participating in the plot, I feel that I need to be there. I don't know how much good my one voice will do, but my wish is for things to be handled fairly." He shook his head slowly back and forth. "A mob mentality can be a terrifying thing to witness. Sometimes all it takes is one lone voice to bring back some reason. Pray I can help."

Butler cleared his throat. "Thank you for riding over to tell me the news. I will be praying for everyone involved. It is a terrible tragedy."

Parker nodded and swiftly took his leave. Zebulon Butler stood in the doorway watching the bearer of the news of this calamity grow smaller and smaller into the distance. He attempted to pull together his thoughts rationally. *Don't let emotion get the better of you. Just think about what needs to be done now to achieve the best outcome possible for everyone involved.*

He knew that Henry would want to be informed right away, and so he dressed quickly. When he arrived at Henry's room in the boarding house, he found that the young man was already awake and dressed. It seemed as if he had interrupted him in the midst of writing a letter. He found his friend to be in good spirits, filled with a sense of purpose.

Henry invited him in, and after depositing his hat and coat, Butler delivered the news to him with the few details that he had at his disposal. He recounted the facts, exactly as they had been delivered to him by Mr. Parker.

Henry's head dropped. Butler had been sure to tell him straight away that Mary was uninjured in the fire, but the news of Martha succumbing to the fire seemed to devastate him. "I saw her once playing with Mary," he croaked.

"Mary loved her so deeply. She'll be overcome with grief."

Henry looked up at Butler, his face stricken. "I have got to see her."

Butler was concerned. "I know that you are concerned for Mary. I understand that. But this is not the time to throw caution to the wind. In fact, it is a time when we need to exercise extreme caution. Emotions are running dangerously high at Prospect Hill in the aftermath of the fire."

Henry's perplexed expression caused Butler to elaborate. "Look Henry, I didn't say anything to you before because I'd convinced myself that there was nothing to it. But now in light of what happened in the early hours of this morning, it seems there might have been something to it after all."

"What?" asked Henry. He was beginning to get a little concerned by the graveness of Reverend Butler's tone.

"Do you recall a conversation we had recently in which you recounted an odd question that Levi had asked you? It was in regards to your comments concerning Mr. Wade. More specifically, getting rid of him."

A horrible realization washed over Henry. He looked aghast at Butler. "Are you saying that Levi and the others thought that I was advising them to get rid of Mr. Wade by murdering him? By burning his house down in the night?"

"It is something I fear, yes. But let's not get ahead of ourselves completely. As of right now, we do not know with anything close to certainty that the slaves were even responsible for the fire. Mr. Parker said that there is talk of it. Hopefully a natural cause can be proven and any doubt that has been cast on the slaves will be lifted."

"But what if the fire is proven to be arson? And the slaves are proven to be guilty of starting the fire?"

Butler replied bitterly, "It won't be a matter of proof, I'm afraid. If sentiment is strong enough that the slaves are responsible for the death of that girl, and the serious injury to Mrs. Richardson…" his voice trailed off.

Henry was truly alarmed now. Sure he had heard accounts of lynching and whipping slaves in his reading of abolitionist materials. But the sudden realization that the people he had come to know and care for were at risk of such atrocities caused a panic to rise in his chest.

"Reverend Butler, you have to continue. What do you fear may happen?"

"Vigilante justice," he replied with a short, caustic laugh. "As if one can apply the term *justice* to such a barbaric concept. The planters will round up any slaves they feel are guilty and deal with them swiftly. More likely they'll have their overseers handle it."

"We have to do something!" Henry was growing agitated now. "We can't just stay here waiting to hear news that Edmond, Wade, Levi, Andrew, Esau and the others were hanged because rumors reached the wrong ears that they've been talking to us. How could we ever live with ourselves if that happened?"

Henry began pacing back and forth out of desperation to do something. Anything. "Especially," he continued, "If they acted on my words." He grabbed the sides of his hair with his fists. "This is all my fault." His looked almost frantic with grief and despair.

Zebulon Butler felt completely impotent. There was nothing within his power that could help either the slaves or

Henry right now.

"Henry, listen to me," he urged. "You have to calm down. Think about our options. I cannot possibly turn up at the ruins of Prospect Hill at this moment. I would be most unwelcome there. Questions would be asked."

A strangled sound came from Henry's throat. He continued pacing back and forth. Butler went on, "And what possible explanation could you offer for showing up yourself?"

Henry offered no answer to his friend's question.

"Mr. Parker is there right now, Henry. He specifically wants to be there in an attempt to be a voice of reason and justice. I believe that he will do whatever is in his power to help the Prospect Hill slaves. If we made the rash decision to go there, we would make the situation worse for them. Trust me. I have lived here much longer than you. I understand the way the system works."

Henry felt truly anguished. He would have given anything he possessed to go back in time and take back his thoughtless comments made out of frustration. *How could I have said something so imprudent, so rash? Comments that could so easily be misinterpreted.*

He would have to take Reverend Butler's advice for now. But he knew that he would not be able to restrain himself for long from seeing Mary. Butler had mentioned the family being at Oak Hill. Whether Mary was still with them, or heading back to Bellevue he didn't know. *Surely they will have a funeral service for Martha. Mary will stay long enough for that, I am sure of it.*

He resolved to see Mary within the next several days no matter what it took. *I owe her an explanation. I have to tell her what I have done.* Fear gripped his heart at the thought of her response to his confession. *I will have to pray that she can find it within herself to forgive me.*

***

Mary had known grief before. She had grieved the loss of her younger siblings. She had grieved family, friends, and relatives. Yellow fever alone had claimed the lives of many people that Mary had loved. But she had never experienced anything as gut wrenching as the morning after the fire at Prospect Hill. It was easy to identify a disease as the enemy—something to despise and fight against. But the loss of Martha just seemed so senseless, so tragic. Who was the enemy? Who was there to fight against?

She longed to be comforted and reassured. She longed to be able to talk about how much it hurt. But Catherine was consumed with her duties to Adelaide, who was severely burned, as well as acknowledging the countless neighbors streaming into Oak Hill. They came to offer their condolences, bring food, and donations of clothing for the family with assurances of, "Anything we can do, please don't hesitate to call on us for assistance." There was no way that Mary could see to interrupt her duties to ask for comfort and companionship. She had barely seen her aunt since arriving at Oak Hill.

Mary tried to keep busy by spending time with the children, who were left dazed and confused by what had happened. They didn't understand that Martha had died in the fire, although they understood something was wrong as Isaac had asked several times where she was. Soon, she found that being with the surviving children was terribly painful as well. When Isaac asked her to finish the story about Katydid and Billydid, Mary could not fight the tears that began streaming down her face. She had managed to say, "We need to wait for Martha to return before we can finish the story, Isaac. She would be sad if we went on without her." Immediately she had excused herself from the room to regain her composure.

The men were back at Prospect Hill now that there was daylight, sorting through the remains of the house with the help of some neighbors. Mary had overheard Catherine telling Isaac that she didn't dare get her hopes up that anything would be found that would be of any use. By the time the family had piled into carriages and made the two mile journey to Oak Hill during the night, it was obvious to them all that the house was completely destroyed. As they had driven away, all eyes had been fixed on the smoldering ruins that had once been their home.

Mary envied the men having something useful to do—a purpose. Something to distract them, if only momentarily from the agony of thinking about Martha. *Did she wake up terrified, desperately trying to escape? Did she simply die in her sleep, overtaken by smoke?* They would never know, but Mary promised that she would force herself to believe the latter. Thinking of Martha dying a horrific death was more than she could bear. Even more dreadful than witnessing the chills, cries of pain, yellowing eyes and frequent vomiting of those suffering from yellow fever.

Mary desperately wanted to see Henry. She needed someone to hold her and allow her to cry. To cry until it was impossible to shed another tear. She needed to talk to him. To tell him about Esau with the axe and the strange way that the others were acting during the fire. She needed to tell him about poor little Martha. Her precious girl, who had enchanted and delighted her since the first time she had laid eyes on her. She wanted to explain to him that she still wanted him to speak with her father, but it would be best to wait and allow the family to recover from this shock. There was so much she needed to say. *I need you, Henry. Please come to me. Find a way.*

Reverend J. R. Hutchinson from the Presbyterian Church in Rodney had been summoned to officiate at the funeral services for Martha. She would be laid to rest in the family cemetery at Prospect Hill, although Mary realized with a shudder that there would likely not be anything left of Martha to bury. But she would have a headstone placed bearing her name and the dates of her birth and death. *So little time to experience life. Just like my little brothers and sisters.*

The aching void that Mary felt seemed impossible to fill. She wanted to rage and scream, maybe even hit something. She cried when she found a private place to do so at Oak Hill. For the first time since leaving Bellevue, Mary yearned for her mother. She desperately wanted to feel her mother's arms wrapped tightly around her, shushing her as she cried and promising that it was going to be all right. In the course of one day, she had gone from feeling like a grown lady on the brink of beginning her own life as a married woman, to a small, terrified, and helpless child.

Mary was standing at a window in the beautiful parlor of Oak Hill. The floor-to-ceiling paper depicting outdoor scenes gave the appearance of being outside in nature. She had heard Uncle Isaac's mother Jane explaining to Mr. Bailey that the wallpaper and furnishings had come from Pennsylvania in 1830. At the moment she heard this conversation, Mary couldn't believe that anyone could possibly be interested in room décor in the midst of such a terrible time. But now she realized that sometimes talking about trivial matters is far easier than discussing things as painful as the death of a young child.

In addition to mindless chatter, she was privy to some of the more serious conversations going on in the aftermath of the fire. She and Walter Wade were the only adults in the home that were not in a groggy state at the time of the fire. After some discussion, it was determined that they were the only two who'd not consumed the coffee served after dinner. Mary was questioned about Esau's actions, which she recounted as accurately as possible. Eventually an outline of a slave plot to burn the house was conceived and speculated about for hours.

Lost in her thoughts, she didn't hear Catherine approaching, causing her to jump in surprise when her aunt laid her hand upon her shoulder.

"Oh, Aunt Catherine! Gracious, you startled me."

Her aunt's expression conveyed her concern at the state of Mary's nerves. "Forgive me please. I didn't mean to sneak up behind you. I came to check on you Mary. I've been so terribly preoccupied with…well, with everything going on here. Poor Adelaide." She closed her eyes momentarily and slowly shook her head briefly.

Then refocusing her gaze on Mary, she simply stated, "Well anyway, I wanted to make sure that you were all right. At least, as well as can be expected after something like this."

"I am fine, Aunt Catherine," Mary lied. She lowered her gaze, unable to face her aunt's concerned, but caring appearance. *I am nothing close to fine. But you have more important things to tend to than me.*

Catherine smiled weakly at her; seeing through the feeble but well meaning attempt at bravado. "You have been so brave and so strong, Mary. If Adelaide survives, I know that she will feel eternal gratitude to you for saving Cabell and Addie from almost certain death."

Mary felt miserable. *But I didn't save Martha. I should have made sure she was with us. I will never forgive myself.*

Catherine's eyes filled with tears. "I know what you are thinking, Mary Elizabeth Girault, and I want you to stop this instant." Her voice was firm but loving.

Does Catherine actually know what I was thinking, or is she imagining something completely different?

Catherine continued in a deliberate and composed tone. "None of us could have ever carried all three of the children down the stairs. Not even Isaac or Walter. You acted so bravely and you remained calm. I couldn't possibly be any more proud of you."

The flood gates that had been holding back Mary's tears were broken open by Catherine's words of kindness. Catherine opened her arms to her niece, who buried her face in her bosom and cried like a child—sobbing and choking, then sobbing some more. Catherine stroked Mary's hair and shushed her the way she had been longing for ever since they had arrived at Oak Hill. When Mary was finished, Catherine gently pushed her back so that she could look into her eyes.

"I want you to promise me that you will never allow yourself to feel any guilt about what happened to Martha. Her death was a senseless tragedy. I fear that Adelaide will not be able to do what I am asking of you. As a mother, I understand too well that she will never forgive herself. But Mary, you did everything you possibly could have done. Not one iota of blame belongs with you. Do you understand?"

Mary nodded. "I just loved her so. I will miss her terribly. It is so easy now to look back and think that I should have made sure that Martha was with Adelaide. But at the time, with the smoke and desperation to get out..." More sobbing. More comforting. It went on like this for the better part of an hour before the tears were spent and the terrible raw gut wrenching pain in Mary's chest had at least diminished to a dull gnawing ache.

"I have an idea," Catherine said following a lengthy silence. Catherine had led Mary by the hand to the sofa, as exhaustion made standing for long periods increasing difficult as the day progressed.

"You can meet with Reverend Hutchinson when he arrives from Rodney. You knew Martha as well as anyone. Adelaide's husband has been sent for, but I don't know if he will arrive before the minister has taken his leave. I think Martha would have wanted you to be the one to plan her service. I think you surely must know how she felt about you, Mary."

The thought of being the one in charge of conveying the family's wishes to the Reverend was slightly intimidating, but the opportunity to feel useful—to have a purpose again—was exactly what she needed.

"Thank you, Aunt Catherine. I would be honored to speak with Reverend Hutchison when he arrives. I will start writing down some thoughts on what would be the most appropriate Scriptures and hymns."

She embraced her aunt for a long moment before setting out with a newfound sense of purpose.

April 16, 1845   Prospect Hill Slave's Quarters

The general mood in the quarters the day following the fire was a mixture of sheer terror and complete shock. The vast majority of the slaves had known nothing of the plot to burn the house. Within just a few hours of the Wade family's departure for Oak Hill, word had spread to every resident of the quarters that the fire was not an accident.

Some of the older slaves had participated in the process of constructing the grand home—the complete destruction of which left them with a profound sense of loss. In addition, many of the slaves who spent time in and around the main house knew Martha in varying degrees. Even though Mr. Wade was not loved among the slaves at Prospect Hill, the death of his niece brought great sadness to them.

It didn't take long for the names of those responsible for the fire to reach the ears of the workforce at Prospect Hill. The Belton brothers, Esau, Andrew, Gilbert, and Old Yeary had all disappeared. Rumors were flying in regards to their whereabouts. Word trickled through the quarters in whispers that Edmond Belton had definitely been making his way to the ferry crossing at Rodney into Louisiana. Wade Belton was reportedly headed to Copiah County to the northeast. Andrew and Gilbert were said to be aiming for Natchez, which had a larger free black population than any other town in the area, making it easier to blend in unnoticed. No one even had an inkling of Esau's whereabouts, nor those of Old Yeary. Some speculated they might be traveling together, but no one knew for sure.

Barely after dawn on the day of the fire, Peter Stampley and a few of the other overseers from the area were in the slaves' quarters pounding on doors and demanding answers. Many slaves were interrogated—many frantic questions lobbed at them.

"Anyone gone missing? You better answer me!" Frantic slaves began attempting to account for everyone, which was made difficult by the number from their community who were still up near the house. It took the better part of an hour, with several slaves being summoned to round up and return anyone not in the quarters, to obtain a general accounting of the slave population.

Stampley, mounted on a horse, made a note of the missing slaves and began shouting out descriptions to his cohorts. Several men rode off with intentions of splitting up to cover more territory. The fugitives had already gotten at least a five-hour head start. The overseer of Prospect Hill knew they could have crossed the river by now. He cringed at the realization, knowing that his only hope of redemption for not successfully sniffing out and thwarting this plot would be his ability to swiftly bring the culprits to justice.

Time was of the essence in rounding up the runaways, but Stampley also wanted to interrogate the remaining slaves privately in case any guilty parties had remained behind. After assuring himself that an adequate search party had been dispatched, he began questioning the slaves he felt to be loyal to him. His mind was reeling from the news that two of the Belton boys had run off—he had never seen that coming. *Both of them boys kept their noses to the ground, and never caused no trouble. And it look like they might of done planned the whole thing.*

He wasn't able to get much information of any use from the slaves. They were scared, and not feeling inclined to talk much. He had left each of them with instructions to come to him at once with any information that could be useful in capturing the guilty parties. *I can't blame 'em for being scared. There's going to be some hangin's for this.*

After getting what information he could, Stampley headed up to the remains of the big house where Wade and some other local planters were still sifting through debris. He shook his head in disbelief at the sight. Several of the first floor fireplaces remained somewhat intact, although chunks of brick were broken off by the collapse of the top floors. They were the only vertical structures remaining of the once impressive home.

Isaac Wade looked up at the sound of his overseer's approach. He stood up and rubbed his lower back which had begun aching from pushing aside large pieces of the home's foundation to search for anything salvageable. Stampley swung down off his horse and walked towards Wade.

"What did you find out?" Wade had an air of mild exasperation in his tone which created in Stampley a desperation to appear useful and efficient.

"We were able to account for the missing ones, sir. I wrote their names down here. Some of 'em come as a surprise." He handed his boss the list of the missing slaves he had made earlier. "We got men trackin' 'em down now. I think we'll get 'em back before long."

Wade took a moment to survey the names on the list and let out a low whistle. He too was astonished at some of the men listed. "Needless to say, I want to see justice served. We cannot allow them to get away with…" he swept his hand to indicate the ruins surrounding him, "…this."

"No sir. I'll do what I can to bring 'em to justice. You got my word on it."

"Thank you, Stampley."

Brusquely, Wade turned from the overseer and returned to his sifting. "I might need a hand moving this one," he indicated to the man standing closest to him as he attempted to push a large piece of the home's foundation aside.

Stampley easily recognized the dismissal. Though irritated by Wade's arrogance, he recovered well. He returned to his horse and led her to the stables. There was still a crop to be planted, still a full day's work to be done around the place. He vowed this would be a regular work day at Prospect Hill.

He realized the cast iron bells had not rung yet this morning. It was getting late. Then, with a shock of realization he understood: Gilbert had been his foreman, but now he was running for his life. One of Gilbert's responsibilities had been to start the work day each morning. *Damn!* He shook his head again. *How could they have pulled this off without me hearin' nothin'.* He rang the bells himself. Soon there was a flurry of activity audible in the quarters. *Last thing we need is a bunch of talkin' goin' on round here today and little to no workin'.* Once he got the day's labor underway, he planned to ride out in search of the missing slaves himself.

Before long he was riding out towards Rodney. He figured they would be making their way to the nearest ferry crossing out of Mississippi. *That's what I'd do if I was runnin'.* When he got to Rodney, he was a bit taken aback that the news of the fire was already spreading through the town. In fact, when he questioned the man operating the ferry crossing, he was told that he hadn't been the first man who'd questioned him about negroes crossing. He confirmed that he had taken a colored man across before dawn, insisting that the man had the proper papers with him.

He went to his ledger and brought it to Stampley for his inspection. "Like I told the other feller this mornin'. The darky had a written letter. Looked like nice writin' too. Said he had an errand for his master to do and needed to git across t' river."

"Did the letter say what the errand was?" Stampley asked.

The operator looked sheepish, a bit of color rising to his cheeks. "Best I could tell, it just said an errand. I ain't too good at that fancy kind of writin'."

"Did the men who were here before me today cross the river to look for this fugitive?" Stampley was hopeful for a moment. *Maybe they could still catch up to him.*

The man shook his head. "Nope. Offered to take 'em

across. But they rode back attaway." He gestured to the main road out of town. Then raising an eyebrow, he added. "This 'bout that fire at the Wade place ain't it?"

Stampley nodded. "'Fraid so." He shook his head solemnly. "Bad business. Little girl dead." Before leaving he made sure to write down the name recorded for the passenger. *Ed Benton. Smart son of a gun. Only changed one letter.*

He asked some questions around Rodney, but as it was pre-dawn hours when Belton came through, he gained no useful information. About half way back to Prospect Hill, he heard a commotion just off the road. There were several voices making their way to the main road. It sounded like someone yelled, "Freeze, boy!"

He rode into the woods to check it out. When he was close enough to make out the scene, he found Esau lying face down on the ground with two drawn pistols aimed at his head.

"Stampley, get over here! We think we got one."

"He's one of ours, all right." Stampley opened his saddlebag and retrieved a coarse rope, unwrapping it as he walked towards the three men; two upright and one face down in the dirt.

"You going to string him up right here?" sneered Jack Miller, one of the overseers at the nearby Hunt Family Plantation.

Stampley shook his head. "Nope. Gonna drag him back closer to Prospect Hill. Others are gonna see what happens when you burn down a house and kill a little helpless girl."

He looked with contempt at Esau. "Git on your knees, boy."

Esau didn't move. Stampley kicked him in the ribs. "I said git on your knees. You got two guns aimed at your face. I suggest you do it."

Slowly Esau pushed himself up off the ground and settled to his knees. Stampley wrapped the rope around his chest, binding his arms. "Stand up."

Esau rose to his feet, a bit unsteady from the jerking of the rope around his middle. "I'm gonna tie this here rope to my saddle. If you keep up, you won't be eatin' dirt all the way back."

"You want us to come with you 'n keep a gun aimed at him?" asked Miller.

"I'll git him on back. You keep lookin' for the others while we got this good daylight."

The men nodded, mounted their horses and rode away obviously pleased with their success in capturing the fugitive slave. They knew that word of this would get back to their bosses, which would give them bragging rights—and hopefully an increase in pay, or at least respect.

When Stampley got back to Prospect Hill, Esau was still on his feet—but barely. He was clearly exhausted—and just as clearly terrified. He had good reason to be. According to Mary Girault, Esau was found standing just outside of the front doors of her uncle's home during the fire. He had made no effort to assist anyone to safety. Instead, he stood with a raised axe as if stationed there to dispatch with anyone who might escape.

The overseer tied Esau securely to a large wooden support post in the stable before tying up his horse. He looked with contempt at his captive. "Don't even think about escapin' boy. It wouldn't hurt me none to shoot you in the back."

Esau didn't offer a response, but he defiantly met the man's gaze refusing to back down. *If I gonna die, then I gonna die with some pride.*

Stampley sneered, "You better watch yourself, boy."

Without a backwards glance, Stampley left to find Mr. Wade. He knew that he would want to interrogate Esau to find out the details of the plot; especially who else in the quarters, or even possibly the main house, was guilty of conspiracy. Since Dr. Wade had concluded that the coffee after dinner had been drugged with a sleep-inducing herb, the kitchen staff were all suspect at this point.

As he approached the pile of rubble and ash which had once been the main house, he saw no signs of his employer. The day was growing quite warm, so he assumed they had returned to Oak Hill to ride out the heat of the day. *Must be nice to be so rich you can just quit workin' when it git hot.* Casting a glance out over the distant fields, he saw the slaves working; preparing the ground for the next crop of cotton. It would be planted within the week. It was clear that he would need to appoint a new foreman to take over for Gilbert. *But which one of 'em can I trust?*

Peter Stampley felt deflated, his confidence shaken by the perceived betrayal of the slaves. Ironically, he never once attempted to understand the reasons behind their desperate actions. Never did he envision what it would be like to wait nine years for a freedom that was just out of reach—so close one could almost taste it, and yet steadfastly unobtainable. What he did see was the negative light it cast upon his job performance. He knew the other overseers in the county were talking amongst themselves about the signs he surely must have missed.

He grimaced at the thought of what lay ahead. In his job as overseer at Prospect Hill, he had never been required to use an excessively heavy hand with the slaves. Captain Ross had earned their respect and loyalty. Even though he knew the feelings did not carry over to Mr. Wade, the slaves had done as they were told for the most part. He had always been secretly grateful that he had not needed to resort to whippings or other sorts of brutal physical punishment up until now; he honestly didn't have the stomach for it, although he would have never admitted that to anyone. He had kicked Esau in the woods out of anger, and hated the way it made him feel afterwards.

There was no way he could see to avoid the ugly truth of what was going to happen to the slaves that were responsible for burning the house. He had yet to receive instructions from Mr. Wade regarding Esau and the others responsible for the fire. However, it wasn't hard to deduce that an example was going to be made of all of the slaves they managed to capture. Graphic images flashed across his mind, before he physically shook his head in an attempt to rid himself of them. *You brought this on yourselves. There ain't no help for you now.*

April 18, 1845   Ross Family Cemetery, Prospect Hill

Mary fixed her gaze on a beetle burrowing under some pine straw near her feet. It was too painful to watch the tiny casket being lowered into the freshly dug grave. Watching the insect gave her eyes a place to focus that didn't cause her heart to ache. The day was overcast and gloomy, perfectly mirroring her internal forecast. She could hear the sound made by the leaves in the surrounding trees as the breeze stirred them, and she was vaguely aware of the same breeze against her tear streaked cheeks. And yet, her senses felt strangely dulled.

The colossal monument bearing the Ross name towered over the small family cemetery where Martha was being laid to rest. *What do you think of all of this, Captain Ross? It must make you very sad, indeed. Your family fighting, the house burning to ashes, and poor sweet Martha.* Mary could almost picture him coming to life—a walking, talking version of his portrait. She had a vision of him looming over the crowd, solemnly reflecting on his legacy at Prospect Hill. Surely when he was approaching his own death, this is not what he expected, not what he had hoped for.

She thought about her own father, and how he had once shared with her his hopes that he had made his father proud of him. *Does Uncle Isaac think the same thing about his grandfather? Does he ever worry about how Captain Ross would react to his contest of the will?*

The realization hit Mary that she desperately wanted her parents to be proud of her. She had always sought their approval, even when chafing at her mother's strict ways. *If they don't approve of Henry, how will that affect me? Would I ultimately give in to their wishes?* Her insides began churning uncomfortably. She didn't know how much longer she could stand in this wretched place, listening to words that brought her no comfort, and fretting about her future with Henry.

The verses read by Reverend Hutchinson reached Mary's ears, but were not fully processed by her mind.

> *At the same time came the disciples unto Jesus, saying, Who is the greatest in the kingdom of heaven? And Jesus called a little child unto him, and set him in the midst of them, And said, Verily I say unto you, Except ye be converted, and become as little children, ye shall not enter into the kingdom of heaven. Whosoever therefore shall humble himself as this little child, the same is greatest in the kingdom of heaven. And whoso shall receive one such little child in my name receiveth me.*

She knew that she was supposed to draw comfort from these scriptures, but she was finding it extremely difficult to do so. She tried her hardest to listen to the words spoken by the minister. He described the great joy which occurred among the saints in Heaven as Martha was received into their midst. He described Martha being cradled in the arms of her Savior, Jesus. He promised the coming day when Martha would be reunited with those she left behind. Mary had been raised to believe that day would come. *But until that day comes, we are left to feel the loss of you here and now.*

Mary glanced at Martha's father, John Richardson, who stood beside her stoic and erect, holding Cabell's tiny hand. Catherine held Addie, as her own three children had been left back at Oak Hill in the care of servants. Uncle Isaac stood next to Catherine, his expression completely unreadable. Adelaide, still clinging to life, was in no state to attend her daughter's service. Friends and neighbors huddled near the family members, listening to the words of the minister.

Most touching to Mary were the number of the slaves who had come up from the quarters, now standing in groups, many of them silently crying. Mary remembered the comfort and aid provided by them on the night of the fire. She was grateful they had come today. Many of them loved Martha too. With a pang, Mary realized that Martha meant more to many of the slaves than to most of the neighbors who'd come to show their support for the family, rather than to actually mourn the loss of the child.

Mary would be leaving for home in the morning. Her journey home had already been arranged. She felt a mild panic thinking that she would leave before having a chance to speak to Henry. *Would he immediately travel to Tuscahoma and visit Father at Bellevue? Or would he realize that the timing is wrong?* The longing to see him again had only intensified with the passing of the days since the fire. It felt like an eternity since he had shared his intentions with her in the carriage house. In some ways the destruction of Prospect Hill had changed everything in her life. But she prayed that nothing had changed between herself and Henry. *I don't know what I would do if I lost him too.*

As the service finally drew to a close, a weary Mary headed to the carriage looking forward to the ride back to Oak Hill. *Anywhere but here. There are just too many painful memories here.* Nellie would not have much packing to do, as all of Mary's belongings had been destroyed in the fire—including the book of poetry that had been her birthday gift from Henry. She was grateful that she had finished it recently, but still regretted the loss of it. Overall, she had given little thought to her possessions. The loss of Martha had caused all other losses to seem insignificant.

Mary took one last glance back at the cemetery. She let out a small gasp when she noticed Henry standing on the periphery of the crowd. Her spirits immediately soared as she made her way towards him. The small, crooked half-smile on his face was so tender and endearing that she felt tears welling up in her eyes. Her emotions were positively raw, and she found herself wondering how she would ever be able to keep from throwing herself into his arms.

When she was in close enough proximity to speak with

him, she said quietly, "I am so glad that you came. I've been longing to see you ever since..." her voiced trailed off. *Ever since what? My life changed forever?*

"The moment I heard about the fire I wanted to rush to your side. But Reverend Butler urged me to wait and find a moment that was less likely to raise questions. For the past hour I've been watching the crowd, and I felt that at this moment my presence would go largely unnoticed." Glancing around to ensure that Isaac and Catherine were still engrossed in conversations, he added, "I will not stay more than a few minutes though. But I wanted to arrange a time that we can meet again."

Mary felt a twinge of desperation welling up inside her chest. "I leave in the morning to go home. My parents are expecting me."

Henry's expression was pained. "I've been afraid of that. I knew you would have to leave soon in light of what is going on here."

Mary thought about the most likely time she would find herself alone before morning. "I will sit on the front porch at Oak Hill tonight. The best we can hope for is that I will be alone long enough for you to come close to the house and summon my attention. It isn't very private, but at least we can talk."

Henry's countenance lightened perceptibly. "I will be there, Mary Girault. You can count on it."

Before turning to leave he added, "I am so terribly sorry about Martha. I know how fond you were of her."

"Thank you. I truly will miss her terribly." Tears began welling up in her eyes again.

He cast her a tentative smile, feeling pained at her tears

but knowing that he needed to clear out before he was noticed. He began casually making his way through the crowds who were milling towards carriages. She stood watching him until he broke for the edge of the woods.
Until tonight, Henry. I finally have something in this day to look forward to.

***

Oak Hill Plantation

The evening seemed endless to Mary. She had barely spoken a word at dinner but, engulfed in the grief of the day, it went entirely unnoticed by anyone. No one at Oak Hill was completely 'in their element'—the guests were displaced by the fire, without even their most basic personal belongings. Jane Ross' home was filled with the refugees of the fire as well as the minister who'd remained with the family for the evening. All of the extra people had thrown off her own comfortable routines, although she was making an attempt at graciousness. In the midst of this chaos, it was easy for Mary to slip unnoticed onto the wide covered porch of the stately home.

She went to the far side of the porch and sat with her legs hanging off the edge, just as she had done at Bellevue as a young girl. Her mother would have cringed and surely chastised her for sitting this way, but Mary didn't care. She swung her feet back and forth, relishing the freedom to do as she pleased. She wanted to be able to speak with Henry. There were trees mere feet from this edge of the porch. In her sitting position, she could see beneath the railing, giving her an unobstructed view of the place he was likely to appear. All she had to do now was wait for him to arrive.

It would have been impossible for her to discern how long she sat there, with her mind full of thoughts and flashing images. Perhaps it was twenty minutes. Perhaps an hour. But she was so lost in thought that she hadn't felt impatient. However, when she caught sight of him, a feeling of sheer elation filled her. *He came!*

"I told you I would come," he said quietly, as though answering her unspoken cries.

"I so hoped that you would," she replied breathlessly. "I have felt so alone. Even with all of these people around me. I cannot explain it, Henry, but I just feel so utterly alone."

He moved closer, leaving the concealment of the trees. There was just enough moonlight coming through the cloud cover to illuminate his face. He was as handsome as ever, but Mary thought he looked older than he had just weeks ago. His features were drawn and tense, even though a slight smile appeared on his face.

"What is troubling you Henry?" she asked, alarmed at her realization.

"Please let me make sure *you* are all right. Do not concern yourself with me. It is you who have suffered and lost someone you loved."

"But Henry, I love you as well. And you are still here to worry about. So please let me worry about you."

He smiled at her. "May I?" he asked, lifting his arms up to her.

She nodded, and he placed his hands on her sides and lifted her gently down off the porch to stand in front of him. He held his arms open and she flung herself into his embrace eagerly. They stood this way for quite some time; neither of them speaking. His embrace provided sheer release for Mary, allowing her pent up anxieties to flow from her. She felt safe for the first time since Dr. Wade woke her in the early morning hours of April 15th.

After some time, they withdrew from their embrace and Henry spoke. "May I still come to your home and speak with your father?"

"Yes, yes of course. But I think you should give it some time. A few weeks perhaps. To allow my family to heal somewhat from this tragedy."

"I understand. I still have much work to do here. I feel that I should stay in Port Gibson working with Reverend Butler until…"

"Until the Prospect Hill slaves are on their way to Africa?" Mary's voice offered no clue as to her feelings regarding his desire to continue helping them.

Henry regarded her for a moment. "Do you think what people are saying is true? About the slaves setting the house on fire deliberately?"

She thought briefly before answering. "A few weeks ago I would have thought it impossible. I have known many of these people since I was a child. But now, I think it could well be true. If you'd seen Uncle Esau that night. He had a look on his face that I will never forget. And that axe…"

Mary recounted the whole event to Henry. From the moment Dr. Wade had shaken her awake until the family had left Prospect Hill hours later. Henry's eyes grew wide several times and he reached down to squeeze Mary's hand in the more harrowing moments of account.

"It must have been so terrible for you," Henry said when

she had finished.

"The moment that I realized that Adelaide did not have Martha was the worst moment of my life." She dropped her head, the tears flowing freely.

Henry pulled her close to him again. "You did all that you could possibly have done. You saved Cabell and Addie."

Mary nodded. When she replied, her voice was muffled by his chest, in which her face was buried, "If I could just go back and do it again. It would only take a second to check that she was coming down with us."

"If I could go back and do things again, there would be things in my life I would change as well," Henry said, recalling the words he spoke to the slaves regarding Mary's uncle. The words that he felt he needed to share with her. *But is this the right moment? She has so much to bear already.*

"Like what? What would you want to change?" Mary looked up at him thoughtfully. She wondered what Henry, who'd lived a seemingly charmed life, could possibly have to regret.

Henry had a gut feeling that the time wasn't right to tell her the truth. But he also wrangled with the fear that if he didn't tell her now, it would grow harder and harder as time went by. He swallowed hard.

"I said something to some of the Prospect Hill slaves when I was there with Reverend Butler that I think might have been taken the wrong way. In fact, I feel partly to blame for the fire."

Mary's heart began to pound furiously. *What is he talking about? How could he possibly be to blame for that horrible tragedy?*

He went on, "I told them that I thought the solution to their problem was to find a way to get Mr. Wade out of the picture. Of course, I meant legally by having a judge intervene or something of that nature."

He looked into her eyes, desperately hoping to read her expression and discern how the news was being received. But Mary's eyes were wide with surprise, and he began to feel panic rise within him.

"Did you make it clear what you meant?" Her voice was trembling. "Or did you leave them thinking that they needed to take drastic measures to remove Uncle Isaac from the situation?"

"Mary, I promise you with God as my witness that I thought I was clear. It never even occurred to me that my words could have been misinterpreted."

"So why do you think they were? Maybe you were understood perfectly."

Henry shook his head. "Levi asked me what I meant a few weeks later. He seemed confused enough to question me about it."

"So what did you tell him then?" She was looking at him hopefully. *Please don't let him be the one who gave them the idea to burn Prospect Hill. Please let him have explained himself clearly.*

"I told him that it was just a careless comment and apologized to him for not thinking it through before blurting it out." Henry let his chin drop to his chest. "I would give anything to go back and change my words."

Mary was thoughtful for a moment. "Henry, I think you might be making too much of this. You don't even know for sure that it was your words that led the slaves to think they should burn a house with people sleeping inside of it. Surely you didn't suggest anything of the sort."

"No, of course not! I would never…"

"I know you wouldn't. That is what I am saying. You can't blame yourself for something that you'd have never imagined they were capable of."

They were silent for a few moments, both of their minds swimming with conflicting emotions.

Finally, Henry looked into Mary's tear filled eyes. "Can you forgive me?"

"Of course I can. Is there anything to forgive? You've been trying to help them. I've known that since the beginning. It makes things hard for us. Sometimes I feel like I am betraying Uncle Isaac and Aunt Catherine."

Henry nodded, his expression pained.

"But Henry," Mary continued, "I could never believe that you would have wanted to bring harm to anyone in my family. Or suggest to the slaves to do so."

A feeling of immense relief washed over him, as if a thousand pounds had been lifted from his shoulders. He held her in his arms and silently thanked God for the faith that Mary had in him.

"I was afraid you would not want to see me again," he said after a few more silent moments.

"I love you, Henry," she replied simply.

"I love you too. And when my work is done here, I will come for you. I want us to spend our lives together."

They stood beside the porch at Oak Hill, clinging to each other for over an hour. Sometimes they spoke, and sometimes they listened to the chirping of the crickets mingled with the other sounds of a clear spring night in Mississippi. Mostly they were just grateful to be together. Their youth and naiveté made it impossible for them to see in the moment that some obstacles are just insurmountable—no matter how much one tries to pretend otherwise.

April 19, 1845   *The J.M. White* Steamboat

Mary stood on the Hurricane Deck of the large vessel, enjoying the steady breeze blowing her hair loose from its pins. It was twilight, and the sunset was particularly glorious from her vantage point near the pilot house. She closed her eyes and inhaled deeply, allowing the fresh air to fill her lungs. She felt more relaxed than she had in days. The cool evening air, the breeze against her face, and the sounds of the engines were a balm for her weary soul. Her future seemed quite vague; exciting perhaps, but fraught with uncertainty. *Is it possible for Henry and I to be together? Will Father ever agree to the marriage?*

   Her mind was swirling with questions which there was no way of answering. Time would answer them eventually, but impatience gnawed at her. She opened her eyes to spot a beautiful tern on a nearby sandbar. The bird's movements were so graceful that she became captivated watching it. She thought back to her departure from Oak Hill. Aunt Catherine's attempts at strength had failed her, and the two had shared a tearful farewell. Uncle Isaac had accompanied her to Rodney where he had booked her passage. The fares to travel upriver were rather costly, but he didn't flinch at the cost.

The J.M. White was a magnificent vessel. It was as fine as the hotel in Rodney. The floors were fully carpeted and there were chandeliers in the dining and common areas. Wood paneling lined the lower half of the hallways leading to the cabins. Meals were served on the finest china. As lovely as the interior of the boat was, she craved the fresh air which aided in clearing her head of nagging thoughts.

Neighbors had called on them at Oak Hill in the days following the fire with clothing, shoes, hairbrushes, and all of the items that the Wade family had lost in the fire. She was quite grateful to have these necessities for her journey home. She had even been provided a new trunk for her possessions. Wistfully she remembered her old trunk, with her birthday gift from Henry tucked inside of the lining; but attempted to push all regrets from her mind. *There is no point in crying for what is lost now.*

As she continued to watch the night fall, she heard music drifting up from somewhere beneath her. Normally, she would have spent her first few hours aboard exploring. But on this journey, she had seen only the parts of the craft that she had to. Her natural curiosity had been dulled by her grief. The music was pleasant, however, and she found herself enjoying the tune. She was glad to be returning home where the constant reminders of Martha would not be surrounding her. It would be good to see her parents and siblings again. Now that she had been away for so long, she realized how much she had missed them. With a sigh, Mary Girault began her descent to the lower deck which housed her cabin; cautiously optimistic about what lie ahead.

***

Port Gibson, Mississippi

Henry sat in the chair beside his bed in the boarding house. He imagined Mary aboard a steamboat returning home full of hopes and dreams of a future they would share together. His complexion was ashen with the dark circles beneath his eyes revealing the scant amount of sleep he had accumulated over the past few nights. He looked as though he had aged ten years in mere days. The guilt he internalized regarding his comments to the slaves was eating him alive. There was only one course of action that he felt could bring him the resolution that he would need to absolve himself of his culpability in the fire. *Or convict me of my guilt.* And that was speaking directly to the slaves remaining at Prospect Hill.

Reverend Butler had immediately dismissed the notion as foolhardy and dangerous. But after a completely sleepless night, adrenaline was all that was fueling his body. To be honest, he felt a bit reckless with little regard for the consequences he might face. He stood up determinedly and left for Prospect Hill.

As he rode into the familiar woods surrounding the slaves quarters, he realized that Levi was still in the fields. It hadn't occurred to him that it would be business as usual on the plantation, and the realization that it was rankled him. He found a fallen tree near enough to the slaves' quarters that he felt he would be able to hear them return.

He tied up his horse and sat down. *What will I say? How can I just ask Levi if he believed that I wanted Isaac Wade killed?*

A part of Henry wished that he had never met Stephen Duncan, never stepped foot in the state of Mississippi, and certainly never decided to remain here and help the slaves realize their dreams of freedom. Such a short time ago, his life had been planned out. He would finish college, become a successful businessman and pride himself on his accomplishments. He would gather in smoke-filled rooms with other prosperous men and discuss politics and religion. They would congratulate each other on a profitable business deal, or a favorable ruling in a legal case. Of course, he would donate to charity and live a moral life. It had all made perfect sense to him a year before.

But now little if anything made any sense to Henry. Even his feelings for Mary, the one thing that felt completely right to him, had become a source of anguish in the early hours of the morning. Sleep deprived and racked by guilt, he had a vision of Mary sobbing and pounding her fists against his chest saying over and over again, "It was all your fault. It was you who made those poor desperate souls think their only choice was to kill us all!"

The word "desperate" replayed in his mind in a loop. Levi was intelligent and one of the most intuitive men he had ever met. Under normal circumstances, Henry would not find it possible to believe that Levi could misinterpret his words to mean murder. But these were not normal circumstances. They were certainly desperate ones. After years of waiting and hoping, the slaves felt no closer to freedom than they did before Henry arrived to assist Reverend Butler. Of course they were desperate. *And desperation can cloud reason.*

It was near dusk when Henry heard the approaching voice of the groups of slaves returning from the fields. He waited for the large influx to pass, before making his way towards the quarters. His stomach was in knots and he was unsure of what his reception would be. Yet, when he caught Levi's eye, a smile broke out over his friend's face. Rachael had met her husband at the edge of their cabin and handed Gabriel to him. After a moment, Levi whispered something into his young son's ear and lowered him to the ground.

As the two men drew nearer to each other, the strangeness of the situation struck Henry. *In the social structure of this society, I am the higher man. And yet I come here seeking absolution from this man who is far greater than I. Being in his presence is humbling.*

Levi greeted Henry enthusiastically. "Good to see you round here again. It been a while."

Henry nodded in affirmation. "It has been. In light of what happened, it seemed to be wise to stay away. That is what I am here to discuss with you though, Levi. The fire. What did happen that night?"

Levi looked as if he had seen a ghost. "I promise you I had no part in it."

Momentary relief washed over Henry. *Maybe it was not an intentional fire at all!*

The brief hopefulness was dashed almost immediately, however, by Levi's words. "As soon as I hear what they goin' do, I wanted no part in it."

Henry's heart sank. *Oh God, there was a plot then. And Levi knew about it.*

"So, Levi," Henry began, deciding that it was best to get this over with once and for all. "Did my comments regarding Mr. Wade give anyone in the group here the impression that I wanted him…"

Levi's eyes had grown big as Henry was finishing his question; his head was already nodding slowly up and down.

"…killed?"

Henry swallowed hard watching Levi's reaction. He waited for him to answer him directly.

"Some of 'em did. I tried tellin' 'em that ain't what you mean. But they decide on it, and they weren't no stoppin' it. That when I got out. It just wasn't somethin' I could be part of."

"But it was me? I am the reason that the house was burned? To get rid of Isaac Wade and get to Liberia?"

Levi didn't answer right away. He studied Henry's anguished features before replying. "I think they would a done somethin' like this anyways. People get tired of waitin' and waitin'."

Henry hung his head. In his heart he already knew the truth.

"You don't need to go blamin' youself now Mr. Henry." Levi's expression conveyed both concern and compassion. "Won't do a bit a good."

Henry nodded. "I will try." He looked around the quarters. The mood was more somber than he had ever seen it. There were no songs floating in the air, no laughter ringing out. "What has been going on here?"

Levi glanced behind him before responding. "People is scared. They got Esau up in the stables. They lookin' for the others. They questionin' everybody. Somebody goin' pay for the fire. That for sure."

Henry felt a shiver of realization that there would be no jury trial, no formal court proceedings of any kind. When whatever passed for justice was carried out, it would be mob rule—vigilantism. *No wonder people are scared. Once again they have no control over their circumstances.*

"Have you been questioned?" Henry felt a lump in his throat. He was scared for Levi.

Levi nodded. "I told 'em I didn't have nothin' to do with the fire. And that the truth."

"I know you didn't. Do you feel like they believed you?"

Levi shook his head. "Ain't got no way to know for sure. Just gotta hope."

Rachael approached from behind her husband. She didn't wear the usual smile that greeted Henry on their previous encounters. She acknowledged him with a nod, and turned to Levi. "Come eat while it hot. You been workin' hard and need a good meal."

Rachael regarded her husband intently for a moment before she turned and walked back towards the cabins without a word to Henry.

Henry was disconcerted by Rachael's reaction to his presence. "Is she all right, Levi?" His tone was concerned rather than accusing.

"She real scared," Levi replied simply. "She think my talkin' to you is risky. And that my bein' in those meetin's gonna come out."

"I should go. She is right." Henry heard Reverend Butler's words of caution ringing in his ears. *Am I putting my own need for redemption ahead of Levi's safety? No wonder Rachael wasn't happy to see me here.*

"It was good seein' you." Levi replied genuinely. "But I'm mighty hungry."

The two men grinned at each other, fleetingly free from the anxiety that had weighed so heavily on them.

Henry mounted his horse and rode back to Port Gibson, the moonlight barely enough to light his way over the now familiar route between the two places he spent most of his time. Sheer exhaustion was overtaking him. He considered removing the blanket he kept rolled up on the saddle and sleeping in the woods.

Ultimately, he plodded along to his waiting bed at the boarding house, wondering if he would sleep even in this state of fatigue and sleep deprivation. As he lay in bed, so far from his home in Pennsylvania, a montage of images played across his mind. Mary's beautiful face, Levi's earnest request for him not to feel guilty, the burned ruins of the once grand house, and the grave of the little girl. Darkness gradually replaced the pictures and Henry slept like he hadn't slept in years. Even though the absolution he had hoped for hadn't come.

April 22, 1845   Port Gibson, Mississippi

Henry sat at the desk in his room absentmindedly twirling his pen between his fingers. He had inadvertently splattered ink on the crisp linen paper in doing so. However, after scanning the letter, he felt his writing would be legible in spite of the black splotches. He was attempting to write his sister, Hannah, in regards to Mary. But Henry was finding it terribly difficult to put into words the feelings that he had for her. He had briefly described their unconventional courtship, the climate which prevented a more typical one, and her agreement to come to Pennsylvania if her father granted his permission.

Somehow the words lacked the fervor that he felt, and he considered crumpling the paper and starting over. The stationery upon which he was writing had been a gift from Hannah. A gift he suspected to be a mild rebuke for his lack of correspondence. Since receiving it, he had made a concerted effort to be more diligent in his letter writing.

With Hannah it was generally easy. They shared a comfortable rapport that did not require hours of effort and thought in regards to the wording of each letter. With his parents, it was much more difficult. The only correspondence he had received directly from his father, in fact, had been the Garrison pamphlet denouncing the Colonization Society—with the brief note scrawled and stuffed in the envelope. His mother's letters were more frequent, but he sensed that she struggled just as much with the content of her letters as he did.

His mother's letters contained detailed descriptions of the weather, the exquisite beauty of her Kalmia bushes, and the large carbuncle on his brother's toe which had required draining by the doctor. Never once did she reveal her disappointment that he had not returned to the University, the embarrassment he had caused the family, or her desire for him to return with haste. She was always careful to include the statement, "Your father sends along his best regards." However, Henry doubted that his father had done anything of the sort. In fact, he was sure that he had not done so.

He sighed and stood up, reaching his hands over his head to stretch out his back muscles. He was still having nights where he tossed and turned, leaving him feeling tired and achy the next day. He walked to the window to gaze down upon the street of his adopted town. *How did I ever come to be here? It made so much sense at the time. But now…*

Just as Henry turned his attention back to his letter to Hannah, he was interrupted by pounding on the door. He opened it to the flushed and anxious face of Mrs. McGregor, the housekeeper employed by Reverend Butler.

"Oh, thank goodness you're here! A Mr. Parker came round a poundin' on the door! I didn't know where the

Reverend went this mornin'. He said it be urgent to get to Prospect Hill straight away! I hoped to find him with you here." She was breathing heavily and appeared quite relieved when she had spilled the news she came to bear, relieving herself of the burden.

"He mentioned to me yesterday that he was planning to make a call to a sick parishioner today. I don't think he mentioned the name to me. Did Mr. Parker indicate the nature of the emergency at Prospect Hill?" Henry made a desperate attempt to quell the panic rising within him. *Levi could be in trouble just as Rachael feared.*

Mrs. McGregor shook her head rather frantically, waving her plump hands as she did so. "He only said to find the Reverend and send him over straight away! So that's what I did."

"You've done well, Mrs. McGregor," Henry replied, feigning a calm he didn't feel. "Thank you. I will do my best to locate Reverend Butler."

She tucked her loose reddish curls back under her bonnet as she turned away muttering in a thick Scottish brogue that interfered with Henry's comprehension. But he wasn't listening anyway, as he was mentally planning the best strategy with which to proceed. *If I waste time looking for him, it might be too late if my fears are founded. Should I ride out myself immediately and determine what the crisis is for myself?*

Afraid that hesitation would be a mistake, Henry left immediately for Prospect Hill. He ran his horse at a steady gallop, his heart racing as fast as the horse. When he arrived at the familiar clearing at the quarters, he noticed immediately that something was wrong. The cabins lay empty, with pots over fires unattended and several of the cabin doors standing open. He debated his options. On one hand he could edge along the woods and attempt to determine the whereabouts of the slaves. On the other hand, he could attempt to find Reverend Butler who would know much better what to do.

His previous experiences at Prospect Hill had taught him that at this time of day the older women and children should be at the quarters, the field hands laboring in the distance, and quite a few more workers busy in or near the house. *But the house is gone.* He decided without much internal debate that he needed to stay and try to help.

He made his way to the edge of the quarters where the closest of the fields were visible. *Empty.* His alarm reached a new level as he noted a few abandoned plows standing in the fields. *Something is terribly wrong. Where are they?*

Henry began making his way towards the main grounds of the plantation. He had learned that when a large gathering of slaves was close by there was a familiar sound composed of talking, singing, and sometimes praying, that indicated their presence. He began straining his ears for anything that would reassure him that they were all right.

But it was not until he was almost to the foundations of the former home that he finally heard something. Yet reassurance was not the emotion that flooded over him in response to the sound. It was that of sheer horror.

"See what happens when you git up to no good? Look good. Every one of ya better look good."

Henry had no idea who was speaking but the menace in the voice carried clearly through the trees. When he came close enough to see what the man was referring to, he clamped his hand over his mouth. Esau and Old Yeary were hanging by their necks from a low hanging branch, clearly dead. He knew it immediately from the way their heads were turned sideways, their faces swollen and distorted.

Esau had obviously been whipped multiple times before his death. His shirt was tattered, revealing the injuries. His wrists and ankles were still bound by ropes that had clearly cut into his flesh, as dried blood was visible on the trusses. Old Yeary seemed to have fared better than his companion, and yet one of his eyes was grossly swollen with globs of congealed blood matted around it.

He reached out a hand to steady himself, determined not to vomit. He didn't see Levi, and his view was obstructed by the people crowded around the hanging figures. The grouping of slaves was ominously quiet, and Henry was filled with trepidation as he slowly edged even closer to the horrifying scene.

Finally he saw Levi, and the sight of him caused his heart to sink. He was tied to a tree, gagged and clearly petrified—eyes as wide as saucers. Scanning the crowd gathered closest to Levi, Henry spotted Rachael clutching another woman silently and sobbing for her husband.

The speaker called out again, "Most of 'em guilty ones run off! But this one here thought he would stay around here and go on 'bout his business like nothin' happened!"

Dread filled Henry as he realized that Levi was the subject of this man's diatribe. *They are going to hang him and there is nothing I can do to stop them!*

Frantically he surveyed the scene. There were at least four men on horseback that Henry could make out, but there could have been even more that were obstructed from view. Each of the four men he could see had weapons visible. He thought he recognized Mr. Stampley, the overseer, but he wasn't the man speaking. Henry did not know who it was, but he felt rage unlike he had ever experienced directed at him.

With a start, he noticed that Rachael's eyes were fixed on him. At first, she looked relieved, even hopeful. But within seconds, her expression hardened and the eyes piercing him appeared cold and indifferent. *She expects me to stay here safely hidden and do nothing. And she despises me for it.*

Shame mixed instantly with the fear that filled Henry. No matter how much rationalizing he did, he was at least partly responsible for what was happening to Levi. He realized with sudden clarity that he could die if he stepped out of the trees. But he knew just as clearly that he wouldn't want to live with himself if he stayed hidden. Henry Willcox made a break for the base of the tree to which his friend was bound.

Under different circumstances, the shock that registered briefly across the faces of the lynch mob would have been humorous. The sudden appearance of a well-dressed white gentleman from out of nowhere clearly rattled them. But it didn't take long for the man who'd been speaking moments earlier to recover, the scorn returning to his face.

"Who are you?" he sneered, revealing his tobacco stained teeth.

"My name is Henry Willcox. And I know this man to be innocent." He pointed in the direction of Levi, who was staring at Henry as though he had never seen him before—

clearly amazed to see him appear so suddenly.

"Well, I ain't never seen you 'fore in my life. An I don't see how this here any of your business." He turned to the group of other men giving Henry the chance to scan their faces. Besides Stampley, he recognized no one. "Any you seen him before?"

One of the men shouted, "He ain't from 'round here! Listen at him!"

With a sneer, the leader said, "Where you from boy?"

Henry debated on whether to engage these men in conversation. But for lack of a better plan, he decided that to keep them talking was his only option at the moment.

"Philadelphia," he answered in a loud, clear voice that sounded somehow unfamiliar. "Pennsylvania."

A smirk spread across the face of leader. "What you doin' so far from home then?"

Once again Henry gauged his options and decided to keep stalling as long as possible. "I took some time off from the university there to work with Dr. Duncan in Natchez." He attempted to give nothing away in his answers that he would regret later.

"You ain't nowhere near Natchez right now. In fact, you right here in the middle of somethin' you need to git out of." His expression was threatening, and his hand moved slightly in the direction of his gun. The movement wasn't lost on Henry.

Stampley spoke now. "We under the authority of the owner of this property to avenge the death of a little girl. This ain't somethin' you want to meddle in." He was much less threatening than his counterpart, but his message was clear.

Henry took a deep breath, bolstering his courage. "In the time that I have spent in Mississippi, I have come to know this man Levi. I'm asking you to give him a chance to prove his innocence before you make a grave mistake."

He knew he had said the wrong thing immediately by the anger that flashed in the stranger's eyes. "You tryin' to tell me my business?"

"I just want to be sure nothing happens here that any of us will regret." Henry was surprised to hear that his voice wasn't shaking, though he could feel his knees doing so.

The man turned back to his friends again. "You hear that? This here boy from the university up 'ere in Pennsylvania goin' to help us make sure we don't do somethin' we gonna regret. Ain't that nice of 'em?"

The men all laughed. *Keep stalling, keep stalling.*

"He had nothing to do with the fire," said Henry simply.

The laughter stopped at once. "What you know about the fire?"

Several of the men further back were slowly making their way closer to Henry. He stood his ground. He could hear Levi's ragged breathing around the gag in his mouth.

"I know that Levi didn't set the house on fire. I am sure of it."

Mr. Stampley spoke again now, while the man who'd been speaking previously spit on the ground less than a foot from Henry's feet. "How can you be sure? You with him at the time of the fire?"

Henry thought of lying, but it would be too easy to prove false. And lying would not help Levi here, but instead would only make it worse for him.

"No, I wasn't with him the very moment the house

caught on fire. But I have had numerous conversations with him. He isn't capable of hurting anyone."

Laughter again. From all of the men except Stampley. Something made Henry wonder if Stampley had the same gut feeling regarding Levi's innocence.

"Stampley, that biggun over there told us that Levi were in on the planning.'" More sneering. More spitting.

Henry glanced towards the gruesome figure of Esau hanging from the branch. *Esau. Oh why would you give up Levi? What good does that do now?*

But even as these thoughts ran through Henry's mind, another quick glance back at Esau made it clear. He was whipped until he gave up a name.

"Are we goin' to string up this darky or stand here talkin'?" The sneering man issued his challenge to Stampley contemptuously.

Peter Stampley had no color left in his face. He looked between Henry and his fellow overseer Jack Miller, whose name remained unknown to the former. At first Stampley had been relieved to relinquish control of this business to Miller, who was much better suited for it than himself. In fact, it almost sickened him how much he seemed to be enjoying it. But now, he regretted the loss of control he felt desperately.

"Well?" Miller said, spitting again. "We ain't got all day. We still got more of 'em to round up. We got plenty a rope and plenty a trees." The sneer spreading across his face disgusted Henry.

Stampley had always respected Levi's attitude and work ethic. He had never once suspected him of any sort of treachery. When Esau said his name, Stampley was sure that he must have heard wrong. But there was no mistaking it. And furthermore, Levi didn't seem surprised when they came for him—as if he had been expecting it. *If word gets back to Mr. Wade that I was told Levi helped plan the arson, but I let him go free, then I'm finished here. It's him or me.*

The crowd on horseback had closed in now around Henry and Levi, pushing back the slaves who were crowded around the scene. Rachael continued her quiet sobbing, watching in horror at the events unfolding around her.

What followed next happened so suddenly that he couldn't be sure what happened first. But the events would be replayed in bits and pieces in Henry's mind for the rest of his life. He remembered yelling, "Stop!" and standing between Levi and the ugly man who was snarling racial slurs and insults, goading Stampley into action. He felt the unseen hands grabbing him roughly and restraining him, pulling him away from Levi. There was a struggle, Rachael's screams, a sharp pain, and then darkness.

***

"Henry!" the rough hands were still shaking him. "Henry, can you hear me?" But the voice was familiar. There was no malice in it. He opened his eyes, but nothing was in focus. He had a blinding pain in the side of his head, and a strange tightness when he moved his jaw. He moved his eyes inside their sockets to try and focus in on something recognizable. Finally Zebulon Butler's face came into view mere inches from his own.

"Thank God," Butler responded to Henry's gaze falling on him. "Thank God you are all right."

But nothing felt further from the truth. The chaos of the last moments of his conscious memory flooded over him, and panic swept through him. "Levi," he croaked, "We have to help him."

Butler's voice conveyed Henry's worst fears. "It is too late, Henry. By the time I arrived, he was gone."

"Gone?" Henry was dizzy even though he was lying on the ground. The world around him was spinning. Yet, he needed to see for himself what Butler meant. He tried to sit up, but gentle hands pushed him back.

"Henry, you should wait before trying to sit up. Here, allow me." Butler placed his handkerchief on the side of Henry's head to stop the bleeding.

"What happened?" Henry asked. His senses seemed to be coming in and out. He heard crying and praying—two of those telltale signs that the slaves were still close by. Noticeably absent, however, was the laughing. There was nothing to laugh about. The images of Esau and Old Yeary once again swam in front of Henry's eyes. His gut clenched violently. *Levi.*

This time he resisted Butler's attempts to keep him supine. He sat up and saw with repulsion his friend Levi hanging at least four feet off the ground in the same gruesome position as the other two men. There was no stopping the tears that flowed freely from Henry as he watched Levi's lifeless body suspended above him. Rachael's sobs added to his anguish. *Levi is dead. And it is my fault.*

There was no sign of the men on horseback. Henry

never saw them again. The rest of the day was a blur to him. Rachael's accusatory stares only compounded his own sense of guilt. The bodies being left to hang following the threats of what would happen to anyone who cut them down only deepened the sense of despair he already felt.

When Henry awoke the next morning, he had no recollection of how he had gotten back to his bed. It had taken a long time after waking to realize where he was and what had occurred the day before. He had wanted to apologize to Rachael, but her countenance had clearly conveyed her opinion of his role in the death of her husband. *I can't even blame her. She tried to warn him about becoming so friendly with me. But he trusted me and wouldn't listen.*

Henry Willcox was a broken man. His intentions had been so honorable, but his failure to help the Prospect Hill slaves was now consuming him. *I cannot stay here another moment.* He knew it with perfect certainty. He got out of bed and went to his desk. He regarded the letter he had begun writing to his sister about his future with Mary. Had it been only one day ago that he had actually had a viable future with her? With a sigh, he balled the letter up and discarded it.

Without stopping to ruminate over it further, he promptly wrote two letters: one to Zebulon Butler and the other to Mary Girault. He assured himself that a clean break from this miserable place was his only option at having any chance of normalcy in his future life. And he vowed to never look back.

The last thing he did before leaving his room was to

carefully pick up the small wooden figures that Levi had carved for him and place them gingerly in his pocket. He had made a promise to Levi once that he would cherish them always. And that was at least one promise that he knew he could easily keep.

April 23, 1845

Dear Reverend Butler,

During the months that I have spent working alongside you in your noble attempts to end slavery, I have learned a great deal about the world and about myself.

I admire your willingness to remain here working for a cause you believe so strongly in. I have watched you work tirelessly to help those enslaved souls whom you aim to free. Believe me when I confess to you that I take no pleasure in admitting that I cannot remain here. The acts that I witnessed yesterday have left me shattered and defeated. I realize now that I am beyond my ability to better the life of any one, even those toiling in slavery.

It is a failure and shame that I will carry to my grave. I ask that you pray for me as I return to my home. I recall the parable of The Prodigal Son as I prepare to throw myself at my father's mercies in hope of being received back into his good graces. I will work hard for the rest of my life in an effort to make up for the harm I have caused here.

With the utmost respect and affection,

Henry

The second letter had been exponentially harder to write. But as difficult as it was to do, Henry believed with complete conviction that it was the only possible course of action he could consider after what happened to Levi. He told himself that Mary would be better off without him. All he could do now was to try to help her see that for herself.

April 23, 1845

My dearest Mary,

Only yesterday I was writing to my sister professing my undying love for you and my desire to have you join me in Pennsylvania. Nothing in regards to my love or desires have changed since then. But Mary, something terrible has happened. And I fear that I will never again be whole and free to love you the way you deserve.

I failed to save Levi from the lynch mob determined to end his existence on this earth. He was one of the finest men I've ever known, and because of his association with me, he is dead. In death he leaves behind a wife and a fatherless child. His dreams of freedom will never be realized, and the fault for that lies directly at my feet.

If I could only take back those comments that I carelessly made to the slaves of Prospect Hill regarding their situation, then maybe I could absolve myself of some of the guilt. In spite of the tragedy, I could move forward with my life—the life I hoped to share with you.

But Mary, as you know I cannot take back those words. Levi's blood will forever remain on my hands. When we look at each other, we will forever be reminded of that shame. And though you feel now that you could forgive me, each time you think of your beloved Martha, I fear that you will resent my role in her death. How can I bear that?

We come from different worlds. I realize it is a cliché and a weak excuse, not worthy of the love we share. Both of us hoped to overcome the tremendous obstacles that our backgrounds placed in the way of our future together. And I believe we could have triumphed over anything put in our path if only the outcome had been different- if the fire had never happened. But it did happen, and that is something that we cannot change or hide from.

I beg your forgiveness, but realize that I

am not worthy to receive it. I pray that you will never doubt my love for you, or the tremendous respect I have for you. I wish for you a life of happiness and prosperity. I will never forget you or the love that we have shared for each other.

With all my love,

Henry

Henry never saw Mary again. He wasn't there to witness her tears as she read his heartfelt words. To feel the grief and sadness with which his letter was received. But months later, when Mary could be honest with herself, she also felt relief. Since she had returned home, her father had made several references, each one full of contempt, for the abolitionist minister he thought may have "stirred up the slaves."

James Girault did not know about Henry or his association with Reverend Butler. But once he found out the connection, the likelihood that he would approve of him seemed highly improbable. Her future with Henry seemed almost impossible, and yet she had held out hope for them until the moment his letter came. She felt no anger or resentment towards him. In fact, she felt as though they were both victims of the world around them. A world that had conspired to keep them apart.

***

May 1845   Prospect Hill Plantation

Isaac Ross Wade gathered his family around him facing the ruins that had once been their home. And his grandfather's home before that. Adelaide was making strides towards physical recovery and there were high hopes that she would survive her physical injuries. Her psychological injuries however, would likely never heal.

Wade realized that he was losing his legal battle to keep the slaves at Prospect Hill. He wasn't ready to give up yet, but he was beginning to devise plans that didn't involve the slaves remaining in his possession. Wade had stashed away enough money to buy the property when it was sold at auction, which it would be if his grandfather's provisions were carried out.

With Catherine at his side, surrounded by their children, Isaac made a promise to his family. "We will rebuild on this very spot. Prospect Hill is not gone forever." He envisioned a phoenix rising from the ashes as described in the mythological tales he had devoured in his youth. In his mind's eye he could see the new Prospect Hill standing proudly on the crest of the hill; different perhaps, but just as grand as the original.

He turned to squarely face Catherine, looking her in the eyes. "I promise you that we will raise our family together here. And eventually, we will be buried together here."

And it was so.

Afterword

The Prospect Hill slaves who chose to emigrate to Liberia eventually were allowed to do so. However, it wasn't until January of 1849 that the last group of 142 slaves set sail aboard the *Laura*. A year earlier 129 slaves had departed for Liberia on the *Nehemiah Rich*. Unfortunately there was to be no "happily ever after" for those who managed to reach the shores of Africa. Letters sent back to Mississippi document disease, lack of supplies, clashes with the tribal peoples of Africa and other tribulations endured by the Ross slaves. No longer enslaved by man, many of them sadly remained slaves to misfortune.

Grace and her children decided to emigrate to Liberia with the other Ross slaves, as they were given the option of emigrating or remaining with Adelaide. Mariah and her younger son William remained behind and worked for a time on Rosswood Plantation. William remained a carriage driver. Eventually after the Civil War, they moved away from Jefferson County.

The plantation known as Prospect Hill was indeed purchased by Isaac Ross Wade when it was sold after all legal appeals of his grandfather's will were exhausted. A fine new house was erected on the site of the original home which had been destroyed by fire nine years prior. The new Prospect Hill was completed in 1854 and was the home to Isaac Wade, his wife Catherine, and their children. The couple is buried at Prospect Hill. Their firstborn son Isaac died in childhood, about a year after surviving the fire which killed his first cousin, Martha. Prospect Hill experienced years of neglect and decay after its ownership passed out of the Wade family. However, at the time of this book's publication, efforts are being made to restore the house to its original condition.

Adelaide Richardson survived her injuries from the night of the fire. She never had more children after Martha's death. Young Cabell went on to marry a Wade cousin and have six children of his own. His sister Addie, who also survived the fire, never married. Adelaide died in 1863, at 51 years of age. She is buried in the cemetery at Prospect Hill near her daughter Martha, whom she had tried desperately to save years earlier. Her gravestone bears the inscription, "To our Mother" on a scroll across the top.

Mary Elizabeth Girault remained at Bellevue with her family until she married Mr. Edward Poitevent on August 6, 1847, just two years after saving the lives of Adelaide's two youngest children in the fire. Mary died in Alabama at the age of 58 in November of 1885.

According to family lore, Edmond Belton and his brother Wade never were captured for their roles in the fire at Prospect Hill. It is believed that Edmond was able to successfully cross the Mississippi River into Louisiana and elude arrest for the remainder of his life. Wade Belton was believed to have moved to Copiah County in Mississippi where he eventually died of natural causes. All other slaves associated with the fire, including Andrew and Gilbert, were either hanged or burned according to accounts. Although the Wade family made claims for years that Isaac Ross Wade knew nothing of these lynchings, his brother's diary seems to suggest otherwise. In truth, we will never know for sure.

Walter Wade, who helped raise the alarm on the night of

the fire, built the grand plantation he named Rosswood a few miles from Prospect Hill. He practiced medicine and managed the plantation, chronicling much of his daily life in a diary which has been widely read today. Rosswood still exists today, although it is not owned by members of the Ross or Wade families. At the time of this book's publication this beautiful home is open to the public for tours and overnight guests.

Reverend Zebulon Butler remained in his position as pastor of the Port Gibson Presbyterian church, where he served for 34 years. He died in 1860 and is buried in Port Gibson. The church which was built shortly before his death still stands today. It boasts the unique feature of a large gold hand pointing to heaven, as Butler frequently did the same during his sermons.

Jane Brown Ross, the firstborn and last surviving child of Captain Isaac Ross, lived at Oak Hill until her death in 1851. She survived both of her parents and her two husbands. Her role in fighting her father's will is clearly documented in the historical record. Several suits and appeals were filed in her name. The egregious nature of the legal tactics and delays employed by Jane Ross and her son Isaac Wade prompted several admonitions from the Superior Chancery Court and the Mississippi High Court of Appeals. Justice Clayton wrote that the "Ross slaves have been detained against their will and the will of society." Justice Clayton actually labeled the lawsuits as fraud, which clearly reveals his contempt for the actions of the heirs in these matters.

Ker, Duncan, and Butler all remained involved in the outcome of the case until the last of the slaves had departed for Liberia. Each of the men had ties with the American Colonization Society, which existed until after the Civil War. It is estimated that 12,000 slaves emigrated to Liberia under the direction of the society during the years of active colonization. There is still debate about the motives of the organization and its supporters.

Two of the characters in *Burning Prospects* were completely fictionalized for the novel. Henry and Levi existed only in the imagination of the author, but are composites of people who lived at the time. The idealism and desire to change the status quo is a characteristic that has existed throughout history. Henry exemplified this desire for change, but also the human frailty that ultimately sent him home in shambles. Levi represents the countless innocent black men who were victims of lynch mobs. As no opportunity would have been provided for him to exonerate himself, it seems plausible that he would have been viewed as guilty by his mere association with the other conspirators.

Ultimately, the estate of Captain Ross, once quite large, was bankrupted by lawyer's fees and the apparent expropriation of the profits from the cotton sales during the years of litigation. The dying wish of Captain Ross for his slaves to begin a new life in Africa equipped with the supplies and raw materials necessary to become established was thwarted by his own family members. The school was never built in Liberia, due to the depleted funds. The Colonization Society was forced to privately raise the funds to pay for the passage of the Ross slaves to Liberia, where the former slaves were sent some items of from the family, but ultimately were left largely to fend for themselves.

Author's Note

I am a descendent of Captain Isaac Ross through my mother's family, and grew up hearing the story of the fire at Prospect Hill. My grandmother spent the early years of her childhood playing at the rebuilt home, as well as Oak Hill and other nearby homes, as they all still belonged to family members at that time. This event in my family history is the source of many conflicting emotions, and obviously was difficult to write about at times. My hopes for fictionalizing the events at Prospect Hill were to bring the story to life for the countless people who've never heard it. Though the events occurred many years ago, the themes are timeless. And the underlying currents that created this situation still simmer under the surface today. As far as we have come with race relations in America, it is obvious that we still have a long way to go. Hopefully, this novel can open the doors to a healthy and respectful dialogue on this topic.

I've made every effort to keep the historical facts portrayed in the novel accurate. However, in researching the accounts of the fire, the court cases, the slaves departure for Liberia and countless other plot elements, I found discrepancies in the records. When discrepancies existed, I chose the one that seemed more likely and went with it. One exception to this was the location of Catherine and Isaac's wedding. It actually took place at Catherine's home in a neighboring county. However, it served the plot better to hold the wedding at Prospect Hill in order to allow the wedding of Levi and Rachael to occur that same evening.

It was not my intention to vilify any of the characters who truly existed in history, but neither did I attempt to shy away from unpleasant details uncovered in the historical record. They were held accountable for their actions, just as I will be for my own. It is my hope that I've created characters that are multifaceted and real—flawed as we all are, but not stereotypical.

Since childhood I have been haunted by the situation that the slaves must have found themselves in, being forced to wait helplessly while others decided their fate. I attempted to bring to life the feelings of hopelessness and frustration that would have led to the ultimate decision to set the house on fire. In reality, there is no way that I could ever fully understand their plight. But even this many years after the fact, my heart aches with remorse that they were ever in this situation. None of us could ever say with certainty what we would do under similar circumstances. In a perfect world no one would ever have to face such choices.

For anyone curious about my own connection to these families, my maternal grandmother Minnie Jane Ross was born in 1905 in Redlick, Mississippi. Her parents were Eugene Allison Ross, born in 1860, and Margaret Idella Wade. Eugene's parents were John Isaac Wayne Ross, born in 1825, and Hellen Perine Green. John Isaac Wayne was a child of his father, also named John Isaac Wayne Ross, born in 1785, and Jane Brown Wade Ross, daughter of Captain Isaac Ross. This makes Captain Ross my great, great, great, great grandfather.

Acknowledgments

First and foremost I am eternally grateful for my husband Lewis, without whom I could never have accomplished this amazing journey of writing *Burning Prospects*. My two children, Rachel and Hank, are by far my greatest accomplishments and inspire me to do my best at everything that I do. I value Rachel's critical eye more than she knows. I've never known a living soul who loves books more than she does.

Also to my parents Bill and Linda Johnston, and my sister Mary Beth Castagnaro, who clamored for new chapters to be written because they really wanted to read the next one! Their enthusiasm for this work kept a fire lit underneath me to finish. Even when the writing became difficult and my emotions got away from me.

Taylor Roosevelt, my wonderful editor and friend, has been invaluable in creating a book that I am proud to publish. She beat the most important deadline to finish editing the manuscript—the birth of her first child! Congratulations.

The records of the Ross family compiled by Anne Mims Wright provided a wealth of information for which I am extremely grateful. Her efforts are appreciated more than I can say.

I'd like to thank Alan Huffman who wrote the amazing book *Mississippi In Africa*, which reignited the spark in me to explore my family's heritage at Prospect Hill. Even though my ancestors were not always portrayed favorably in his book, they were portrayed in a fair and balanced way that I appreciated. The information he presented in his book sent me hunting for more. Eventually it led to me writing my own fictionalized account of the same events he did such a great job of describing in a non-fiction format.

Dr. Kirk Michael Steen's Master's thesis from the University of New Orleans studied the Ross and Reed wills, and provided a trail of breadcrumbs for me to follow in the footnotes. Without this thesis, I would have missed out on a great many documents that made my narrative richer. Thank you also to Mr. Jewell Ross for sharing the copy of this manuscript with my family.

Shirley and B.V. Cooper have been supporters of my writing ever since they read my first novel. Their encouragement and enthusiasm have been a treasure!

My mother-in-law Jean Miles tracked down the information on the Girault family which led to the discovery that I am also descended from that line. I appreciate her time and dedication in this task!

The Belton Family maintains a website with a wealth of information regarding the family's history. The details of Mariah and her sons came from this site. I appreciate the efforts of the family to maintain this site so well.

Finally, to my friends of all races who took the time to discuss their feelings on the subject matter. Our racial background plays a large role in how we view both historical events and the events of the modern world. I'd especially like to thank Betty L. Oliver, who is a descendant of both slaves and sharecroppers. Our conversations on this novel guided me as I wrote the scenes in the slaves' quarters. Her knowledge of literature and history on this time period was a great help to me, and I am extremely grateful for her willingness to impart it to me.

Questions For Consideration and Discussion

1. What do you think motivated Captain Isaac Ross to take the course of action that he did in freeing his slaves posthumously? Did he have any other viable courses of action at that time?

2. Why was it so important to Captain Ross that his slaves be able to read and write and manage their own affairs while still slaves? How did this ability shape the slaves' actions in this situation?

3. Throughout the novel, characters used arguments to justify actions that would otherwise have seemed unjustifiable in other situations. Consider the actions of Captain Isaac Ross, Isaac Ross Wade, Jane Brown Ross, the Prospect Hill slaves, the vigilantes. How did each of these justify their actions?

4. What were the forces supporting the institution of slavery in the South? If any one force had been missing, do you think that slavery could have developed and survived?

5. Most slave owners saw slaves as a sub-human species. How did this impact their relationships with slaves? With slavery in general? Do you think that slavery would have taken root in the South if the slaves had not been devalued in this way?

6. Why do you think that other slave owners were so violently opposed to Isaac Ross' will? What fears do you think led to their opposition?

7. Most plantation owners owed their fortunes to the establishment of cotton, a very labor intensive process which depended upon slave labor. Can you think of other times in history when economics led to practices that might otherwise not have been considered morally acceptable?

8. Consider the comment by Margaret Reed related to her own status in her patriarchal society and that of her slaves. In your opinion, was this a valid comparison? Do many women still live in situations in which their abilities are negated by their gender? Can you think of some? Would you agree with Margaret that women throughout history have been an oppressed group?

9. Consider other oppressed groups throughout history. What perceptions on the part of the oppressors as to the status of the oppressed do these have in common with the slaveholders in this novel?

10. Jane Brown was also a female in a male dominated society, but how did her actions compare to Margaret's? Would the phrase "steel fist beneath a velvet glove" apply to Jane?

11. Isaac Ross chose to free his slaves through the American Colonization Society. Why do you think that he chose this group? Knowing that the group included mixed motivations for returning free blacks to Africa, which group do you think he identified with? Can you make a comparison to the interactions of the current American political parties?

12. What do you think that Africa represented to the slaves? Ancestral home? Freedom? Independence? Why do you think some of the slaves chose not to leave with the others? How does this compare with the volunteer emigration of citizens of other countries to new worlds throughout history?

13. What was the influence of the church in the South related to slavery? Consider your own personal faith; how do you think your faith would have influenced your actions in this situation?

14. How was Mary's acceptance of slavery influenced by Henry? How often are our positions held based upon misperceptions and lack of knowledge? Are you influenced more by opinions of others or do you try to determine all the relevant facts before forming your own opinion?

15. Why do you think that Henry was unable to forgive himself for his role in the slave's revolt? Do you think that he was really responsible for what happened? Have you ever known a situation in which someone's actions led to outcomes that "went beyond intent?" In your opinion was there any possibility of a future for Henry and Mary? Or was he right to return home and end their relationship?

16. History can often be one's best teacher. Have you learned anything from reading this novel that might influence your future decision making?

Appendix

The Ross Family:

Captain Isaac Ross was born in 1765, and married Jane Allison before moving to Mississippi in 1808. He built Prospect Hill with his slaves. Isaac and Jane Ross had five children. However, only two of the five were still alive at the beginning of this novel. Their children are listed here:

—**Jane Brown Ross** was born in 1786. She married her first husband, Daniel Wade in 1807. He died in 1820, only two years after moving from South Carolina to Mississippi to join Jane's family. Before his death, they had the following children: Lawrence Wade, **Walter Wade, Adelaide Wade**, Martha Wade, **Isaac Ross Wade,** Mary Belton Wade, Wilson Wade. After Wade's death, Jane married her first cousin, John Isaac Wayne Ross Jr. They had three children together: Jane Brown Ross, John Isaac Wayne Ross, and Frances Toledo Seaborn Ross.

—**Margaret Allison Ross** was born in 1787. Her first husband, Dr. Archer died and she married US Senator Thomas Buck Reed. Widowed twice, Margaret never had children of her own. Although after the death of her brother-in-law Daniel Wade, Margaret took a large role in raising Adelaide.

—Martha B. Ross was born in 1793 and also died childless. She died of yellow fever tending to her second fiancé. Her first fiancé was killed in a duel near Rodney.

—Isaac Ross was born in 1796. He married Sarah Elliot and had one son, Isaac Allison Ross. He died in 1832. Records indicate that he also freed his slaves in his will, although I did not locate detailed records of it.

—Arthur Allison Ross was born in 1800 and died in 1834. He married Octavia Van Dorn two years before his death, but they did not have children.

Captain Ross lost his wife and three of his children within a fairly short window of time. Speculation has been made that he left in a fit of despair, and it was during this time that he began entertaining notions of freeing his slaves.

Some of the Ross slaves who appear in the historical record were **Grace, Enoch**, Hanibal, **Esau, Old Yeary, Gilbert, Andrew**, Daphne, **Dinah**, Rebecca, Merilla, and **Thomas**.

The Wade Family:

The branch of the Wade family discussed in this novel descend from the union of **Jane Brown Ross** and Daniel Wade, son of Captain George and Mary McDonald Wade. All of their children are listed under the Ross family, but three of those children played a role in this novel.

—**Walter Wade** was born in 1810 and died in 1862. He first married his cousin Martha Taylor Wade and the couple had four children together before her death in 1848. He married again to Mabello Chamberlain and had two additional children. His plantation Rosswood still stands today.

—**Adelaide Wade** was born in 1811. In 1836, she married John Crowley Richardson. They had three children: Martha Ross Richardson (who died in the fire at Prospect Hill), Cabell Breckenridge Richardson, and Adelaide (Addie) Richardson.

—**Isaac Ross Wade** was born in 1814. He married **Catherine Elizabeth Dunbar** in 1845 at Belmont on Pine Ridge, even though in this novel, the wedding took place at Prospect Hill (See Author's note). Three of their children were alive the night of the fire at Prospect Hill: Isaac, Dunbar, and Catherine. Young Isaac, however, died in August of 1846. They had at least five more children after the fire, although records vary. According to family genealogical records, additional children included Willie Dunbar Wade, Benjamin Young Wade, Battaille Harrison Wade, and Thomas Magruder Wade. He went on to become a judge.

Major, was listed as Isaac Wade's manservant, and according to the family account, was present at Prospect Hill on the night of the fire.

Through Catherine Dunbar's sister Susan Dunbar Girault, we have **Mary Elizabeth Girault**, a major character in the novel. Mary's father James Augustus Girault was a land speculator who helped found the town of Tuscahoma. It would have been a terribly arduous journey from there to Prospect Hill. One can only speculate on why Mary would have been staying there on the night of the fire. Obviously, creative license was taken to give Mary a good reason to want to be in Jefferson County. Mary's grandfather Colonel John Girault was on the Rogers and Clark expedition.

The Belton Family:

According to the Belton Family Reunion Website, **Mariah Belton** was a mulatto woman born in 1785 in South Carolina. Three of her sons feature in this novel**. Edmond (Ed) Belton, Wade Belton,** and **William Belton**. The exact years of birth are not known for her sons. None of the Belton family members from the novel made it to Africa. Ed and Wade ran for their lives after the fire and apparently were never captured. Mariah and her youngest son William eventually became free after the Civil War and moved to Union Church, Mississippi not far from Prospect Hill. I was not able to find out any information about Ed or Wade having a family, however it was likely. I created the character of Sadie Belton to show, in part, what Edmond Belton was willing to risk his life for—to give his family a shot at freedom. William did marry, and according to the family site, his wife's name was also Mariah. Mariah Belton died in 1897.

CPSIA information can be obtained at www.ICGtesting.com
Printed in the USA
LVOW05*1334270414

383413LV00001B/1/P

9 780991 211715